HARVEST OF BLESSINGS

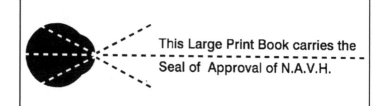

This Large Print Book carries the
Seal of Approval of N.A.V.H.

SEASONS OF THE HEART

HARVEST OF BLESSINGS

CHARLOTTE HUBBARD

KENNEBEC LARGE PRINT
A part of Gale, Cengage Learning

GALE
CENGAGE Learning·

Farmington Hills, Mich • San Francisco • New York • Waterville, Maine
Meriden, Conn • Mason, Ohio • Chicago

GALE
CENGAGE Learning·

LIBRARY OF CONGRESS CATALOGING-IN-PUBLICATION DATA

Hubbard, Charlotte, 1953–
    Harvest of blessings / Charlotte Hubbard. — Large print edition.
        pages cm. — (Seasons of the heart ; 5) (Kennebec Large Print superior
    collection)
        ISBN 978-1-4104-8513-7 (paperback) — ISBN 1-4104-8513-7 (paperback)
        1. Amish—Fiction. 2. Large type books. I. Title.
    PS3613.A277H37 2016
    813'.54—dc23   2015035730

Published in 2016 by arrangement with Zebra Books, an imprint of
Kensington Publishing Corp.

Printed in the United States of America
1 2 3 4 5 6 7 20 19 18 17 16

For Mom

ACKNOWLEDGMENTS

Thank You, Lord, for yet another time when I've turned a ream of blank paper into a story. It's an act of faith each time I begin, and I couldn't do it without Your help.

Many, many thanks, Alicia Condon, for continuing this series beyond the four calendar seasons to embrace the seasons of many hearts in Willow Ridge! And thank you, Evan Marshall, for your continued guidance in my career. This is the tenth book we three have worked on together, and that's very special to me.

Neal, you're the best.

My ongoing gratitude to you, Jim Smith of Step Back in Time Tours in Jamesport, Missouri, for your gracious help with all matters Amish and for your friendship. And a wave to Joe Burkholder and Mary Graber of Jamesport, as well! I cherish the way you've welcomed me with open hearts and smiles.

And forgive us our debts, as we forgive our debtors.

Matthew 6:12

A new commandment I give unto you, That ye love one another.

John 13:34

CHAPTER ONE

"Welcome back to Willow Ridge, Nora. It's a pleasure doing business with you."

How weird is this? Sixteen years ago, Nora Landwehr had never imagined herself returning, much less accepting the keys to a prime property from the man who'd been the bishop when her father had sent her away. But this little Amish spot in the road had changed a lot. And so had she.

"Thanks, Hiram," Nora murmured. "I hope I've done the right thing."

"At least you've arrived while your parents are still alive — if you can call it that." His gaze followed the road toward where the Glick house stood a ways back from the county blacktop. "Mending fences in your situation will be much like opening Pandora's box. Once you raise the lid, all your secrets will swarm out like hornets, whether you're ready or not."

His choice of words made her wonder if

she'd been wise to confide in Hiram Knepp, or even to go through with this transaction. But it was too late for second-guessing. As her gaze swept the panorama of Willow Ridge farmsteads, Nora was amazed at what she could see. From this hilltop perspective, Willow Ridge looked like an idyllic little town where nothing hostile or cruel could ever happen — like Mayberry, or Walton's Mountain. But appearances could be very deceiving. "So, does Tom Hostetler still live there where all those buggies are parked?"

"He does. He's the bishop now."

"This being Thursday, is that a wedding or a funeral?"

Beneath Hiram's short laugh, Nora imagined the *bwah-hah-hah-hah* of a melodrama villain. "As you probably realize," he replied wryly, "a wedding, in retrospect, might indeed be a funeral of sorts, depending upon how it all works out. Annie Mae's marrying Adam Wagler today."

Nora thought back, waaay back, to when Adam must've been about school-age and Annie Mae Knepp had been a toddler —

And you're not there to see your daughter marry, Hiram? She bit back her retort. Her Realtor had hinted that Hiram had committed even more heinous sins than she had — and after all, her father hadn't attended *her* wedding, either. If Hiram had been run out of Willow Ridge, she and this man with the devilish black goatee had a lot in common.

Nora didn't want to go there.

She was looking for a way to move Hiram along, so she could figure out where her major pieces of furniture would fit before the moving van arrived. And yet, if everyone in town was at the wedding, this would be a fine time to look around . . .

"I'll have my crew remove the Bishop's Ridge entryway sign tomorrow." Hiram's voice sliced through her thoughts. "That way you won't be living in my shadow."

Nora didn't miss the irony there. Every Amish colony lived in its bishop's shadow — and she sensed the cloud over Willow Ridge, Missouri, had gotten a whole lot darker of late, even if Hiram no longer resided here. "That'll be fine. Thanks again."

"What will you do with that big barn? I miss that more than the house."

Nora smiled. No need to tell this renegade everything, for who knew what he'd do with the information. "I have some ideas," she hedged. "Figured I'd live here a while before I committed to any of them."

Finally, Hiram was headed down the road in his classic, perfectly preserved black

Cadillac. Nora closed her eyes as the summer breeze caressed her face. She'd really done it. She'd spent her divorce settlement on this house and acreage with the huge barn, in the town where she'd probably be greeted with hatred and hostility as she stirred up old grudges like muck from the bottom of a farm pond.

But blood is thicker than water. Isn't it?

Once the shock and accusations ran their course, Nora sincerely hoped to reconnect with her family. To ask forgiveness and make her peace while creating a purposeful, productive new life. Was she being even more naive and fanciful than when she'd believed Tanner Landwehr was her ticket to a storybook ending?

Nora glanced at her watch. She still had an hour until the van was to arrive. She slid into her red BMW convertible to cruise town while she could still pass as an English tourist — not that anyone would see her. Everyone from Willow Ridge and the nearby Plain settlements would be at Adam and Annie Mae's wedding.

Once on the county blacktop she turned left, away from town, and drove past a timbered mill with a picturesque water wheel. With its backdrop of river rocks, wildflowers, and majestic old trees shim-

14

mering in the breeze, the Mill at Willow Ridge was a scene straight out of a Thomas Kinkade painting.

Nora turned back toward town. Henry and Lydia Zook's home looked added-on-to yet again, and Zook's Market had expanded, as well. The white wooden structure sported a blue metal roof that glimmered in the afternoon sunlight. A handwritten sign on the door proclaimed the store closed for the wedding.

Purposely not looking at her childhood home yet, Nora focused on the new house built on what had been the northeast corner of her father's farm. Across the road sat the Sweet Seasons Bakery Café and a quilt shop — more new additions, although she recalled the blacksmith shop behind them, and the large white home down the lane, which had belonged to Jesse Lantz. From what she could tell on the Internet, Jesse had passed on and Miriam had opened a bustling business. Who could've guessed an Amish woman would have a website with pictures of her meals and bakery specialties?

Down the road stood the Willow Ridge Clinic, with what appeared to be a horse-drawn medical wagon parked beside it — yet another startling change. Nora headed down the gravel road on the left, past the Brenneman Cabinet Shop, which looked the same as always. So did Tom Hostetler's dairy farm, where black-and-white cows grazed in the pasture near a red barn that sat behind the tall white farmhouse. Dozens of buggies were parked along the lane and around the side of the barn, yet the place looked manicured. Not so much as a scrap of paper marred the Plain perfection of this scene.

The sound of a hymn drifting out Tom's windows compelled Nora to stop. She'd all but forgotten the German words, yet the power of hundreds of voices singing in one accord made her swallow hard. The melody seeped into her soul, its slow, steady cadence stilling the beat of her heart.

Nora sighed and drove on. Could she *really* go back to three-hour church services, hard wooden pew benches, and endless, droning sermons? She couldn't recall the last time she'd attended a worship service. You couldn't consider a quickie ceremony in a Vegas wedding chapel *worship,* after all.

Maybe you won't have to worry about sitting through church. You haven't been allowed back into the fellowship yet. Haven't been forgiven.

Nora drove past the Kanagy place and

16

then a few homes where the Zeb Schrocks and other Mennonite families lived. She passed the fork that led to her brother Atlee's farm — she wasn't ready to go down *that* road yet — and followed the curve that meandered in front of the Wagler place and then past her own new residence. Definitely the finest house in town.

But what shall it profit a man, if he shall gain the whole world and lose his own soul?

Nora let out a humorless laugh. Her father, ever the sanctimonious Preacher Gabe even among his immediate family, had often quoted that verse when she'd wanted new dresses or some doodad she'd seen at Zook's Market. The memory of his harsh discipline tightened her chest even after sixteen years of living in the English world. If that was her gut reaction without even seeing him, how did she think she could face him in person? So much water had gone under that proverbial bridge that Gabriel Glick would never, *ever* cross it to see his errant, banished daughter.

Nora brought herself back into the present. The moving van hadn't yet arrived, so she pulled back onto the county highway where she'd begun her trip down memory lane. While everyone in town was at the wedding, she had the perfect chance to revisit her childhood home. To prepare herself for the ordeal she would soon face.

She pulled into the lane and parked behind the house, somewhat surprised to see the surrounding pastureland planted in tall corn that shimmered in the breeze. Knowing it wouldn't be locked, Nora slipped into the back door. The kitchen appeared smaller and shabbier than she recalled, as though it hadn't seen fresh paint since she'd left. How odd to stand in this hub of the house and not detect even a whiff of breakfast.

Nora moved on before she lost her nerve. She felt like an intruder — and she wanted to be long gone before anyone came home from the wedding. She peeked into the small downstairs room where she and her mother had sewn the family's clothes on an ancient treadle machine —

Nora gaped. On a twin bed lay a motionless female form, like a corpse laid out in a casket. Was this what Hiram had meant by implying her parents were barely alive? Did she dare approach, or would this woman pop up like a zombie from an old horror movie and leer at her with hollowed eyes? Nora wanted to bolt, yet she felt compelled to look the sick woman — surely her mother — in the face. If Mamma was so ill, why wasn't someone sitting with her? Or was she merely napping, too tired to attend the wedding? The way Nora had it figured, her mother was in her early seventies now — several years younger than her *dat.* Why did she look so far gone?

Holding her breath, Nora slipped to the bedside. The room felt stuffy in the July heat, yet a faded quilt covered her mother's shriveled form up to her chin. A *kapp* concealed all but the front of her white hair, so all Nora saw was a pallid face etched with wrinkles. The eyes were closed, and again Nora felt she was observing a stranger in a casket rather than her own mother. Last time she'd been here, Mamma's face had been contorted with indignation as disgust hardened her piercing hazel eyes —

And suddenly those eyes were focused on her.

Nora froze. Not a muscle moved in her mother's face, yet Mamma's gaze didn't waver — until her eyes widened with recognition. Or was it disbelief, or fear?

Nora didn't stick around to figure that out. Hurrying from the airless room and through the kitchen, Nora burst through the back door. She couldn't gulp air fast enough as she climbed into her car and sped down the lane. She felt as though she'd stared Death in the face and Death had stared right back.

Her tires squealed on the hot blacktop as she sped toward her new home. What a relief to see the moving van lumbering across the bridge by the mill. Nora made the turn onto Bishop's Ridge Road too fast and fishtailed in the gravel. She steered up the driveway and then pulled around behind the huge barn — to be out of the movers' way, but also because she felt compelled to conceal her car.

Better get over that. You live here now, whether the neighbors like it or not.

Nora was walking toward the house when a tall, broad-shouldered figure stepped out of the shade behind it. His straw hat, broadfall pants, and suspenders announced him as Plain, and there was no mistaking the fascination on his handsome face. Yet Nora hesitated. Had this stranger been roaming around inside her house? *Note to self: call a locksmith.*

"Something I can help you with?" she asked breezily. Better to believe in basic Amish honesty than to accuse him of something he might not have done. It wasn't as if he could take anything from her empty house.

"Just coming over to meet my new neighbor," he replied in a resonant voice. "I'm Luke Hooley. That's my gristmill on the river."

"Great place. Really scenic setting," Nora replied. Even though the brim of his hat shaded his features, it was easy to see Luke Hooley was a looker — and that *he* thought he was, too. "So why aren't you at the wedding?"

"Didn't want to waste a perfectly fine July morning in church."

Now *that* was different. But when he cocked his hat farther back on his head, the flirtatious glint in his deep green eyes was the same as any player's on the prowl — and that was not what she needed right now. Nora was glad to see the moving van lumbering up the driveway. "Well, there's my furniture. Nice to meet you, Luke."

"I'd be happy to help you unload. That's quite a job for a gal —"

"I've paid these guys big bucks to do the heavy lifting," Nora insisted as she waved to the van driver. "It would become an insurance issue if you got hurt."

"Been hefting furniture all my life. I won't get hurt," Luke replied with a cocksure grin.

Careful there, big boy. You don't know the meaning of hurt *until you've tangled with me.*

"Sorry," Nora insisted. "That's the mov-

21

ing company's policy, not mine. But thanks for stopping by."

Nora walked around to the other side of the van to greet the driver. Hopefully her neighbor could take a hint and wouldn't make a pest of himself. Luke was a fine-looking fellow, but she'd been married to one of those and she wasn't in the market for another one.

As Luke hiked back toward the mill, he couldn't quit grinning. The fox with the auburn ponytail bouncing behind her spar-kly blue ball cap had been well worth a few moments of his time. She was a sizzling English chick — maybe his newest, best reason not to join the Amish church. And the way she'd squealed her tires coming out of the Glick place suggested she was keep-ing secrets other than her name. Secrets he would *so* enjoy coaxing her to confess.

Now he was glad he'd opted out of Annie Mae's wedding — not that he'd remained interested in Hiram's daughter after she'd taken in her three little brothers and two sisters. She'd gone from being a wide-eyed adventuress to a mother hen clucking over her brood, and what man needed that? He'd just turned thirty and still felt no need to fill a bunch of bedrooms with kids. He did miss their dates . . . those times he and his brother Ira had run the roads with Annie Mae and Millie Glick —

Luke halted in his tracks, thunderstruck. With her catlike hazel eyes — *tigress eyes* — and that red hair and stunning body, his new English neighbor could pass for Millie Glick's twin.

But Millie was sixteen. This gal was *his* age.

And she'd come racing out of the Glick place as though she'd done something she didn't want to get caught at.

Very interesting. Very, *very* interesting.

CHAPTER TWO

Millie Glick grinned as Ira Hooley winked at her from the pew bench directly across from hers. They were serving as side-sitters for Annie Mae and Adam, so only about twelve feet of hardwood floor separated them — as well as Preacher Ben, Bishop Tom, and her grandfather, who'd been conducting the church service.

As the wedding began, the couple rose to repeat their wedding vows. Millie's heart thumped so hard she barely noticed all the folks crowded into Bishop Tom's home. Nor did she pay any mind when her grandfather scowled at her from the preachers' bench. Of *course* Preacher Gabe Glick was frowning at her for flirting with Ira — that's all he knew how to do, it seemed. But this wedding was such a welcome morning away from caring for her grandmother, Millie didn't care.

Soon she'd have to return to that stifling

house — unless she dared to accept the invitation to adventure that sparkled in Ira's eyes. She'd catch a lecture when she got back, but so what? The monotony of caring for a grandmother who drifted farther away with each passing day made Millie almost welcome her grandfather's tirade. It was a sign he was still breathing.

And isn't that a fine picture of your life at sixteen? Checkin' to see that two really old people are still breathin' as they nap?

"Adam and Annie Mae, as ya repeat your marriage vows," Bishop Tom was saying, "you're not to forget, in the intense love ya share for each other at this moment, that the promises ya make today bind ya together as man and wife *forever.* Other than the vows ya made when ya joined the church last month, these promises are the most important words you'll say in your entire lives."

Despite the bishop's solemn warning, Annie Mae's face radiated a joy Millie envied. As best friends, they'd shared many exhilarating, life-altering moments, but their relationship wouldn't be the same now that Annie Mae was marrying Adam. Millie sighed. Her circle of girlfriends was shrinking, and living with her grandparents hadn't exactly improved her social life. *Rumspringa* was feeling like a huge letdown.

Ira blew her a kiss and Millie choked on a laugh. When Preacher Ben and her grandfather glanced her way, she gazed demurely at her lap. Oh, but she was going to catch it after the wedding let out. She forced herself to listen to the same questions and answers Old Order brides and grooms had exchanged for centuries.

Will you ever get the chance to marry? Will Ira keep comin' around, or will he lose interest while ya live under an old preacher's watchful eye? He's twenty-nine. Handsome. Plenty of other gals would jump into his buggy without bein' asked twice.

Millie stole another glance at Ira. His mop of rich brown hair glimmered in the sunlight that poured through the windows, and he looked very much like a groom in his black trousers and white shirt. But would he ever settle down? Ira's aversion to joining the church was no secret, so maybe he and his older brother Luke would remain bachelors together in their apartment above the gristmill. Or maybe they'd jump the fence and live English, despite the way their older brother, Preacher Ben, kept after them to commit to the Plain faith.

Millie's morose thoughts vanished the moment Bishop Tom gave the benediction. As everyone stood up, Ira strode over to grab her hand.

"Let's sign the marriage certificate and make ourselves scarce," he murmured. "I can think of better ways to spend this summer day than hangin' around with all these folks watchin' us."

Millie's eyes widened as he bussed her cheek. "What about the dinner? We can't leave our places beside Annie Mae and Adam empty, or people will —"

"*Can't* we?"

As Ira gazed playfully into her eyes, Millie's heart danced. He *did* want to spend time with her, private time like they hadn't enjoyed for weeks! Yet the idea of skipping Annie Mae's wedding feast seemed like a betrayal — not to mention a missed opportunity to eat a delicious meal she didn't have to cook.

"Can we eat and *then* leave?" she pleaded. "I'm starved half out of my mind."

Ira's sigh sounded impatient. He led her through the crowd that had gathered around Adam and Annie Mae, to the small table where the certificate awaited them. Bishop Tom was signing it. He smiled as he handed Ira the pen.

"Well, it's another happy day in Willow Ridge," he remarked. "It means Annie

Mae's younger brothers and sisters have a stable home with a man in their lives. And another fine young couple's stayin' here in town to make our district stronger."

Ira pressed his lips together, considering his reply. "Adam's a better man than I am, takin' on four little kids and a sixteen-year-old sister-in-law." He signed his name with a flourish and then handed the pen to Millie. "Let's hope this'll keep Hiram in Higher Ground and out of our hair."

Millie winced at Ira's choice of words. Poor Annie Mae had suffered the ultimate humiliation when her father had whacked off her long, braided hair last spring. Although the excommunicated bishop of Willow Ridge had started a new colony — under dubious circumstances — no one really believed that Hiram Knepp would mind his own business, even if he had a new home and a new woman.

"We don't know who's bought his house," she remarked. "Let's hope it's not somebody who got the place because of some sort of crooked connection to Hiram."

"Let's think positive," Bishop Tom insisted. "All our speculatin' won't change God's will for us, so I'm for sittin' down to a feast with our families and friends."

"And did ya make ice cream to go with

the wedding cake, Bishop?" Ira asked. "*That's* a treat worth lookin' forward to."

Millie chuckled at the way Ira had changed the subject — but Bishop Tom did make the best ice cream ever. "And Miriam baked the wedding cake, so we know there'll be none better."

"Ya got that right," Tom agreed. "While a white cake's not my favorite, Miriam bakes it up moister than anybody else. It'll be perfect with the peppermint stick and chocolate ice cream I made. I'll see ya there."

As the bishop went over to greet other folks, Millie elbowed Ira. "See? We don't want to miss the meal —"

"But the cake and ice cream won't be served until suppertime," Ira reminded her. "If we hang around that long, we'll miss out on a *sweeter* way to spend the afternoon, ain't so?"

Millie smiled. "So we can have the kind of sweets you're talkin' about after dinner, and then come back later for cake and ice cream? Like havin' our cake and eatin' it, too, *jah*?"

When Ira laughed, Millie's heart danced to the music in his voice. This day was shaping up to be one of the best she'd had in a long time, and she was determined to enjoy every moment of it.

"And where do you think *you're* going, Millie? Your grandmother's home alone and she'll be needing a bite to eat by now."

At the sound of her *dat*'s voice, Millie bit back a retort. She waved Ira ahead to hitch the horse to his buggy. They'd eaten their wedding dinner quickly and then mingled with folks while they'd inched toward the back door, but her watchful father had caught them. It wouldn't be a good idea to smart off, so Millie worded her request carefully.

"Dat, would ya mind too much takin' a plate over? *Please?*" she asked. "It's been *weeks* since I've gotten out to —"

"If you want to be treated like an adult, you've got to put your responsibilities to others first, young lady." Her father's hazel eyes hardened like marbles. "When you agreed to take care of your grandmother —"

"I had no choice!" Millie blurted, even though it was the wrong thing to say to this man who constantly reminded her of her duty.

"Life doesn't usually let us *choose,*" her father replied stiffly. "We must learn to bear our burdens, and the burdens of others —"

"And besides," Millie continued in a rush, "Mammi would be glad to see somebody besides *me*. She's been askin' where you and Mamm have been keepin' yourselves, and —"

"That'll be enough of your sass." Dat's face was getting nearly as red as his hair. "You *know* I don't approve of you seeing Ira, because he's nearly twice your age. Now fix your grandmother a plate and —"

"Miriam's packed your parents enough food to last several days," Millie's mother interrupted as she joined them. As she shifted year-old Ella on her hip, she pointed to a cardboard box on the table where women were cutting pies. "I told her I'd take it over while it was still warm. But I'd be glad to let you carry it, Atlee."

"That's not the point," Dat stated in a rising voice. "If you keep covering for Millie every time she falls short, and condoning the company she keeps —"

"Why is it such a chore for you to visit your mother? She's only a block away — and she always perks up when she sees Ella." Mamm flashed Millie a tense smile. "Go have your fun, honey-bug. I know you'll be back to get your grandparents ready for bed."

Millie didn't wait to be told twice. "*Denki*

so much, Mamm. Mammi's been sleepin' a lot lately, so don't be surprised if she won't eat much. Bye, honey-bun," she added as she kissed her baby sister's chubby cheek.

As Millie scurried away from the wedding crowd, she tamped down her rising distress. Was it her imagination, or was Dat's fuse getting shorter? Or was *she,* being a teenager, to blame for his moods? She hoped her mother wouldn't catch a lecture from Dat — and that she wouldn't have to load the heavy box into the rig by herself. Millie paused in the yard. Maybe she should offer to deliver that food.

But Ira's wave made Millie jog faster, until she was springing up into the rig beside him. "Sorry," she murmured.

Ira clapped the lines lightly across his horse's back. "Hope your *dat* didn't give ya too much grief," he said. "I figured I'd best get out of the way, or I'd only provoke him."

It occurred to Millie that a different sort of man might've stuck around to help her, but she'd known all along that Ira Hooley was only out for a good time. "It's behind us now. Mamm sidetracked him."

"Is it just me he doesn't like? Or does he have a burr up his butt, in general?"

Ira's imagery made Millie laugh, although he'd hit upon a subject that wasn't funny.

As the *clip-clop, clip-clop* of the horse's hooves took them away from Willow Ridge, she relaxed into the arm he'd slung around her shoulders. "I don't know," she said with a sigh. "He must've had his reasons for buildin' his house practically in the Morning Star district — away from the rest of the family — back when he married Mamm. I suppose it's closer to the sale barn he runs with Zeb Schrock —"

"And far enough from his folks' place to keep the peace," Ira remarked. "Can't say I'd like havin' a preacher for a dat."

"*Jah,* the way I understand it, Preacher Gabe was none too happy when Dat partnered with Mennonites to become an auctioneer. But that's history," Millie said with a lift in her voice. She smiled at Ira, hoping to change the topic of conversation.

Ira kissed the tip of her nose. "It's that redhead thing," he teased. "You and your *dat* are too much alike, both of ya wantin' to have your way. It's a fight you'll never win, Millie, goin' up against an Amishman. They've got to be *right,* ya know."

Millie looked away. She didn't need to be reminded that Atlee Glick, as the head of the household, did indeed have the upper hand. And what did it say about Ira, that he spoke of Amishmen as though they were a breed apart . . . as though he didn't consider himself one of them?

"So why're we talkin' about my *dat*?" she muttered. It wouldn't do to let Ira know she was upset, so she started a different topic. "Couldn't help but notice your brother wasn't at the wedding."

Ira let out a grunt. "Luke wasn't wild about watchin' his old girlfriend get hitched. They had a tiff when Annie Mae wanted some things out of the Knepp house a while back, so he wrote her off."

Millie rolled her eyes. Annie Mae had told her, in no uncertain terms, that *she* had been the one to end that relationship. Millie was glad her best friend had found a much better man than Luke Hooley to hook up with. Even knowing that Hiram Knepp would probably use his youngest kids as an excuse to cause more trouble, Adam Wagler had willingly taken in the four children, not yet in school, as well as Nellie, who'd just graduated from eighth grade. Adam was head-over-heels for Annie Mae.

Once again Millie felt a rush of yearning, wondering if such a wonderful fellow would ever court her. How long would she have to live in her grandparents' home, hidden away from potential boyfriends as her *rumspringa* passed her by?

A few moments later they were rolling past Millie's house, where the treetops swayed gently in the breeze and the porch swing rocked as though someone invisible sat in it. It wasn't a large house by Amish standards, but there'd been no need to add on to it after she'd been born because nearly fourteen years had passed before baby Ella came along a couple of years ago.

Millie blinked. For a moment, she'd been looking at her home with a sense of utter detachment, as though she'd never been inside it. She'd lived in this place on the far edge of Willow Ridge forever, yet the windows gazed back at her like empty eyes, devoid of feeling.

"Ya got quiet on me," Ira remarked. "Need to go inside for anything? Or for a little smoochin'?"

"*No,* let's — well —" Millie flushed, wondering how to give him the answer he wanted. She craved the kisses Ira was hinting at, yet the scrap she'd had with Dat had set her on edge. "Who knows when my parents might come home? They weren't exactly enjoying the wedding celebration when I left."

"Sorry," he replied with a shrug. "I thought —"

"*Jah,* well, thinkin' can get ya in trouble,"

35

Millie quipped. "You've told me so your-self."

As the next several minutes passed in silence, Millie kicked herself for acting like such a wet blanket. Was it her imagination, or was this outing with Ira getting more awkward by the moment? She racked her brain for something safe to talk about. "So how's your new mill comin' along? Will your store open soon?"

"Got the gas refrigeration units installed this week. The shelves for the bulk foods are all set, too. So, *jah,*" Ira said with a confident nod, "we'll open in a week or so. How many dozen eggs can I sell ya, girlie? Laid by certified free-range chickens that're eatin' organic feed."

Millie let out a laugh. "Why's it such a big deal that chickens are peckin' in the yard instead of livin' in coops?"

"Lots of English are convinced the eggs taste better if the hens aren't confined," he explained with a rise of his dark eyebrows. "They think cages are inhumane — so Luke and I are sellin' them what they think they want. Organic specialty grains are all the rage, too. Along with millin' local farmers' corn and wheat, we're offerin' spelt and millet and quinoa we get from Plain mills around the country."

Millie's eyes widened. "If I have no idea how to cook with that stuff, does that make me stupid?"

Well, ya just begged to be made a fool of. What's with ya today?

Ira squeezed her shoulders. "Nah, it makes ya Plain, Millie. Simpler. Nothin' wrong with that."

And yet, as they circled the outer limits to the north of Willow Ridge, past homes that belonged to Schrock cousins and other Mennonite families, Millie sensed that Ira *did* find something wrong with being Plain. She wondered if the Hooley brothers might drift all their lives, never committing to the Old Order or to marriage. Maybe her *dat* had known that all along, even if her *mamm* allowed her to go out with Ira.

Why does this have to be so complicated? Why am I not having the fun I'd hoped for today?

As the rig headed back toward town, the Wagler place came into view. Millie sat taller, taking in the two-story structure with an addition that had put on a porch and extended the front room and the kitchen, years ago. "Adam and Matthias have done some painting and fixin' up," she remarked, gazing eagerly at the home where Annie Mae and her sibs would live. "Used to be, you could tell by the difference in paint colors which was the old part and the newer part. It'll make them all a real nice home now," she added wistfully.

Ira glanced at her as though she'd sprouted a second head. "That's what happens when a woman enters the picture," he teased. "Adam painted all the rooms and refaced the kitchen cabinets, too, usin' the money he got from sellin' that antique motorcycle he'd stashed in his barn. And who knew about *that*?"

Annie Mae knew. And she believed Adam was sufferin' deep down inside, the same as she was. And now they're both so happy I can hardly stand to watch them.

Millie sighed, but then her breath caught in her throat. The house up the hill, which had once belonged to Hiram Knepp, was buzzing with activity. "Looks like your new neighbor's movin' in. That's a mighty big van."

"It's a big house to fill with furniture." Ira, too, gawked at the men who were wheeling tables and couches out of the truck. "Can't help but wonder what sort of folks bought it, because I doubt any Amish or Mennonites would've coughed up the bucks for that custom horse barn and the land that mansion's sittin' on. My oh my, would ya look at *those* wheels!"

Millie frowned, not seeing any vehicle other than the moving van. There was, however, a woman wearing tiny jean shorts and a clingy lime T-shirt, with a sparkly blue ball cap and big sunglasses. As her auburn ponytail swung with each step she took, Millie's heart sank lower.

Ira was spellbound, and he'd not even spoken to this stranger. He was so far gone, he probably wasn't aware that he'd stopped the buggy in the middle of the road to gape at this woman.

"Wonder what her *husband* does?" Millie speculated in a purposeful tone. "It's not like Willow Ridge has a lot of high-dollar occupations for him to —"

"Who cares?" Ira spouted. "That red BMW convertible parked around the side pretty much says it all."

Once again Ira's conversation left Millie feeling clueless and inept. "Careful, Ira. She's another one of those *redheads,* ya know."

"Yeah, but rich chicks go to salons to get their hair colored. That shade of red comes from a bottle, most likely. Not that I mind."

Millie frowned. Ira was already adrift in his imaginings, to the point he'd forgotten all about *her.* How did he know that lady got her hair colored? Her bouncy ponytail was the same shade as Millie's own hair — but of course, Plain girls wore buns with *kapps* covering most of their heads, so hair color wasn't a big deal. Millie smoothed her white apron over the royal-blue dress that fell mid-calf, over black stockings that ended in simple black shoes. Even dressed in her very best, she felt mousy compared to the woman Ira was ogling.

"Maybe ya should take me back now," she murmured.

Ira blinked as though coming out of a trance. "Oh. Yeah, if that's what ya want," he said as he got the horse going again.

Millie pressed her mouth into a tight line. She'd hoped to stay out all afternoon and then return to Annie Mae's wedding celebration for cake and ice cream, but she'd lost her appetite. If Ira dropped her off at her grandparents' place, it seemed likely that Mamm — and maybe Dat — would still be there. And once Mamm asked why Millie had returned so soon, her father would resume his tirade about the company she was keeping.

Past tense. Ira's history now. I'm invisible to him.

CHAPTER THREE

As Miriam stacked takeout boxes and foil-wrapped packets of wedding food in the Glicks' old refrigerator, the conversation from the front room made her stiffen.

"I'm telling ya, sure as you're starin' at me, Gabe, Nora was *here*!" Wilma Glick rasped. "She was standin' over my bed, lookin' right at me."

"That's crazy talk and you know it!" Preacher Gabe replied gruffly. "And I'll remind you that in this house, we don't speak that name. I have no daughter named Nora. She's been dead to me for more than sixteen years."

Miriam gripped the top of the refrigerator door, her heart thudding. When she and Ben had driven Gabe, Lizzie, and the baby over here with food for Wilma, she'd had no idea what they were walking into. Poor Wilma had been at death's door for months, barely existing and bedridden, yet they'd found her sitting in the front room, wildly excited. What if Wilma had gone over the edge, mentally?

But what if she hasn't? What if Nora was peering at her — and where in the world did she come from? And why? Oh, but this is a big can of worms to be opening —

"Are you *sure*, Wilma?" her daughter-in-law asked in a tight voice. "It's a hot day, and when you're dehydrated you get confused —"

"I'm not confused!" the old woman insisted. "Do ya think I don't know my own child?"

Miriam's hand went to her belly, where a new baby grew. Her maternal heart sympathized deeply with Wilma Glick's predicament. She, too, had lost a daughter — had watched her toddler Rebecca get washed downriver in a flood, more than nineteen years ago — so she knew the gut-wrenching pain of such a loss in a way Preacher Gabe would never understand. Every day she thanked God that Rebecca had miraculously returned to her last fall, after being rescued and raised by English parents.

Was there a way to save this situation, as well? Gabe, in his Old Order male insistence on having his way, might never change his mind about having sent Nora away in her shame. But didn't Wilma deserve to know the truth about her long-lost daughter?

"Maybe it was Millie you saw checking on you," Lizzie suggested gently. "She left the wedding a little bit ago —"

"Why does no one believe me?" Wilma said, sounding close to tears. "This woman was older than Millie. It — it was like looking in a mirror, seeing myself at that age, I tell you. Except she was wearing a blue baseball cap."

Miriam closed the refrigerator and went to the doorway of the front room. Preacher Gabe sat in a straight-backed chair, his arms crossed tightly as he scowled into space. Lizzie stood beside her mother-in-law, rocking little Ella from side to side to keep her from getting fussy. She looked very worried. Scared, even. Ben sat with his elbows on his knees, trying to sort out the details that hadn't been mentioned, because the scandal that had rocked Willow Ridge and the Glick family years ago predated his coming here.

And then there was Wilma. The poor old soul looked a hundred years old, so thin and frail she resembled a skeleton wearing clothes a couple of sizes too big as she sat in an old sewing rocker. But her eyes were alight with a fire Miriam hadn't seen there for years. She was rocking so fast that the sound of the wooden rockers on the hardwood floor filled the front room with her nervous energy.

As Miriam joined her husband and the Glicks, the tension in the front room seemed as thick as sausage gravy with too much pepper. It was pointless to talk with Preacher Gabe, whose face remained stony as he glared through his rimless glasses, so Miriam leaned over Wilma to stop her frantic rocking. "This is a matter for you Glicks to figure out — and Ben and I need to return to the wedding," she said as she rubbed the woman's bony shoulders. She glanced at Lizzie. "Have you and Atlee ever mentioned Nora to Millie?"

Lizzie shook her head. "Atlee went along with his *dat*'s insistence on silence, tryin' to minimize the damage and the tongue-waggin'."

"*Jah,* my husband Jesse was the deacon then. I recall how all the church leaders agreed it was best to put Nora out of our thoughts," Miriam replied with a sigh. "But the same sort of secret came to light when my Rebecca turned up last summer, after she'd discovered that the English woman who'd raised her wasn't her birth *mamm.* I will never forget the pain on that poor child's face," she added emphatically.

"I suggest ya deal with this sooner rather than later," Ben remarked as he rose from his chair. "If our faith and our families are truly foremost in our lives, we need to fix what's broken so we can keep rollin' on, livin' out God's will for us."

Miriam straightened, nodding her agreement. "Not my place to tell ya what to do, but you three and Atlee need to be prepared. This is a skillet full of hot grease that'll splatter on all of ya. But meanwhile, Wilma," she added as she grasped the woman's skeletal hand, "it's real *gut* to see ya up and around again. I hope you'll enjoy that food we brought ya from Annie Mae and Adam's wedding feast."

Wilma's eyes shone like tawny marbles in her withered face. "*Denki* for all ya do, Miriam," she murmured. "Don't be a stranger."

"If ya need anything, I can be here in two shakes of a tail." Miriam sent up a prayer that the Glicks would rely on God's love and comfort and direction to —

"What's goin' on?" came a shrill voice from the kitchen. "And who is *Nora*?"

Miriam turned to see Millie standing in the doorway. As she crossed the front room ahead of Ben, wondering how much of their conversation the girl had heard, her heart rose into her throat. Millie's freckled face, hazel eyes, and deep red hair marked her as Wilma and Atlee's kin, as surely as Miriam's own triplet daughters resembled their blue-eyed *dat. Bless your heart, Millie, you're the picture of your mother, last time any of us saw her,* she thought.

But she couldn't say that out loud.

Miriam gazed into Millie's sweet face, which was taut with a sense that something immensely important had been discussed, and that she had been purposely left out. "Never forget that God loves ya — we *all* love ya — and that you're not alone," she murmured. "If ya need to talk, come see me. My Rebecca could help ya, too."

Millie's eyes widened as she looked from Miriam to Ben. She was trembling like a frightened rabbit. "What's goin' on — *really?*" she rasped.

"Ya need to hear about it from your family. It'll all work out, if ya give it a chance, honey-bug." Miriam hugged the girl and then headed for the kitchen door. Her pulse raced as she wondered how this situation might end. The outcome all depended upon how Lizzie, Atlee, Wilma, Gabe — and Nora — handled it.

Once outside, Ben reached for her hand. "Okay, so who *is* Nora?" her husband asked quietly.

Miriam gazed across the road, past her Sweet Seasons Café and Ben's blacksmith shop, to where dozens of buggies were still parked at Bishop Tom's place. Dressed-up folks chatted in the shade around the Brennemans' cabinetry shop, where they'd eaten their dinner. The people of Willow Ridge had banded together in support of Annie Mae and Adam, who had no parents to help with their wedding — and who'd come through some tough crises in their young lives to stand together in love and faith. Miriam believed her friends and neighbors would also rally around Millie and the Glicks when their story came to light, but some bumpy roads and stormy weather loomed ahead.

"Nora is Millie's mother. Wilma and Gabe's daughter," Miriam replied, gripping her husband's hand. "She was about Millie's age when she got pregnant. Gabe sent her out of town to Wilma's sister's house to have the baby —"

"As often happens when an Amish girl's not married," Ben remarked.

"*Jah,* and I suspect words got said and feelings got hurt before she left home. Nora had a stubborn streak every bit as deep as Gabe's," Miriam continued as they walked down the driveway. "He and Hiram agreed that no more was to be said about Nora in her shamed state — but about nine months later, a redheaded baby showed up on Atlee and Lizzie's porch, in a basket. No doubt in anyone's mind whose baby she was, and that Nora had no intention of raising her."

Ben's brow furrowed as he followed these details. "So Atlee is Nora's brother, and Millie's uncle. And he and Lizzie have raised the girl as their own child."

"That pretty much sums it up," Miriam said with a sigh. "But it's a tangled web they've been weavin', goin' along with Gabe's demand for silence and not tellin' Millie the truth as she got older."

"It's a shame Atlee's distanced himself from his *dat* and *mamm,* too," Ben said. "When ya mentioned his name — back when we were votin' on new preachers after Tom became the bishop and Gabe retired — I hardly knew who ya were talkin' about."

Miriam smiled ruefully. "Atlee's got the Glick stubborn streak, too. When he graduated from eighth grade, he started workin' at Zeb Schrock's auction barn, like he couldn't get away from Preacher Gabe or the farmin' life fast enough. Went to auctioneer school so he could take on a partnership with Zeb," she explained. "And with the Schrocks bein' Mennonites, Gabe considered Atlee's career choice a slap in the face."

Ben thought about all these details as they crossed the county blacktop. "So who was Millie's *dat*? I get the feelin' he either had nothing to say about these events, or that he ducked his responsibility."

"That was another subject Gabe refused to discuss." Miriam shrugged. "Could be that Nora wouldn't tell who he was, to protect the boy from her *dat*'s anger. But truth be told, I was surprised when Nora got — She made *gut* grades. Got a little lippy as a teenager — like a lot of us did — but far as I know, she wasn't datin' anybody steady. It was a mystery. A sad chapter in the lives of the Glicks."

"A mystery," Ben echoed in a lighter tone. He slipped an arm around her shoulders. "God works in mysterious ways, pretty girl."

"We know all about *that,* ain't so?" Miriam asked as she grinned up at him. "Last year at this time, who would've believed I'd be married to the likes of *you,* Bennie, much less carryin' your baby?"

"You're the best thing that ever happened to me, Miriam. Have I told ya lately that I love ya?" Ben bussed her temple and then stopped on the shoulder of the road to kiss her full on the lips.

Miriam felt color spreading across her face. Her younger husband's expressions of affection still made her feel as giddy as a girl, and more blessed than she could ever have imagined. "Not since, oh, maybe noon," she teased.

"I can't say it too often, how you've turned my life around," he murmured as he gazed into her eyes. "We can only hope that if we two love each other so much, so that all the world can see it, maybe other folks will catch on and be just as open about their feelings. Hidin' our light — or our love — under a bushel wasn't what God intended."

"Maybe it'll be you who helps Gabe and his family accept that idea, Preacher Ben. You're a *gut* man and I'm proud of ya."

As they approached the Brennemans' yard, Miriam listened to their friends' laughter drifting on the breeze. She delighted in the smiles of so many folks who'd been a part of her life nearly forever. "If Nora's really back, we're gonna need all the love we can muster. A big pot's about to boil over, and a lot of folks might get scalded — and I see the fella who needs to know what's goin' on."

Miriam waved her hand high above her head to catch Tom Hostetler's attention. He was coming up the road from his farm with a pull cart, bringing bins of his homemade ice cream to serve with the wedding cake outside the Brennemans' shop.

"If I didn't know better, I'd think you two lovebirds were slippin' away for some spoonin'," Bishop Tom teased as he met up with them.

"We could say the same about you and Aunt Naz, the way ya gawk at each other," Ben countered with a chuckle. "But we drove Gabe home just now —"

"Along with Lizzie and little Ella," Miriam continued urgently, "and we found Wilma out of bed and in quite a state. She was carryin' on about how Nora had leaned over her bed and gazed into her face —"

"*Nora?* Why would Nora come back after all these years?" The bishop scratched his silver-shot beard. "Do ya think Wilma was in her right mind?"

Miriam let out a little laugh. "We haven't seen Wilma so perky in a long time. She was so excited, thinkin' her girl had come to see her — but of course Gabe reminded her and Lizzie that they were still not discussin' that subject. And about that time Millie was at the kitchen door, askin' who Nora was."

"Uh-oh. Atlee and Lizzie have some talkin' to do. No matter how ya slice it, Millie's the one who's gonna get cut." Tom gazed out over the farmsteads around them, as if the peaceful, rolling landscape held the answers he was seeking. "If Nora wasn't at the house when ya got there, where do ya suppose she is?"

CHAPTER FOUR

The *hisss-POOF!* of the burner on her new gas stove made Nora jump back with a startled cry. *You're going to blow this place sky-high before you even get unpacked! What were you thinking, buying a house without electricity?*

As she put a small pan of soup on the burner, Nora shook her head. She was surrounded by her microwave, her electric can opener, her blender — all of them useless now. And why had she bought a house with such a huge kitchen? Tanner had entertained his clients in upscale restaurants, so she'd done little cooking since she'd lived in Willow Ridge as a girl. Thank goodness the real estate agent had suggested that she get a gas fridge and stove, along with some battery lamps. He hadn't questioned her insistence on moving back to this little Amish speck in the road — because he'd been laughing all the way to the bank with his hefty commission.

Just like Hiram's laughing. Waiting for this situation to explode in your face.

"Get a grip," Nora muttered. Then she realized she'd been talking to herself ever since the moving van had pulled away an hour ago. Maybe, along with plunking down all her money on this big, impractical piece of property, she was also losing her mind.

She stirred her soup, reminding herself that she'd handled far worse crises than a hissing gas stove and living alone. Tanner had traveled more than he'd stayed home — before he'd announced he was divorcing her to hook up with someone else. Someone more *sophisticated* and *interesting,* he'd said.

Nora swiped at her eyes, stirring faster as the soup bubbled in the pan. It was the stress of moving — the overwhelming prospect of unpacking all these boxes — that was upsetting her. Not to mention how dead her mother had looked in that bed, in that dreary house with all the windows shut tight.

Toughen up. This is nothing compared to living at Aunt Elva's and giving birth at sixteen, when you were clueless and scared to death. If you're to ask forgiveness for dropping Millie on Atlee's doorstep, you've got to face them all. Are you ready for that?

Not a day had gone by that Nora hadn't regretted abandoning her baby, but she'd been too young and upset to foresee the consequences — afraid she'd spend the rest of her miserable life without any way to support a child, beholden to her mother's *maidel* sister. She'd also been too terrified to name the man who'd taken advantage of her, because he'd promised she'd go straight to hell if she did.

You came back for Millie. To make amends . . . to tell her you love her. She's the reason you'll endure whatever flak they throw at you.

What sort of a girl had Millie grown up to be? Had she done well in school? Was she happy, with lots of friends? How had she handled the chip on Atlee's shoulder — *and what if Dat never claimed her as his granddaughter? What if they all poisoned Millie's mind against you, so she'll never want to —*

Nora stiffened as male voices drifted through the kitchen window.

". . . better keep your paws off her, Ira, because *I* saw her first."

When she caught sight of her too-friendly neighbor Luke approaching with a shorter fellow, who was dressed in black-and-white church clothes, Nora groaned. Wolves coming to the door, ready to paw at her, indeed.

Note to self: get real curtains. The narrow pulled-back panels at the edges of each window were *so* Amish, because they bespoke total openness and allowed no secrets — yet another irony in her life. But if she closed the windows and kept full-size curtains drawn against Luke's curiosity, she'd get claustrophobic and die of the heat. *And why, again, did you buy a house without central air?*

"Hey, new neighbor lady!" Luke called out. "We came to see if you need any help yet."

Nora nearly choked on laughter — but maybe if she kept quiet, these rubes would go away.

"I know you're in there," Luke teased in a singsong voice. "Smells like chicken noodle soup."

Nora swore under her breath as she turned off the burner. Her hair was a mess, she was wearing no makeup, she was hot and tired and testy — and she *would* find a way to convince these two turkeys to leave her alone. When she opened the back kitchen door, however, Luke walked inside as though he owned the place, followed by his companion.

"This is my little brother Ira," he said as

he nailed her with a green-eyed gaze. "And we're pleased to make your acquaintance, *Nora.*"

"H-how'd you know my name?" she stammered.

Luke's lips flickered wryly. "Hiram stopped by to tell us you'd moved in."

The blood rushed from her head as she caught a whiff of wintergreen on his breath. What else had Hiram revealed about her — and her past? What if these guys went blabbing to everyone about how she'd —

"Hey, nice stove," Ira remarked as he looked around the cluttered kitchen. "So, do ya like to cook, Nora?"

Their hopeful expressions brought Nora out of her panic. Here was her chance to get rid of two nosy Amish bachelors looking for home-cooked meals. "If I can't microwave it, I can't cook it," she replied plaintively. "But there aren't any plug-ins. So I'm figuring out how to open soup with a manual can opener and —"

"Nobody told ya about the solar panels?" Ira blurted.

Luke was staring at her as though he couldn't believe she hadn't noticed the lack of electricity when she'd bought the place. Nora found herself way too riveted by his intense gaze, so she watched his brother open the pantry door. "Solar panels? That sounds too progressive for an Amish town."

"Ah, but see, Hiram had more gadgets than he was supposed to," Ira replied as he held up two cables with electrical adapters on the ends.

"Which is why those solar panels are on the back side of the roof, away from the road," Luke explained. "Knepp arranged his power cables so they came into closets, so any visitors from the district wouldn't see his TV set and the computer that hooked up to the security system in his barn. He's a real piece of work, Hiram is."

Nora was so ecstatic about having power for her small appliances that she momentarily set aside her concern about any information the former bishop might've revealed to Luke Hooley. She could plug in her microwave and blender and blow dryer! She could make toast for breakfast! Maybe these guys were worth knowing, after all, if —

"Annie Mae used to tell us about her *dat*'s gadgets when Luke and I were runnin' the roads with her and Millie Glick," Ira said in an offhand voice. "And gee, now that Annie Mae's married to Adam Wagler, they'll be your neighbors on the other side."

Nora had lost him at the mention of her

daughter's name. Once again she fought waves of panic, wondering if these brothers knew more about her than they were letting on — maybe baiting her to reveal more answers. *I remember Annie Mae when she was in diapers! What kind of losers are these guys, if they're nearly my age yet dating girls young enough to be my daughter — not to mention running the roads with my Millie?*

She struggled to keep a straight face. These chatty brothers might be rubes, but they were also potential fonts of knowledge about Willow Ridge and its inhabitants. "So, what else can you tell me about this house and —"

Luke's catlike eyes narrowed as he walked around her, looking her up and down. "You could pass for Millie's sister," he murmured in an appreciative voice. "Don't you think so, Ira?"

Ira studied her face and hair, his thumbs hooked behind his suspenders. "Millie'll never have this much *class*," he declared. "But that's because she doesn't get out much, what with takin' care of her grandmother, and livin' under old Preacher Gabe's nose."

"But since you're not Amish, you'll not have much reason to get acquainted with him," Luke added matter-of-factly. "Except for eating at the café most mornings, he doesn't get out much anymore, either. Gabe's so old and crippled up, he's retired from preaching."

Again Nora fought to maintain her neutral facial expression. She'd never known an Amish preacher to retire — it was a lifelong commitment — so her father must be severely disabled. While the Hooley brothers were fascinated by her resemblance to Millie, they seemed to have no clue that Gabe Glick was her father . . . *so if Dat has claimed Millie as his granddaughter, she surely believes Atlee and Lizzie are her parents. But if Millie's living with Dat and Mamma, how will I ever reconcile with them first, without her being in the middle of it?*

This was no time to get lost in such concerns, however. If she was to get any more information about Willow Ridge and the people here, she had to ask questions as though she were a newcomer. "So is there a real grocery store anywhere close?" Nora asked. "Or is that little place with the blue metal roof where you do your shopping?"

Ira rolled his eyes. "Zook's Market's the closest thing we've got to a store —"

"There's an English supermarket in New Haven," Luke cut in suavely, "but we usually eat at the Sweet Seasons. Our older brother Ben's married to the woman who runs the place, and it's where most everybody goes for breakfast and lunch —"

"The guys do, anyway," Ira agreed, "on account of how the buffet, along with the pies and rolls in the bakery counter are the best anywhere. We bring home enough for our supper, usually. If it weren't for Miriam's place, a lot of us single fellas would starve."

Note to self: don't eat at the café. The Hooley brothers are always there.

Nodding, Nora feigned ignorance again. "So, what do people around here do for entertainment?"

The brothers looked at each other and burst out laughing. "Oh, honey, if ya think there's movie theaters or miniature golf," Ira began with a chuckle, "ya moved to the wrong spot in the road."

Luke was studying her closely. "Didn't you check out any of this stuff before you bought a house in an Amish town?" he quizzed her. "The nearest place with anything going on is Warrensburg, where there's a college —"

"I did enough homework to know I could find some peace and quiet here," Nora retorted, hoping her tone would shut them up — and cover the irony of that statement.

Peace was the *last* thing she'd experience once her father and brother found out she'd returned. "Willow Ridge is a quaint little town in the countryside, and the house was a steal, compared to what such a place would've cost in Saint —" She stopped before she revealed where she'd previously lived. "Anyway, I figured I'd get an electrician out here, and have cable installed —"

"Hiram had a satellite dish," Ira said.

"Yep. Attached it to the back side of his barn," Luke clarified. "But of course, since we could see it from our apartment above the mill, he told us it was part of the security system for his Belgian breeding business rather than for watching TV."

"Like he thought we were too stupid to know better," Ira chimed in.

Although Nora chuckled with them, she realized that too much chitchat with these nosy neighbors wasn't in her best interest. Luke and Ira probably couldn't wait to spread the word about their new neighbor when they went to the café for breakfast tomorrow morning — where her father might be eating.

Nora suddenly felt overwhelmed by the many repercussions of her return she hadn't anticipated. She had very little time left to remain anonymous, or to tell Mamma or

Millie about her return before the grapevine buzzed like a swarm of hornets. Longtime residents would remember who she was and why she'd left, and when they quizzed Dat about her return, he would *not* be happy. *Forgive and forget* might be the key to the Amish faith, but unless her father had undergone a personality transplant, he would never welcome her back.

With a sigh, Nora glanced at the soup congealing in the saucepan. "It's been a really long day, guys. How about if I visit with you again some other time?"

One of Luke's eyebrows rose in a distinctive curve, accentuating his furtive green-eyed gaze. "You sure you'll be all right here without any lights, or —"

"Or any company in this big ole house?" Ira asked. "Might get kinda spooky here, all by your lonesome."

Nora caught herself before she revealed that she knew quite well how to get by with lanterns. She pointed to the two battery lamps on the counter. "I'll be fine, really. But thanks for asking."

"And your bed's put together?" Luke asked with another of his suggestive gazes.

With an exasperated gasp, Nora pointed to the back door. "Who do you think you're dealing with? I *really* don't need your help."

The brothers exchanged a knowing look as they put on their straw hats and left.

Nora felt a tension headache coming on. Would her words come back to haunt her once Luke and Ira knew who she really was?

CHAPTER FIVE

As they left her grandparents' house to return to the wedding festivities, Millie had to walk very fast to keep up with her *mamm.* Her heart throbbed painfully from overhearing just enough of the adults' conversation to be bothersome — and she felt as though she'd explode because of what she had *not* heard.

"So who's Nora?" she demanded in a strained voice.

Mamm glanced up the county highway in one direction and then down the other before they crossed it. Her face nearly matched her white *kapp* and light blond hair, and she was clutching Ella so tightly that the poor little girl's eyes were wide. "We'll talk about it when we get home," she answered stiffly.

"But I'll be going back to take care of Mammi tonight, so —"

"Nora is your *dat*'s sister," her mother

snapped. "He needs to know she's in town — or else we need to take your *mammi* to a doctor, if she's been hallucinatin'."

Millie frowned. "If Dat has a sister, why have I never heard about her? And why doesn't she live here in —"

"Enough already!" Mamm stepped in front of Millie, stopping her on the shoulder of the road. "Not a word of this to *anybody* until we can be sure what's goin' on, understand me?"

Millie's heart shriveled. All her life she'd endured her *dat*'s temper and her grandfather's brusque manner, so her mother's angry demand sliced her heart like a knife. "I — I only asked," she whimpered, "because it sounds like everybody but me knows what's going on and — and because of what Miriam said before she left. She was *worried* about me, Mamm. Because of this Nora."

Suddenly Mamm's face fell and she let out the breath she'd been holding. She caressed Millie's cheek. "I'm sorry it's come to this," she murmured. "We can't understand why the Lord allows things to happen the way they do. If I'd had my way, you would've been told about Nora long ago."

Her mother appeared torn between what she knew and what she wasn't ready to reveal, so Millie sensed she'd better keep her questions to herself. She swallowed hard, but the lump remained in her throat as they resumed their rapid stroll to the Brenneman place. Clusters of wedding guests dotted the lawn beneath the big shade trees, some of them in chairs and some of them standing. Farther across the lot, the little girls were squealing in their best pastel dresses while the boys darted after them, playing tag. Millie had the feeling she'd never again feel that carefree, once the family secret had been revealed to her.

With an odd expression on her face, Mamm passed baby Ella to Millie and then made a beeline toward Dat. He was visiting with Adam Wagler's brother, Matthias, about retired racehorses that were being sold at an upcoming auction — a topic of interest to Amish men, who bought these beautiful horses and retrained them to pull their buggies.

"I might be in the market for a couple of geldings," Matthias was saying. "What with Adam and Annie Mae moving in, I suspect we'll be needing another —"

"Excuse me, Matthias," Mamm said as she strode up to the two men. "I've got to talk to Atlee. *Now.*"

Matthias's eyes widened. "Sure thing,

Lizzie. Thanks for the scoop on this next auction, Atlee. See you there," he said as he walked toward the Brennemans' shop.

Millie cooed to Ella when the baby started fussing, sensing she should hang back even as she desperately wanted to hear what her parents were about to discuss. Dat's frown warned her to make herself invisible, too. She ambled off as though she might help Miriam's daughter Rhoda set up a croquet game for the kids, but not so far off that she couldn't hear.

"What's with you?" her *dat* demanded. "I was talking business with Matthias —"

"Nora's back," Mamm said nervously. "She — she went to see your *mamm,* so now —"

"She *what?*"

Her *dat*'s tone of voice made Millie turn. His face, burnished by years of outdoor work, had turned so white that his freckles looked ready to pop off as he stared at her mother.

Mamm looked terrified. "When we took that box of food for your folks," she went on in a rush, "Wilma was in the front room, sayin' Nora had been leanin' over the bed lookin' at her —"

"That's crazy," Dat argued. "Surely you didn't believe —"

"Hear me out," Mamm insisted, stepping closer to him so her voice wouldn't carry to the other guests. "Your *mamm* seemed totally rational — excited, even — but your *dat* refused to talk about it. And then Millie —"

"It's all fine and *gut* for him to hide behind his silence," Dat muttered. "He hasn't had to live with Nora's mistakes all these —"

"Atlee!" Mamm's voice cracked. When she saw that Millie was still standing nearby, she swiped at tears and quickly focused on Dat again. "Think about what you're sayin', *before* ya say it," she pleaded. "Millie walked in and the conversation came to a halt —"

"And Miriam and Ben were there? It'll be all over town by —"

"Which is why we need to talk to Millie —"

"No, *we* do not," Dat blurted as he took off his straw hat and then crammed it back on his head. "We're goin' home. *Now.*"

As her father strode across the yard toward the parked buggies, Millie could barely breathe. Why was it such a big, secret deal that Dat's sister had come back to Willow Ridge? And why did Mamm's face look like a crumpled wad of paper as she glanced

Millie's way? Millie forced her feet to move despite the confusion that was making her heart constrict. "Mamm?" she murmured, tightening her hold on wiggly Ella.

Her mother quickly kissed her cheek as she took the baby from Millie's arms. "I don't know what to say, what to do just yet," Mamm rasped. "It's best that ya go back to look after your *mammi* tonight, because ya can see what a state your *dat*'s in."

Millie nodded solemnly. She and her mother had gotten a lot of practice at tiptoeing around Dat's moods over the years.

"Your *dawdi* won't want to discuss this, either," Mamm warned, "so don't push your luck by askin' Mammi to explain things. Be patient, all right? I wish this was goin' differently, honey. I — I love ya, Millie."

As her mother rushed off toward the buggy, Millie stood awkwardly in the yard. The playing children and the other guests on the lawn seemed to disappear in the haze of despair that enveloped her. While she had never doubted her mother's love, they seldom put their affection into words — and this, after Miriam had told her that everyone loved her, just moments ago.

A familiar voice cut through her thoughts. "Millie! I thought ya might still be out with Ira!"

Millie blinked. Annie Mae — now Mrs. Adam Wagler — rushed up and grabbed both of her hands. "We're cuttin' the cake! Come on, ya gotta be there with me!"

"*Jah,* sure," Millie murmured. She allowed Annie Mae to lead her toward the shop building because it gave her something real to do, instead of drifting off in a confused daze. But just short of the door, Millie stopped. "Annie Mae, do ya know anything about a gal named Nora?" she asked urgently. "I guess she's Dat's sister, but I've never seen her."

Annie Mae frowned. "Well, *that's* odd. Never heard of her. Why?"

Millie shrugged. It seemed wrong to bother her best friend about this situation on the biggest day of her life, so she forced herself to smile. "Never mind," she said as she opened the door. "We don't want Bishop Tom's ice cream to melt while everybody's waitin' for it."

A few hours later, when Millie returned to her grandparents' house, *melting* was something her *dawdi* was obviously not going to do. As she entered the front room, he rose from his chair to stand behind the rocker where Mammi sat, as though she'd been there all afternoon. She still appeared alert,

71

but her expression — the shining hazel eyes that blazed in her wrinkled face — warned Millie not to make any waves.

Mammi winced, probably because Dawdi was squeezing her bony shoulders too hard. "And how was the wedding?" she asked in a voice that sounded raspy from lack of use.

Millie walked as close as she dared, considering her grandfather's harsh expression. "It was a fine day," she murmured. "I brought ya both some cake, and some of Tom's peppermint-stick ice cream. So how come you're still up and sittin' in here, Mammi? Ya must be feelin' so much better —"

"A bee got under her bonnet," her grandfather muttered, "and once it gets loose, we'll all get stung. I'm puttin' her to bed, and you're to go to your room, Millie."

Millie blinked. It wasn't nearly dark yet, but she knew better than to argue that Dawdi might not be able to help Mammi into her nightgown, as he wasn't very steady on his feet. As she trudged up the creaky wooden stairs, she wondered yet again about the strange situation, and about this Nora who seemed to be overturning everyone's apple carts.

She thought about slipping out after her grandparents were settled in bed, but whom could she talk to? Her parents didn't want her around. If Annie Mae had no idea about Nora, none of her other friends probably knew her, either. She hated to bother Miriam, because she and Ben would be clearing away the food from the wedding supper. And Ira was too moony-eyed over his new neighbor to listen to her concerns.

As dusk fell, Millie sat on her bed watching the shadows fill her tomblike room. *I've got to hear this Nora story from somebody. But who?*

CHAPTER SIX

At five o'clock on Friday morning, Nora strode across the parking lot of the Sweet Seasons Bakery Café. The lights were on in the back of the building, and while she hated to interrupt Miriam's baking, this seemed like her best opportunity for some damage control. It was only right that her parents, Atlee, Lizzie, and Millie hear about her presence before the grapevine blazed with news of her return, just as it was a sure thing that Luke and Ira Hooley would be blabbing about their new redheaded neighbor when they came here for breakfast. Nora hoped Miriam was still the level-headed, compassionate woman she'd been years ago, when she'd been raising school-aged Rachel and Rhoda.

But a lot of things had changed in Willow Ridge. Nora was finding out the hard way that she hadn't anticipated nearly enough of the complications she would cause when she showed her face. She knocked on the back door.

"*Jah?* It's open," Miriam called out.

Such a lack of concern for security took Nora back to her childhood, when nobody had locked any doors. As she stepped into the kitchen, a warm sweetness redolent with yeast and sugar and cinnamon wrapped around her like a cozy shawl. Miriam stood at the back counter arranging rolled-out pie dough in the metal pie pans that covered most of her work area. She was thicker in the middle than Nora remembered, but she worked with the same cheerful energy and efficiency. When Miriam looked up, her brown eyes widened. The crust she'd been lifting dropped into the nearest pan.

"So it's true," she murmured. "Wilma said you'd been to see her yesterday, but nobody wanted to believe her. Hello, Nora."

"Hi," Nora murmured. "I was hoping you'd help me with — see, I bought Hiram Knepp's house —"

"*Did* ya, now?"

"— and Luke and Ira Hooley have already introduced themselves —"

"*Jah,* I just bet they have."

"And, well . . ." Nora lost track of what she'd intended to say. Miriam's expressive face embodied the best of Amish simplicity,

75

concern, and wisdom, which reminded Nora yet again of the life she had fled — and the family she might not be able to reconcile with, no matter how sincerely she wanted to. "Mamma recognized me?"

"Oh, *jah,* and now your *dat* and Lizzie are flustered right along with her," Miriam replied in a low voice. "And then there's poor Millie, who walked in when my Ben and I were leavin'." Miriam came to stand in front of Nora, her face solemn as she crossed her arms. "That girl has no idea about who ya are, Nora, but all the adults she loves and trusts are in a dither over ya. I hope ya know what you're doin', comin' back to town this way. I want no part of breakin' Millie's heart or tearin' her life apart."

A sob escaped Nora and her hands fluttered to cover it. "This is *not* the way I'd intended to come home — honest to God, I came back to ask their forgiveness. To reconcile with Mamma and Dat before they — and to be Millie's mother."

Miriam's brow arched sternly. "But see, Millie already *has* a mamm, and as far as she knows, it's Lizzie. And don't be talkin' so fast and loose when you're usin' God's name, either. I won't stand for it."

Nora swallowed so hard her throat clicked.

It seemed the dominoes were already falling in a chain reaction that she'd lost control over. "I came here to ask for your help, Miriam," she pleaded, "because I remember you as calm and supportive and — and loving, when other people —"

Miriam's face remained taut.

Nora wiped her eyes with her hand and then realized she'd smeared her mascara — just one more point this steadfast Old Order woman would chalk up against her. "I suspect Luke and Ira will come here for breakfast. They'll start blabbing about the neighbor who's bought Hiram's place —"

"*Jah,* that'll be big news around here."

"— and I didn't want Dat to hear about it secondhand. But if he already knows . . ." Nora shook her head, gazing sadly at the plank floor. "I should've stayed at the house yesterday until folks got back from the wedding. But when I saw Mamma in that bed, looking like a corpse — and then when she opened her eyes — I got so startled, I ran out. I hope I didn't . . . finish her off."

Nora focused on Miriam through her tears. "I've really, *really* made a mess of things, haven't I?"

Miriam stepped forward to wrap her sturdy arms around Nora's shoulders. "Now you're talkin' like the gentle, sweet Nora I

77

remember," she murmured. "You're on the right path, but it's not gonna be a walk in the park. When ya left, your *dat* insisted that none of us speak about ya ever again, and he's maintainin' that silence now. Your *mamm,* bless her heart, is out of bed for the first time in months, *so* excited that she saw ya."

Nora eased away from the embrace that felt so welcoming. "She knew me?"

"For sure and for certain." Miriam's face creased with her smile. "You'll always be her little girl, Nora. And *your* little girl is the spittin' image of ya when ya went away."

While that information formed a sweet, sentimental picture in her mind, it didn't make her situation any easier. "What'll I do?" Nora whispered. "How can I tell Millie about why I left her with Atlee and Lizzie? And what if she won't have anything to do with me, or —"

"One thing at a time," Miriam murmured. "If God has brought ya to this situation, He'll get ya through it. Ya believe that, don't ya?"

Nora sensed she was being tested, yet hadn't she known she would have to deal with the Old Order faith if she was to reconcile with her family? "He's about the only chance I've got left, ain't so?"

The words sounded lame as they tumbled from her mouth, yet Miriam's lips lifted. "Most of us find ourselves in that position at some time in our lives. But when you've landed at the bottom of the pit, the only way to go is *up.*" She glanced toward the back window. "Ben just went into the smithy. Let's go introduce ya."

Nora wasn't all that comfortable with spilling her story to a total stranger, but she didn't argue. "Ben's your husband now — Luke and Ira's brother, right?" she asked as they stepped out into the pale daylight. "Some of the stuff those guys told me yesterday might not have sunk in. I was pretty tired by the time the moving van pulled out."

"Being Luke and Ira's brother doesn't mean Ben'll have any control over what they say this morning," Miriam added with a short laugh. "He's a *gut* man, though. He's a preacher now, on account of how your *dat*'s retired because of his failin' health —"

Nora sighed as they approached the small white smithy she remembered from her childhood. "I had no idea he and Mamma were doing so poorly," she remarked. "I wondered about them and Millie the whole time I was away, but one thing and another kept me from getting here any sooner."

"That's a story best saved for another day," Miriam said as she swung open the smithy door. "Bennie, this is the Nora that the Glicks were buzzin' about yesterday," she said as she approached the man at the forge. "She's come back to make peace with her folks, and we're hopin' you'll keep Luke and Ira quiet during breakfast at the bakery so she can meet up with Gabe. She's bought Hiram's place, ya see, so they've been over to meet their new neighbor." Miriam smiled at Nora. "This is my husband of seven months, Ben Hooley."

"Nora," Ben said with a cautious nod. He looked somewhat younger than Miriam, as vibrant as his brothers. The sandy-brown hair and open smile he had in common with Luke looked more compelling on a face framed by a beard. "And ya want to speak with your *dat* at the café? Why not over at the house?"

Miriam fitted herself against Ben as he slipped an arm around her shoulders. It was an affectionate gesture Nora had never seen her parents share — nor did she recall Miriam getting this cozy with her first husband, Jesse Lantz. It gave her hope that maybe things in Willow Ridge had loosened up since she was a kid.

"When Dat sent me away from home

sixteen years ago, he told me I was never to show my face there again," she explained. "When your brothers told me he often eats breakfast at the café, I was hoping that if I met him in a public place —" Nora crossed her arms, hugging herself as though to hold body and soul together. "It's probably another one of my bad ideas."

"Well, you've got grit, facin' him in front of everybody," Ben remarked. "And Tom Hostetler, our bishop, usually sits with your *dat*, so —"

"Why do they eat in the café?" Nora blurted. When she realized that Miriam might take offense at her question, she said, "I mean, when I was a kid everybody ate at home."

Ben chuckled. "The Sweet Seasons is where I met Miriam," he replied with an endearing smile. "For a lot of unattached fellas, it's the best place for miles around to get a *gut* meal — and eatin' breakfast here is a way for your *dat* to get out amongst other people. Even with Millie lookin' after him and your *mamm,* he's been pretty much housebound for the last few years."

"And we can hope that if he sits with Bishop Tom this morning," Miriam went on in a pensive voice, "he'll not be as inclined to — well, we can't predict what Gabe might do. But I'm glad you're givin' it a try, Nora. Stay brave and pray."

Nora's heart shriveled when she pictured her father's negative reaction to seeing her, yet Miriam's words rang with an air of confidence. *Stay brave and pray.* Hadn't such a sentiment kept her going through a lot of tough times, even if she hadn't expressed it so succinctly? Even if she hadn't prayed as often as she should have?

"No matter how your *dat* reacts, though," Miriam continued as she gazed at Nora, "it's your *mamm* and Millie and Lizzie who need to know why you're back in Willow Ridge. Your return's gonna tear their lives apart in different ways, but it's always the women who can put the pieces together again and move on. Where there's a woman, there's a way."

Nora's mouth opened and then closed. How had Miriam managed to portray the most dismal storm and then paint a rainbow arching over the clouds? "Thank you," she murmured. "No matter what happens, I appreciate your help."

Luke entered the Sweet Seasons in fine fettle Friday morning, itching to tell Matthias Wagler and the Brenneman brothers that he'd met the mystery person who'd bought Hiram's house — mostly to let them know he had first dibs on her. Matthias, the local harness maker, was Nora's neighbor on the other side, and a widower. He was likely to be feeling more pinched by his single state now that his younger brother Adam had married Annie Mae and brought her five younger siblings to live with them. Luke hoped to dissuade Matthias's interest in the sizzling redhead who was keeping more secrets than she could cram into her red BMW's trunk —

"So where do ya suppose Nora got off to so early?" Ira was saying as the café's bell jingled above their heads. "Seems odd that she didn't have any lamps lit —"

"That's none of your beeswax," Luke muttered, grabbing his brother's arm. "And if she figures out you've been peering through her windows —"

"Like *you* haven't!" Ira retorted, jerking away from Luke's grasp. "You're so far gone you're gonna trip over your tongue and —"

"Mornin', fellas. It's *gut* to see the two of ya ready for another day of workin' together at the mill." Ben rose from a table near the door with a purposeful smile. "I was hopin' you'd join me for breakfast. My treat."

Luke's eyebrows rose. Though he got along fine with his older brother, Ben's generosity struck him as . . . fishy. "What's the occasion?"

"Do I need a reason to buy you boys a meal?" Ben asked as he gestured toward the buffet line at the other side of the dining room. Then he smiled at Rebecca, Miriam's English-raised daughter who often waited tables during the early shift. "Coffee all around, and a big glass of milk for Ira. He's a growin' boy, ya know."

As the three of them made their way between the tables, Luke looked around. All the regulars seemed to be in their usual places. He nodded when Seth and Aaron Brenneman greeted him, and noted the table of English fellows from down the road who often ate here. Bishop Tom and Gabe Glick were headed for their habitual corner table. The retired preacher seemed more stooped this morning, and he didn't argue when Tom offered to carry his steaming plate from the buffet.

"Happy Friday morning to ya," Miriam called out as she bustled from the kitchen with a basket that held three brown, rounded loaves of bread. "We're featurin' the five-grain bread mix from your mill today, Luke — and Naomi's stirrin' up more sausage gravy, scrambled eggs, and onions so ya can make haystacks with the hash browns, too."

Luke snatched three slices of the bread, which were so dense with grains and dried fruit that he nearly crammed a slice into his mouth on the spot. As he mounded hash browns on his plate, Seth Brenneman joined them at the steam table for his second plateful. He seemed particularly cheerful as he greeted the three of them.

"*Gut* thing I got here before you Hooleys loaded up," he teased.

"Unless I miss my guess, you'll be tankin' up at your own breakfast table before long," Ira replied. "You and Mary looked mighty tight at the wedding yesterday."

Seth couldn't hide his grin. "We'll do the finishin' work on her house this week, so she and the kids'll be movin' into it by next weekend. Yesterday I asked her if I could join them as the man of the family, and Mary said yes!"

"That's *gut* news even if it comes as no surprise," Ben replied, clapping Seth on the back. "I figured it was a go when she came to town with Sol and Lucy last Christmas, when ya helped deliver baby Emmanuel. Givin' yourselves plenty of time to get acquainted was the best idea for all of ya."

As his brothers chatted with Seth, Luke filled his plate and returned to the table. He recalled how Seth had rescued Mary Kauffman mere hours before she gave birth at the local clinic — and how the idea of getting romantically involved with a widow who had three little kids had repelled him. It was nearly the same situation Adam Wagler had married into yesterday, agreeing to raise Annie Mae's four little siblings and take in her teenage sister, Nellie. Adam was asking for trouble, too, because Hiram Knepp wouldn't leave well enough alone. What was it with these bachelors who'd sacrificed their happy lives to raise other men's kids?

Well, now that you're thirty, what sort of women are left to hook up with? They've all been married, and they all carry baggage —

"Here you go, Luke." Rebecca set their three mugs of coffee on the table along with Ira's milk. "I'll be back in a few to be sure everything's the way you like it."

"*Denki,* Rebecca," Luke murmured. He'd had his share of fantasies about their waitress — Miriam's daughter had been raised by adoptive English parents after they'd rescued her during a flood years ago. She was a looker, she was single, and she made no bones about keeping her computer business rather than joining the Old Order. It was a combination he found very attractive.

And yet, as Ben and Ira took their seats at the table and began to eat, Luke's thoughts wandered toward his new redheaded neighbor. Nora Landwehr was divorced, Hiram had said, but he hadn't revealed why a woman who could afford such a prime property would choose to move to Willow —

Luke's fork stopped halfway to his mouth. Nora was standing in the kitchen doorway!

She wore a brown cape dress with a matching apron and a white *kapp.* Her pale face and tight expression quelled Luke's urge to blurt out a greeting, but he watched her pass between the tables with great interest. Why was she dressed Plain? And why would she be heading toward the corner where Bishop Tom and Gabe Glick were sitting? Ira was digging into his breakfast, but Ben sat taller, watching Nora as though he sensed something intense was about to happen.

The chatter around them masked what Nora was saying. Bishop Tom's eyes widened in recognition as Gabe Glick threw down his fork and struggled to his feet. His scowl could've soured cream — and Nora stepped back when he flashed it at her. She said something else to the old preacher, pleading with wide eyes that spoke of great pain and remorse, but Gabe pointed vehemently toward the door.

"Get thee behind me, Satan!" he snapped.

The dining room went silent. As all eyes turned to witness the drama unfolding in the corner, Luke didn't care what quarrel the old preacher had with Nora. A protective urge surged within him and he stood up so fast, his chair fell over backwards.

Ben grabbed his wrist. "Leave it be, Luke," he murmured. "We need to let God's will run its course."

The bell above the door jangled, but Luke didn't turn to see who'd come in. His list of reasons for not joining the Old Order had just gotten longer. Gabe began to hobble from the table, slapping Nora's arm when she tried to assist him. Murmurs rose around the room and Tom stood up.

"Gabe, there's a better way," the bishop insisted as he caught up to the preacher. "Maybe it's time to reconsider —"

"I don't *have* a daughter," Gabe huffed as he shuffled toward the door. Then he raised his head. "Millie. Take me home, child. *Now.*"

Luke turned in time to see Millie's hands fly to her mouth. She was staring so intently at Nora that she didn't realize the door was opening behind her, or that Hiram Knepp couldn't come inside. As the excommunicated bishop of Willow Ridge took in the scene, his coal-black mustache and goatee made him look downright wicked. A grin lit his chiseled face. He knew exactly what was happening, and he was delighted to be watching it play out.

Did he orchestrate this scene? Luke mused. Hiram had surely seen Millie entering the café. Perhaps he'd been lurking near the smithy or peering into the window of the Sweet Seasons kitchen, aware that Nora was inside. Luke wondered how long Nora had been back there with Miriam and Naomi, but he had no such questions about Knepp's motives. Hiram's devious ways knew no limits.

Millie backed away from her grandfather, as though his scowl and words frightened her. Hiram stepped in then, offering the preacher a steadying arm. "Got you covered, Gabe," he murmured. "We keepers of the faith have to stick together."

And what did *that* mean?

When Luke looked from Millie to Nora, his previous speculations about his new neighbor began spinning in his gut. Gabe might have just denied that he had a daughter, but there was no getting around it: Nora and Millie were kin. Luke doubted the old preacher would be making such a fuss if

Nora were Millie's aunt, so did this mean . . . ?

This was no time to ponder such a startling idea, however. As Ben and Ira made their way toward Millie, Luke strode between the tables to where Miriam had slung her arm around Nora's shoulders. "Are you all right?" he asked earnestly. "I don't know what that was all about, but —"

"You will," Nora rasped. "You and everybody else have just witnessed my humiliation —"

"Honey-bug, ya did your best," Miriam insisted. "Ya made the first move, tryin' to make peace with your *dat* about your daughter, and ya knew it might not go so well."

So there you have it. Nora is *Millie's mother.* Luke fought the urge to grasp Nora's shoulder. Miriam's protective tone implied that Nora was no stranger to her. The recollection of her red BMW racing away from the Glick place took on a whole new meaning for him: Nora had grown up in that house and had been banished. Yet she'd come back.

From across the crowded café, the expression on Millie's face tore at him. She didn't know Nora, but on a gut level she was piecing this puzzle together, just as he was.

"Nora, how can I help?" Luke murmured. "If you want to speak with Millie —"

"We could let ya into the quilt shop, where it's private," Miriam suggested. "The Schrocks won't open it until nine."

When Nora gazed again at the girl who could be her double, Millie pivoted toward the door. Ira and Ben went outside with her, talking in low voices.

"I've blown it again," Nora whimpered. "Why did I think this reunion was a good idea? Or that it would go as I'd seen it in my mind, hundreds of times?"

"Seems to me you've got two choices," Miriam insisted gently. "Ya can catch Millie now, while Ben's with her. Or ya can wait. I can understand why you'd like some time to get your nerves together again. And I can see where leavin' this to hang — takin' your chances that other folks might tell her things ya wish they hadn't — might make it even harder to approach her next time."

"I'll go with ya, if ya want," Bishop Tom offered as he approached them. "This isn't an easy situation you've set yourself up for, Nora, but I believe you've done the right thing."

"I'll go with you, too, if you'd like," Luke murmured. "Or I can get Ira out of your way so you and Millie can talk. He means well, but sometimes he doesn't have a clue."

When Nora gazed up at him, Luke's stomach did a flip-flop. Her eyes shone like honey mixed with cinnamon and gratitude. Red flags flapped in his mind, warning him that he was getting way too involved in a sticky situation, yet he held her gaze, awaiting her answer.

Nora grabbed his hand. "Let's catch them before they cross the road, or — well, before Millie gets hurt any further."

Luke followed her outside, sucking in fresh air to fortify himself. Nora's hand felt like a branding iron but he couldn't let go. They spotted his two brothers walking on either side of Millie, slowly heading up the lane toward the Lantz house. Ira was holding her hand while Ben was talking to her, his head bent near the *kapp* that covered her auburn bun. When they stepped into the grass near the apple trees, Nora clutched Luke's hand.

"Wait!" she called out. "Millie, *please* wait for me."

CHAPTER SEVEN

Millie stopped. The woman's voice sounded achingly familiar even as she knew that was impossible. Surely the thudding of her heart and the rush of her thoughts were affecting her hearing because — except for a glance at this woman yesterday, when she'd worn shorts and a sparkly ball cap instead of a cape dress and a *kapp* — Millie had never seen this stranger.

But deep down, Millie vibrated with the truth.

She closed her eyes. Maybe if she pretended this wasn't happening, she'd awaken to find she'd been caught up in a bad dream. She could forget that yesterday she'd learned her *dat* had a sister, yet moments ago her grandfather had denied he had a daughter. She could chalk it all up to a huge misunderstanding or a coincidence that someone who looked just like her had bought the house on Bishop's Ridge Road.

That someone was approaching her now, even as Millie squeezed her eyes tighter.

"Come on, Ira. Let's make ourselves scarce," Luke said from a few feet behind her.

How ironic that yesterday Ira had been drooling over this woman — *Would ya look at those wheels!* — yet now he was standing with *her.* Millie released his hand when he eased it away.

"This'll all work out the way it's supposed to, Millie," Ben murmured as he went with his brothers. "We'll all be prayin' for ya."

Millie nearly begged Ben to stay, but her throat was too tight to say anything.

So she stood alone, with the breeze teasing her skirt and her *kapp* strings. The apple trees whispered in the morning sunlight that warmed her face. Millie sensed this moment would be etched in her memory forever, whether or not she wanted it to happen. She'd once considered herself reasonably intelligent and perceptive, yet the knots in her stomach suggested that she'd remained blissfully unaware of the unspoken truth, like a mushroom growing in a dark cave. *How is that you're the last one to know?*

"Millie. I . . . I don't know what to say, honey. But I love you *so much.*"

"Who *are* you? Why are you here?" Millie

blurted. She crossed her arms tightly, in case this woman tried to grasp her hand.

"I'm your mother, Millie," the woman replied in a breathless voice. "I'm sorry we got off to a rough start. I never intended to hurt —"

"*You* got off to a bad start!" Millie retorted. "I was minding my own business, taking care of my grandparents and —"

"Thank you for doing that. I admire you for giving up your *rumspringa,*" the woman continued in a voice that hitched a time or two. "It should've been me taking care of them in their old age."

"So why didn't you?" Millie demanded.

The stranger sighed. She was still standing behind Millie, not touching her but so close that the heat of their bodies mingled. "Your grandfather ordered me out of the house when we learned you were on the way," she murmured. "He said I was evil. Told me never to come back again."

Millie winced. She had no trouble believing that stern, stoic Dawdi had said such awful things, but she wouldn't give this stranger a moment's sympathy. "So why did you?"

"I — I wanted to make amends. Wanted to ask forgiveness, especially of *you,* Millie, because I was hoping we could be together.

Not a day has gone by that I didn't think of you, or wish I'd done things differently."

Millie pivoted. "So ya bought Hiram's house? And ya came here with your shiny red car and your English clothes, thinkin' that would make everything *right* with me?" she demanded shrilly. "Let me tell ya somethin', lady. Lizzie Glick is my *mamm,* and she would never *ever* do those things to make me love her. Leave me alone! Get out of my life!"

With no idea of where she might go, Millie took off across the Lantz orchard. She passed beside the big white house where Miriam's daughter Rachel and her husband, Micah Brenneman, now lived, then curved left at the pasture where Dan Kanagy's sheep watched her through the fence as they chewed their grass. She kept going, past the new house Seth Brenneman was building for Mary Kauffman and her kids, without really seeing any of these things through her tears.

Except for Mary, who was new in town, did *all* of these neighbors know that Atlee and Lizzie Glick weren't her birth parents? Did they remember that *Nora* woman from when she'd lived here, and recall the reason she'd left town? *Why didn't anybody tell me the truth? I've trusted everyone in town —*

*especially the people I believed were my
parents — only to find out they've been keeping a huge secret about who I really am.*

"Liars," Millie muttered as she continued
past Bishop Tom's dairy farm and onto the
gravel road. *Every last one of them's a liar —
my grandparents, the bishop, Miriam, Mamm
and Dat. It would serve them right if they all
went to hell for their lies!*

Blinded by tears, she stopped where the
road forked. One path led around in a circle
that defined the edge of Willow Ridge and
then ran in front of the Wagler place and
Bishop's Ridge to the Hooleys' new mill,
while the other path led toward home and
eventually to Morning Star and Higher
Ground. *But is that really home now? How
can ya face those people again, knowing
they're not really your parents? Knowing
they've kept the truth from ya for your entire
life?*

For a brief moment, it comforted Millie
to realize that Atlee Glick wasn't her father.
He was a difficult man, with a chip on his
shoulder and a short fuse. She had his red
hair and freckles, but he was actually her
uncle.

*No, you got your looks from that Nora
woman. Who was your father, really?*

Millie mopped her face with her apron.

So many questions overwhelmed her that she couldn't think straight. She didn't want to return to her grandparents' place, because Dawdi would be in a foul mood and Mammi would be upset — and *they* had kept the truth from her, too. And she certainly didn't want to deal with Mamm — *um, Aunt Lizzie?* — even though she'd had the decency to look upset yesterday when she'd heard Nora had returned. And she'd at least hinted to Millie that something huge was about to happen.

So where should she go? What should she do until she could figure out how to handle this life-changing information?

Millie walked slowly along the road that circled Willow Ridge. She passed a few neatly kept places that belonged to various Schrock families, including the three women who ran the quilt shop next door to Miriam's café. In her present state of mind, a stroll along the river sounded like the best way to deal with her churning emotions. As she got closer to the mill, maybe she would confide in Ira, who'd so gallantly held her hand and taken her side — and maybe she wouldn't. In his way, he'd betrayed her, too, by ogling his new neighbor . . . *who is my mother.*

It was all so confusing.

CHAPTER EIGHT

Nora dropped onto her couch, feeling as wrung out as an old dishrag. Could her encounters this morning have gone any worse? As she sat in the big living room that was still strewn with half-unpacked boxes, she felt the overpowering urge to stuff her belongings back into them — to call the Realtor and stick a For Sale sign in the yard and get out of Willow Ridge in a hurry.

But that couldn't happen. She had nowhere else to go, and no savings left to take her there. And now that she'd opened the Pandora's box Hiram had talked about, there was no turning back. No coaxing the secrets into hiding again, and no erasing the way she'd disrupted everyone's lives, thinking her need for reconciliation was noble enough to warrant the pain and upheaval she would cause.

Millie, I'm so sorry I've hurt you.

If she sent out that mental message, would

her daughter receive it? And if she did, what would stop Millie from turning away again? If she lived to be a hundred, Nora knew she'd never forget the anguish that had puckered Millie's sweet, innocent face this morning. And she hadn't anticipated the depth of the torment she'd opened herself to, either, when Millie and Dat had refused to accept her.

"Nora? You in there?"

Nora grimaced. Luke Hooley was the last person she wanted to see, but she didn't have the energy to send him away. He was standing at the screen door, gawking this way and that to find her in the shadows of the house. It occurred to her that she hadn't hooked the screen door — that she was already slipping back into the Willow Ridge level of home security. "Yeah. Come on in."

He entered cautiously, sensing she was in an iffy mood. He was holding a handful of Queen Anne's lace and black-eyed Susans she'd seen growing along the riverbank. Even clad in broadfall trousers with suspenders and an unironed yellow shirt, Luke possessed a confidence — a trace of class — that set him apart from the Amish guys she'd known as a kid. He lowered himself to sit on the floor in front of her. "How'd it go with Millie?"

"Badly."

Luke sighed. "For what it's worth, I was ready to clobber Gabe when he called you Satan and then shoved you aside," he said in a rising voice. "That whole shunning thing is exactly why I can't join the Old Order. It's the most unforgiving attitude in the world, yet the Amish supposedly base their faith on forgiveness and living Christlike lives. Go figure."

Nora smiled weakly. She really did appreciate his supportive attitude even if she wasn't in the mood to discuss Amish theology. "Technically, I wasn't shunned, because I hadn't yet joined the church. I was only sixteen when my parents sent me away to an aunt's house to have my baby."

"But for your father to claim he never had a daughter — and with Millie standing right there," Luke protested. "That was just *wrong,* Nora."

She shrugged. "Old Order men stand by their right to be *right* — to dictate the script their families will follow," she replied with a sigh. "And while I anticipated my father's reaction, I didn't realize how crushed I would feel, even after all these years. I've been so naive, thinking I could make this work."

"Will, um, Millie's father help you out?"

"He's dead."

When Luke's eyes widened, Nora hoped he'd take her unspoken hint and not ask any more about that part of the story. Though her new neighbor piqued her interest, some information just couldn't be entrusted to a man she'd only known for twenty-four hours — especially considering how the Hooley brothers thought they had dibs because they lived next door.

"So what will you do now?" Luke asked in a low voice. "Not intending to be nosy, understand. Just . . . interested. There's a lot more to you than meets the eye, Nora."

She let out a humorless chuckle. Allowing Luke's curiosity to evolve into a romantic entanglement wasn't in her best interest. "I have no idea. I'm so drained, I might just sit here on the couch for the rest of the day, surrounded by all this *stuff,*" she blurted, gesturing at the mess around them.

When Luke smiled, Nora thought she saw a gentle sadness etched around his eyes — not an emotion she'd expected when he'd first introduced himself. "Well, I'd better get back to the mill," he said as he stood up. "I wanted to be sure you weren't in the mood to self-destruct, or to give up on reconciling with Millie. She's a sweet girl —"

"And she's what — *half* Ira's age?" The words sounded harsher than Nora had intended, but guys at the Hooleys' life stage had certain needs.

Luke looked her straight in the eye. "He's never taken advantage of her innocence, if that's what you're thinking. Maybe having Millie's mother next door will make him quit sitting on the fence and commit. They've been dating for a long while."

Nora sensed Luke was the sort of big brother who thought it'd be right for Ira to follow the rules — to remain sexually honorable — even if he himself showed no inclination to settle down. But she wouldn't raise that issue while she had so many other emotional fires to put out. "Thanks for the wildflowers. That was sweet of you."

His lips curved. "I'll stick them in water and get out of your hair. Take care, Nora."

"Yeah, you too."

She heard water running in the kitchen and then the closing of the back door. Nora let her head fall back against the couch. She hadn't felt like chatting with Luke any longer, but the silence of the house closed in on her after a few minutes of being alone. What *would* she do now? How could she possibly believe anything positive would come of the fiasco she'd caused this morning?

When you've been knocked to the bottom of the pit, the only way is up.

Nora chuckled glumly. Miriam's words had rung with the staunch belief that all things worked out to the good for those who loved God, but Nora wasn't setting her heart on a happy ending. Not anymore. Her original good intentions had gone so wrong she didn't see any way to reclaim them or to start her reconciliation efforts again.

Figuring it was better to move than to remain mired in her defeat, Nora went into the kitchen. If she emptied a box of towels and moved a bunch of gadgets from the table into the drawers, she would have the satisfaction of a single room that looked settled. She gazed at Luke's bouquet of wildflowers, sitting by the sink. If only the beam of light shining through the window, making the water glow in the drinking-glass vase, could be a ray of sunshine for her soul, as well.

Luke's not as shallow as I thought, Nora mused. But she knew not to count on him. She'd be better off getting some sort of business established in that huge barn, creating a badly needed income —

"Nora? The men will be here soon to

remove my Bishop's Ridge sign from your driveway," an all-too-familiar voice said through the screen door.

Nora scowled. *You forgot to hook the screen door — again!*

This morning's scene in the Sweet Seasons had rushed past her in some ways, but she hadn't missed seeing Hiram Knepp in the doorway, smiling smugly when Dat had shoved her aside. And then Hiram had helped Dat go home. Who knew what he might have told her parents about what she'd paid for the house, or what other damning details he'd shared with them?

"All right, fine," she called out, hoping that was the end of the conversation. She had nothing more to say to the former bishop.

She slit the tape on the box of kitchen towels with a paring knife and then stiffened. The screen door creaked. Footsteps echoed in the entryway.

Hiram poked his head into the kitchen. He smiled slyly as he took in her Plain attire. "It's good to see you've not let the incident at the café defeat you, Nora," he declared. "I figured you'd handle it — that you'd lick your wounds and try again. You've always been a survivor."

Where does this guy get the nerve to just

walk in? Nora nearly told him to leave, but she sensed it was a bad idea to unleash her frustration. She'd heard that Knepp was adept at using incriminating evidence when it would most affect the person he was trying to control. "Yeah. Thanks."

Hiram walked toward the sink, as though the wildflowers were a magnet. "You should be careful of the company you keep, however," he continued in a sinuous voice. "You don't realize it yet, but the Hooleys have taken over this town. Ben's gotten himself selected as a preacher, while his aunts, Nazareth and Jerusalem, have insinuated themselves into two bishops' lives — Tom's, as well the fellow from Cedar Creek."

Nora frowned, thinking back. "Tom's wife died? Her name was Lettie, wasn't it?"

"She ran off with an English fellow, and then got killed in a car crash," Hiram replied. "Nazareth Hooley was waiting in the wings to latch on to Tom, just as Ben wasted no time in claiming Miriam. But more to the point, the younger brothers who live next door to you came here from Lancaster County under . . . suspicious circumstances," he went on with the rise of one eyebrow. "They left a couple of young ladies in the lurch. And if Ben had to finance the building of the mill — for men

106

of Luke's and Ira's age — their ability to run a business seems doubtful, as well."

Hiram paused to let all these details sink in. "I phoned some of my family in that area of Pennsylvania, as part of my responsibility to the souls I was shepherding here in Willow Ridge at the time," he explained matter-of-factly. "What my kin said about the Hooleys wasn't very complimentary."

Nora's thoughts whirled faster. She found it ironic that Hiram was coming down on the Hooleys, yet he'd been relieved of his position as bishop — which had never happened in any other Amish settlement that she knew of, because bishops were ordained for life. Hiram's insinuations didn't have a lot of bearing on *her,* but what if Millie was unaware of Ira's past?

"And your point would be?" she asked archly. For all she knew, Hiram was making this stuff up. She was getting more annoyed with every tick of the kitchen clock.

Hiram smirked. "I'd hate for Luke to pull the wool over your eyes while you're in such a vulnerable state, Nora. I was aghast when he began dating my Annie Mae — she was only seventeen while he was pushing thirty. As a parent, I'm sure you're just as concerned about Ira being alone with your naive young daughter. You're well aware of how *that* can play out," he added quickly.

Nora's cheeks flared. Hiram was insinuating that someone she'd been dating had caused her fall from grace — but no one knew all of those details, because she hadn't revealed them. The man who'd taken advantage of her had promised she'd go straight to hell if she told his name, and she'd been terrified enough to believe him. In the years that had followed, she'd learned that hell wasn't necessarily a place where lost souls suffered torment after they died. They could experience hell every waking moment, every day of their lives.

At the sound of machinery revving up, Nora glanced out the window. "Your sign guys are here," she said, pointing toward the front door.

Hiram plucked a stem of Queen Anne's lace from the water glass and tickled her nose with its airy white bloom. "Takes more than that to get rid of *me*," he teased. "I've made it my mission to be sure you succeed here, Nora. When I learned it was *you* buying this house, I cut the price considerably."

As Hiram walked out the front door with the flower he was whistling, which irritated Nora even more. Where did he get off, thinking she'd feel beholden to him for supposedly lowering the price of this house? Or thinking she'd appreciate the information he'd shared?

Snake in the grass. Like another man you knew.

But which of the details Hiram had given about the Hooleys were fact and which were fiction? Nora went back to her unpacking. It wasn't even noon yet, but such mindless tasks were all she had the energy for.

She was arranging the last of the folded towels in the drawer beside the sink when a movement caught her eye. Nora leaned closer to the window. A girl dressed in a *kapp* and a pale peach dress was walking awfully close to the river's edge — and then, thank goodness, a fellow came out of the mill to capture her attention.

Nora nipped her lip. Millie and Ira were clasping hands like a couple who'd known each other for a long while. *Better choose your battles carefully,* her thoughts warned. She felt uncomfortable about their age difference — about Ira's intentions — but this was no time to further alienate her daughter by expressing her disapproval of the relationship.

Some things you can't control — as you've found out the hard way. Get used to it.

Through the window of the gristmill's main

workroom, Ira had spotted a solitary figure walking along the bank of the Missouri River. He'd immediately engaged the brake on the big mill wheel and left the dried corn he was grinding into meal. With her head bent low and her shoulders sagging, Millie had been the picture of dejection, walking so near the rushing current on the sandy riverbank. He'd had a sudden vision of her being sucked underwater by the pull of the mill wheel — maybe knocked unconscious when one of the paddles struck her head. He could not let that happen.

He'd rushed down the stairs and out the back door, then slowed down so he wouldn't startle Millie into falling in the river when jumping in hadn't been her intent. "Millie!" he called out. "It's *gut* to see you, sweetie. Can I walk with ya?"

Millie raised her head. "I've just been walkin' and walkin' with no idea where I'm headed. Maybe sittin' a spell would be the better idea."

Millie seemed more sad and confused than distraught, so perhaps he'd overdramatized her mood. Or maybe he cared about her more than he'd admitted to himself. "Let's sit on the rock under this tree, in the shade," Ira suggested. "It's gotten awfully hot."

"*Jah,* you can say that again."

Ira helped Millie clamber onto the flat river rock, telling himself not to say anything he'd someday regret. But how could he not commiserate with this young woman after the ordeal she'd endured today? "I — I hope ya don't mind that I stuck around in the orchard for a bit," he murmured. "To be sure ya did all right while Nora was talkin' to ya."

Millie's golden-brown eyes widened. "So ya know who she is, then? Or have ya known for a long time — like everybody else — and ya didn't tell me?"

The pain in her voice pierced Ira's heart. "I'd never heard of her before yesterday," he insisted. "I thought she could've been your sister or your cousin or — the thought of her bein' somebody's *mother* never occurred to me."

Millie rolled her eyes. "Too busy lookin' at her *wheels,* were ya?"

"Okay, I deserve that." He lifted Millie's hand to his lips. "I'm sorry I act like a jerk sometimes, Millie. It's a guy thing."

She smiled glumly. "Your brother's got the same silly grin on his face when he looks at her —"

"Which means if Nora's turnin' our heads, and ya look just like her," Ira pointed out, "*you* are just as pretty and just as —"

"Stop right there!" she bleated. "Ya don't understand, Ira. That woman's my *mother,* yet she dumped me off when I was a wee little baby, and everybody's covered for her! They've all kept her secret — and kept me from knowin' who I really am."

They had drifted into dangerous emotional waters — the sort of intensely personal conversation Ira had avoided with girls because he'd wanted no part of getting serious. But this felt different. Millie's beliefs about who she was and who had raised her had been totally overturned. He'd never witnessed anything like this.

"From the way Gabe shoved Nora aside this morning, I'm guessin' she didn't have a lot of options back then," he murmured. "What would *you* do if ya had a baby ya couldn't support, and your *dat* had sent ya away —"

Millie's cheeks reddened. "Whose side are ya on?" she snapped.

"*Yours!*" Ira replied just as vehemently. He took a deep breath to settle his nerves. "I'm not sayin' Nora's done everything right. And what she admitted to ya this morning has turned your life upside down," he said more gently. "But she told ya the truth, Millie. A gal who can afford Hiram's place could be livin' *anywhere,* but she came here. Plunked down her money to be with you and her parents, so she could set the record straight."

Ira wasn't sure where his thoughts were coming from, but he'd seen and heard enough in the past several hours that his perception of Nora — his thoughts about a *lot* of things — had changed. These revelations were stirring him on a very deep level, much like the mill wheel churned up sand and debris from the river bottom.

"She's been livin' English, but she's bought a house without electric power, to live amongst folks who've cast her out — knowin' her father might treat her the same way he did all those years ago." Ira squeezed Millie's hand between his. "And what your *dawdi* did in the Sweet Seasons got me to thinkin' about other things, too."

A hint of a grin played on Millie's face. "I never knew ya to be such a *thinker,* Ira. The philosopher of Willow Ridge."

He chuckled, relieved that her sense of humor was returning. Millie was still upset, but she was listening to him, which meant he had to express his churning thoughts carefully. "Gabe didn't even give Nora a chance to say hello when she went to his table," he recalled. "What if she's sincerely

113

tryin' to make amends, and he won't let her?"

Millie didn't answer, and Ira didn't really expect her to. He searched for another way to express ideas that were rising to the surface now, even though he hadn't been aware of them before. "Do ya remember that sleigh ride we took last winter, when we caught Rhoda Lantz kissin' Andy Leitner in his parked car?"

Millie's brows flickered, as though she wondered where this conversation was leading. "How could I forget? All folks could talk about was Rhoda's sin. Everyone said she shoulda known better than to ride in a car with an English fella, let alone kiss him, because she was a member of the church."

"And did ya think that reaction was right?" he quizzed her. "I mean, look at them now. Rhoda's already like a *mamm* to Andy's two kids, and he's given up everything in his English life to be with her. He's changed *who he is* to join the Old Order Amish church because they're so much in love. But I could never do that."

Millie's breath escaped in a rush. "Are ya jumpin' the fence, then? Not gonna take your instruction to join the church?" she blurted. "That means you're goin' to hell, Ira."

"Does it?" Ira clutched her hands. For most of the time he'd been dating Millie, the difference in their ages had been something they'd used to defy her *dat* — a game that bound them together rather than a number of years that might keep them apart. Now, however, Ira felt more aware of his responsibility. He was a man whose maturity should determine his relationship — his future — with a younger girl who was very vulnerable.

"What about folks who go to other churches, like Mennonites?" he murmured. "Or even English folks who belong to completely different denominations? Do ya think God's damned them all because they're not Amish?"

Millie looked dumbstruck. "I — I've never thought about it. I've always believed what the bishop and the preachers say, because God chose them to lead us."

"And I understand your way of thinkin', Millie. But today it was like I got hit upside the head with a brick," Ira said carefully. "I believe there's gotta be different ways to worship God and still live a *gut* life. And it doesn't include shuttin' out folks like Nora for makin' one mistake. *Not* that you were a mistake, Millie."

She gazed at him solemnly. "I'm too upset

to think about all that," she replied after several moments of silence. "But — but if ya don't want to see me anymore —"

"That's not what I meant," he whispered, cupping her precious face between his hands. "And you're right. This isn't the time to be talkin' religion." Ira cleared his throat, again hoping the right words would come to him. "I'm *with* ya, Millie. No matter what happens — or what we decide to do about our relationship — I hope ya realize I'm your *friend* as much as I'm your boyfriend. Ya know that, right?"

Awe and disbelief softened Millie's sweet, freckled features. Then her smile came out like the sunshine after a storm. *"Jah,"* she murmured. "We have our squabbles, but I've always figured that when push came to shove, you'd be shovin' the same direction I was."

Such a simple statement of faith in him made Ira's heart pound. As Millie's eyes closed, he kissed her. "Keep that in mind if this thing with Nora gets sticky," he murmured. "Who knows what other secrets might jump out now that she's come back?"

CHAPTER NINE

As Miriam pulled seven loaves of bread from the oven early Saturday morning, she savored the silence of the Sweet Seasons kitchen. This time before her partner, Naomi Brenneman, and her waitresses arrived was always her chance to think things through, and the past twenty-four hours had given her quite a lot to consider.

Lord, I hope You'll hold Nora and Lizzie and Wilma and Millie in Your healin' hands, she prayed as she measured flour for the day's piecrusts. *And I hope You'll open Gabe and Atlee's hearts, as well. But Your will be done.*

Miriam chuckled, at herself mostly. It seemed that *telling* God what to do rather than asking Him was an easy habit to fall into. Her visit with Nora yesterday, followed by the unfortunate scene with Gabe in the dining room, had made her think a lot about whether some of the Old Order ways came more from men's insistence on control than

117

from consulting God about the right way to handle their children's mistakes. In some districts, expressing such an idea out loud might be considered reason for requiring a member to repent. But that didn't stop a lot of Plain women from wondering if things couldn't be different. Kinder. More loving.

"Miriam, when I die and go to heaven, please God, I believe it'll smell a whole lot like your kitchen," came a voice through her open window.

Miriam laughed. "Tom Hostetler, I believe you're beggin' for a sample," she called out. "My stars, I can't think you've already milked your cows."

"I get up earlier when I've got a lot on my mind."

"*Jah,* I know all about that." As the bishop walked in, Miriam gestured toward a tall stool near her work area. "And between you, me, and this countertop, my heart's achin' for the Glick women. Every one of them had their lives turned upside down sixteen years ago when Gabe sent Nora away, and now they're goin' through it again."

Tom smiled ruefully. "I knew you'd see it that way, just as I could've predicted Gabe's reaction when Nora asked for his forgiveness," he murmured. "That's where the fish bone gets caught in my throat. She *did* ask.

And her father flat-out refused to even give her the time of day."

"And then there was Hiram, appearin' from outta nowhere to get right in the thick of it," Miriam said with a grimace. She passed Tom a serrated bread knife and went to the refrigerator for a stick of butter. "Somebody's gotta see if this bread's fit to eat. Might as well be us."

Tom chuckled and selected the round, golden-brown loaf nearest him. "How much do ya recall from all those years ago?" he asked as he positioned the knife on the bread. "Hiram was the bishop then, and Gabe and I were preachers, with your Jesse servin' as our deacon."

"It was all so hush-hush. Nora'd already been gone a week or so before I realized it," Miriam replied in a faraway voice. "Wilma looked like she'd been hit by a truck, and wouldn't — couldn't — let on about the details Gabe forbade her to discuss. So we were left to assume that Nora was pregnant. Then, when Atlee and Lizzie suddenly had a redheaded baby — as newlyweds, without her bein' pregnant — that pretty much told the tale."

"Gabe insisted that the less folks knew, the less they could gossip — and other girls wouldn't follow Nora's sinful path." He slathered butter on a generous slice of dense, grainy bread and handed it to Miriam. "And while Hiram and Jesse and I went along with that age-old strategy, I wondered what would become of Nora . . . how she would ever join the church or reunite with her family."

He paused to close his eyes over a big bite of bread. "But I hadn't been a preacher very long, so I didn't make waves," he went on. "Eventually the whole episode faded away, and Millie grew up as Atlee and Lizzie's child."

"Well, our days of sweepin' it under the rug are over. Mmmm," Miriam murmured as she took a big bite of the warm bread. "Your fresh butter almost turns this bread into dessert, Tom."

"Nah, it's your way of puttin' the ingredients together that makes it special," the bishop insisted. He closed his eyes over a second bite and chewed it slowly. "What's in this, anyway?"

"A nice five-grain cereal Luke and Ira are gonna sell in their mill store — rolled oats, barley, rye, and wheat flour — along with a handful of golden raisins and dried cranberries. I made some the other day, but now I've actually gotten a taste of it." Miriam studied the color and texture of her bread, pleased with the way this new recipe had turned out.

"You'll not have to worry about it goin' stale before folks snatch it up," Tom predicted. He polished off his slice and looked at her, his brows arching over his expressive eyes. "I'm goin' to visit Wilma, Lizzie, and Nora today. What would ya think if I took them each a loaf —"

"Oh, please do! What a fine idea."

"But I don't want to run ya short for your menu."

Miriam squeezed his wrist and then cut them both another generous slice of the bread. "If anybody could use some lovin' from the oven, it's those gals. I'm glad you're talkin' them through this tough time."

"Mainly I want to ask if they'll all meet together at my place — with Millie and the men — so everybody can find a way to . . . mend fences," he said with a sigh. "Except the fences need to come down. Separation from each other — especially within our own families — is akin to separation from God, the way I see it."

"I agree a hundred percent," Miriam whispered. "But do ya figure on Atlee and Gabe goin' along with it? If they get wind of Wilma, Lizzie, and Nora gettin' together, they might well nix the whole thing."

"As the bishop of Willow Ridge, I see it as my mission — my duty to God — to bring folks closer together instead of allowin' old attitudes and habits to keep us apart," he replied in a low voice. "If *I* call a meeting, Gabe and Atlee will need to be there, ain't so? And with tomorrow bein' a non-church Sunday, the afternoon will be a *gut* time to get this process started."

"Oh, Tom, I'm so pleased to hear ya sayin' that," Miriam insisted. "I was thinkin' on that very subject when ya came to the door. Let me know what I can do."

"I'll be countin' on you and Ben — askin' him, as a preacher, to help persuade Atlee and Gabe to at least hear Nora out," Tom said as he slathered butter on his bread. "If she's willin' to talk about what happened all those years ago, maybe we'll see her situation in a different light. And I for one want to know what sort of life she's been livin' since she left."

Miriam began cutting shortening into the flour in her big wooden mixing bowl, for her piecrusts. "As I've been thinkin' back to when Nora left town, I had a real hard time believin' she was pregnant," she mused aloud. "Nora grew up right across the road. She was back and forth with my girls even

122

though they were a few years younger, so I thought I *knew* her. She didn't go chasin' after the boys. She wasn't the sort to hide English clothes or jewelry and wear them when she was out of her parents' sight. Truth be told, she'd barely gotten into her *rumspringa* and then she was gone."

"That's how I recall it, too." Tom tucked the last chunk of bread into his mouth before he spoke again. "I'm thinkin' Ben will be a *gut* candidate for keepin' Atlee and Gabe at least civil, on account of how he's a newcomer. Doesn't have any preconceived notions or family biases."

"And Ben wants the best for Millie, too. She's the one most likely to feel betrayed and hurt."

"Millie needs our prayers," the bishop agreed as he slid off the stool. "I'll leave ya to your work now, Miriam — and I'll take those loaves of bread after I've had my breakfast. I'm hopin' Gabe'll eat here this morning so I can sweeten him up," he added with a smile. "But he might stay away, thinkin' that's what I intend to do. He's a crusty old character."

"*Gut* luck and Godspeed with your visits." As the door closed behind him, Miriam placed a ball of dough on the countertop and began to roll it flat. Sweet Seasons customers always bought more whole pies — more of everything she baked — for the weekend, so she wanted to be ready. The July heat and humidity had already made the kitchen feel sticky, so she switched on the exhaust fan. The midsummer weather seemed a good reason to serve chilled salads and lighter fare on the day's menu, but with so many of the local men eating breakfast or their noon meal here, the steam table would have to offer solid meat-and-potatoes fare, as well.

As Miriam considered stirring up a batch of whole grain pancake mix from the Hooley mill, the shifting in her abdomen made her grin and place a floury hand there. "*Gut* mornin' to ya, wee one," she murmured.

Once again she considered what a major change this baby was going to make in her life, now that she was forty-one with a busy preacher and farrier for a husband, grown triplet daughters, and a restaurant to run. This child was a miracle she welcomed, however, even as she realized young Nora Glick had experienced these same fluttery sensations as a terrified teenager who'd been cast out of Willow Ridge.

What a difference a baby makes, Miriam mused as she resumed her baking. With all her heart she hoped the Glick family would be reunited, and she prayed that Millie would come to feel she'd made a *positive* difference in the lives she'd touched since she'd been born.

Chapter Ten

When Nora stepped into the Schrocks' quilt shop early on Saturday afternoon, she stood for a moment to gaze at the bolts of fabric arranged by color families on the shelves along the wall. She inhaled the scent of dyes, made more pronounced by the mid-day heat, and rejoiced that she'd found a source for embroidery floss, thread, and other supplies within a five-minute walk of her new home. Standing in a large room surrounded by so much color made her believe she could survive in Willow Ridge — could thrive here, if she applied her best artistic instincts and business sense.

Nora wandered over to where full-size quilts hung from heavy rods that extended out from the wall. A log cabin quilt was displayed on a double bed, and Nora paused to admire the unusual gradations of green, blue, and purple prints that formed the traditional design.

A pleasant voice interrupted her reverie. "How can I help ya?"

Nora smiled. She had dressed Plain again today, in a solid-color cape dress of goldenrod she'd sewn in anticipation of moving to Willow Ridge. "I've come for some materials, and maybe some advice," she replied as she studied the woman before her.

Was this Mary Schrock, Zeb's wife? Or was she dealing with Priscilla or Eva, one of Zeb's aunts? As a kid she'd been acquainted with the Schrock family who lived on the road to Morning Star, because Atlee had been apprenticed to Zeb. But in sixteen years they — and she — had matured. "I need some fabric and crochet thread to finish some hangings, but I'm also gathering information about whether a gift shop might be a feasible venture here in Willow Ridge," Nora explained. "I'm hoping to repurpose the big barn on Bishop's Ridge Road — to turn it into an outlet for locally made Plain items."

The woman sucked in air. "You bought the Knepp place — which means you're Wilma Glick's girl. Oh my."

Nora kept her smile in place, hoping she wasn't already condemned as someone a decent Mennonite woman shouldn't talk to. "Word travels fast," she murmured.

"Atlee's sister, then. He works at my Zeb's auction barn —"

"*Jah,* Mary, I'm Nora and it's *gut* to see you again. A few years have separated us, but as I look at these fabulous quilts," she said, gesturing toward the display, "I'm hoping I can sell some of them for you in my store. Surely other folks around these Plain settlements have handmade items they'd like to consign, too. But it'll take a lot of merchandise to fill that big barn and make it look like we mean business!"

Mary's gray eyes sparkled. "My stars, just a few weeks ago Eva and Priss and I were wonderin' where we'd put some of our quilts. Our space is gettin' too full to really see some of the details our gals put into their hand quilting."

As her heart began to dance, Nora willed herself not to get too excited yet. It would take a tremendous amount of work to convert the two-level barn into a store, but if she could convince local crafters and artisans to participate, wouldn't it be *something*?

"I'd guess the Brenneman boys would have some furniture to display, and Matthias Wagler might have some leather saddles and tack," Mary said as she counted these folks off on her fingers. "And over

Morning Star way, there's a fella who makes rockin' chairs and wooden toys. And Miriam's husband, Ben, makes the prettiest rose trellises and garden gates you ever did see, out of wrought iron."

For the first time in days, Nora felt she was in the right place at the right time. "You can't know how glad I am to hear these suggestions," she murmured as she pressed her hands together.

Mary cocked her head, studying Nora. "From what I was hearin', I didn't expect ya to show up in Plain clothes or to be talkin' about our handmade merchandise," she said. Her eyebrows rose, questioning Nora.

"It's true that I've been living English — was married to an English man before he divorced me," Nora admitted, watching for signs of Mary's disapproval. "But during that time I got considerable experience in consignment shops. I'm a fiber artist — which is yet another difficult subject to discuss with my Amish family."

Mary looked puzzled, but then she giggled. "For a wee moment I thought ya made things out of bran flakes and beans," she said as her cheeks grew pink. "Never you mind, Nora. Takes me a minute to catch on to new ideas."

Nora began to laugh along with Mary. To Plain women whose ways hadn't changed much in the last century, the term *fiber* was dietary rather than a reference to fabric, yarns, and other needlework materials. She welcomed this moment of humor, sensing a barrier had come down between her and this middle-aged Mennonite lady.

A slow smile lit Mary's face. The hair tucked beneath her *kapp* was steely gray, and her dress of muted blue calico was pressed to perfection, yet Nora sensed this prim and proper shopkeeper might overlook some of Nora's personal issues . . . or even help her with them.

"Never let it be said that ya chose an easy path," Mary remarked. "But a store like you're dreamin' of is more likely to happen now than it was even a few years ago. What with Miriam next door bein' Amish, and we Schrocks bein' Mennonite, and the owner of our building bein' the nice English fella who raised Miriam's daughter, Rebecca," she added with a grin, "we've had some practice at gettin' along with all sorts of folks. There's a place for every soul and work for every hand, the way I see it."

Nora almost grabbed Mary in a hug — except the bell above the door jingled as a couple of English women entered the shop.

"Thank you so much for saying that," she whispered. "I'll look around while you help these ladies. I hope we can talk more about my consignment store idea."

Her heart was thumping as she made her way to the shelves of quilting fabrics. Instinctively pulling out bolts of prints that would complete her hangings, Nora realized she had some catching up to do. Her tiny hometown had undergone several radical changes: the former bishop had been excommunicated, Preacher Tom had remarried after his first wife, Lettie, had run off, and the Lantz girl who'd been washed away in a flood-swollen river had returned to live here.

There's a place for every soul and work for every hand.

Nora had been about eleven when toddler Rebecca had broken away from Miriam, who'd been hurrying her triplet daughters away from the rising river while calling out to her husband about an approaching storm. Miriam had lost the baby she'd been carrying, too. And after the local men had searched for Rebecca and decided the police were not to be notified, Miriam had grieved the lively little girl everyone believed was dead. Yet now Rebecca was waiting tables and assisting at the new clinic down the road.

Rebecca came back after being raised English. She wears jeans and lives near her family and designs websites. Everyone loves her even though she'll never become Amish. Maybe there's hope for me.

Nora piled her bolts of fabric on the cutting table and then grabbed a shopping basket. As she quickly selected tubes of fabric paint, skeins of cotton crochet thread, and some fat quarters from a bin of fabric remnants, she eased into her creative zone — that state of mind where she intuitively chose materials that appealed to her, without thinking too much about how she'd use them. It was this innate artistic ability that had given her a purpose, a focus, after she'd left Millie with Atlee and Lizzie. She'd blended the practical sewing skills Mamma had taught her with so many other techniques she'd picked up in craft classes, to create a lucrative hobby while Tanner had been traveling so much. More than once in her lifetime, crafting items to sell had been her salvation — in a personal sense if not a religious one.

But it was *art*. And art for decoration — art for art's sake — was forbidden in the Amish culture because it called attention to the artist.

On impulse, Nora grabbed two more bolts of fabric — a vibrant pink, red, and orange plaid and a calico of muted red shamrocks on a beige background. She could envision cape dresses with matching aprons she would wear when she opened her shop. Such un-Amish prints wouldn't be suitable while she tried to reconcile with her family, but this new clothing would fit the woman Nora thought she could become, given a chance.

When Mary had rung up the other customers' purchases, she joined Nora at the cutting table. "I can't wait to tell Eva and Priss about your idea for a store," she said as she measured the fabrics. "If you'll jot down your phone number, I'll tell our friends at church tomorrow, too. I bet you'll get calls from folks all over mid-Missouri once word goes out, on account of how there are so few places to sell our work, aside from our own little shops."

"I can't wait to get going on this store now," Nora replied as she grabbed paper and a pen from her purse. "But it's going to take a lot of cleaning. I'll need shelves and display tables, and —"

"Many hands make light work," Mary reminded her. "Seems only right that anybody wantin' to consign pieces to your new store should have a hand in gettin' it ready. Set some dates and times. Ya might be surprised at who-all shows up."

Nora's mouth dropped open. Half an hour ago she'd ventured into this shop, and she was leaving with a contact list and a store preparation plan she believed would work. "I can't thank you enough for your help, Mary," she said as she paid for her supplies.

Mary handed over Nora's bulging sack with a bright smile. "I wish ya all the best, Nora — with your family and your new store, as well," she said. "And if you'd like to meet some of those folks I was tellin' ya about, our church is right out there on the road that runs past my Zeb's auction barn. We'd love to have ya."

And wasn't *that* a pleasant surprise? While outsiders occasionally attended Amish weddings or funerals, Nora had never known an Amish person to invite anyone except members of the Old Order to worship with them.

"I might just show up one of these Sundays," Nora replied. "I could use some help from higher up, that's for sure."

" 'And from whence cometh my help? My help comes from the Lord, who made heaven and earth,' " Mary paraphrased as she gently grasped Nora's wrist. "You'll figure that out eventually, Nora, just like you'll figure out where ya fit in. Really ya will."

Nora nodded, fervently hoping Mary Schrock was right.

As she hurried home with her purchases, Nora felt certain she could make a go of a consignment store. When she entered her kitchen through the back door, the house's relative coolness felt good after the heat outside. Hiram had built this home on a hill to catch the breeze from the river, and its well-placed windows allowed her to create a cross current by opening them in the basement as well as on the first and second levels.

When she'd raised her upstairs windows, Nora went into the room she'd chosen as her studio — it had a fabulous view of the river and the mill. As she opened a couple of big cardboard boxes, it was almost like Christmas in July, seeing the hangings she'd packed away.

Nora carried her pieces downstairs, arranging them on the backs of her sofas and chairs so she could remember what she'd made and decide on new items to design for her store. It was no coincidence that the people on her pieces were Plain. She'd harkened back to her early years for inspiration, so these quilted, appliquéd pieces featured buggies and little Amish boys and girls because those subjects sold very well to English shoppers. No two of her pieces were alike, but as she created her three-dimensional hangings she repeated the themes and scenes that her customers bought most often.

Nora grabbed a notepad from the kitchen. *Barefoot girl in a garden,* she scribbled. *Another washday clothesline. Scenes from Willow Ridge — dairy farm/cows, mill on the river.* Instinct told her she'd just purchased the right fabrics to begin a couple of these projects, which suddenly felt much more pressing — and much more fun — than unpacking the boxes that were still stacked in some of her rooms.

A confident knock on the front door brought Nora out of her artistic musings. *Oh, just leave me alone,* she thought with a sigh — until she caught a glimpse of a straw hat and a graying beard through the glass panel in the entryway. Her visitor wasn't Hiram or any of the Hooley brothers, so as she opened the front door she reminded herself to be patient and polite.

"Tom Hostetler," she said as a kindly

smile lit his weathered face. "I hope you've not come to warn me of any wrongdoing, after I've only been in town a couple of days."

That was a presumptuous, smart-aleck thing to say to the bishop, her conscience warned as she held the screen door open for him.

Tom studied her for a moment. "My reputation precedes me," he replied with a chuckle. "Truth be told, I've come with an apology and an invitation — and a loaf of Miriam's bread, baked just this morning," he added as he offered her a white paper bakery sack.

"I'd be silly not to accept any of those," Nora replied as she took the solid, round loaf. "I didn't mean to sound offensive or —"

"No offense taken, Nora." The bishop paused in the entryway to gaze into the kitchen and the living room. Then he focused on her, his eyes clear and direct. "I wanted to say how sorry I am for the way your *dat* treated ya yesterday. It took a lot of courage to approach him after all these years — and to that end, I'm hopin' you'll join your *mamm* and Lizzie at my place tomorrow afternoon to talk things out."

Nora blinked. This bishop's energy was so different from Hiram Knepp's that she sensed Willow Ridge had entered a new era . . . perhaps an atmosphere of co-operation rather than condemnation. "Will Millie be there?"

"I'm hopin' she will, *jah.* I've asked her to come."

Nodding, Nora tried to keep up with her racing thoughts. "Will Dat be there? And Atlee?"

"I've expressed my opinion that their presence would be beneficial," Tom replied earnestly. "With those fellas, the old sayin' of leadin' the horse to water applies."

"You can't make them drink," Nora agreed with a sigh. Tom's simple, homespun philosophy was no threat to her. He was trying to make things right, in compassionate ways that were foreign to her father and brother. "Speaking of a drink, can I pour you some iced tea? It's awfully warm today."

"That sounds real refreshing. *Denki,* Nora."

She gestured toward the living room with an apologetic chuckle. "Feel free to move stuff so you can sit down. I'll be back in a few."

As Nora carried the bread to the kitchen, she opened the bag enough to inhale its grainy-sweet fragrance — and realized she was easing back into the local dialect. Years had passed since she'd said *in a few,* but she knew better than to assume that talking the Amish talk would lead to walking that straight-and-narrow path required by their faith — and Tom was now a witness to the artist she'd become. Nora paused in the door way to assess his reaction to her hangings before joining him with their glasses of tea.

"These are like nothin' I've ever seen," he murmured as he stepped closer to touch a hanging of a courting boy and girl seated on a bench. "Who'd think to put real suspenders on a fella, and part of a straw hat — and a real *kapp* on the girl? Most pieces just show those things as flat fabric cutouts. Did *you* make these, Nora?"

It was a moment, a subject, which would make or break her return to Willow Ridge.

"I did, *jah,*" she murmured. "And if it's permissible — if it's all right with you, Bishop — I'm hoping to open a consignment store for Plain crafts in the barn. I know how a store selling art might be a problem in an Amish town."

Tom focused on her as he took a long sip of his iced tea. "And if I say no?"

Nora swallowed hard. It was time to fish or cut bait. "If you won't permit me to operate such a store, where Amish and Mennonite folks can sell their handmade wares to help support their families," she said softly, "then I have no idea what I'll do with that monstrous barn — or how I'll support myself, either, truth be told."

Tom's lips flickered. "Ya said a mouthful there, Nora. And I truly appreciate your *askin'* me instead of just figurin' to do things your way," he replied. "When ya were growin' up here, a store like you're describin' wouldn't have been appropriate. Nowadays, though, our men can't always support their families just by farmin' or workin' at their home-based trades," he explained. "If we're to keep our members in Willow Ridge, and financially stable, it's in our best interest to expand our ideas of what's *gut* for the community as a whole."

Nora nodded. The bishop hadn't given her an answer, but experience had taught her that the Amish took their time about arriving at conclusions. Tom moved slowly past the couch and the two armchairs, fingering some of the dimensional details of her designs.

"I like it that ya don't show these folks' faces," he remarked. Then he grinned. "And look at these little wooden clothespins hangin' the laundry on the line, and the way the dresses and shirts seem to be flutterin' in the breeze. I've never seen the likes of it. You've probably done pretty well at sellin' pieces like these, ain't so?"

"*Jah,* I have," Nora murmured. Tom's noticing such details tickled her, but that didn't mean he'd give his blessing to her artistic pursuits. "All things Amish hold a huge appeal to people who think they'd like to try the Plain lifestyle — or who just want mementos of it hanging in their electrified, computerized homes."

Tom chuckled and sipped his tea. "Ya got that right. Most of my hand-carved Nativity scenes aren't displayed in Plain homes, on account of how much Henry Zook tells me to charge for them in his market — and probably because the figures gathered around the manger are dressed as Amish folks rather than in biblical clothing," he remarked. "But carvin' helps me pass the cold winter days. And like ya said, it's extra income."

"Your Nativity sets sound awesome," Nora replied. "Mary Schrock told me about them — and about other items folks around here make — so I'm really hoping you'll consign some sets in my store. If it's all right to open one."

"Ya realize, Nora, that some of the older folks in the district will see your work as decoration — as *art* —"

"*Jah,* there's no way around that."

"— so if you're plannin' to join the Amish church, what'll ya say when those members disapprove of your livelihood?" Tom gazed at her over the top of his glass as he drained it.

The clinking of his ice cubes accentuated the pounding of her pulse. Nora wanted to be totally honest with this man, because he was giving her the benefit of the doubt — and he was so much more compassionate and understanding than her father. But she wasn't ready to let her dreams cave in yet, either. "What do *you* do when members criticize your work?" she asked. "I'm not trying to dodge the issue, understand."

"I didn't think ya were." Tom thought for a moment. "I suppose because my Nativity sets represent the birth of our Jesus, nobody Plain has objected to them. But if your *dat* were to see these hangings, he'd consider them yet another reason not to accept ya into the Amish faith. Or maybe back into his family."

"I am who I am, Tom. And I believe I'm a child of God, the same as he is," Nora insisted quietly. "I know Dat's set in the Old Order ways, so my main mission is to reunite with Millie and Mamma, no matter how he treats me."

"But see, I don't accept that." Tom came to stand in front of her. When he wiped his cool glass across his forehead, Nora sensed he was sweating from more than the heat of a July day. "*My* mission is to bring your *dat* around to the forgiveness our faith demands of him. So don't write him out of your story too soon, all right?" he asked earnestly. "Don't let him off the hook by acceptin' anything less than his full acknowledgment that you're his daughter, and that ya expect to be a part of his life again."

Nora's eyes widened. "*Gut* luck getting *that* to happen," she murmured.

Tom's eyes took on a boyish shine. "I'll need all the *gut* luck the *Gut* Lord can bless me with. And I give ya permission for your new store, too, as long as ya honor whatever form of faith ya take to," he said with a decisive nod. "If you're gonna join the Old Order, you'd better remove the fancy computer surveillance system Hiram installed in the barn. And while I really like your hangin's, Nora, I couldn't condone your makin' them if ya joined the Amish church," he continued. "You'd need to stick to quilts or clothing. Practical pieces."

Nora nodded. She'd anticipated his stating the *Ordnung*'s principles, as a reminder

143

to one who'd lived outside of Plain teachings for all of her adult life.

"Or, you could partner with Mennonites, the way Miriam has at the Sweet Seasons," Tom went on. "If *they* have computers and electric lighting and such in the store, I can go along with that. And their definition of acceptable creativity is freer than ours."

Bishop Tom had just defined her future. Nora sensed he already knew which direction she would go. "Where there's a woman, there's a way," she murmured.

"So you've been talkin' to Miriam," he said with a chuckle. "Model yourself after her example, and you'll be on the right path, Nora. Can I count on ya to be at my place tomorrow around two?"

Nora smiled. Tom Hostetler might seem to amble along a conversational trail, the way his dairy cows moseyed around his pasture, but he hadn't forgotten his question — and he wouldn't leave until she gave her answer. "I'll be there," she said. "I appreciate your getting my mother and Lizzie and Millie together on neutral turf so we can talk things out."

"If ya could tell us what went on all those years ago, the details of what led to your *dat* sendin' ya away, it might shed some light on our current situation," the bishop said softly. "That's askin' a lot, I know. I'm not keen on airin' your dirty laundry, understand, but your *dat* refused to talk about the circumstances. Gabe forbade any of us to so much as say your name after he banished ya, and Hiram went along with that."

Nora's throat tightened. She wasn't surprised that she'd gone unmentioned in her long absence, but to reveal the damning details of her encounter — even to her family — would require some real gumption. "I refused to give Dat any names — for reasons that were impressed upon me by the um, other party involved," she murmured. "I've never told *anyone* about what happened."

"I'll be holdin' ya up in prayer while ya figure out what to say," Tom said. "Ask for the strength to clarify your situation, and you'll receive it, Nora. God's will be done."

Nora nodded. There was a time she would've resisted talk of everything being God's will — especially when situations were manipulated by people who proclaimed themselves morally upright. Tom Hostetler had never impressed her as that sort of man. "I — I'll do my best," she hedged. "With Millie being only sixteen, I hesitate to get into too much of the down-and-dirty."

"I can understand that. When I was at the house earlier, talkin' to her and your *mamm,* she seemed skittish about this whole situation," he said. "We don't want to scare Millie so bad that she won't want to know ya better."

Tom handed her his empty glass. "*Denki* for the *gut* tea and talk, Nora. I'll get out of your way now, as I know you've got a lot on your mind."

Nora accompanied him through the living room, enjoying Tom's smile when he glanced back at her hangings. She was glad she hadn't confided her dream of a consignment store to Hiram, because she sensed the previous bishop tended to twist things around to his own advantage — a tendency she should probably know more about, considering the way he liked to pop in uninvited.

"What's the story on Hiram Knepp getting excommunicated?" she asked as she and Tom reached the door. "I've heard bits and pieces, but I figured he'd stretch the truth if I asked him about it."

"You've got him figured right. First off, Hiram was shunned for ownin' a car and havin' a driver's license — offenses he chose not to confess. But there's more to the story."

Tom cleared his throat, gazing out over the front yard and the expanse of Willow Ridge that stretched before them from this hilltop vantage point. "Last winter his young twins, Joey and Josh, were in a sleighin' accident on the road in front of Miriam's café. The fella who skidded on the ice and hit them with his car was the real estate agent who sold ya this house. He also happens to be a county politician."

Nora's eyebrows rose. She'd suspected Conrad Hammond had a story he wasn't telling, and Tom's tone suggested the Realtor might be cut from the same slippery cloth as Hiram.

"To give ya the short version, we found out that Hiram convinced Hammond to pay the twins' hospital bills and then to cut him a sweet deal on the tract of land where he's built his new colony, Higher Ground," Tom explained. "In exchange, Hiram didn't press charges, and he kept Hammond's name out of the papers. He was talkin' on his cell phone when he hit the sleigh, ya see."

"Ohhhh," Nora breathed. This was even more twisted than she'd expected.

"Watch yourself around Hiram," Tom warned in a low voice. "Not long after he moved to Higher Ground with his four littlest kids, his Annie Mae saw a young gal chasin' them around in the snow without their coats, with a paddle in her hand. After Annie Mae brought them back to Willow Ridge, Hiram used her previous boyfriend to trap her. And he whacked off her hair."

Nora sucked in her breath, appalled by the depth of Hiram Knepp's depravity. *Note to self: get those new locks.*

"That's how I came to be bishop," Tom explained. "We don't tolerate Hiram's shenanigans around here. If he starts actin' suspicious, you let me or Ben Hooley know about it, all right? It's a sorry state of affairs, tryin' to keep Hiram out of our little town, but that's the way of it."

"I'm glad I asked," Nora murmured. "I'll see you tomorrow — and thanks again for trying to bring my family together again, Tom."

"Faith and family. That's what life's all about," he replied.

Nora watched the bishop walk down the semicircular driveway. Tom was a lithe, slender man whose sweat-stained straw hat and faded broadfall pants proclaimed him a humble, hardworking servant of God. Now that he'd issued her an invitation and a challenge, she had about twenty-four hours to figure out how she would respond. It would mean dredging up memories of the day when she'd learned the meaning of terror and humiliation — a day that had defiled her and ruined her relationships with her family and friends.

It means bringing your darkest hours into the light — coming clean, and then facing a new set of consequences. Dat used to harp on the Bible verse about how the truth would set you free, so here's your moment of truth. And his.

CHAPTER ELEVEN

Millie held out her arm to steady Mammi, but her grandmother grabbed the handrail and took the steps up to Bishop Tom's house on her own. "It's the day I've been waitin' more than sixteen years for," her grandmother murmured. "Praise be to God that I lived to see it."

"Stuff and nonsense," Dawdi muttered. "Nora hasn't changed one bit. She's still sneakin' around, wormin' her way back into Willow Ridge. Do ya really trust anybody who'd buy that house from Hiram? And where'd she get that kind of money?"

"Hush, Gabe! Here comes the bishop," Mammi replied.

As Tom Hostetler opened the door, Millie felt the urge to flee. She didn't really want to see that Nora woman again — she'd only come to hear secrets she'd never suspected while she'd grown up believing Lizzie and Atlee were her parents. She was gathering evidence, determined to remain silent and unmoved — *stoic* in the face of painful revelations. Wasn't that the Amish way? To accept such misfortunes as God's will and then move on in spite of them?

"*Gut* to see you folks," the bishop said as he waved them toward the front room. "Looks like Atlee and Lizzie are comin' right behind ya."

"We've got fresh lemonade and cookies," Tom's wife, Nazareth, added with a smile. "I put pans of ice in front of the fans to keep the room cooler. Sure has been muggy lately."

Millie was relieved to see fans on either side of the front room, plugged into sockets from Bishop Tom's solar panels. Her grandfather scoffed at such modern conveniences, while her grandmother was so skinny that the midsummer heat didn't seem to bother her. At the sound of Lizzie and Atlee entering the house, Millie stalled, waiting to see where the adults would sit . . . which seat would be left for Nora.

"Millie, how are ya? I'm sure this feels a little awkward," her *mamm* — or the woman who'd pretended to be her *mamm* — said softly.

Millie pivoted to face Lizzie. "A *little* awkward? It wasn't much fun to find out —

from a total stranger — that she was my mother and that she *dumped* me. And you said nothing about it."

Lizzie's face fell. She held Ella tighter, grasping the baby's puffy quilt in her other hand. "I never meant for it to happen that way," she murmured. "Never meant to hurt ya, Millie."

"Could be we'll hear things that'll set the record straight today," Atlee remarked stiffly. He glanced at the horseshoe-shaped seating arrangement, grabbed a glass of lemonade, and sat down in the upholstered rocker nearest the top of the curve.

Lizzie sat next to him, arranging Ella's cheerful quilt on the floor beside her, while Millie's grandparents chose the loveseat. Millie considered her options, figuring Tom and Nazareth should have the other chairs at the top of the horseshoe . . . which left a straight-backed wooden chair beside Mammi and a padded rocker beside baby Ella. As Millie settled into the rocking chair, the front door opened again.

"Nora, it's nice to meet you," Nazareth said in her polite way. "If it makes ya uncomfortable havin' me sit in on this family talk, I'll go to another room or —"

"Please stay," Nora insisted calmly. "You're a relative newcomer to Willow

Ridge, so your perspective — your objective viewpoint — might be helpful."

"I said the same thing," Bishop Tom remarked. "Nazareth was a schoolteacher for years before she married me, so she asks relevant questions, and she has a way of seein' through excuses and poor logic. Or at least she figured *me* out pretty quick," he added with a chuckle.

Millie glanced toward the door, and then focused on her hands, which she'd clasped in her lap. Nora was wearing a pumpkin-colored cape dress and a fresh kapp, appearing cool and collected even though she'd apparently walked rather than drive her flashy red car.

Pretender, Millie thought. *Nora looks properly Plain for this Sunday visit, but at that fancy house she wears short-shorts and a sparkly ball cap.*

"Oh!" Mammi stood up, blinking back tears. "Oh, Nora, it's so *gut* to see ya, child."

"And look at you, Mamma!" Nora said as she rushed into Mammi's open arms. "Last time I peeked in on you, I was afraid you were nearly gone."

"I was. Millie's been takin' *gut* care of me, but I haven't given her much to work with." Mammi's reply was muffled because she stood with her head buried against Nora's shoulder, hugging her as though she'd never let go.

Millie looked away. While she was glad her grandmother had been improving with each passing day — which might mean she wouldn't need a caretaker much longer — Millie didn't give this prodigal daughter all the credit for Mammi's recovery. Nora didn't deserve to be considered a miracle worker for sneaking into the sickroom and then ducking out, leaving chaos in her wake.

"This isn't the time or the place, Wilma," Millie's grandfather scoffed. "The bishop didn't invite us here to watch ya carry on."

Nora eased away from the intense embrace. She smiled and nodded at everyone, but Millie stared at her lap rather than make eye contact. She had no intention of acting like Nora's long-lost daughter.

"Let's invite the Lord amongst us with a prayer," Bishop Tom suggested as he and Nazareth took the seats between Atlee and Millie's grandfather. "We've set ourselves up for potential healin', but there's bound to be some heartache that comes with it."

Millie spent the next few moments of silence peering through the slits of her eyelids at Nora, who sat across the room from her. Once again she had the impression that the stranger in their midst knew the right *look,* all the right Amish attitudes and postures, while deep down she was still English to the core.

Bishop Tom cleared his throat. "I'm pleased to see all of ya here, hopin' to reacquaint yourselves with Nora. And we should help Millie figure out where she fits into the picture, now that she's dealin' with several unexpected pieces of the puzzle," he began as he looked around the room. "We all come to this situation with different perspectives, and we all have different emotions. I'm gonna ask that we respect each other's opinions and feelings. Flyin' off the handle — or leavin' in a snit — will only delay the resolutions we seek. And such behavior dishonors God."

Millie felt a glimmer of smug satisfaction when Bishop Tom gazed directly at Atlee and her grandfather as he gave these warnings. Beside her, Lizzie fished a folded piece of paper from her apron pocket.

"I brought along the note that was pinned to Millie's little gown, the morning Atlee and I found her in a basket on our porch," she murmured. She smiled at Millie, looking as though she might cry. "It says, *Since nobody loves my mamma and she can't raise me alone, I'm yours. Millie.*"

When Lizzie handed her the yellowed

note, Millie accepted it rather than risk hurting Lizzie's feelings again. The handwriting was loose and loopy, appearing rather immature — especially considering how sleek and pulled-together Nora was now. It seemed ironic to Millie that when she was a wee babe in a basket, her mother had signed Millie's name to notes an infant couldn't have written — and had expected other folks to deal with problems she didn't want to take responsibility for.

"I lived at your *mammi*'s sister's house in Bowling Green while I was carrying you, Millie," Nora explained. "It was the common thing to send a girl away to have a baby out of wedlock. Aunt Elva and I got along all right during my pregnancy, while she could hide me away in her little house, but she was a middle-aged *maidel* and she didn't like babies much. Once you were born, she made it clear that you and I were upsetting her routine, and that she'd fulfilled her duty as my caretaker."

Nora sighed as she looked at Lizzie and Atlee. "I didn't know what else to do," she said in a faraway voice. "I had no way to pay rent or to buy what you needed, Millie, so I left you with a couple I believed would take care of you . . . who could raise you as their own. With your mop of carrot-colored hair, you looked like a Glick from the beginning."

"I had no idea Elva turned ya out that way," Mammi fretted. "Her letter just said ya were gone."

"You were such a sweet baby," Lizzie reminisced as she gazed fondly at Millie.

"You cried like a fire siren," Atlee piped up. "And with us being newlyweds, we had no idea how to settle you down or —"

"But ya did the right thing," Bishop Tom interrupted earnestly. "Ya took on the sleepless nights and the tough decisions every set of parents faces, to do right by a helpless child."

"And you did a wonderful job of raising her," Nora said in a voice that didn't sound quite so confident anymore. "I thank you from the bottom of my heart, no matter what you must think. Millie has had a stable life — a home and a family I couldn't have given her."

"And that was because your own family cast ya out when ya needed us most." Mammi shifted in her chair, shaking her head sadly. "From the moment your *dat* ordered ya to leave, Nora, I believed we'd done somethin' that God surely wouldn't have wanted. But he was a preacher and he said he was obeyin' the rules of the *Ord-*

nung. And as his wife, I had to submit to his will."

"*Jah,* I knew that, Mamma," Nora murmured. She reached for Mammi's hand and the two of them held on to each other so hard their knuckles turned white.

"Nothin'll come of gettin' all teary-eyed about the past," Dawdi remarked sternly. "Girls who get themselves in trouble need to experience their family's disapproval — the wages of their sin — so they can repent and return to the path of salvation —"

"But you told me I couldn't come back," Nora insisted. "You said the door was closed, and that I wasn't to darken it ever again. I had no home, no family. No place to go when Aunt Elva shut me and Millie out."

Millie crossed her arms, uncomfortable with the turn this talk had taken. She knew of a couple girls in other towns who'd gotten in the family way, and they'd both returned to their homes after putting their babies up for adoption. She didn't want to think about what might've happened to her if Nora had done that. Millie was trying very hard not to sympathize with Nora, but Dawdi *had* shut her out . . .

Dawdi let out a humorless laugh. "Seems ya made a pretty *gut* life for yourself in spite of that," he retorted. "Ya didn't let your Amish upbringin' stand in your way when it came to acquirin' a fancy car and that big house on the hill!"

"So how'd ya manage that, little sister?" Atlee demanded. "You've obviously jumped the fence to live an English life —"

"I didn't see that there was a fence to jump," Nora said softly. "I couldn't be so much concerned with religion when my day-to-day survival was at stake."

Nora looked at Lizzie and Mammi then, entreating them with her eyes. "I found work cleaning at a motel. It was an honest job and the family that owned the place let me have a room there as part of my pay. When the eldest son took an interest in me, we started dating . . . eventually got married," Nora summarized. She let out a long sigh, looking at Dawdi. "I'd have probably joined the Amish church, had you allowed me to come home. So yes, I've lived English because that was the path that opened to me."

"Huh," Dawdi said. "The path of least resistance."

"Isn't that the way a lot of Amish gals meet the men they marry? Workin' for their families?" Nazareth asked in a purposeful voice. "When I came to Willow Ridge I'd

been a *maidel* schoolteacher all my life —
and Tom's wife had left him, so we figured
a permanent relationship wasn't meant to
be. But circumstances changed, and God's
will was done. Sounds like God's will has
worked out for Nora, as well — just not the
way you'd rather have it, Gabe."

Atlee let out an exasperated sigh. "That
has *nothing* to do with Nora latchin' on to a
rich English fella who —"

"Who found himself another woman he
felt was more sophisticated and interesting,"
Nora blurted as she held her brother's gaze.
"So Tanner divorced me. Had I not hired a
competent lawyer, I would've been left
without a home *again.*"

When little Ella began to pat Millie's leg
and chatter, Millie was glad for the distraction of lifting the baby into her lap. She was
tired of Atlee and Dawdi speaking in such
critical tones. Nora was replying to their
objections matter-of-factly — not making a
play for anyone's sympathy by sniffling or
blinking back tears.

"Well then, Nora," Dawdi said in a rising
voice, "it seems that you've not only turned
your back on the faith you were raised in,
but you married an English fella and then
you divorced him —"

"No, *he* left *her,*" Lizzie pointed out.

160

"— so you've committed a number of major sins," Dawdi went on doggedly. "And what with ya buyin' a high-and-mighty house and drivin' a fancy car, it seems ya have no intention of repentin' or changin' your ways, either."

"Which brings me to the fact that Nora asked for your forgiveness at the Sweet Seasons, Gabe," Bishop Tom pointed out as he sat forward on his chair. "She asked ya in all humility — I witnessed the whole thing. And what was your response?"

Dawdi crossed his arms, muttering something. When his rimless glasses caught the light from the picture window, the reflection hid his eyes.

Mammi, however, sat up much straighter in her chair. "I've not heard about this," she said as she glared at Dawdi. "How did Gabe respond, Tom? He's not gonna tell us the whole story, it seems."

"He said 'Get behind me, Satan,' and then he shoved me out of his way as he left." Nora pressed her lips into a tight line, looking into her lap.

"*Jah*, that's how it went," the bishop said ruefully. "I felt mighty bad for Nora, and I was appalled that a fella who'd been one of our preachers for most of his life showed such disregard for his own flesh and blood

— and for the most basic tenet of our faith."

The room got quiet, except for the whirring of the fans. It seemed obvious that her grandfather wasn't going to offer up any excuse for his behavior, so the bishop went on.

"In the prayer our Lord taught us, He tells us to ask for our daily bread and to not be led into temptation, and to be spared the evils of this world," Tom recounted in a quiet but firm voice. "And when it comes to askin' the Lord's forgiveness, we agree to do likewise — to forgive the folks who've done us wrong. It's the *only thing* we're expected to do in return for God givin' us the rest of the benefits outlined in His prayer."

Dawdi's face was growing ruddy, but he appeared more contrary than contrite. "Let's hear the rest of the story, so we can place the blame where it belongs," he said gruffly. He leaned forward to look around Mammi, focusing on Nora. "Back when I asked who got ya in the family way, ya refused to tell me — which was the main reason I sent ya packin'. Ya defied me, Nora, and ya gave me no way to demand that the boy take any responsibility."

Nora's expression turned grim. "I haven't told a soul to this day — mainly because the *man* in question informed me that I'd go straight to hell if I revealed his identity," she said in very small voice. "I was naive enough — terrified enough — to believe him at the time. But he's dead now, so it does me no good to keep his secret any longer. It was . . . the bishop of Morning Star."

"What?" Dawdi blurted. "Don't think for a minute I'll believe that Jeremiah Shetler —"

"No, back then Tobias Borntreger was the bishop," Tom pointed out with a frown. "Jeremiah was a preacher, just like you and I were."

"And ya expect me to go along with *that*?" Dawdi retorted. "Tobias was a *gut* friend of mine, and a devout man of the faith! He would no more have touched Nora than —"

"See there?" Nora blurted, throwing up her hands. "You don't believe me now, and you certainly wouldn't have believed me when I was sixteen — which was *exactly* what Tobias was counting on."

Everyone in the front room sat wide-eyed, as though the air had been sucked out of them. Nora slumped in her chair, shaken from the strain of her revelation. Lizzie's hand fluttered to her mouth, while Mammi's face fell and she fished a handkerchief from her apron pocket.

"Did this happen while ya were helpin' at the Borntreger place?" Mammi asked in a voice they could barely hear. "That was the summer Tobias's wife was laid up with a broken leg, and in the family way, too, as I recall."

"It did, Mamma," Nora whispered. "More than once. I — I didn't know what to do. Tobias insisted that God had brought me there to be helpful, and that I wasn't to say anything to you or Dat, because if I did, he'd deny it. He said I'd go to hell for disobeyin' him, too."

"Oh, you poor dear girl." Mammi rose from her chair to stand behind Nora, hugging her shoulders. "I am so sorry. All these years wasted."

"Tobias made some inappropriate remarks to me a time or two." Lizzie grimaced as though the bishop's name tasted bad when she said it. "But I was married, and old enough to brush him off —"

"You were imaginin' things," Atlee interrupted with a roll of his eyes. "And it was me who drove Nora over to work at the Borntreger place, and I picked her up at the end of the day. *I* never noticed anything was goin' on —"

"You were clueless," Nora replied with a

sigh. She patted Mammi's skinny arms, wrapped around her shoulders, as Mammi remained behind her chair. "You were so engrossed in your auctioneering work, proving yourself to Lizzie's *dat,* it was only an annoyance to you when I cried all the way home."

"You're *still* clueless," Lizzie muttered. "And at that age, Nora was innocent and sheltered and had no idea what to do when a man in authority — a man she was supposed to *trust and obey* — took advantage of her. I'm sorry, Nora," she added as she shook her head sorrowfully. "I had no idea. This changes the way we all see —"

"No," Dawdi insisted. "It's Nora's word against a dead man's. She's been tryin' for your sympathy, and she's got it." He rose unsteadily, grasping the arm of the loveseat to boost himself up. "I've had all of this nonsense I can stomach. We're headin' home, Wilma."

"Run along," came Mammi's reply.

Millie's mouth dropped open. Once again the room got very quiet, and the fans seemed useless against the stifling heat of this confrontation. Mammi's tone wasn't sarcastic or defiant, but Dawdi wasn't accustomed to his wife disobeying him. Her grandfather began to shuffle the length of

165

Bishop Tom's front room, muttering under his breath as he put a hand to the curve of his back.

It was startling, the way Dawdi's posture and attitude had declined nearly as much as Mammi's had improved these past few days. Millie didn't feel compelled to assist him. It seemed clear that he'd brought this whole situation on himself before she was even born. Millie sensed Nora had a few more secrets up her sleeve — revelations that might affect her future. So she sat tight.

"Well, it's obvious Dat's not gonna make it home by himself," Atlee snapped as he stood up. Glaring at Millie and Lizzie and then at Mammi, who still clung to Nora, he strode across the room and took his father's arm. Everyone remained silent until the two men had gone out the door and were clumping down the wooden porch stairs.

"Is it my imagination, or did a black Cadillac just pull away from the Riehl's lane next door?" Nazareth murmured.

Lifting a sleepy-eyed Ella to her shoulder, Millie stood up to gaze out the picture window behind Nora and Mammi. "*Jah*, there he goes," she confirmed. "Do ya suppose Hiram was eavesdroppin' at one of the windows and then slipped away when he knew Dawdi was leavin'?"

Nora let out an exasperated sigh. "Why wouldn't that surprise me? From what I've seen of Hiram since I bought his house, he's an even sneakier snake than Tobias was," she muttered. "That pointed black goatee just *fits* him — but here I go, passing judgment." She paused, shaking her head. "I'm sure folks here in Willow Ridge have had similar thoughts about the way I was dressed when I arrived, not to mention about the car I drive."

Bishop Tom's expression remained solemn as he considered what had just happened. "We'll ask the Lord to oversee our dealings with Hiram," he said as Nazareth poured refills of lemonade. "And I'm trustin' Him to guide my words as I keep talkin' to Gabe and Atlee. I'm truly concerned that Gabe might still have this burden on his soul when he goes to meet his Maker. It's hardened his heart for far too long."

"But in spite of his orders, Nora's come home," Mammi declared. She squeezed Nora's shoulders one more time before she sat down on the loveseat. "Seems to me we should be countin' our blessings today, rather than allowin' Gabe's stubbornness to diminish our joy. In learnin' the truth about the past, we've seen how God's been with Nora all along, guidin' her back to Willow

Ridge. Praise His holy name!"

"Amen to that," Nazareth murmured as she started the cookie plate around.

Millie resumed her seat, amazed at how her grandmother was speaking out. Wilma Glick was known for being the reserved wife of a preacher, not physically well, yet she was glowing as she gazed at everyone around her. When Lizzie held the treats in front of her, Millie chose a frosted sugar cookie to share with Ella.

After she'd passed the tray back to Nazareth, Lizzie reached for Millie's shoulder. "These past few days have been hard for ya, Millie. But do ya recall how, through the years, I've said ya were such a blessing to me?" Lizzie's eyes shone with tears. "With each time I miscarried, and with both stillborn wee ones we laid to rest, *you* were the reason I gathered myself together again and found the strength to go on. I considered ya a gift from God even more than ya were a gift from Nora."

Millie blinked rapidly, glad she had Ella in her lap as a distraction. "*Jah,* you've always said that."

Lizzie let out a shuddery breath. "Without you in my life, my days would've been sad and empty. I know you're upset because I kept the truth about Nora from ya, but I *wanted* ya to be my daughter, Millie. I always will."

The breath rushed from Millie's lungs. She hugged Ella fiercely, trying not to cry — trying not to let Lizzie's heartfelt words penetrate the emotional defenses she'd put up. But her heart could no longer shut out the love this quiet, caring woman had always shown her. Millie blotted her wet cheeks on her sleeve. "*Jah,* I know that, too," she murmured.

"It's not my intention to come between the two of you, either," Nora spoke up. "I know you'll never love me the way you do Lizzie, because in every way that matters, she's your *mamm,* Millie."

When Nora crossed the room to stand before her, Millie looked up at her. She saw the face of the woman she would someday become . . . the trembling chin and wide hazel eyes of the girl who had given birth to her and then given her to Atlee and Lizzie Glick — not as a careless, trifling act, but as the sacrifice that would allow both of them to live stronger lives.

"I'm sorry my return has caused so much upheaval," Nora went on. She stroked Ella's cheek, gazing at each of them in the room. "I knew it would be tough for all of us at first, but I had faith that once the initial pain passed, we could make our peace and figure out how we fit into each other's lives. I've come to realize that I need this family every bit as much as you do, Millie. I'm so glad I got back to Willow Ridge to make amends before your *mammi* was no longer with us."

When Nora gently squeezed her shoulder, Millie felt a confident strength — a determination that seemed to run in the Glick family. She'd always considered this trait as stubbornness in Dawdi and her *dat,* but Millie felt that for her *mamm* and Mammi this tenacity fed the faith that had seen them through disappointments and heartaches — which had often been the result of their men's refusal to see anyone's viewpoint but their own.

Millie still had a lot of feelings to sort out, but the warmth and commitment she felt in this group of women seemed strong and right. Her emotions had undergone a radical change, coming almost full circle in the last hour. When Ella giggled, Millie fed her another chunk of the sugar cookie.

"Maybe this is a good time to clear up another potential misconception," Nora began as she returned to her chair. "Tom and I talked yesterday about what I plan to do here in Willow Ridge. He has generously agreed that the big barn on my place would make a good consignment store for crafts and handmade items produced by Plain folks around the area."

"Oh!" Lizzie said. "I've wondered what would become of Hiram's huge horse barn —"

"That seems like a real *gut* idea," Nazareth chimed in cheerfully. "I've not seen any sort of shop for handcrafted gifts around this area."

"You need to know," Nora continued in a determined tone, "that while Bishop Tom was admiring the hangings I've made to sell in the shop, he told me I'd have to choose my faith and operate my store accordingly. I've thought about what he said, and he's right. A lot of people in this town will consider my dimensional fabric pieces *art.*"

Nora paused to allow everyone to absorb what she'd just said. Millie fed her sister another bit of cookie, intrigued by Nora's statement that she was an *artist.* She wasn't minimizing her talent or trying to pass it off as acceptable to folks like Dawdi and Dat, either. What did that mean?

"I hope you'll understand that after a lot of prayer and soul-searching," Nora continued in a lower voice, "I've decided that joining the Old Order isn't right for me. Even though, technically, I wasn't shunned, I'm a poster child for the way shutting folks out can shatter families —"

"I can see why you'd feel that way," Nazareth remarked.

"— and I believe that God allowed me to develop my artistic talents so I could support myself," Nora continued. "So thank you, Tom, for insisting that I commit one way or the other, without waffling or making excuses."

"I respect your comin' out and sayin' that." Tom's smile hinted at disappointment, but he nodded. "That means your family'll have to decide how they'll handle your choice, but I think it was the right one for ya."

"So what'll ya *be* then, Nora?" Mammi asked. "When I saw ya in a solid-colored cape dress, I figured —"

"I made a few Plain dresses before I came, out of respect for the way you raised me, Mamma," Nora replied, reaching for her hand. "And I've adjusted to living in a house that's not electrified. And I'll probably put my car up for sale soon."

"You're goin' back to a horse-drawn rig?" Millie blurted. Wouldn't *that* take Ira and Luke by surprise?

Nora chuckled, her eyes lighting up. "I

172

don't know yet. I might trade the convertible for something more practical, with room to haul merchandise for the store," she said. Then she turned to Mammi again. "I'm thinking to become a Mennonite, Mamma, like the Schrocks who run the quilting shop. Can you accept that?"

Lizzie chuckled. "It's Mary Schrock's husband that Atlee's partnered with all these years, ya know. Mennonites are just as committed to their faith — and to the same God — as we are. They're *gut* people."

Mammi looked a little perplexed. "After all these years of wonderin' what's become of ya, I can adjust my thinkin' if ya choose Mennonite ways over ours. But I doubt your *dat* will accept it."

"That's how I see it, too." Nora sighed, but then she shrugged. "Dat will be Dat, and I can't change that. I can only follow what I believe God's telling me to do."

The room went quiet, with only the soft whirring of the fans. Bishop Tom's ice rattled in his empty glass when he set it down. "I feel we've accomplished a lot, talkin' these things out amongst ourselves," he remarked. "If ya feel the need to meet this way again, let me know. You're all welcome in my home anytime."

"It was *gut* of ya to look after us this way,

Bishop Tom," Lizzie said. She gathered the puffy baby quilt from the floor and then opened her arms to take Ella. "We've still got some issues to iron out, but at least we women are willin' to make Nora welcome and to keep our family movin' forward."

"Thank you all so much for talking to me, and for seeing my side of things," Nora said as she, too, stood up. She smiled over at Millie. "I'll need a lot of help setting up displays and getting the store ready to open, and I'll need someone to help me run it, too. If that would interest you — and if your grandparents can spare you — let me know, okay?"

Millie's heart skipped rope. She wasn't ready to accept Nora as her full-time, for-real mother, but working at a craft consignment store would be a lot more fun than hanging around at her grandparents' house. "*Jah,* I'll think about that," she replied.

"We'll see what Gabe says — and what sort of schedule we can work out," Mammi said with a nod. "We'll let ya know, Nora. I think that's a real *gut* idea, for the two of ya to spend time together."

"Even if helping in the store won't work out," Nora added, "you're welcome to come over anytime, you know. Don't be alarmed if the door's locked, though. Hiram let himself in the other day, and I've installed new dead bolts to put a stop to that. I'm not keeping *you* out."

As Bishop Tom walked them all to the front door, he frowned. "I don't like the sound of that, Nora. There seems to be no limit to Hiram's arrogance."

When they got outside, Millie saw that her *dat* had driven Dawdi home in her grandparents' buggy. As she helped her grandmother into Lizzie and Atlee's rig, Millie saw that Nora was walking on down to the road. "Can we give ya a ride?" she called out. "It's awful hot."

Nora stopped, shading her eyes with her hand. "*Denki* for the offer, but I need the exercise. It's so *gut* to see you, Millie!" she called out.

Millie realized that Nora had slipped into the local Deitsch dialect, and it sounded totally natural. She returned Nora's wave, watching her as she strode along the gravel road.

That's your mother. She's slim and pretty and energetic. She's an artist who's opening a store no matter what Dawdi says. Your life — life in Willow Ridge — is about to change in a big way.

CHAPTER TWELVE

As Luke walked slowly around the displays in the mill's sales room, he couldn't help grinning. It was a fine Friday morning, the first of August, and the Mill at Willow Ridge had officially opened for tourist business today. He wanted to be sure all the refrigerated cases and shelves lined with bags of baking mixes and grains looked just right before anyone else came in. It wasn't yet six in the morning, but most folks in Willow Ridge had been up for hours tending their livestock, so it was anyone's guess when somebody might peek in to wish him and his brother well. Or at least Luke hoped they would.

"Well, Brother, it's been nearly a year in the making, but here we are," he said to Ira with a grin. "When we lived in Lancaster, who would've believed we'd be operating our own gristmill and store?"

"It's been an adventure," Ira agreed. "Better than anything we ever could've had if we'd not taken Bennie's advice and come to Willow Ridge to —"

"Is that *my* name somebody's takin' in vain?" a familiar voice teased. Ben peered around the door frame before stepping inside with a large box. "I've got some little loaves of bread and fruit bars Miriam made up with your grains. And she sent ya a pie in honor of your openin' today."

"Great! I'll put her goodies by the checkout," Luke said as he peered into the box. One whiff of the grainy, spicy-sweet aroma told him that all of Miriam's little packages would be gone by the end of the day.

"And I'll relieve ya of that pie," Ira chimed in. "Someone we know was too excited to make us any breakfast this morning."

Ben laughed as he clapped Luke on the back. "If ya can't get excited about your own store openin', then why bother bein' in business?" he asked. "You boys've outdone yourselves. When word gets out about all the local specialties you've got to offer, you're gonna be runnin' a gold mine here. Really."

Luke plucked the two forks from the box Miriam had sent. Though he got along well with his older brother, Ben's praise and encouragement felt especially sweet on this momentous occasion. "It was Ira's sales skills that convinced some of the area farmers to raise the cage-free chickens so we could sell their eggs," he said, gesturing toward the refrigerator case. "And he was *gut* at gettin' other fellas to grow us some organic oats, rye, wheat, and other grains — along with corn and popcorn."

"Your packagin' looks mighty nice, too," Ben remarked as he took a bag of coarse-ground cornmeal from the shelf. "And there's a recipe on the back. That'll appeal to folks who've not cooked with these kinds of grains before."

"The idea for usin' recipes — and all our labels — were Rebecca's work," Luke replied as he approached his younger brother. "Ira, if you think that pie's all for you, think again."

"It's cherry — and still warm, too." Ira snatched one of the forks from Luke's hand.

As his younger brother gouged the pie from one side, Luke dug into it from the other. For a few moments, the two of them forked up huge bites of the tart cherry filling and Miriam's flaky pastry while Ben made his way around the shop, chatting as he went. The *clip-clop* of an approaching horse made them both glance toward the door.

"We should probably set this behind the counter, in case it's our first customer," Luke murmured, but Ira held fast to the glass pie pan.

"This early, who's gonna care if we're eatin' our breakfast?" Ira teased. "And unless my ears are foolin' me, it's the two aunts comin' with their goat cheese."

Moments later, as their chatter and laughter preceded them, Jerusalem and Nazareth stepped inside, carrying a large cooler between them. Their steely-gray hair was pulled into perfect buns beneath their starched *kapps,* and their dresses of magenta and deep green looked freshly pressed.

"Would ya looky here!" Jerusalem crowed as she gazed around at the shop. "You boys've been hard at it since last time I saw this place! Are ya ready for your big day?"

"We didn't want ya to think we forgot the goat cheese we promised ya," Nazareth chimed in as they set down the cooler. "But we wanted it to be real fresh, and we got the labels on just so — and the little plastic tubs for Tom's fresh-churned butter finally came yesterday. So ya should be set for a while."

"*Denki,* aunts," Luke replied as he bussed their temples. "This is turning into quite a

Hooley enterprise, with you two helping us."

"And who knew we'd be gettin' into such a thing when we left our classroom behind in Lancaster?" The crow's-feet around Jerusalem's eyes deepened with her glee. "It's the hand of God leadin' us all."

"Or proddin' some of us in the backside to get a real life," Ira remarked with a chuckle. His fork stopped halfway to his mouth. "I could offer you aunts a bite of Miriam's fresh cherry pie, I suppose. We need to get out the forks for the sampling table anyway."

"*Jah,* we're not really as crude and unmannerly as we appear, wolfing this down in front of you," Luke added.

"Hah! We know you boys better than that," Ben teased. "For some protein, ya ought to spread a little of the aunts' goat cheese on that pie."

"Did somebody say goat cheese?"

The melodic lilt of Nora Landwehr's voice made Luke's heart sing along, and when he turned to greet her, his eyes widened. She had a roll of fabric tucked under her arm and a secretive smile on her face. Though she was dressed Plain today, the bright orange, red, and pink plaid of her cape dress made a statement he couldn't miss. No woman who aspired to join the Old Order

Amish would wear such a colorful print.

"Nora, *gut* morning!" Ben called to her. "Have ya met our aunt, Jerusalem Gingerich?"

Luke handed Ira the pie pan to take over the introductions. Or so he thought.

"It's a pleasure to meet you, Jerusalem," Nora said as she came forward with her hand extended. "Tom's told me you and your sister both married bishops this spring, and that you're living in Cedar Creek now."

Smooth. That was the word for Nora even at this early hour, even wearing clothing that concealed her curves and covered most of her skin. While he had enjoyed her jean shorts and tank top, Luke was secretly pleased that his new neighbor appeared more appropriate this morning — or at least his aunts would think so.

"*Jah,* Vernon and I came up for the mill store's opening today," Jerusalem replied, gripping Nora's hand between her two larger ones. "Naz tells me ya bought the place next door, thinkin' to open up a big outlet for handcrafted stuff that Plain folks've made. I can't wait to go shoppin' there!"

Luke blinked. How had he missed hearing such important news? "Seems a lot happened this week while Ira and I have been

181

setting up."

"I've been a busy bee, *jah.*" Nora focused on Luke, widening her tigress eyes. "Thanks to Mary Schrock, I've got several folks from around here and Morning Star, New Haven, and other little burgs ready to consign all sorts of neat items. They seem really excited about having a central place to sell what they make, and I think this sort of store will bring a lot of tourist trade to Willow Ridge — and to your mill, as well," she added with a smile.

Was it his imagination, or was Nora making her expressive eyes glimmer just for him? Luke set his fork in the pie pan Ira held, his breakfast forgotten as he reached toward the big cooler his aunts had carried in. "Did I hear you say you were interested in goat cheese?" he asked. "Just so happens I have fresh bread from the Sweet Seasons and little tubs of my aunts' cheese, from the goats they keep over at Tom's place. You can be our first official taster, because we're ready to set up a sampling table."

"That would be fabulous," Nora replied. "I saw your lights on over here, so I left home before I ate any breakfast."

Fabulous. No one else around Willow Ridge used that flashy word much, yet Nora had slipped into the local dialect and its rhythm since he'd last seen her. Luke clearly had some catching up to do . . . later, when his aunts and his brothers weren't hanging on their every word.

Nora set her rolled bundle on the nearest table and grinned at the little plastic cup of goat cheese Luke showed her. "Now is this cute, or what? You've got a goat face on your cheese containers — and a cow face on Tom's butter. Where'd you find these adorable labels?"

Luke's two aunts lit up like stars. "We asked Miriam's Rebecca to help us. She's really *gut* at all this packagin' and advertisin' stuff," Nazareth replied.

"*Jah,* she found the faces and designed the labels, and whenever we need more she'll print them out for us," Jerusalem chimed in. "They're already sticky on the back, too, so ya don't have to lick anything."

"Nothing's nastier than a paper cut on your tongue," Nazareth said with a nod.

Nora chuckled. The sisters were a charming pair, and like most Amish ladies their age, they were easily amazed by such simple advancements as sticky notes or anything generated by a computer. "Seems Rebecca is the go-to girl for all sorts of great ideas," she remarked. "I'll have to talk to her about

— oh, *denki,* Luke!"

He handed her a small disposable plate with a slice cut from a grainy mini-loaf that smelled of oats and cinnamon, along with a generous clump of goat cheese and a plastic knife. The bread was still slightly warm, so the cheese oozed into its little crevices as she spread it. Nora closed her eyes over the first bite, savoring a robust yet simple goodness . . . something she could never bake herself.

"Oh my," she murmured. "If Rebecca's done your advertising and you plan to have samples of this luscious cheese and bread out today, I predict that the Mill at Willow Ridge is going to be a *huge* success. This is absolutely divine."

Nora didn't care that the two sisters and the three Hooley brothers were watching her as she chewed her second mouthful of bread and goat cheese. When she finished her sample, she let out a satisfied sigh. "Now *that* was a gift. *Denki* to all of you for sharing it with me — and I brought a little something, as well," she added as she handed the rolled fabric to Luke. "Consider it a shop-warming gift."

Luke's eyes widened as he took her offering. He still smelled fresh from a shower, and with the neck of his pale green shirt open lower than most Plain men would dare, he looked extremely appealing. As he unfurled the hanging, his mouth dropped open. "Would you look at — it's the mill, Ira! With the paddle wheel —"

"And the river rollin' along, and the wildflowers in bloom on the riverbanks," his brother added in an awed voice. "And it says 'The Mill at Willow Ridge' along the top."

"Where'd ya get this, Nora?" Luke gazed at her as though he might kiss her in front of his whole family. "This is to hang on the wall, right?"

"Over here above the display table, where folks'll see it as soon as they walk in," Ira said, pointing to a spot near the cash register.

"My stars, would ya look at this perty appliqué quiltin'," Jerusalem exclaimed as she held one side of the hanging so everyone could see it better. "I like the way the mill wheel stands out, catchin' the water. Looks so real it could start turnin'."

"And the flowers have beads for petals, with embroidered stems and leaves," Nazareth murmured, running her finger over these details. "And the ripples on the calico river are fringed, to look frothy."

Nora chuckled. "If I'd had a little more

time, I could've gotten a small motor and designed the mill wheel so it *would* move," she replied. She'd been struck by the inspiration for this gift just a few days ago, so everyone's enthusiasm made the late-night hours worth the effort she'd put into finishing it for the store's opening.

"That's the perfect spot for it, Ira," she remarked as Luke's brother went to the back room. Then she smiled up at Luke. "I'll have several of my hangings displayed in the consignment store when it opens, so maybe — if your customers notice this banner — you can send them next door? I'll certainly rave to my clients about your organic grains and local dairy treats."

Luke appeared stunned. "*You* made this?"

"I did." Nora's cheeks went hot with the intensity of his gaze. "Just as you and Ira know how to get the best out of the grains you mill, I combine all sorts of fabrics and sewing techniques to make my hangings."

"This is really something," Ben said as he stood back a few feet to admire the banner. "I've been around quilts all my life, but I've never seen the likes of this, Nora. Would ya make something for Miriam's kitchen at home — when ya get a chance?" he added quickly. "If you're figurin' to get a store up and runnin', you'll be mighty busy, so

186

there's no hurry."

Nora smiled. This was working out even better than she could've planned it. "Ben, I'd be willing to barter however many hangings you'd want in exchange for a decorative metal sign for my store," she suggested. "From the way some of the locals have described your wrought iron garden gates and trellises, I bet you could make me a sign that's as unique as the shop will be."

Ben waved off her compliment. "It's just metal put to the flame and I bend it around a bit," he remarked.

"Don't fall for that modest act," Luke said. "Bennie made the sign above our shop's door, from a template Rebecca designed to match our website's home page. He's got a really *gut* eye and the strength in his hands to make whatever you'd want."

"I figured he'd made your sign," Nora replied. "I'd be tickled to sell your gates or trellises or whatever else you'd care to display in my store, Ben," she added as she smiled at the eldest Hooley brother. "I'm going to carry merchandise that appeals to both men and women. Matthias Wagler's consigning a saddle or two, as well as some of his leather horse collars. And the Brennemans have furniture for me, so your metal work would be a great addition."

"You got *Wagler* to put stuff in your store?" Luke said. "That took some doing. Matthias has pretty much been a hermit since his wife died."

Nora's lips lifted. Was that a little competitive jealousy she heard behind Luke's remark? "Truth be told," she murmured, "Matthias brought me home from a few singings when we were kids. Had that, um, other man not gotten me pregnant and banished from Willow Ridge, who knows? Matthias and I might've courted and married."

"*Jah,* Nazareth and Tom told me about that unfortunate situation," Jerusalem said with a cluck. She gently grasped Nora's wrist. "I'm real sorry your *dat* sent ya off, and real glad, for Wilma's sake, that ya found your way back to Willow Ridge."

Nora squeezed the older aunt's sturdy hand, considering Jerusalem's gesture the ultimate badge of acceptance. The expression on Luke's face was priceless, too.

"You and I need to talk, Nora," he murmured. "Real soon."

Ira laughed from across the room as he leaned a ladder against the wall. "Let's don't forget we've got a store to run, brother," he called out. He ascended the wooden steps to hold the new banner

188

against the wall. "How high? Is this about right?"

"Down about a foot, and a few inches to your left," Nora replied.

Ben stepped over to help Ira position a couple of wooden pegs he'd fetched, and then the pounding of a mallet rang in the high, beamed ceiling. A few minutes later Nora's work was brightening the wall — the entire shop — and she thrummed with pleasure. The calico fabrics she'd chosen in blues, greens, and browns looked bold and masculine, depicting the mill as a work site rather than a romanticized scene, and the beaded flowers picked up on the colors of the grains displayed on the shelves beneath it. The banner also hung low enough that her potential customers could get a close look at it.

"Isn't that *something*?" Nazareth exclaimed, clasping her hands to gaze at Nora's hanging.

"I'm thinkin' such a piece might dress up the butcher shop," Jerusalem murmured. Then she smiled at Nora. "My Vernon raises Black Angus cattle, you see, and his nephew Abner runs the local butcher shop and meat locker. The meat case is a sight to behold with the cuts of beef and local pork they sell, but the shop itself —"

"Looks like a couple of hayseed farm fellas did the decoratin'," Nazareth added with a girlish giggle.

Ben laughed along with the rest of them. "Wouldn't it make for a great banner — Vernon's stone silo, alongside some of his sleek black cows peerin' over the white plank fence by the barn?" he remarked. He smiled at Nora. "How about if ya count a banner like that against the metal sign I'll do for ya? I can sketch ya a picture of Vernon's place —"

"Or I could take you there. How about Sunday afternoon?" Luke asked in a purposeful voice. "Who knows what *inspiration* a ride in the country might provide?"

Nora laughed. She could envision the banner perfectly from Ben's description, but nothing was better than an on-site visit to provide the details she liked to include on her pieces. She could read Luke's face clearly, too. He was a man determined to hear the details of her past while he scored his own points.

"It's a church Sunday," Ben remarked offhandedly.

"*Jah,* and I'll be going to the Morning Star Mennonite Fellowship service with the Schrocks," Nora said. She focused on the two aunts and Ben, figuring it was best to spell out her intentions. "After talking with Bishop Tom and praying on it, knowing in my heart that I don't want to quit making my hangings, I've decided the Old Order's not right for me."

"And what's Preacher Gabe sayin' about *that*?" Jerusalem asked. She didn't look critical; just sincerely interested.

"He still doesn't allow me in the house," Nora replied ruefully. "But Mamma told him it was *his* fault that the Amish ways wouldn't become my ways. He didn't want to hear that, of course."

"But you've been open and up-front about it," Nazareth pointed out. "While I'm sure your *mamm* wishes she could spend her Sundays in church and then visitin' with ya at the common meal, I could see during our meeting that she's ever so grateful to God that she can visit with ya at all."

Nodding, Nora turned to look up at Luke again. "You can come to the Mennonite service with me, if you care to. I'm leaving around eight."

Luke leaned down until his nose nearly touched hers. "You'd fall over if I said I'd go. Wouldn't you?" he challenged in a suggestive whisper.

Nora refused to drop her gaze. "Try me — but only if you're sincere about following

Jesus," she added. "I don't see church as a place for flirting and dating."

Jerusalem began to laugh and her sister joined in. "We'd best get our cheese and butter into the refrigerator case," she teased. "What with all the *heat* in here, we'll soon have a melted mess on our hands."

"Our nephew doesn't stand a chance," Nazareth remarked as the two of them carried the cooler over to the glass refrigerator cases. "It's Nora who's holdin' the hoops and Luke who's jumpin' through them, far as I can see."

When Nora said her good-byes and left the mill store, a big grin overtook her face. The banner she'd sewn for the Hooley brothers had reaped even more rewards than she'd hoped for. Besides bringing in more orders for hangings and getting Ben to make a sign for her store, she'd won over Luke's aunts, and she had a date with a man who was keenly interested in her.

Not a bad day's work, considering it's not yet seven in the morning, Nora mused as she strolled home along the riverbank. As her skirt swished through the tall grass, she smiled at the colorful wildflowers . . . saw patterns swirling in the river's currents and got an idea for a new dress. She could have it pieced and sewn by Sunday if she started on it this morning — just as she could cobble together a satisfying life here in Willow Ridge, if she focused on her strengths and the talents God had provided her.

For who could walk in this scenic, peaceful countryside without feeling His presence? Nora inhaled and slowly let out her breath, finding utter serenity in the river and the sight of her big red barn silhouetted against the sunlit horizon. True enough, she had a long way to go to reconcile with her father and to have a solid relationship with Millie. But she'd made great progress in other areas this week — and this morning.

And those were truly blessings to be grateful for.

CHAPTER THIRTEEN

"I don't see Luke here today," Millie remarked as she scanned the folks coming out of Micah and Rachel Brenneman's house after the church service. It was a bit cooler on this August Sunday, so the women had suggested putting blankets and lawn chairs between the apple trees in the orchard and serving the common meal as a picnic buffet.

Ira chuckled as he wrapped his hand around hers. "Can ya believe it? Luke went to the Mennonite church with Nora this morning. Then they're drivin' to Cedar Creek so she can get an idea for a banner she's makin' for the butcher shop Vernon's nephew runs."

Millie let out a startled laugh. "Your brother went to *church* with her? I thought maybe he'd slept in after your big opening for the mill store," she teased. Then she thought for a moment. "My word, it's what

— a couple of hours to Cedar Creek from here? That's a long way to go, I'd think."

"Not if you're Luke and you're tryin' to get Nora all to yourself for the day." Ira, too, looked at the crowd. The men were milling around in the shade of the main yard, waiting for the women to set out the food on some long tables that Preacher Ben and the Brenneman brothers had set up. He smiled at Millie. "Did ya know Nora and Matthias Wagler used to be sweet on each other? I think that was another reason Luke was hot to trot — especially when he heard Matthias was going to consign some items in Nora's new store."

"No! But then, I wasn't even born when that was goin' on," Millie murmured. Then she considered another interesting detail. "Must be bothersome to Luke that the Waglers live on the other side of Nora's place. Next thing ya know, your brother'll be keepin' a set of binoculars by his window upstairs."

When Millie considered how the August afternoon would drag by — especially because Annie Mae and Adam had gone to visit out-of-town relatives to collect some wedding presents — she suddenly longed to be anywhere except in the Brennemans' yard, swatting the flies and honeybees that would buzz around their food. "What if I fetched a cooler and we took our lunch on the road?" she hinted. "I've felt so cooped up all week —"

"You're wantin' to chase them down, aren't ya? To spy on them!"

Millie laughed. "Well, Sunday *is* the day for visiting with family," she pointed out. "I suspect Dawdi kept me so busy reorganizin' the canning shelves in the cellar this week because he knows I'm itchin' to go to Nora's house — just to get a look inside it, ya know? And to get better acquainted with her. Is that so wrong?"

"Not that I can see," Ira replied. "She's your mother, after all."

"She asked if I wanted to work in her store," Millie went on in a hopeful tone. "Mammi thinks it would be *gut* for me to spend a few days every week helpin' Nora get that big barn cleaned up — and then helpin' her wait on customers."

She could tell by the shifting smile on Ira's face that he might go along with her idea if she gave him another nudge or two. He was in fine spirits today, telling everyone how busy the mill store had been, and how they'd run out of Bishop Tom's butter and his aunts' goat cheese as well as several of their bagged baking mixes. Millie had also heard people talking about the banner her mother had made for the mill store, and she longed to hear more about these hangings — how Nora decided what to put on them, and how she chose her colors and fabrics. Now that Millie knew the story of her mother's unfortunate past, she felt a lot more forgiving about the way Nora had deposited her on Atlee and Lizzie's porch.

"I'll run across the road and fetch us a cooler and some ice, while you decide what-all we should take along to eat," Millie said. "We can be on the road in ten minutes!"

"And what'll you say to Luke and Nora if we *just happen* to meet up with them?" Ira quizzed her. "They'll figure out that you're bein' nosy — just like Luke'll know it was *me* who told ya where they were goin'. He won't be keen on that."

"Puh! Who is he to tell us where not to go for a drive?" she asked. "And why does he think he's got a corner on my *mamm*'s time and attention? It's not like I've gotten to see her all that much."

Ira kept hold of her hand, studying her intently. "You've really changed your tune about Nora. Not that long ago ya wanted nothin' to do with her."

Millie shrugged, unsure of what to say. How could she explain the impact of their meeting at Bishop Tom's to someone who hadn't been there? "Now that Nora's explained why Dawdi booted her out, I see her side of the story," she murmured. "And I feel bad about the way things've gone for her . . . how the folks she's loved and counted on have left her to fend for herself, time and again."

After a moment, Ira kissed her knuckles. "All right then, get us a cooler —"

"Oh, Ira, *denki*!" Millie exclaimed. "If we happen to see your brother and Nora, I won't call out to them — unless *you* want to stop them, or *they* want to visit," she assured him. "Mostly, I just want to get away for a while."

Millie dashed down the long lane, which ran past Ben's smithy and the Sweet Seasons Café, and then sprinted across the county highway. A few minutes later she hurried back to the Brennemans' with the cooler, which held some ice and two cans of the cola she kept on hand as a special treat. She let Ira choose their food while she told her grandmother they were going for a ride. Soon Millie was seated beside Ira in his open rig, all smiles as the *clip-clop, clip-clop* of his mare's shoes rang out on the hot blacktop road.

"This is fun," she said. Millie gazed

eagerly down the road, glad for the breeze that teased at her *kapp* as the horse trotted faster. What time had the Mennonite service let out? It was probably silly to think they'd come across Luke and Nora, who could've taken two or three different routes to Cedar Creek — or might even have changed their destination. "I really appreciate your goin' along with my wild-hare idea, Ira. You've been a real *gut* friend while all these important, scary things have been happenin' to me."

Ira took the lines in one hand and slung his arm loosely around her shoulders. "Seems to me ya took some pretty hard knocks, findin' out ya had a different mother than ya grew up with," he remarked quietly. "If I'd learned that my *mamm* or *dat* had been holdin' out on the truth — or that a preacher and the bishop had hush-hushed the circumstances — I'm not sure I would've handled it too well."

Millie nodded. "Do ya *like* Nora? I mean, I know ya think she's really pretty —"

"And I acted like a jerk that first time I saw her in the driveway, too." He kissed Millie's forehead. "I've backed off now. But *jah,* I think Nora's a nice gal and she's got a steady head for business — and she's all for helpin' out the other shops around

Willow Ridge. That makes her a *gut* neighbor in my book."

Millie nodded, savoring Ira's nearness despite the heat of the afternoon. "Do ya think your brother's serious about her? I mean, he chased after Annie Mae for months, yet he never came close to settlin' down — even before she left her father's new colony and snatched her little brothers and sister back to Willow Ridge."

"I don't know, and I'm not gonna ask him," Ira teased. "But I think it's interesting that he went to the Mennonite service with her this morning, after she challenged him to go. I don't think he would've done that for Annie Mae."

They rode in silence for a while, out in the countryside where the houses got farther apart and fields of tall corn whispered in the breeze. It seemed her mother was becoming a vital member of the Willow Ridge community, despite Dawdi's objections to her presence. That took some strength — some faith — that other folks around town wouldn't turn against Nora to show their support of Preacher Gabe's longtime convictions. When Ira's rumbling stomach brought Millie out of her woolgathering, she reached down to the floor for their lunch.

"What did ya pick out for us?" she asked as she peered into the cooler. It felt good when the coldness of the ice drifted around her face. "Looks like some sliced ham, and a few of the deviled eggs Mammi and I made —"

"Hope they didn't slide out of the waxed paper," Ira remarked with a chuckle. "I was hurryin' to stick stuff in the cooler before too many folks asked where we were goin'."

"Wish I'd thought to bring us a couple of plates," Millie murmured. "Guess I'll just hand you this and that. Feed ya while ya drive."

"We could pull over," Ira suggested playfully. He pointed to a grove of trees off to the side of the road. "We haven't shared a picnic for a long while —"

"But we haven't seen Luke and Nora!" she protested. "I want to wave at them, just to see the looks on their faces."

Ira shook his head good-naturedly as he took a bite of the deviled egg she held in front of him. "Whatever you say, Millie," he teased. "Your wish is my command, it seems."

Giggling, she grabbed a can of the cola from the bed of ice cubes. "That's what I like to hear — a fella *submittin'* for a change, instead of that just bein' something only the women do."

Millie yanked at the can's pull tab and then cried out as it hissed and fizzed, shooting a shower of foamy soda out the front of the buggy. The startled horse neighed, bolting wildly down the road even as Ira tugged on the lines. The rig began zigzagging across the center line, just as they spotted a car coming around the curve up ahead.

"Whoa there, Dinah!" Ira called out as he grabbed the leather lines in both hands. "Gee, girl! Steady now — steady —"

Whack! With a loud, sickening crack, one wheel of the buggy ran over a rock as they went off the side of the road. Millie dropped the soda can to grab Ira and the back of the seat, letting the cooler slide off her lap as they lurched to a halt behind the snorting, stomping mare. The car whizzed past them.

Millie's heart was pounding so hard and fast, she could barely breathe. "Oh, Ira, I'm sorry!" she wailed. "The soda can must've gotten all shook up when —"

"Just be thankful we're still in the buggy," he rasped. "I wasn't sure I was gonna get Dinah off the road in time. We'd better climb out, in case that wheel decides to give. Sit tight — I'll help ya down."

The buggy was tilted precariously toward the ditch, so Ira stepped carefully over

Millie's lap and jumped to the shoulder of the road. He reached up for her, his face taut. Once her feet found the pavement, Millie dared to think about what might have happened. She envisioned Ira and herself flung out into the bushes, maybe thrown against the thick trunks of the trees, perhaps with the buggy overturned on top of them — with Dinah crying out in agony. It happened sometimes.

She grabbed Ira around the waist and buried her face against his chest. "This was all my fault. And now we're out in the middle of nowhere —"

"Shhh," he murmured as he held her close. "It was a close call, *jah,* but the thanks go to God for gettin' us out of it unharmed. Not the first time I've had a horse spook on me, and it won't be the last."

Millie inhaled deeply to get control of her tears and her racing pulse. It wasn't Ira's way to talk about God's assistance, yet it soothed her to hear such reassurances and to know he wasn't angry about the shaken-up soda. After he released her, Ira settled Dinah, stroking the mare's muscled neck and talking softly to her. When he went around behind the rig, his groan told the tale.

"We're goin' nowhere on this busted

wheel," he announced. "It took a nasty hit when we went over that rock."

Millie drooped. The breeze had stopped, and even though the roadside was shady, the afternoon heat and humidity were becoming very uncomfortable. "Um, got your cell phone?"

"Nope," Ira replied with a rueful chuckle. "I know better than to let Aunt Naz or Ben see it on me during church. It's at home on the charger."

Millie sighed. Even though it was getting more common for kids in their *rumspringa* to carry cell phones, Atlee and Dawdi had strictly forbidden her to have one. Ira and Luke got by with having cell phones because they used them for their business calls. If they joined the church, Bishop Tom would expect them to forego the portable phones in favor of a landline in a phone shanty by the road.

"So I guess we'll wait for somebody to stop," she murmured. Millie glanced into the tilting rig, where the overturned cooler lay in a puddle of melting ice. Slices of ham, smashed deviled eggs, and several broken cookies were strewn on the floor around it. "I sure made a mess of your rig. Not to mention our lunch."

Ira glanced at their ruined picnic, shrugging. "We can clean that up — but we'd better start walking. Who knows how long we'd have to wait? And what would we do about Dinah, if a car stopped for us?"

He squinted up through the sun-dappled canopy of the trees. "It's nearly two o'clock. The buggy will roll along all right without our weight in it. Maybe by the time we reach that gas station we passed a while back, somebody'll be home from church to answer their phone and help us."

Or not, she thought glumly. When Ira got the horse turned around, Millie fell into step beside him, hoping a car wouldn't come around the curves too fast while they walked along the shoulder of the road.

A fine sight we make in our church clothes, gettin' all sweaty. These Sunday shoes are startin' to pinch like the dickens. Sure wish I had a cup to catch some of the ice on the buggy floor . . .

CHAPTER FOURTEEN

Luke steered his gelding onto the county blacktop that would be the final leg of their trip home from Cedar Creek. While Nora's earlier offer to drive them in her car had sounded like fun, she'd told him flat out that he wouldn't be taking the wheel even though he'd been a pretty fine driver when he'd had a car as a teenager. She'd said it was a matter of insurance, but he figured it for a control issue — so he'd taken control by driving a rig today.

"Are you going to sit with that sketch pad in your lap for the rest of the way home?" he hinted. "By my last count you had at least a dozen new hangings drawn out."

Nora's smile teased at him. "*Denki* for suggesting this field trip. I'd forgotten how scenic these back roads are — and when I make hangings that include specific objects or places that local folks recognize, they sell better," she remarked as her pencil moved across the page. "Vernon's stone silo is a great example of that, just like your mill is. It reminds English customers of simpler times and a lifestyle they'd like to try. Or they can say they've been to the place on the hanging."

Luke couldn't help himself. Little beads of moisture dotted the rim of Nora's upper lip, and he wanted to keep her talking so he could watch her mouth. Had she been any other woman, he would already have kissed her several times, but something in Nora's tawny eyes warned him that she wasn't the type to suffer fools or to give in to every guy who wanted a sample. Her crazy-quilt cape dress pieced in prints of blues and greens announced that she was artsier than most folks, yet in her crisp white *kapp* she'd looked as demure as any other woman sitting in church. Even though she wasn't wearing a trace of makeup, he'd found Nora the most desirable woman in the Mennonite congregation this morning . . . the most enticing female he'd met in a long, long while.

"And then there's Vernon himself," Nora continued as she flipped to a fresh page. "Had I grown up with him for a bishop, I might have returned to Willow Ridge after Millie was born. Maybe joined the Amish

207

church," she speculated in a faraway voice. "Your Aunt Jerusalem's lucky to be married to him. They seem as happy as a couple of kids."

Luke immediately recognized the face, hair, and beard taking shape as her pencil flickered across the paper. No two ways about it: Nora was a talented artist who could probably make a living with her pencil if she hadn't chosen to open a store.

Nora sighed as she sketched in the details of Vernon Gingerich's crow's-feet and wispy white beard. "I think I could've gone to Vernon after my ordeal with Tobias Borntreger and I believe he would've listened to me. What a wise, patient man he is. What a compelling, eloquent voice he has — and those baby blues!" she added with a rise of her eyebrows. "Why, he could pass for Santa Claus or — or God! When I imagine what God looks like, He has a very similar appearance, except He's more stern and forbidding."

"That's how the Old Testament and the preachers present Him," Luke remarked, although religion wasn't what he wanted to talk about. "After all, He wiped out all but Noah's family with a forty-day flood, and ordered Abraham to kill his son. And He gave Moses that list of thou-shalt-nots, which pretty much guaranteed that every-one thereafter would lead guilt-infested lives."

Nora's laughter did funny things to Luke's insides. She looked up from her sketch, her hazel eyes aglow. "I just met Vernon today, yet I sense he cuts through the guilt and gets right to the forgiveness part." She let out a pensive sigh. "My life would be so dif-ferent now if my father had had the same sort of mind-set sixteen years ago."

Luke nodded, focusing on the road. How could he change the subject? Once Nora had shared her unfortunate fall from grace with him, along with a sketchy account of her marriage and divorce, he'd figured she was lonely, rattling around in that big house . . . eager for company. Never had he guessed that a sketch pad would beat him out for her attention today — especially after he'd gone to church with her!

"Where'd you learn to draw so well?" he asked, figuring a compliment would appeal to her.

Nora shrugged, flipping to another fresh page in the spiral-bound pad. "I loved fid-dling with art supplies when I was growing up. But of course I did my drawing in the privacy of my room because Dat thought art served no practical purpose for an Amish girl."

"Ah, the things we did in our rooms when we were kids," Luke murmured.

Nora's knowing smirk made him laugh. "I bet you and Ira were incorrigible as teenagers. *Puh* — you still are!"

"What can I say? We Hooleys kept the roads hot and we never left singings — or any other activity — alone." Luke sucked in his breath and let it out slowly. "Okay, I'm just going to flat out ask you. What's it take to get to first base with you, Nora? You've been deflecting my —"

"What do you consider first base?"

The wide-eyed expression on Nora's face made Luke kick himself for asking such a crude question. Did she expect him to spell out every little detail? Or was she covering for not knowing what *first base* meant? Maybe being sent away at sixteen to have a baby had robbed her of that experimental dating time in her life.

Her English husband had surely put some moves on her while they were dating.

"Maybe I'd like to be . . . wooed," Nora murmured, lingering on that final word. "This time around I'm not going to accept everything an eligible guy dishes up just because he can. Seems like every man I meet expects me to respond with a passion that matches his, even if that's not what I feel."

She put her pencil down to nail him with a direct gaze. "I have a lousy track record when it comes to romance, and I've finally realized it's because the men got to do all the choosing," Nora confided in a low voice. "Well, no more. From here on out, Luke, it's all about me. And if that means you don't want to take me out anymore because I'm a waste of your time and effort, then that's the way the cookie crumbles. Just sayin'."

So much for Nora being lonely. Or needy. Luke looked straight ahead, keeping his expression unchanged. He wanted to set this outspoken, self-centered, arrogant woman out on the side of the road, because *nobody* turned him down that way.

Yet Nora's candid words resonated with a challenge, just as they had when she'd teased him into taking her to church. Luke relaxed, his gaze following the steady movement of his gelding's sleek, muscled haunches. *She probably thinks* I'm *acting like a horse's backside.*

Nora's voice cut into his thoughts. "Thanks for asking about my preferences, Luke." She sounded wistful rather than willful. Totally sincere. "You've probably saved us both a lot of stupid moves and heartache. I hope my response didn't —"

Nora leaned forward, shading her eyes with her hand. "Looks like somebody's had buggy trouble."

Luke, too, was gazing at the pair leading a horse ahead of an open rig that was missing a back wheel. "Is that Ira and Millie? Not many fellows wear their straw hats cocked back at that angle."

Nora sat on the seat's edge, her face tight with concern. "Awfully hot to be hiking along this blacktop. We don't have room for both of them in your buggy —"

"We'll figure something out." As he clucked for his gelding to go faster, Luke thought of a way to make this situation work to his advantage. He put two fingers to his lips and whistled loudly. "Ira Hooley!" he hollered.

The two walkers turned around. Relief and another emotion he couldn't yet identify lit their sweaty faces as Luke pulled his rig ahead of them. He stopped on the shoulder of the road.

"Millie and Ira! What happened?" Nora asked as she stepped down to the blacktop. "Are you all right?"

Millie's eyes were wide and her freckles

looked ready to pop off her nose. "I was openin' a can of soda and when it sprayed, the mare spooked —"

"And you *just happened* to be out riding on this road this afternoon?" Luke quizzed his brother as he, too, hopped down to the pavement.

Ira bit back a grin, knowing he'd been caught, while Millie gawked at her black shoes. "That's my doin', too," she confessed. "So now you'll think I'm a nosy, pryin' —"

"I think you and I will stand in the shade while the guys figure out how to get us home," Nora interrupted smoothly. She slung her arm around Millie's shoulders and steered the girl into the shadow of some nearby cottonwoods and cedars.

Ordinarily Luke would've accused Ira and his girlfriend of spying, yet he held his tongue. Mother and daughter were together, speaking in low tones as their *kapps* bobbed in unison. Here was his chance to earn a few points, because even if Nora insisted she wasn't into game-playing, she *was* keeping score. Every woman did.

"So what happened?" Luke asked his younger brother. As Ira recounted the accident that could have had much nastier consequences, Luke fished around in the back compartment of his buggy. "Here's enough rope to hook your rig to my trailer hitch," he said, pointing to the metal ball mounted on his rig's underside. "Will you be all right riding Dinah without a bridle?"

"I've got a halter and a lead rope in the back of my rig, so I can make do," Ira replied. "But what about Millie? I don't think Dinah will tolerate havin' both of us on her back."

"Millie's riding with us." Luke glanced toward Nora and her daughter, lowering his voice. "I see it as a way to finally get her gorgeous, skittish, *willful* mother to sit close to me — but you didn't hear me say that."

"Ah. Slow date, eh?"

"It's picking up. Let's go," Luke murmured as the two of them unhitched Dinah from the crippled rig. "The sun's going to fry us if we're out here much longer. Glad I brought an enclosed buggy today."

After they fastened Ira's rig to Luke's and adjusted the halter and lead rope into a makeshift bridle on Dinah, they were ready to roll. Luke smiled to himself as Millie preceded her mother to sit against the left side of the rig. When three people rode in a vehicle this small, the middle one had to sit forward on the seat. Nora would have no choice but to ride with her hip against his thigh, in constant contact with him all the way back to Willow Ridge.

"Geddap, now," Luke called his gelding. It would be slower going because they were hauling the extra weight of Ira's rig, but he was enjoying the sound of Nora's voice — the expressions on her face and Millie's as they looked at Nora's sketches, and the way her clean fragrance wafted around him. The only way to make a little more space was for Luke to turn slightly sideways and slip his arm behind Nora as he took the lines in his right hand.

"So you make your sketches and then trace the main pieces to cut out the appliqués?" Millie asked. "Oh, look at these cute cows! Sort of like Bishop Tom's herd — except he doesn't have such a pretty wooden fence."

"*Jah,* Vernon's cows are Black Angus, and I figure to cut them from different black calicos and little prints," Nora replied eagerly. "The red barn with the gambrel roof and the stone silo will look *so* cool alongside them! I'll get some little silk flowers to sprinkle in the grass after I embroider it with different shades of green, and —"

"How do you think of this stuff?" Millie asked. Her eyes, so like Nora's, were wide with wonder.

Nora shrugged modestly. "I've been making dimensional banners and hangings for a long time," she replied. "I don't know exactly how my pictures fall together. My mind just works that way."

"Wow." Millie sighed. "I didn't get any of that talent from ya, I guess."

"As we spend more time together, though, I bet we'll find we have a lot of things in common," Nora said tenderly. "Even though I've not been around my *mamm* for a good many years, I still find myself doing and saying things like she does. Little stuff, mostly. There's no getting away from it."

Luke couldn't help feeling good about the way Nora and Millie were sharing this quiet conversation. Maybe it was one of those instances where fate and faith had stepped in — even though he knew Ira and Millie had been hoping to spy on him and Nora. When they came to a long straightaway without any oncoming traffic, he pivoted to peer through the open rear window. "You all right, Ira?" he called out.

His brother waved. Despite his hat, his face was getting sunburned and he looked awfully hot in his black vest and trousers. "I'm thinkin' a stop at the ice cream place up ahead would be a *gut* idea," he replied. "I'll treat. And maybe we can find a hydrant so the horses can drink."

"Ice cream!" Millie said. "Now *that's* the best idea I've heard all day. Our picnic got tossed to the floor when we went off the road."

"Truth be told, I could use a burger, some fries, and a tall, cold soda before I enjoy that ice cream," Luke remarked. "The picnic your *mamm* and I shared is long gone, and it'll be a while before we're home."

"Fabulous! And we can sit indoors where it's air-conditioned," Nora said. She flickered her eyebrows at him. "I don't know about you, Mr. Hooley, but I could use some cooling off."

Luke laughed out loud. While he'd never considered going on a double date with a mother and her daughter, the day was working out better than it might have.

When they pulled off the road at the Jerzee Creem, Luke assumed that Nora dashed inside because she had to use the restroom — but she came out with two big plastic bins they could use to water the horses, from a spigot on the side of the building.

"And how'd you get ahold of *these*?" he asked her.

Nora shrugged. "I asked. The young man at the counter was obviously a victim of my freckle-faced charm and persuasive ways."

Luke could've kissed her. He loved the playful tone of Nora's teasing, and the way she and Millie stayed outside with him and Ira until both horses had drunk their fill and been tied to trees, in the shade. Did he dare think of this as a family gathering? Could he dream ahead to spending more time with Nora and Millie keeping him and his brother company? It wasn't the sort of date he would have found appealing when he was younger — but then, he'd not found himself in such a compelling situation before.

He'd never gone out with a woman who wasn't eager to do whatever he wanted — or eager for his kisses — either. Luke realized that in her subtle way, Nora was exerting her control over him. But he was willing to play along for a while. The payoff seemed so tantalizing, even if Nora had chosen to sit across the table from him, beside Millie, as they ate their early supper. He found himself watching the way she bit into her burger and licked the melting cheese from the bottom of the bun. He wished he could be her napkin when she wiped her mouth.

"You know, we could've left my broken wheel at James Graber's carriage shop," Ira murmured. "We weren't but a couple of miles away when we pulled over. And now I'll have to take it there, as nobody closer to Willow Ridge can fix it."

Luke considered this as he noted how sunburned his brother's face was becoming. "That would've meant doubling back, and a longer trip home," he pointed out. "With Graber's shop being closed today, it's not like you'd have gotten the wheel back any faster."

"I'll take it in tomorrow, then." Ira gulped some of his cold soda. "Guess that means you'll have to watch the shop and grind that load of dried corn —"

"I'm really, really sorry I made us wreck," Millie mumbled. "I didn't intend for my can of soda — our spur-of-the-moment picnic — to cost ya a day of work."

Ira reached across the table to grasp Millie's wrist. "You've already apologized," he insisted. "Even with our rig incident, isn't this fun supper — gettin' out for the day — a better time than we would've had hangin' around for the common meal after church?"

Luke was slightly amazed at how tenderly his brother was treating Millie. Though the two of them had been dating for nearly a year, Ira had always been inclined toward impatience and more impetuous behavior than he'd displayed the past few weeks. Was he becoming more seriously involved with his girlfriend? Or was Ira on his best behavior to impress her mother?

Across the table, Nora's furtive smile told Luke she was either scheming or —

"What if *I* take your wheel to Cedar Creek tomorrow?" she volunteered. "At church, folks were telling me about a gal there who braids rag rugs, and another lady whose pottery would be a good addition to my shop. I could toss the wheel in my trunk and save you a day on the road — and if you want to, Millie, you could go with me! The mercantile looks like a fine, fun place to shop."

Millie's eyes widened. "I'd have to ask Mammi. Monday's when I do the laundry."

"We'll visit with her when we get home." Nora smiled first at her daughter and then at Ira. "Are you *gut* with that, Ira? I'm not trying to interfere with —"

"It's a generous offer. *Denki.*" As he picked up his second cheeseburger, Ira flashed her a grin. "I'd like to ride along to Cedar Creek myself, but I'd better not push my luck with the boss. We've got a lot of grain mixes to bag up, to refill the shelves after our big opening weekend."

"So it's all settled," Luke said. "Mighty

nice of you to help us out, Nora." He care-fully caught her two feet between his under the table without Millie or Ira being the wiser. The flicker of a sly smile was her only response, but it was enough. A few moments later Luke inched his hand across the table to sneak her last onion ring, delighting in the way she slapped his hand.

"All you have to do is *ask,* Luke," Nora scolded playfully.

Desire slammed into him as he thought of all the implications her statement might have. Luke released the onion ring, holding her gaze. "I won't stop asking until I get what I want," he challenged in a low voice.

Ira choked on his soda. Millie's eyes wid-ened.

Luke felt odd making such a remark to her mother while Millie looked on, but they would all have to get past that mother-daughter detail. After all, Nora had started this train rolling by playing hard to get ever since church had let out, while Millie and Ira had come looking for him and Nora. *He* had just come along to be the driver . . . and he intended to keep the lines — the leather ones and the psychological ones — in his own hands.

After they had all enjoyed double-dip ice cream cones, they began the last leg of the trip back to Willow Ridge. With Nora again settled so close to him, Luke thought ahead to when he might take her out — or stay in. Even when there was a breeze from the river, the upstairs mill apartment got stuffy on these humid August days, so he was looking for any excuse to spend time at Nora's place when he wasn't running the mill or keeping the store open.

"Did your *mammi* make it to church this morning?" Nora asked Millie. "She was looking so much perkier when we were at Bishop Tom's house last week."

"She did," Millie replied. "She was lookin' forward to seein' everybody and chattin' with her friends at the common meal. Figured she'd go home for a nap if the day started wearin' on her."

"Sounds like a fine plan," Nora replied. Then she brightened. "Would you want to come to my place when we get back to town? You could see my hangings —"

"Oh, that would be wonderful-*gut*!" Millie blurted.

"— and we could talk about what working in the consignment shop would involve," Nora continued. "Then I could walk you to Micah and Rachel's place to visit with folks who're still there. It's time I got back in touch with everybody — and time they got used to seeing me around, too. And we'll talk to Mamma about our trip tomorrow."

Luke was careful not to show his disappointment. He'd hoped to be with Nora this evening when it was cooler, because once the new workweek began tomorrow, he'd have little time to socialize with his attractive neighbor until next Sunday. He didn't want to wait that long. Didn't think he *could* be away from the mysterious, intriguing Nora Landwehr for seven days without suffering withdrawal pangs.

When they reached Willow Ridge, Luke pulled into the mill's parking area and smiled at his two riders. "I hope you girls will have a *gut* visit for the rest of the day," he said as he stepped to the ground. He was pleased when Nora allowed him to lift her down from the rig — and more pleased that Millie scrambled out of the buggy to see how Ira was faring after his hot ride.

"When can I see you again?" Luke murmured, keeping his hands lightly at Nora's waist.

She flashed him a smile and eased out of his grasp. "I have a lot of folks to contact this week, about putting merchandise in my shop. I'll be in and out."

Luke's lips curved. "Surely you'll not be busy in the evenings, or —"

"*You* burned some midnight oil getting ready to open your shop, as I recall. And it's all about me, remember?" she reminded him with a rise of one provocative eyebrow. "*Denki* for a great day, Luke. You rock, you know it?"

As he was catching on to what she'd said, Nora stood on tiptoe to place a quick kiss on his cheek. Then she strode down the driveway toward the county road. "See you in a few, Millie!" she called out. Then she wiggled her fingers at Luke.

He raised his hand in response, and then touched his face where Nora had kissed him. *You rock, you know it?* echoed in his mind as he watched her dress swish with her energetic stride, until she disappeared around the bend. Was he losing his touch? He hadn't seen Nora's kiss coming at all — would've grabbed her and claimed her lips until she surrendered, if he had.

You really think so? his thoughts taunted. Luke laughed at himself. He'd been kissing women for more than half his life, but it seemed Nora was showing him how much he really didn't know about *wooing* as opposed to winning.

He'd have to work on that.

CHAPTER FIFTEEN

Millie held her breath as she knocked at Nora's door. Even though she and Annie Mae had been best friends since childhood, she had rarely set foot in this large, glorious house when Hiram Knepp and his family had lived here — because the former bishop had discouraged visitors, and because Millie had felt too intimidated. Unworthy.

"Come on in, sweetie," Nora called from the front room.

Millie smiled in spite of her jitters. She'd have to start thinking of this woman as her mother — would have to call her something besides Mamm, because that name had always belonged to Lizzie. And calling Nora by her first name would be unthinkably rude.

When she stepped inside, Millie forgot her nerves and just gawked. Plush store-bought rugs adorned the hardwood floors, and they coordinated with sofas and overstuffed chairs that looked fresh from a furniture store in royal blue, magenta, and tan. The chair arms weren't covered with hand towels. Nothing was slipcovered or draped with a sheet to hide the worn spots. The wooden tables gleamed in the sunlight without any white rings from wet glasses or scuffs and scratches from years of use.

But it was the hangings that made Millie suck in her breath. "These are *so cool,*" she murmured, drawn to the image of a clothesline with garments that appeared to be fluttering in the breeze. "How did ya — why, those are real clothes pins and a rope instead of just appliquéd pieces cut from fabric!"

"*Jah,* they're little craft-size clothes pins," Nora replied as she came to stand beside Millie. "I sell a lot of Amish wash-day hangings. You'd think folks would want something more exciting, but English women have forgotten how to hang laundry. They think dresses and broadfall trousers flapping in the breeze are quaint. Charming."

Nodding, Millie stepped sideways to admire a banner of a little Amish girl running her finger over a kitten's fur. The girl's white *kapp* was cut from a real one, to show the profile view. "So, have ya had a shop before? It must've been hard to close the place up to come here."

"I had some of my hangings in other people's shops, and I sell a lot of pieces from my website," Nora replied. Her chuckle told of mixed emotions. "I'm almost ashamed to say it, but one of the reasons I can't commit to joining the Amish church is my online business. I've supported myself with Internet sales for the past year, since Tanner left, and I . . . don't have enough faith to believe I can earn a steady living from a shop."

Millie frowned. "But you'll do really *gut* with all the different stuff you've been talking about, from so many folks around the area," she countered.

"It's a tricky business, selling gifts," Nora explained. "Most of the money for a consigned item goes to the person who made it. And after the crafters set their prices high enough to be paid fairly for their time, and the storekeeper adds her percentage, customers sometimes think they're being overcharged. And if a shopper returns a couple of times without finding anything she thinks is worth the money — or if it's always the same old stuff in the displays — she won't come back."

Millie considered this as she looked at Nora's other hangings. Even with her limited experience at quilting, she could tell her mother was a true artist rather than someone who always followed a pattern or who was using up scraps of material she had on hand. Living among women who made crazy quilts and hot pads from pieces of old clothing had taught Millie the same sort of thriftiness, yet she couldn't fault Nora for choosing new fabric for her special hangings.

"If ya ever want to get rid of leftover fabric pieces, I'd be glad to take them off your hands," Millie said with a tentative smile. "I'm thinkin' to make Annie Mae and Adam a flower-basket quilt for their wedding present —"

"What a lovely idea!" Nora's smile made her eyes sparkle. "And if you'd ever want to put a quilt in the shop, I'd be pleased to have it. If you decide to help me run the place, you could work on quilts when we aren't busy. The folks who come in would love to watch you work."

Millie envisioned herself sitting in the shop, surrounded by beautifully crafted items and admiring customers as she pieced fabric baskets and flowers — which seemed so much more exciting than doing that same sort of handwork at Mammi and Dawdi's house. When she realized Nora was gazing at her, her face got hot. "Um, what-all would ya have me doin' in your store? I've never had a real job."

"I don't believe that for a minute!" Nora replied as she squeezed Millie's shoulder. "You've been cooking and doing laundry and looking after your grandparents when your *mammi* was very sick. I can teach you how to run the cash register," she went on, "but I bet you're already very good at straightening shelves. And you have a smile customers can't help but love."

Millie felt herself glowing, caught up in Nora's enthusiasm.

"If you can help me set up the store before we open, you'll get to really *look* at all the merchandise so you can answer customers' questions about it," Nora went on. "Even if Mamma can only spare you for a few hours a day, it would be a tremendous help to me, Millie."

As Millie gazed into a face that could almost be her own in a mirror, her spirits took wing. "I — I'd love to work in your store! Let's go talk to Mammi right now, before she's tired out from visiting."

"We're on our way." Nora grabbed a key ring from a peg by the door and tucked it into her dress pocket. She turned then, her hand on the door handle, and gazed deeply into Millie's eyes. "I'm so glad you're giving me a chance, Millie," she murmured. "It means more to me than I can say."

Millie's throat tightened. She couldn't find words, so she nodded.

"And whatever happens — whatever Mamma's answer is — I'll understand," Nora insisted earnestly. "We'll ask her about going to Cedar Creek tomorrow, too."

Millie's heart skipped rope. When they stepped out onto Nora's big porch, she was amazed at how much of Willow Ridge she could see from this hilltop — and surprised at how many people were still sitting beneath the shade trees at Rachel and Micah's place. Even though all the men wore straw hats and all the women were in *kapps,* she could distinguish who most of them were. "There's Dawdi," she said, pointing to a cluster of older men seated in lawn chairs. "If he's still there, Mammi most likely is, too."

It was a new experience, walking with Nora — her mother! — beside her. As they passed her grandparents' home, Millie realized how dusty and careworn it looked compared to Nora's, and when they entered the long lane at Rachel's place, she felt folks gawking at them. Everyone had heard about Nora's return by now, and after church some of them had speculated about her store and her refusal to join the Old Order. When Millie waved to some of the men seated beneath the trees, they nodded but their eyes were on Nora — assessing her crazy-quilt dress, no doubt.

Spotting her grandmother, Millie walked faster. "She's on the porch in the swing," she said as she and Nora strode past the serving tables. Everything had been put away except the remaining cookies and cakes.

"She looks like she's having a *gut* time, and she's in the coolest spot, out of the sun," Nora remarked. Then she sighed. "Not everyone here is thrilled about me coming over. I'm sorry if this bothers you, Millie, or if I . . . embarrass you."

"No! It's not like that," Millie insisted. "It was the same way when Miriam partnered with the Schrock women so she could have electricity to meet health department requirements."

"Change doesn't come easy for most folks," Nora replied. As they approached the porch, where several women sat talking, her face relaxed into a smile. "It's *gut* to see you talking and laughing, Mamma. And hello to the rest of you ladies, as well!"

Miriam and her partner, Naomi, scooted

their chairs to allow Millie and Nora room to step onto the wide wooden porch. Lizzie sat in one of the chairs, smiling as little Ella babbled a greeting to Millie. Beneath the overhang of the roof it felt cooler, although several of the ladies fanned themselves with flat cardboard fans from the funeral home in New Haven.

"How was your ride with Ira?" Mammi asked. "You must've gone quite a long way — and ya brought somebody back with ya, I see."

Butterflies filled Millie's stomach. She sensed she'd better chat a bit before she sprang her questions on her grandmother, but she wasn't keen on having these neighbor ladies know her business just yet. "It was a more eventful ride than we figured on," she replied, and as she recounted the rig wreck everyone agreed that she'd been very fortunate — that God had been watching out for her and Ira when his mare had spooked.

"Luke and Nora gave us a ride back into Willow Ridge," Millie continued in a hopeful tone. Impulsively she grabbed her mother's hand. "She's takin' Ira's broken wheel to the carriage shop in Cedar Creek tomorrow, and she's asked me to ride along, Mammi! Is it all right if I go?"

"The Cedar Creek Mercantile's right across the road from the carriage shop," Miriam said with a warm smile. "They carry such a variety of —"

"Don't even *think* about gettin' into that car, missy," came a gruff male voice from behind them.

Millie's heart sank. Even before she turned to face Dawdi, she heard him huffing with the effort it had taken to come up the long lane.

"You'll be tendin' the laundry tomorrow," her grandfather continued tersely. "What were ya thinkin', to bother your *mammi* with such an impertinent question?"

Millie's eyes closed in humiliation. All around her the women kept quiet, fanning faster, waiting to see how this scene would play out. Beside her, Nora kept hold of Millie's hand and turned to face Dawdi.

"I'm coming first thing in the morning to help with the laundry," Nora replied. "We won't leave until the clothes are hung out and the kitchen's cleaned —"

"No, you've got it all wrong." Dawdi glared at Nora and then looked away, as though the sight of her would contaminate him. "Don't be comin' to the house, hear me? You're not welcome there."

Mammi let out a little cry as the other

women sucked in their breath. Millie wanted to melt and trickle between the floorboards of the porch. She tried to ease her hand away, but her mother held on with gentle strength.

"How many times must I ask your forgiveness, Dat?" Nora murmured. There was a hitch in her voice, but she stood firm. "Seven times? Seventy times seven?"

"Don't you go mockin' me nor the *Gut* Book, neither!" he snapped. When he grabbed the bottom of the porch railing to keep his balance, his face grew as ruddy as a raw steak. "I made it as plain as the nose on your face that I wanted no part of —"

"Gabe, I don't like what I'm hearin'. Not one little bit," another male voice interrupted.

Millie nipped her lip. Bishop Tom was striding toward them, wiping his damp face with a bandanna as he focused intently on her grandfather.

"I couldn't help but overhear what ya said to Nora," the bishop continued. His expression was as stormy as Millie had ever seen it, for ordinarily Tom Hostetler was a mild-mannered fellow. "I've already warned ya — twice — that nursin' this old grudge is arrogant and sinful. As your bishop, I'm sayin' you're to make a kneelin' confession

234

before the members in church, two Sundays from now," he said sternly. Then his face softened. "But as your friend, I'm beggin' ya to come clean before Jesus right this minute. *Please,* Gabe. Your stubborn pride's takin' ya down the same broken road Hiram Knepp chose."

Millie held her breath, along with the other women around them. The chain of the porch swing stopped creaking. The birds stopped singing in the orchard, and she sensed the menfolk in the yard had ceased their visiting to follow this confrontation. It was a serious matter when a bishop told someone to kneel and confess in front of the congregation, and a grievous offense when that someone refused — especially since Dawdi had served as a preacher for most of his life.

But her grandfather didn't reply. He looked off toward the apple trees as though he was intent on watching the fruit ripen.

Bishop Tom stepped around to the other side of Dawdi to look him in the eye. "Ya know as well as I do that the next step is shunnin', Gabe," he said in a rueful voice. "Is that what ya want? Really?"

Dawdi turned to glare up at Nora. "See the trouble you've caused us?" he muttered. "If you're not gonna follow our Old Order ways, then leave us be. And leave Millie to grow up the way we raised her instead of leadin' her into your English temptation."

At that, her grandfather turned stiffly and hobbled down the lane, grabbing his back. Millie choked on a sob, bitterly disappointed — and heartsick for Nora, whose face crumpled as her head fell forward.

"I'm sorry ya had to go through this yet again," the bishop murmured. "If I can help ya, Nora — or Millie or Wilma — I'll do my best. Meanwhile, I hope all of us will keep prayin' about this unfortunate situation. God knows best how to handle it, and we need to be open to His guidance."

Bishop Tom sighed, returning to where the men sat beneath the trees. Most of them were standing up, folding their lawn chairs. The women on the porch rose, as well, maintaining a silence that felt as stifling as the late-afternoon heat.

"Millie, I'm so sorry," Nora rasped. "This isn't what I intended."

"I know." Millie's voice cracked as she broke into tears. "I know."

CHAPTER SIXTEEN

"*Denki* again for takin' my busted wheel," Ira said as he closed the trunk of Nora's BMW. "Hope those folks in Cedar Creek will want to put stuff in your store, too."

Nora put on a smile as Ira returned to his work inside the mill. She was hoping to get on the road rather than lingering with Luke, but he had other ideas.

"So are you going to tell me what's wrong, or do I have to nag it out of you?" he asked in a low voice.

Nora sighed. Why had she thought Luke wouldn't notice the dark circles under her red-rimmed eyes? Her pale complexion had never allowed her to hide crying jags any more than she could keep her temper from flashing in her eyes. "Just another run-in with my *dat* yesterday." She shrugged, hoping he'd get the hint.

"And that's why Millie isn't going with you? Because Gabe got all bent out of shape about her riding in your car, picking up on your English ways?"

There you have it. In Willow Ridge, your business is everyone's business — or else Luke's a really good guesser.

"Everyone at the Brennemans' witnessed our confrontation, and listened as Bishop Tom threatened to shun Dat for not forgiving me," she added in a voice that sounded dangerously close to breaking. "But worse than that, he shattered Millie's hopes — and Mamm's — because he still forbids me to go to the house. And — and —"

Nora folded in on herself, covering her face with her hands as her shoulders began to shake. "I'm sorry, Luke. I didn't mean to burden you with —"

"Burden me?" He exhaled his frustration and wrapped her in his arms. "What is his *problem*? Why can't your father let go of something that happened more than sixteen years ago — especially because you couldn't control what that perverted bishop did to you?"

"Ah, but Dat thinks I surely must've brought it on, because Tobias Borntreger was a friend of his. There were no witnesses, and Tobias is dead, so of *course*, since Tobias couldn't have been the villain, I made up the whole story," Nora explained shrilly. "As *if* I would seduce a sneaky, manipulative, *smelly* old geezer who was my *dat*'s age. Yuck!"

For a few moments Nora allowed herself the luxury of being enveloped in Luke's strength and warmth, even though she sensed she was becoming dangerously infatuated. Luke Hooley was a nice guy, but he didn't have the best reputation for committing himself to anyone — not that she wanted commitment from another man. She wasn't sure *what* she wanted right now, except a glimmer of hope that she could become close to her daughter and could reunite with her mother, who were every bit as stymied by her *dat*'s behavior as she was.

"Well, at least Millie looks like you instead of like her father," Luke replied in a lighter voice. "But I'm not going to let go of this, Nora. It's not fair that your father can ruin everything you've come back to reestablish, and —"

"Please don't get involved," Nora pleaded as she wiped her eyes. "It'll only make things worse."

"Too late," Luke murmured. He gently lifted her chin and thumbed away some stray tears. "I'm already involved, Nora."

She *wanted* to believe in Luke, to place her faith in him even though all the other men in her life had let her down. After Borntreger had stolen her innocence, her father had cast her out, and her husband had abandoned her, Nora had a very dim view of men in general. As the river shimmered with the morning sunlight, she just wanted to drive — to think her thoughts and figure out what to do next. She was hoping the excitement of opening her new store would carry her through these emotionally turbulent times.

"I appreciate your support, Luke," she murmured. "I just want to go now, okay? Catch you later."

"Maybe I'll catch you first."

Nora felt a grin tickling her lips but she got into her car before this little exchange led either of them to say anything that might feel . . . binding. She preferred to think of their relationship as a sticky note, something she could put in place and focus on when she chose to, yet peel away when Luke Hooley became too insistent. Too intimate.

Nora cranked up the air-conditioner and the radio, blasting out all thoughts that threatened to depress her. It was a beautiful summer morning and she had business to attend to. She couldn't give the folks in Cedar Creek the impression that she was a shrinking violet or a pansy. She preferred to think of herself as a surprise lily — a sturdy stem that shot up without preamble and burst into a bright eyeful of color.

Nora chuckled at the thought. Luke more likely referred to surprise lilies as *naked ladies.* And maybe his irreverent way of looking at life was exactly what she needed right now.

She just wouldn't tell *him* that.

After taking Ira's buggy wheel to the carriage shop, Nora met young Zanna Ropp, who was thrilled to be consigning her crocheted braided rugs to Nora's store. Then she drove on down the county highway toward Bloomingdale to speak with Amanda Brubaker, who'd made the exquisite pottery she'd seen in the Cedar Creek Mercantile. As Nora followed the winding road, her thoughts turned toward transportation, because the fellow in the carriage shop and the owner of the mercantile both had raised their Amish eyebrows at her red sports car.

She'd known all along that even the local Mennonites would frown on her ostentatious car, but reverting to a horse-drawn vehicle raised a number of issues. If she bought a horse, she would need to build a small stable for it, and find hay and rations to feed it, and keep it shod and vaccinated and on and on — not to mention buying a surrey, a double-door rig big enough to haul things for the store.

Nora sighed as the dollar signs flew through her head. She didn't even *like* horses much. It seemed more practical to trade the BMW for a small van — something black, with the chrome painted black, as well, because that was the style the Mennonites around Willow Ridge allowed.

What did *God* think about the distinctions the various groups of Plain folks made? Some groups refused to operate motorized vehicles. Some allowed only steel-wheeled farm implements without any rubber tires, and some stipulated that kick scooters with bike tires and baskets were allowable but bicycles were not. To the outside English world, these religious differences seemed to point up discrepancies and inconsistent beliefs, yet the members of each colony worshipped and honored the same God. Nora knew she would have to fit in, to conform to a particular Plain religious community, or she would never be considered a member anywhere.

In Plain congregations, you were either in or you were out. *And where Dat's concerned, you'll be* out *no matter what sort of vehicle you drive.*

Once again Nora's desperation threatened to choke her. Maybe she'd been stupid to move back — to invest all her money before she'd known how her family would react. Maybe she should be looking for somewhere else to live instead of believing she could make a life for herself or build a business among the Amish in Willow Ridge. Maybe she should tell Millie and Mamm good-bye and put a For Sale sign in front of the house and just —

Be still and know that I am God.

Nora blinked. The resonant voice in her head had sounded so near and clear that Cedar Creek's bishop, Vernon Gingerich, might've been talking to her from the passenger seat. Or perhaps the words had come to her from God Himself.

Nora nipped her lip. Was she stretching the truth, thinking the Lord would speak to *her*? He had to know how she'd avoided organized religion for years . . . how unfamiliar she was with His word, the Bible. Was it heresy to believe she could appeal to Him and He would respond, even though she hadn't been baptized into the church?

The concept of coming to God just as she was — right this minute — seemed so compelling that Nora pulled over to the side of the road. She turned off the radio and the engine. She rolled down her window and sat with only birdsong and the whisper of the breeze drifting in around her. She wasn't praying, exactly, but maybe if she opened herself to the message she'd just heard, she would receive the guidance she needed. After all, it had been a still, small voice that had urged her to come back to Willow Ridge . . . to the daughter she'd loved and left behind. And that had been the right thing to do, despite the consequences she'd suffered.

What does the Lord require of you but to do justice, to love mercy, and to walk humbly with your God?

Nora sat absolutely still. Verses from the Bible didn't just occur to her, and this voice didn't quote from the stern King James version she'd grown up with in the Old Order church, but from the more modern version written on decorative placards —

Like the ones you just saw in the Cedar Creek Mercantile.

Nora frowned. Now she was second-guessing herself. If the words of those wooden signs were coming to her, they were merely a matter of her visual memory and surely couldn't be inspired by God.

Yet it seemed *right* to think about justice

and mercy. She was trying to do justice to the bond she shared with Millie and Mamm, trying to right a wrong from their past — just as she could show mercy and forgive her father for his hard-hearted attitude, if only he'd give her the chance . . . and even if he didn't forgive *her*.

That was a new bone to gnaw on. If she forgave her father — no matter how he treated her — she'd be doing what the Lord's Prayer required, as Bishop Tom had pointed out. She could go about her life with a clear conscience, even if forgiving Dat would require a lot of conscious effort. But she could do it. In her heart of hearts, Nora had always known that Dat might never change his opinion of her, yet she'd made her new home in Willow Ridge anyway, hoping for a new start.

The part about walking humbly could certainly refer to getting rid of this flashy red BMW.

For what shall it profit a man, if he shall gain the whole world and lose his own soul?

Nora looked around to be sure Vernon Gingerich wasn't standing in the woods, or hovering above her like an angel in a religious painting — which made no sense at all. Three times she'd heard Bible verses in a voice that sounded like his, rich and melodious and so very compelling. Was it a sign? In the Bible, the number three had always been significant . . .

She started the car and made a U-turn. Maybe she was hearing this voice because she'd come to Cedar Creek to accomplish more than taking Ira's wheel to the carriage shop. Maybe God had led her here, not only to speak with crafters but also to visit with Vernon Gingerich, to seek his counsel. When she'd met him yesterday, he'd seemed so loving and gracious. Even though Jerusalem had probably told him the down-and-dirty about her situation, he'd gazed at her with open acceptance — with genuine goodwill.

Nora exhaled, releasing a lot of tension as she drove to the other side of Cedar Creek. If there was anything that had been in short supply in her life lately, it was acceptance and goodwill. A smile found her as she turned down the gravel lane that ran between the picturesque stone silo and the white board fence she'd sketched yesterday. Vernon Gingerich would listen and give her his opinion in a positive way, even if he had some tough things to say to her. She just knew it.

When Nora knocked on the door, the bishop answered it as though he'd been expecting her. "Nora, it's so *gut* to see you again," he said as he stepped out to the porch. "Did you get the details you needed yesterday for the butcher shop banner, or have you returned for more inspiration? Even after living on this farm for so many years, I marvel at the beauty of the pasture-land and the cleanness of the air here — sure signs that God lives in every blade of grass and that He's never finished with His creating."

Vernon's face lit up in the morning sunlight as he gazed out over his farm. "In the book of Revelation, it says, 'Behold, I make all things new.' If we accept God's forgiveness, every day's a clean slate. What a gift!"

Vernon's childlike excitement was contagious, even as Nora wondered how he'd provided her such a perfect segué. Had he sensed her inner turmoil yesterday? Or was he just that good at seeing into a person's soul? "It's forgiveness I've come to ask you about," she murmured. "Forgiveness and faith. I've reached the end of my rope with Dat, and — and I don't know what to do."

Vernon's blue eyes glimmered as he gazed at her. "When you come to the end of your rope, tie a knot and hang on," he quipped, although his tone was serious. "Let's walk, shall we? Oftentimes, forward motion begets forward thought."

As they stepped off the porch, Nora dared to hope that she would receive the answers she sought. While the Gingerich farmstead, with its added-on-to white house and classic red barn, appeared far less prosperous than the property she'd bought, Vernon's love for his home place shone in the vivid red roses that climbed the trellis, the neatly clipped lawn, and the perfectly maintained white fence with sleek ebony cattle watching them from between its slats.

"How's your father doing, Nora? And by that I mean how do *you* feel about his physical and mental well-being?" the bishop asked. He strolled with his hands clasped behind his back as they followed the gravel lane past his cattle barn.

"When I returned to town, my first thought was that he and Mamm have gotten so *old*," Nora murmured. Then she chuckled. "Of course, Dat's nearly fifteen years older than Mamm, and he was nearly fifty when I came along. Yet it seems Dat has gone downhill since my return, while Mamm has come back from what appeared to be her deathbed. I — I'm grateful they're both alive, and both still mentally alert."

Vernon stroked the nose of a curious black cow that was keeping pace with them on the other side of the fence. "I'm gravely concerned about the burden of your *dat*'s attitude toward you, Nora," he murmured. "Although he's right to hold to the principles of the Ordnung, it's another thing altogether for him to dig a trench so deep that it may well become his grave."

"Bishop Tom has said as much. And yesterday, when Dat forbade Millie to come here with me — and told me again that I wasn't welcome at the house — Tom told Dat he'd need to confess at church in a couple of weeks. And if he won't make a confession, he'll be shunned," Nora recounted in a tight voice. "But Dat walked away. Wanted no part of what Tom was telling him."

Vernon's eyebrows rose. "I'm sorry it's come to this," he murmured. "And I'm sorry Gabe's hardened his heart toward you, Nora. I believe you have the best of intentions —"

"But when I was driving through town this morning, I felt ready to pack it all in," she blurted. "It seemed so *stupid,* to have invested everything I had in Hiram's house, and to move back to Willow Ridge without considering the consequences for Millie and Mamm — and to not have a plan B in case things didn't work out," she went on in a rising voice. "What if I'm stuck there? What if it's all been for nothing?"

Vernon stopped walking. He gazed at her with eyes that seemed to see everything — all her doubts and fears, her needs and dreams. "On the contrary, the fact that you've risked everything, without providing yourself an escape route, is an act of great *faith,* Nora," he insisted. "You trusted God to guide you back to your family. You've opened yourself to the blessing of knowing your daughter along with the bane of your *dat*'s bitterness. I admire you, dear Nora. Most folks wouldn't have taken such a risk."

Nora's heart swelled. Surely if Vernon Gingerich — the most sincere, righteous man she knew — claimed she'd shown great faith, she should believe him. "*Denki* for saying that. Some might call it rushing in where angels fear to tread," she said hesitantly. "My Mennonite leanings haven't helped my cause where Dat's concerned."

Vernon smiled as he started strolling again, toward a small building behind his cattle barn. "God gave us free will, just as He created us all for different work in His kingdom," the bishop pointed out. "I believe He loves his English and Mennonite children — His children of every color and creed — every bit as much as He cares for

250

Amish folks. He loved us long before we began categorizing ourselves according to our differing beliefs. After all, we humans created organized religion more to accommodate our limited understanding of God than to honor Him."

Nora's mouth opened and then shut. She had sensed Vernon was a more progressive bishop than most in the Old Order, but she'd not expected him to expound upon a God who showed such boundless acceptance of His children.

When Vernon opened the door to the small building they'd reached, Nora stepped inside. The air was redolent with the aromas of fresh-cut wood and varnish. Saws, mallets, and other tools of the woodworking trade hung neatly along a large pegboard. Several pieces of furniture in various stages of construction filled most of the floor space. Nora sucked in her breath and walked over to a large rolltop desk that appeared to be finished. "Did you make this, Vernon? It's absolutely beautiful."

"It's what I do when I'm not tending my cattle," he replied. "There's an old saying that to pray is to work, and to work is to pray. I feel closest to God with tools in my hands, and I often find solutions to my knottiest problems out here."

"I know exactly what you mean," Nora murmured as she walked around the room. She admired a set of walnut dining room chairs with burled inlays, and a bird's-eye maple china hutch that appeared so sturdily crafted yet so feminine. Every piece in this shop attested to Vernon's attention to detail and his love for his work.

"When I lost my first wife, Dorothea, my desire to make furniture went to the grave with her," Vernon continued in a pensive voice. "I thank God every day that Jerusalem has inspired me to work with my hands again, for I was born to make things of wood as surely as you were meant to fashion items of colorful cloth."

Again Nora's heart beat with the gratification Vernon's words brought her. *And I thank You, God, for leading me here today — for causing me to listen to what You were telling me in the car,* she prayed silently.

The bishop ran his hand along the glossy top of the desk, with its louvered rolling top and interior compartments of various sizes. "I think God's love is a lot like this desk," he mused aloud. "Even though we humans tend to compartmentalize our beliefs into pigeonholes like I've made here, all the spaces are still housed in the same structure — like the many mansions He prepares for us in His kingdom."

Vernon paused to gaze at Nora. "Most bishops preach that the Old Order is the only way to salvation, but I believe God's love for us is much broader and deeper than we can possibly comprehend," he murmured. "If I'm wrong, He'll judge me accordingly — and only He has the right to pass such judgment."

Nora nodded, wide-eyed. Vernon's statement of belief was exactly what she'd needed to hear — and the opposite of what she'd grown up with.

"It's the same for you, Nora. Jesus gave us a new commandment, to love one another," he went on in a voice that rang around the shop walls. "And if you love those who persecute you, you've done as the Lord instructed even if those others remain too focused on the laws of the Old Testament — or the Old Order — to return your love."

Vernon placed his hands lightly on Nora's shoulders, very much resembling God in the way she'd described Him to Luke: a benevolent father figure, filled with compassion for His wayward children. "That love is the knot you tie in your proverbial rope, to hang on to while God works out His will in your life."

"So simple, yet so complicated," Nora

replied with a sigh.

"That's the way of it, yes. But your faith will see you through, and Tom and I will stand with you every step of the way, Nora." Vernon squeezed her shoulders, a benediction that brought his counsel to a close. "When will you open your store?"

Nora pulled her thoughts from the spiritual realm he'd invoked back to the present. "September sixth. I have a lot to do before then, but it seems like a good birthday present to myself."

"An auspicious time for a new beginning," he agreed. "It's wonderful that you're showcasing Plain craftsmen and creating an outlet for their work. I predict your store will bring many new opportunities to Willow Ridge — just as Luke and Ira's mill has provided a new income stream for several area farmers. I understand the boys got off to a better start than they'd anticipated."

"*Jah,* they sold out of several things, including Nazareth's goat cheese and Tom's fresh butter." Nora hesitated, but then sensed Vernon wouldn't be offended by her idea. "If this rolltop desk — or any of these pieces — don't have homes, I'd be honored if you consigned them to my store. You can set whatever price you choose."

Vernon's smile lit up his round face,

reminding her of cherubs she'd seen in religious paintings. "That's a high compliment, dear, but when I returned to my woodworking, I dedicated my pieces to Jerusalem's years in the classroom," he replied. "I'm donating my work to our district's annual auction, so the money they bring will help support our school."

"What a lovely tribute," Nora murmured.

"Jerusalem's a lovely woman. I'm blessed to have her in my life."

Wow. If more men loved their wives the way Vernon cherishes Jerusalem, what a different world it would be.

Nora let out a grateful sigh. "I can't thank you enough for the way you've helped me. I'll let you get back to your day now —"

"And I look forward to that hanging you're making for the butcher shop," he said, his eyes a-twinkle. "Jerusalem is so tickled to be giving it to me, I can't help being tickled, as well. And *you* have brought about all this happiness, Nora, just doing what you do best. Don't forget that, when the situation with your *dat* overwhelms you. You were born to be a blessing."

After Vernon walked her to the car, Nora drove down his lane with a sense of great relief. He hadn't given her step-by-step instructions or promised that her *dat*'s attitude toward her would improve, yet he'd bolstered her self-confidence. He'd assured her that her faith was strong enough to see her through whatever ordeals might lie ahead.

Love is the knot you tie in your proverbial rope, to hang on to while God works out His will in your life. You were born to be a blessing.

As she again followed the county blacktop toward Amanda Brubaker's place to ask about consigning some of her fabulous pottery, Nora decided to look online when she got home, for places to sell the BMW. She would get a better price for it if she contacted dealerships in larger towns — and she'd have a bigger selection of used vans to choose from, too.

If she trusted God to work out His will, she could remain patient — to see whether Dat made his confession, or whether the congregation would vote on shunning him if he didn't comply. In two weeks she would know how it all shook out, and in the meantime she had a store to organize. September sixth was less than a month away.

Nora pushed the button to fold down the top of her convertible. She put on her sunglasses and smiled up into the sunlight, reveling in these pleasures one final time before she sold her red car. The despair that had filled her an hour ago had been replaced by a sense of celebration that made her heart play hopscotch.

It'll all work out. Vernon believes it, and I do, too!

CHAPTER SEVENTEEN

As Luke bagged freshly milled whole wheat flour on Thursday morning, he felt a deep sense of satisfaction. Seeing *The Mill at Willow Ridge* printed on these brown paper sacks, along with a sketch of the mill, was a longtime dream come true; he and Ira couldn't possibly have set up such a business in Lancaster County because even if land beside a waterway had been available, it would've been too expensive. This morning his brother was out checking the acres of organic corn around the area, which was now in the tasseling stage. He was also collecting crates of eggs laid by the cage-free chickens that some of their other contracted farmers raised. Ira, with his happy-go-lucky personality, was so good at convincing old-school farmers to raise new-fangled products — and every one of them was pleased with the profits they were making on their first harvest.

Luke preferred the milling work, grinding the grains and packaging them for the store. As he filled another sack, he inhaled the nutty-sweet aroma of the flour and knew good cooks like Miriam would appreciate its texture and freshness. His worktable was nearly covered with filled sacks ready to be sealed when he heard the snappy *tap-tap-tap* of feminine footsteps.

"Luke, may I ask a favor?"

Nora's voice sent a lightning bolt up his spine. When he turned to greet her, he beheld a knockout of a woman who could have had anything in the world from him without having to ask. With her auburn hair artfully layered around her face, and wearing a cedar green jacket and matching skirt that showed off her stunning legs, Nora Landwehr might've stepped out of a fashion magazine or a big-city office. "Wow," he murmured. "You look like a million bucks."

Her smile appeared sophisticated. Self-assured. "Thanks," she replied. "I've got an appointment in Columbia to sell my car. And I've found a couple of used vans to test drive before I take the best one to the Mennonite body shop over past Cedar Creek for a coat of black paint. If I call you when I'm en route to the shop, could you possibly meet me there and bring me home?"

"Sure I'll meet you there. I can pick up Ira's repaired wheel while I'm at it," he replied with a chuckle. "But we might not come straight home."

Nora's lips twitched. She was wearing a dusky reddish-brown lipstick that made Luke want to kiss it off her immediately, but he knew better than to mess up her flawless makeup . . . at least until they were on the way home.

"We'll stop for lunch somewhere," she said. "It's the least I can do after bumming a ride."

And what's the most *you'll do?* came his wayward mental reply. But Luke reminded himself that a woman like Nora suffered no fools, so he tried to make conversation that sounded rational. "I've heard that car salesmen are notorious for taking advantage of women who don't have a man along. Want me to go with you?"

"I appreciate your offer," she replied without missing a beat. Then she plucked some papers from her purse. "I've printed out the data from the Kelley Blue Book website and some other sources that say how much my BMW should sell for, and how much I should expect to pay for the vans I'm going to test drive. If the van sales-man acts like I've got *sucker* or *clueless little woman* written across my forehead, I'll walk away. That strategy — and cash in hand — always gets their attention. There are plenty of other places to buy vans, after all."

Nora gazed at him with her tawny tigress eyes, which were fringed with long, dark lashes. "I'm meeting with the owner of the BMW dealership, and he's said he already has a potential buyer for it, so it's in his best interest to take me seriously, too. All things considered, both transactions should be pretty straightforward."

Luke's mouth opened and closed again. "Why on God's green earth do you want to be Plain, Nora?" he blurted. "You could succeed at *anything* in the English world —"

"Don't judge this book by its cover," she replied softly. "I've returned to Willow Ridge to be with my family again."

Luke kicked himself for asking such an intrusive question, yet he couldn't deny that the *cover* of Nora's book was all the incen-tive he needed to jump the fence and go English, to be with her. It would settle a lot of the conflicting thoughts he'd had lately.

And what makes you think she'd be with you? A woman like Nora doesn't need a man to support her or complete her.

Does she?

Luke cleared his throat. "Got my cell number?"

"From your website," she replied pertly.

He sighed to himself. Did he really need any further proof that Nora had all the answers before he could think up the questions? "See you in a few hours then. I'll wait for your call."

"Fabulous."

Luke's mind lingered over his own definition of that word as Nora carefully lifted an open paper bag from his worktable. "So you've milled this whole wheat flour? Fresh this morning?"

"From the crop we planted on your parents' place," he replied. "It's organic and locally grown — two key words these days — and we got a bigger yield than we anticipated, so everybody's happy. Your *dat* even smiled when I handed him the check for it."

Nora's sigh filled the space around him. "So he remembers how to do that?" she asked wistfully. "That's good to know. Gives me hope that someday he'll smile at *me*."

"Maybe I can help."

"Yeah. Maybe." Nora squared her shoulders and slung her purse strap over one of them. "Thanks again, Luke. Be thinking about where you'd like to do lunch."

As her tall, skinny heels tapped a seductive tattoo across his workroom floor, Luke watched the sway of her backside. Just as he knew he wanted to do a whole lot more than lunch, Luke realized that he was probably the one with *sucker* written all over his face. Of all the women he'd known, how did this girl-next-door-turned-temptress make him feel so dynamic, yet so defenseless against her allure?

Don't ask the question if you don't want her honest answer.

Luke laughed, at himself mostly. He knew he'd better finish up with his flour and hitch up his rig soon, if he was to meet Nora when she was ready for him — because once she was ready, he might only have one chance to prove he was worth her while.

Nora stood outside Stutzman's Body Shop, looking up and down the county highway for Luke. As the hot noon breeze riffled her hair, she felt too warm in the long-sleeved green suit, but it had served her well today: she'd gotten a few thousand dollars more than she'd expected for her BMW and had then negotiated the price of her used van down by a few thousand dollars — mostly because the men she'd been dealing with had been attracted to her.

Flash some leg and they'll follow you anywhere, she mused. But Nora wasn't comfortable using her looks as a bargaining tool anymore. She'd reached a point where being accepted as a simpler, unadorned woman suited her better. It was time to clear her closets of all her sleek, shimmery clothing — time to appear as Plain on the outside as she wanted to feel on the inside.

As a buggy approached, Nora enjoyed the *clip-clop, clip-clop* of the horse's hoofbeats. She congratulated herself for recognizing Luke's gelding, because all the rigs in this area still looked the same to her until she saw who was driving them. Waving, she headed toward the blacktop and waited for the buggy to stop.

Luke hopped out, but he didn't put the metal step down for her. "Going my way?" he quipped as he gave her a rakish looking-over.

"In your dreams," she shot back. Luke wore the broadfall pants and suspenders that announced him as Plain, but underneath he was no different from any English fellow: if things were going his way, he was as happy as a dog with a bone. "How's your morning been?"

"Finished bagging all that flour, then fetched Ira's wheel, and now I'm a man about to take a hot woman for a ride," Luke replied as his eyes narrowed. "What's not to love about that?"

Hot woman. Luke's compliment and low, rugged voice suggested he was going to race right on past that proverbial first base today. While that idea assuaged her bruised ego over the way Tanner had cast her aside, she knew she'd regret letting him go as far as he wanted to.

"Up you go," Luke said as he lifted her effortlessly into the rig. His large hands lingered at her waist. "I'm way too hungry to wait any longer."

Red flags flapped in her conscience. As she scooted across the buggy seat, Nora searched for a proper response. "Where would you like to go for lunch?" she asked in a purposeful tone. "Cedar Creek has a couple of —"

"Let's try that place in Higher Ground," Luke said as he joined her on the seat. He took up the lines and got his horse going. "With everybody there coming from some-place else, we won't have folks we know spying on us."

"Except maybe Hiram," Nora pointed out.

"I suspect he's not around," Luke said.

"When Ira was over that way checking our popcorn crop, he heard that Hiram's live-in girlfriend, Delilah, has taken off. So he's out on the prowl, looking for another bed warmer, I'm guessing."

Nora gaped. "He wasn't married to her? That's awfully fast and loose for a man who claims to be Mennonite."

"Oh, he had a slick line about it, something like they were one in the eyes of the Lord," Luke replied with a snort. "But Bishop Tom didn't buy it, and neither did anyone else. Delilah's not much older than Annie Mae — which is why she and Adam have the younger Knepp kids living at their place."

"Ah," she murmured. "That explains Hiram's short English haircut and the dye job."

Luke laughed out loud. "Do you really think there's an explanation for Knepp? Not that I want to talk about *him*," he added quickly. "How'd your car dealing go?"

Nora decided not to get specific about how many thousands of dollars were in her purse after her two transactions. "As well as I'd hoped," she hedged. "The van I bought was a demo the sales guy had used — only has ten thousand miles on it. But with several new-model vans and SUVs on the lot, he was glad to let this one go."

Shaking his head, Luke slung his arm loosely around her shoulders. "No doubt in my mind you drive a hard bargain, Nora-girl," he murmured. "Makes me wonder why you want to spend time with the likes of me."

It was a bid for a compliment — or for a declaration of affectionate intent — yet Nora smiled. "You're a man immersed in honest work, who insists on providing his customers with high-quality food," she replied as she studied the large, work-roughened hand that held the leather lines. "The guys I dealt with this morning might have manicured nails and pricey clothes, but they consider it their job — their *right* — to upsell every person who walks through their doors, and to make a huge profit from it."

Nora gazed out at the passing countryside, allowing the sway of the buggy to bump her against Luke's muscled body. "I understand their methods and motives, but I don't respect them," she murmured. "Car dealers cover their butts with so much fine print and legal mumbo jumbo, the average Joe doesn't stand a chance of getting a fair deal. I want no part of that world anymore."

When she met Luke's gaze, he kissed her.

It was quick, accompanied by a soft sigh. Feathery gentle and wintergreen fresh.

Nora's breath escaped her. Before she could protest, Luke kissed her again, longer this time. While his arm remained loose and his lips merely skimmed hers, he was making her tingle all over as though this were her first kiss ever. She'd often anticipated this moment, but she'd had Luke Hooley figured all wrong. He wasn't the aggressive, possessive kisser his come-on comments had suggested. It seemed he might actually be *wooing* her. And she hadn't felt this responsive in a long, long time.

"More where that came from," he whispered, sounding every bit as rattled as Nora was. He released her shoulders, holding the leather lines with a wolfish smile. "But I'm gonna make you come after it."

"Teaser," Nora muttered.

"Yup. Take some of your own medicine, woman."

"Puh!" Nora scooted across the seat, but they both knew it was only the next play of the game. And the game was *on*.

They drove the rest of the way to Higher Ground with a charged silence thrumming between them. Luke pulled the rig up to the diner's hitching rail, and after he'd secured the horse he put down the metal step. Nora smiled when he reached for her hand this time, playing the gentleman. He kept his fingers entwined with hers as they entered the restaurant.

It was a fifties-style diner, and the Mennonite waitresses wearing *kapps* looked a little out of sync moving among the red leatherette booths. Their athletic shoes squeaked on the black-and-white checkerboard floor as they poured water and handed out menus. Luke quickly decided on the chicken-fried steak special and Nora chose the grilled chicken salad.

"Time to powder my nose," Nora murmured as she stood up.

"No need to do that for *me,*" Luke teased. "I think your freckles are sweet just the way they are."

Her thoughts raced as she entered the restroom. The air-conditioning was a welcome relief from the day's sultry heat, and as Nora washed her hands she tried to corral her thoughts. She intended to donate her English clothes to the thrift store in Morning Star, but she knew Luke would pursue her no matter how modestly she dressed — and she wanted him to. Today's new twist on their cat-and-mouse game intrigued her.

When she looked in the mirror, Nora

couldn't miss the heightened color in her cheeks. She didn't bother to comb her windblown hair. One last time, she would allow her auburn waves to fall in tousled layers around her face. She didn't freshen her lipstick, either, because she wanted it to get kissed off. Just for the ride home, she would enjoy the sight of her bare legs beneath her short skirt . . . the way her strappy heels accentuated her ankles.

Then she would become Plain Nora, forever.

When she swung open the door, she nearly ran into Hiram Knepp before she saw him in the shadowy hallway. He was leaning against the wall as though he'd been waiting for her to come out. He shifted quickly so he was blocking her exit.

"Looking *good*," he murmured with a devilish smile.

Nora somehow contained her irritation. "Hiram," she said with a curt nod. "If you'll excuse me —"

"Oh, there's no excuse for you today," he quipped as his gaze roamed the length of her. "You and Hooley are as mismatched as a thoroughbred racehorse yoked to an ox. What do you see in him, anyway?"

Nora didn't try to break past him, because that would bring her into contact with the arm he'd planted against the wall, right at her chest level. "You're entitled to your opinion," she muttered, "but —"

"But I'm really here with a proposition," Hiram interrupted. "A business proposition, that is."

As he moved closer, Nora had nowhere to go but backwards, into the deeper shadow. As her back found the wall she instinctively bent one leg up so her knee was in a strategic position. She remained silent, making Hiram talk while she figured out how to get out of this trap he'd set.

"Several friends have told me how excited they are to be consigning items to your new store," Hiram continued. "What a shame it would be if your business went belly-up. Most small businesses — especially those owned by women — fail within the first year because they're undercapitalized. I'd like to help prevent that."

I just bet you would, Nora thought, but she kept her mouth shut. Anything she said would give him more ammunition.

Hiram smirked. "Miriam Hooley and Andy Leitner can attest to that," he stated. "They couldn't keep their doors open if they didn't have a benefactor who owned their buildings and relieved them of all that overhead. So what if I bought my barn back?" he asked. "What if I became your silent partner, Nora?"

"No *way,*" she muttered. "I don't care to pay the sort of *interest* you'd expect."

Hiram's chuckle echoed in the small hallway. "Nora, my dear," he protested in a silky voice. "You misunderstand my —"

The door to the men's room swung open so hard it hit the wall.

"The lady said *no,* Knepp," Luke snapped as he stepped into the hallway. "I've got zero tolerance for snakes, so you'd better slither back into your hole. Got it?"

Hiram backed away from her. His jet-black goatee rippled with his grin as he pointed first to Nora and then to Luke. "There's just no accounting for taste, I guess," he said with a shake of his head. "If you care to reconsider my offer, Nora, my door's always open."

As Knepp strode away, Nora let her foot slide back to the floor. Her knees felt so wobbly she wondered if she'd make it back to the table. "Can't thank you enough, Luke," she rasped.

"Good thing I took a notion to powder my nose, eh?" he asked as he offered his arm. "I had no idea he was here until I heard him, uh, *propositioning* you outside the john."

Nora's face went hot. It was bad enough that she'd had to endure Hiram's come-on, but even worse that Luke had been listening to their conversation. She gulped air to settle herself, happy to hang on to his arm as they returned to their table. Their orders arrived, but even though the grilled chicken salad looked really fresh and smelled delicious, she'd lost her appetite.

Luke, however, cut into his chicken-fried steak with gusto. "Has he done that before? Pestered you about your store, I mean."

Nora sighed. "He came to the house once. Let himself in without being invited — so I've now installed dead bolts." She watched as Luke forked up mashed potatoes and gravy, envying the way he was enjoying his meal. "Was it true, what he said? About Miriam and Andy having a benefactor who owns their buildings?"

"Yup. But it's not Hiram — although he tried his best to finagle Miriam's bakery away from her as revenge for not marrying him." Luke sawed off another big bite of his meat.

"Ew," Nora murmured. "I can't picture them as a pair — not as sweet and honest and down-to-earth as Miriam is."

"Hiram needed somebody to raise his younger kids," Luke explained. "He was really mad when he found out that the English fellow who raised Rebecca had bought the place out from under him, with an assist from the banker.

"His name's Bob Oliveri," he went on after he'd chewed for a moment. "He bought the clinic building and helped with its renovation, too, so Andy Leitner — our local nurse — could become Amish yet still have the electricity he needs to run some of his medical equipment. Good guy, Bob is," Luke added with a nod. "Willow Ridge is a better place because of him."

Nora had to agree. Her pulse was returning to normal, but her thoughts wandered. If Hiram had told the truth about Miriam and Andy having a benefactor, should she believe what he'd said earlier about Luke and Ira leaving previous girlfriends behind — in the lurch, as he'd put it — and then being able to open the mill only because their brother Ben was bankrolling it?

A tapping sound brought her out of her woolgathering. Luke was gazing intently at her as the tines of his fork repeatedly struck the edge of her plate. "Do *not* let Knepp ruin your lunch, Nora," he insisted. "He's not worth your time, and he's full of bull. Nuff said."

Nora began to pick the chicken from her

salad, sensing Luke would make her sit here until she ate most of it. And wasn't that sort of nice? He was being a friend — even if he eventually wanted to be a friend with benefits. She wouldn't ruin the moment by quizzing him about his past, especially considering *who* had insinuated such questionable details about it.

When she'd eaten most of her salad and had downed a couple of glasses of ice water, Nora felt much better. She and Luke climbed into the buggy again. They chatted about the fields of corn they passed, which would soon be harvested by the Hooley brothers' Mennonite farm helpers to make cornmeal and yellow corn grits. Nora enjoyed listening to Luke discuss the details of his milling work, and she was impressed with how many acres around these Plain settlements he and Ira had under contract. Even so, in the back of her mind she realized that the minutes were ticking by. And once they returned home, they both had work to do.

Nora's hand found the inside of Luke's elbow. His skin felt smooth and warm beneath the short sleeve of his tan cotton shirt. His eyes were the deep green of the shaded cedar trees along the road, and the intensity of his gaze unnerved her. "Um, maybe before we get to Willow Ridge, we could . . ."

"Shall I pull over?"

Nora's breath escaped her as she nodded. She felt like a nervous girl on her first date. Her heart hammered as Luke brought his horse to a halt on the side of the road. He just kept looking at her, waiting for her to make the first move. Nora was once again impressed by Luke's control, because even as desire danced in his eyes, his hands remained on his lap.

When she reached for him, Luke pulled her close and kissed her for several long, lovely moments. His soft sighs mingled with hers as he explored her mouth. When she eased away, Nora knew she'd followed a path from which there was no retreat. No turning back.

"Wow," Luke murmured as he caught his breath. *"Wow."*

"You got that right," she murmured. "This is the first time I've ever been kissed in a buggy — which sounds odd, considering the reason Dat sent me away. But before Borntreger took what he wanted, I'd led a very sheltered, good-girl life."

"Maybe I can reintroduce you to Plain dating," Luke replied as he took the lines in his hands again. "The basics between a man

276

and a woman don't require a car or cell phones or electricity, after all."

Nora grinned, for it seemed they had generated their own type of electricity — and it was very different from what she'd known with Tanner.

"Will you need a ride to pick up your painted van?"

"No, the Stutzman brothers offered to deliver it, to be sure everything drives the way it should after they've checked it over," she replied. "Poor planning on my part, eh?"

Luke wrapped his hand around hers as the horse clip-clopped along the blacktop again. "The best parts about getting to know someone usually don't follow a plan. Although I'll confess that I accomplished everything on my agenda today. And I liked it. A *lot.*"

Nora smiled. Who could've imagined that cool, self-assured Luke Hooley would admit such a thing in a way that seemed so guileless? So sweet and open.

When the mill came into view, Luke kissed her once more, gently guiding her chin with his finger. He drove her to the front door of her house, and as Nora got out of the buggy, she felt so giddy she wasn't sure what she said to him. When she entered her front room, the fabric hangings stacked on her couch reminded her that she had a million things to do to get ready for her store's opening, but she went straight upstairs. She changed into a cape dress and pulled her hair into a bun with a *kapp* over it. In the bathroom, she washed off her makeup.

Grabbing the wardrobe boxes she'd used for her move to Willow Ridge, she went to her closet and quickly took out every pencil skirt, silk blouse, and pair of tailored slacks, plus all the sundresses and suits and high-dollar shoes and purses that went with them. She bagged her jewelry and colorful scarves, and yanked her T-shirts, jeans, and shorts from her dresser drawers. Waves of emotion rolled through her as she recalled the occasions when she'd worn some of this stylish clothing, but before she lost her resolve, Nora sealed the boxes shut with packing tape. She would haul this stuff to the thrift store in Morning Star as soon as her van arrived.

She felt purged. Clean. Her English wardrobe represented a life she felt good about leaving behind, even though she'd known some shining moments and had gained a world of experience that would never leave her. But it was time to move forward, even if that meant stepping back in time to the simpler life she'd known as a girl.

Nora looked in the mirror and smiled. The woman gazing back at her belonged in Willow Ridge. No matter what her father thought of her, she had come home. To *stay.*

CHAPTER EIGHTEEN

Miriam opened the windows in the Sweet Seasons kitchen and dining room, welcoming the fresh breeze that came with a cool, rainy afternoon. This summer had seemed hotter and more humid than any she remembered, possibly because she was five months along in her pregnancy. A break in the heat had put her in a better mood after a very busy day.

Or was she smiling because all three of her girls were here? Rachel, beautifully round with her first child, sat in the kitchen beside a large crate of carrots, peeling them, while beside her, Rhoda peeled potatoes and dropped them into a big pan of cold water. Rebecca was wiping down the tables and chairs in the dining room.

"What a picture," Miriam remarked as she gazed around the café. "Can't recall the last time all three of ya were in the same place at the same time, even though I see each of ya nearly every day. *Denki* for bein' here with me."

Rachel looked up, her peeler poised over another carrot. "What with Micah and his brothers workin' over in New Haven today, it's better that I'm here helpin' ya with this mountain of carrots than lookin' for things to do. Aunt Leah must have a bumper crop of root vegetables in her garden this year."

"*Jah,* she didn't sell as much at the farmers' market this mornin' on account of the rain," Miriam replied. Her sister, Leah Kanagy, who raised vegetables and kept bees, often sold Miriam the leftover items she'd harvested. "I've been wantin' to try a new carrot soup recipe Rebecca found, and this seems like a fine time for it. And I'm gonna slice some of those onions Leah brought to make that cheesy onion casserole the fellas like so much."

"You'd better enjoy your last weeks of peace and quiet, Rachel," Rhoda teased. "Andy thinks your wee one'll be here by the middle of September. That gives us a bit of time to spoil your baby and practice our diaperin' technique before Mamma's comes along."

"It'll be a new experience, havin' my first grandchild and then birthin' another baby of my own after all these years," Miriam remarked. "I'm glad I've got you girls close at hand. I'm not sure how I'll manage a wee one while Naomi and I keep the Sweet Seasons goin'. But I'll figure it out."

Humming, Miriam took a stockpot from a hook on the ceiling. She was in the mood to cook most of these carrots and make the soup for tomorrow's lunch menu, and then simmer the onions for the casserole . . . maybe get a few pans of cornbread casserole in the oven while it was so pleasantly cool. These days, her energy seemed to come and go on its own schedule, so cooking ahead gave her some leeway for those days when she wasn't as bouncy.

When the bell above the door jangled, she looked out to see Nora entering the dining room, wearing a speculative expression.

"Hope I'm not interrupting anything," Nora said as she smiled at each of the girls. "I thought if I came after you closed, I'd not cause a scene with Dat."

Miriam's smile fell a notch. She sensed Nora was hurting inside even though she'd put on a good front. "Gabe's not been here all this week," she remarked. "I suspect he's avoidin' the lectures he'll get from Bishop Tom — and me. Why he has to be so hardheaded is beyond me."

"I can't change him, so I've stopped fretting over it. I hope he realizes how hard it'll be on Mamm and Millie if he gets shunned, though." Nora peeked into the kitchen and her mouth dropped open. "That's the biggest pile of carrots I've ever seen!"

"Mamma's trying a new recipe for tomorrow's lunch menu," Rachel explained. She shifted her bulk, adjusting her posture in the chair. "Can't say I'm looking forward to slicing all of these before she cooks them, though."

"You don't have a food processor?" Nora gazed around the kitchen, taking in the array of appliances.

"Nor a blender for after the carrots are cooked," Miriam said, frowning at the recipe. "*Ach,* if I'd paid closer attention to *that* detail, I might've started something different. Sometimes I think this baby's makin' me absentminded."

"Not to worry, Miriam," Nora said as she headed for the door. "I've got a food processor I never use, and an extra blender that's never been out of the box. I'll be back in a few."

"Talk about good timing," Rebecca remarked as the bell above the door jangled again. She ran water in a bucket to mop the floor. "I think it's so cool that Nora's opening a store in that big barn. Can't wait to see all the stuff she's going to sell."

"And it would be such a blessing for her and Millie if they could work together," Miriam said. She shook her head as she grabbed a knife to peel onions. "Gabe's got no idea how many lives he's puttin' on hold because he won't let go of his old grudges."

Silence filled the café as each of them went about their separate tasks. Rebecca made quick work of mopping the floor while the peelers went *flick-flick-flick* in Rhoda and Rachel's hands. Time and again Miriam had wondered how she could convince Gabe to relent, but he seemed oblivious to everyone's pleas. Thick white onion slices piled up in her metal pan as she wielded her knife, lost in thought.

"Here you go!" Nora crowed as she came in through the back kitchen door with a box under each arm. "Let me show you how to feed those carrots into the food processor and you'll whip through them in no time."

Once again Miriam gave thanks for Bob Oliveri, Rebecca's English *dat,* who'd bought the building so her restaurant could have the electricity that health department standards required. Nora's slicing demonstration took only a few moments, and then Miriam began feeding the carrots through the food processor's top opening with an amazed grin.

"Can't thank ya enough for lettin' me borrow this handy-dandy contraption," Miriam said above the *whirrrr* of its motor. "Come by for your lunch tomorrow when ya pick it up, all right?"

"Oh, keep it — and the blender," Nora insisted. "I rarely use them, but I couldn't bear to leave them behind when I moved here. And now that you're going great guns with the slicer, I'll talk some business with Rebecca. If I'm to open the store by the first weekend in September, I've got to get my website up and running."

"She's a *gut* one for doin' that," Miriam agreed. By the time she'd dumped a couple of bowls of sliced carrots into a stock pot, her English daughter and Nora were heading for the back kitchen counter, where Rebecca had stashed the laptop she was never without.

It made Miriam smile to watch the two young women discuss the website Nora wanted, using terms no Amish woman would ever understand. Rebecca plugged a little gadget of Nora's into the back of the computer, and then began clicking to bring photographs onto the screen.

"Oh, look at this pottery!" Rebecca said. "And these look like quilts from the

Schrocks' shop next door."

"They are," Nora said as she leaned over Rebecca's shoulder. She scooted aside as Rachel and Rhoda came to gaze at the pictures, and Miriam joined the cluster gathered around the computer, too.

"And those look like the horse collars Matthias makes," Rhoda remarked. Then her eyes widened. "Oh, but look at these hangings! I've never seen the likes of that one, with the laundry on a real clothesline —"

"And these black calico cows looking over the fence are *too cool*," Rebecca joined in.

"Those are Vernon Gingerich's Black Angus, and that's his silo," Nora said as her cheeks turned a pretty shade of pink. "I made a banner for his nephew's butcher shop and it was so cute I made a second one to put in the store."

Rebecca clicked to make the picture bigger. "Just my opinion, but that cow design should be the header on your home page, Nora. And whenever you get the sign for your store, we could use that as the name for your website, as well."

"Ben's making my sign now, from wrought iron," Nora replied. "I decided to call the place Simple Gifts. Do you think that'll work?"

Miriam sucked in her breath, and so did her daughters. "Oh, but I like the sound of that, Nora!"

Nora watched Rebecca open more of the photographs, her expression waxing more serious. "Um, any idea how much my site will run me? I'm being careful with my —"

"Not one penny," Miriam insisted as she slipped her arm around Nora's shoulders. "That blender and food processor'll more than cover whatever Rebecca's gonna charge ya, honey-bug. She and I will work it out between us."

Nora gasped. "But I couldn't let you —"

"Don't argue. It's a done deal — *jah,* Rebecca?"

"Yup," her daughter replied. She had already cropped the image of the cow banner so it would fit across the top of a web page and was experimenting with different colors for a background.

Miriam laughed at the expression on Nora's freckled face. She looked younger, sweeter, in her *kapp* and a calico dress of little pink roses and green leaves. "Consider it my homecomin' gift for your store, Nora. I'm so tickled you're back amongst us. What with you and all three of my girls livin' within a hoot and a holler, it's just like old times."

A smile stole across Miriam's face then, and goose bumps tickled her skin. "I can still hear my little triplets gigglin' at the songs ya sang for them when you'd come over so's I could get some housework done."

"Wow, I'd forgotten about that. I couldn't have been but nine or ten," Nora mused. "It was a treat to cross the road and come to your place. Nobody else had three cute toddler look-alikes."

"That was before Rebecca washed away in the flood," Rhoda murmured in a faraway voice. "I don't remember us all being together when we were that little."

"Me neither," Rachel said. "Far back as I can recall, it was just you and me, Rhoda."

Miriam wrapped her arms around as many shoulders as she could reach, drawing all four of the young women into a close huddle with Rebecca in its center. "Just goes to show ya how we made it through tragedies that tore both of our families apart," she said in a voice that hitched a little. "But here we all are, together again. It's God's doin'. He's never failed me, girls. And He's not finished lovin' us."

As they let out a collective sigh, Miriam gave thanks for these kindred spirits — the daughters and the neighbor girl who were sharing this new life she lived with Ben, running her café. A year ago, she'd had no idea such joy and satisfaction awaited her.

"I was too young to realize it then," Nora murmured, "but what a *loss* you suffered, Miriam, when Rebecca washed away in the river during that storm. I recall the men searching along the riverbanks downstream, but when they didn't find her, no more was said about it."

"It's not our way to involve the police — then or now," Miriam recounted in a tight voice. "Hiram and my Jesse and your *dat* declared that we'd done all we could do and the rest was up to God. We didn't have a funeral, and we didn't question the men's authority. It was like my little girl had never existed — but of course I never stopped missin' her, even though I still had Rachel and Rhoda to look after."

"That must've been so awful, Miriam."

The five of them turned to see Millie standing in the doorway between the kitchen and the dining room. She so closely resembled Nora that Miriam had to smile as she opened her arms to the young girl. "It was much the same when your mother left town, carryin' *you,* honey-bug," she said. "Our Nora just disappeared. The women could only speculate about why she left until Wilma finally broke down and explained the predicament her daughter was in."

"I don't like it that the men make all the rules and tell us what to think and how to act," Millie blurted. "It's makin' me think I don't want to join the Old Order. I can see why Ira and Luke have dug their heels in about joinin', too."

Miriam closed her eyes, hoping God would approve of her reply to this vulnerable teenage girl. "Our faith has always been that way and I don't see it changin'," she murmured. "But in the meanwhile, we women learn to work within the Ordnung's framework even as we handle our day-to-day livin' in our own ways. Your *mammi* never stopped thinkin' about Nora — or lovin' her — just because she'd left town to have a baby without bein' married. But Wilma kept the silence. She kept the faith, and she carried on."

"And your *mammi* will love you no matter what you decide about your religion," Nora said as she eased away from the group around the computer.

"When Mammi saw you gettin' out of your black van over here, she told me to slip on over for a visit," Millie replied with a grin. "Dawdi fell asleep in his chair, so here I am."

Miriam's heart thrummed as she watched

the redheaded mother and daughter embrace. Rebecca turned from her laptop then to smile at the pair.

"If you ever want to talk about what you've gone through, Millie, finding out you had a different mother than you'd believed," she said in a pensive voice, "I know all about that. You have a lot of conflicting feelings to deal with, and you don't have to keep them inside just because your grandfather refuses to talk. Okay?"

Millie nodded shyly. "Mammi's told me the same thing. We talk a lot more now that she's doin' so much better." Her eyes lit up when she saw the images on Rebecca's computer screen. "Is this gonna be your website, Mamma? I still hope I can help in your new store."

Nora's expression was priceless. Miriam could guess, by the profound mixture of love and joy and gratitude that lit up her freckled face, that Millie had just called Nora her *mamma* for the first time. It was the sweetest word Miriam knew, and she was so pleased that Nora thought so, too.

"We'll work it out as best we can," Nora insisted as she kept her arm around her daughter's waist. "A lot depends on how your *dawdi* responds at the next church service — whether he confesses, or if Bishop

Tom calls for a vote to shun him."

"My word, it'll be a busy Sunday and a long Members' Meeting," Rhoda remarked. "My Andy has finished takin' his instruction, and that's the day everybody'll vote on whether he can become a full member of the Amish church."

"I don't know a soul who's gonna say no to *that*," Miriam remarked. "What with him runnin' the clinic and his kids takin' to our ways so quick, it's like the Leitners have lived here a long time."

"And then ya can set your wedding date!" Rachel piped up as she grabbed Rhoda's hands.

"Shall we make it before ya birth your baby, or after? I couldn't have anyone but *you* for my side-sitter, Sister," Rhoda replied. Then she chuckled. "I've been havin' odd dreams about the wedding, where ya let out a holler and then Andy has to deliver your wee one right there in church. Kind of crazy."

As laughter filled her kitchen, Miriam put her hand on her swelling belly, where the baby was kicking, joining in their mirth. Mothers and daughters . . . was there a deeper, sweeter bond on this earth?

While the younger women kept visiting, Miriam poured a couple of gallons of chicken broth into her stockpot and turned on the burner beneath it to start cooking her sliced carrots. It seemed that while she was trying out a new recipe for soup, their little group had cooked up a fresh understanding of what it meant to nurture each other . . . to strengthen their relationships, which in turn strengthened their faith.

The more things changed, the more they stayed the same. And for that, Miriam was grateful.

CHAPTER NINETEEN

Around ten thirty on Sunday morning, Nora started toward Ben and Miriam's house for what she sensed would be a monumental day in Willow Ridge. The low gray clouds intensified her unsettled mood as she walked up the county highway. She could have attended the Amish church service, but her presence would've set her *dat* on edge and thereby upset her mother. She'd watched Luke and Ira walk this way a few hours ago.

The new Hooley house was built on what had once been part of the Glick farm. Selling this property had probably provided the largest lump sum her parents had seen since Dat retired from raising crops several years ago. The income from renting out several acres of his land to the mill was a godsend, but Nora suspected her parents had jars of home-canned food on their cellar shelves and meat in their deep freeze mostly because Lizzie and Atlee — and other families around town — had shared what they'd preserved from their gardens and what they'd butchered. The Amish took care of their own, even as they believed God would provide for their needs.

Singing drifted from the open windows of Ben and Miriam's home — the final hymn. Soon the nonmembers of the congregation would step outside while her father's fate was decided. Nora intended to join Millie, Luke, and Ira when they came outside — not to eavesdrop, exactly, but hearing the words of the Members' Meeting would prepare her for the events to come.

After the hymn ended, Vernon Gingerich delivered the benediction in his rich, resonant voice. Nora was grateful that he was assisting with the service, providing his calm wisdom. While she hoped her father had experienced a change of heart since she'd last seen him, she asked God to guide all of those present as Dat responded to the kneeling confession Bishop Tom had prescribed.

"As the nonmembers leave the room," Tom said, his voice carrying through the windows, "let's prepare ourselves for the two very important matters before us today, the consideration of Andy Leitner as a new member of the Old Order, followed by Gabe Glick's confession."

The back door flew open and several little boys whooped as they ran into the yard. The girls were more demure but equally eager to be playing after a three-hour church service. A few teenagers came out next, followed by a nice-looking fellow and then Ira, Luke, and Millie.

"Nora, this is Andy Leitner, the nurse who runs the new clinic down the way," Luke spoke up. "Andy, Nora has bought Hiram's place —"

"Ah, the gal who's to open the new store," Andy said as he shook her hand. "Sounds like you've taken quite a step, coming back to Willow Ridge."

"And you've made quite a life change, joining the Amish church — and bringing your medical expertise to town," Nora replied as she took in his black broadfall trousers, matching vest, and white shirt. While his Sunday clothes and straw hat made him appear Plain, the final decision wasn't his to make. He'd taken a considerable risk to come this far in his quest to join the Amish faith. "I wish you all the best."

In the house, one male voice followed another as the members voted on whether to accept Andy into the church. "Aye . . .

296

aye . . . aye . . ."

It was gratifying to hear lifelong Amish folks accepting an Englischer, after Andy had sold his previous home — given up the life he'd always known — and taken his instruction in the Amish faith so he could marry Rhoda Lantz. Soon the vote continued on the women's side of the room, and Nora's heart thrummed as the ayes kept coming. It gave her hope that this community might accept *her* presence even if she couldn't follow the strict doctrines and principles that formed the backbone of the Amish faith.

The Hooleys' back door swung open. Rhoda stepped outside, beaming as she wiped her eyes. "You're to come inside now, Andy," she announced. "You're one of us! A member in *gut* standing."

Rhoda and Andy's embrace made Nora envious of the affection this couple shared — and when a school-age boy and girl who resembled Andy ran over to join their hug, the family picture was complete. Nora shared a smile with Millie as Andy and Rhoda went inside.

"That's fabulous," Nora murmured. "You can feel the love and the respect they have for each other. They just *glow.*"

"*Jah,* it's *gut* to see that everybody wants

Andy here," Millie agreed. "He's had half of the clinic building made over into their new home, so things would've gotten sticky if he and Rhoda couldn't get hitched after all Andy's given up to be with her."

Nora nodded. She found it heartening that a good man like Andy Leitner had sacrificed so much to be able to marry the woman he loved. Such things did happen, even if she'd not had them happen in *her* life. As Bishop Tom's voice rose again, she listened closely.

"We've a more serious issue to consider now, concernin' the return of the Glicks' daughter, Nora," he said in a solemn voice. "More than once Nora has asked for her *dat*'s forgiveness for the circumstances sur-roundin' her unwed pregnancy, but Gabe's turned away from her. Because this goes against Jesus's teachings about forgiveness, I've asked him to give a kneelin' confession today, to cleanse his heart so their family can reunite in God's love and —"

"But see, that's where I've got a problem with this whole procedure."

Nora's eyes widened at the defiant edge in her father's voice. She heard a lot of whis-pering because Dat had dared to interrupt the bishop, and to defy him.

"What do you not understand?" Vernon's

voice rose above the murmuring of the crowd. "You've spent most of your life as a preacher of the Old Order —"

"And Tom here was a preacher just like me when I sent Nora away," her *dat* protested. "He and Hiram went right along with sendin' Nora to her aunt's house to have her baby. It's still the way we separate these girls, to give them time to consider their sin and to find a home for the child. So if my decision was right back then, why am I gettin' called out for it now?"

"Ah, but let's remember that ya sent Nora away without consultin' me or Hiram or Jesse Lantz," Bishop Tom pointed out. "And *jah,* while it's the way we've historically handled that situation, the issue *now* is that Nora has asked ya to forgive her, and you've refused. More than once."

"Not my doin' that she came back," her father retorted. "And not my doin' that she dumped Millie on Atlee's porch instead of adoptin' her out, either."

Wincing, Nora slung her arm around Millie's shoulders. "I'm so sorry you heard that," she murmured.

"This is just wrong," Luke muttered as he and Ira huddled around Nora and her daughter. "I can't believe Gabe's picking at these straws."

"And the way I see it," Vernon spoke up in the house, "God's will has been at work all along. Where would you and Wilma be, if it weren't for your granddaughter caring for you? And Nora, who was lost to you for so many years, has returned, wanting to reunite with your family. I see that as a tremendous blessing."

"Had she done it right all those years ago — come home and joined the church, like she was supposed to — we wouldn't be havin' this discussion," Dat ranted.

"Forgiveness, Gabe. It starts with *you*," Bishop Tom stated. He sounded a lot less patient now.

"Our faith is all about forgiveness," Vernon chimed in. "Forgiveness and following God's will rather than being misled by our own willful ways. You've been given this chance to start fresh, Gabe. What's your response to God's call?"

Nora held her breath as silence ensued — until the back door flew open and her father limped out. Anger contorted his weathered, wrinkled face when he saw the four of them standing together. "Eavesdroppers, the lot of ya!" he spat as the sunlight flickered on his glasses. "No respect for your elders or the ways of the church."

When Dat lurched, Nora started over to

catch him, but Luke held her fast. Her father regained his balance by leaning against the side of the house for a moment. Then he hobbled toward the lane to walk home.

"He's gonna fall," Millie whimpered as she watched her grandfather's unsteady progress.

"And whose fault is that?" Luke muttered. "But for you, Nora, I'll see that he makes it to the house."

Nora watched, her heart in her throat, as Luke caught up to her father — and then saw Dat swat away the arm Luke offered him. She turned to follow the words that were drifting through the window.

"Much as I regret takin' this course of action," Bishop Tom was saying, "I warned Gabe that he'd be shunned for six weeks if he didn't confess. I'm askin' everyone to keep Wilma and Millie, Lizzie and Atlee, and Nora in your prayers during this difficult time, and I'm askin' God to shine His light on Gabe's heart and soul."

As the Members' Meeting adjourned, chatter rose inside the house. Nora had thought she was immune to Dat's bitterness by now, but when she saw the anguish on her daughter's face, she reminded herself that this shunning wasn't about *her*. Mamm and Millie, as the ones who saw to Dat's day-to-day living, were the most affected. The most *afflicted.* How would they handle the in-house separation that shunning required? Dat's meals were to be served at a separate table, and they were to limit their speaking to him, except to exhort him to seek the path of salvation.

Men emerged through the back door carrying long tables to be set up for the common meal, talking earnestly among themselves about what had just taken place. It had been unusual enough when Hiram Knepp, their previous bishop, had been cast out — and now, less than a year later, a retired preacher had been shunned, as well. It didn't look good that longtime leaders of the Willow Ridge church district needed such discipline.

Nora saw her mother slipping out the back door, her hand at her mouth as though she were ready to cry. She and Millie hurried toward her with Ira following close behind.

"Mamma, I heard it all from out here," Nora murmured as she grasped her mother's hands. "I — I'm sorry I've caused so much trouble —"

"Puh! The trouble is inside your *dat*'s hard head. There's been no gettin' through to him of late," Mamm muttered as she also reached for Millie. "I wanted to crawl in a hole. I can't be in that house with him after what-all he's said today. He'll have to make do by himself until he comes to his senses."

Nora gasped. Her mother had always followed the Old Order ways of a submissive wife who obeyed her husband and the church's leaders. Mamma looked worn around the edges, yet she showed no sign of backing down from the stand she'd just taken.

Millie licked her lips nervously. "Where'll we go, Mammi? What about when Dawdi needs meals or his clothes washed or —"

"He'll have to humble himself and ask someone for help — or live hungry, in his own stink," Nora's *mamm* answered. "I've wasted all the breath I'm goin' to on that impossible man. Don't know what's come over him."

"Come to my house," Nora blurted. "I've got plenty of room for both of you."

"Or you can stay with Atlee and Ella and me," Lizzie said as she joined them. "This is just — I can't believe Gabe's let it go this far."

Mamma stared at the grassy ground for a moment. "I'm not sure Atlee'll be any too happy to have me under his roof —"

"Well, it's my roof, too," Lizzie insisted as

she shifted Ella to her other shoulder. "After all the times I've urged Atlee to spend more time at your house, helpin' with things, it's only right that he provide ya a place. It's only for the six weeks of Gabe's shunning, after all."

In the expressions that flickered across her mother's drawn face, Nora detected a hint that her parents' separation might not end when the shunning did. She felt surprised at her mother's determination, but it stemmed from a deep desperation that appalled her even more. Her heart faltered when her mother gazed up at her.

"Are ya sure it'd be all right to stay at your place, Nora?" Mamm asked in a breathy voice. "I don't want to impose —"

"It's all settled," Nora insisted. "You can stay as long as you need to."

"*Denki,* Daughter," her mother murmured. "When Gabe launched into his hardheaded excuses, all I could think was how I could *not* endure six weeks of his attitude," she added in a rising voice. "He brought this on himself. I'm not lookin' after him again until he apologizes to you girls and gets himself right with God. And if I get shunned for disobeyin' my husband, well — so be it."

Nora held Millie's wide-eyed gaze as they

both gripped Mamma's withered hands. She certainly hadn't anticipated her mother's declaration of independence — nor had she figured on having two houseguests, although the idea made her smile. "I'd better not help you with your packing. Dat'll accuse me of luring you into my English ways."

"I'll help ya," Ira insisted. He'd been listening to their conversation from a respectful distance. "I'll go in with ya while ya pack, and I'll have a rig ready to take ya to Nora's. I think it's a great idea that you're goin' to her place, considerin' how Gabe won't let her into your house. The three of ya can catch up with each other — as well ya should."

Nora appreciated the heartfelt, sincere way Ira wanted to help them. Was it her imagination, or had he matured a lot in the past few weeks? As it sank in that three generations of Glick women would be together at last, Nora knew she could be ready — knew she could somehow put her new consignment store together, as well — while they all weathered this emotional storm.

For the first time in years, Nora felt she had a family who loved her and would stand by her, just as she would shelter them during their time of trial. It seemed right somehow, and she intended to make the most of the time she'd share with two people she wanted to know a lot better.

CHAPTER TWENTY

Ira felt like the can of soda that had spooked his mare a few weeks ago — so fizzy and full of pent-up energy that he'd spew if he didn't speak his mind. His thoughts had been evolving lately, and this morning's church service had put the final spin on them. He grabbed Millie's hand. "Let's find Ben and meet up with Luke," he said to her and Nora and Wilma. "There's something on my mind, and I only want to say it once."

Millie's eyes widened, but she didn't hang back as Ira started through the crowd of men who were setting up the tables. He spotted Ben among them, and saw that Luke was leaving the Glick house after following Gabe to his door. Was he being stupid? Speaking too soon? Or was this the sort of moment that came over folks when they finally realized the path they were meant to follow?

"Bennie," Ira said as he swatted his older

brother's arm in passing. "I need your ear. Now that Gabe's been shunned and Wilma and Millie are gonna bunk at Nora's place, I've got something that needs sayin'."

Ben joined their group as they walked toward the lane. "You gals are sure that goin' to Nora's is the right idea?" he asked quietly. "That leaves Gabe to fend for himself —"

"As well he should," Wilma interrupted. She walked between her daughter and her granddaughter, clutching their hands. "He's chosen to separate himself with his hard-hearted attitude — just like when he sent our Nora away years ago, with no regard for the details of her situation."

Ben sighed loudly. "Somebody'll need to look in on him. Miriam and I can do that, and I'll let Tom know."

"I'll take a turn, too, if he'll tolerate me," Nora spoke up. "I'd never forgive myself if he got sick because I've caused so much commotion."

Ira gazed at Nora with great admiration. She was a much deeper person than he'd imagined when he'd first seen her wearing shorts and a ball cap, driving a shiny red car. He probably wouldn't tell her so in as many words, but she'd been an inspiration to him. A wake-up call.

"Luke!" Ira hollered. "It's a family meeting."

When they met up with Luke at the bottom of Ben's lane, everyone gazed expectantly at Ira. For a moment Ira wondered what he'd gotten himself into, but his heart told him to go with the flow of *rightness* he felt.

"I've decided to join the Old Order church," he blurted. "Ever since Nora showed up, and Gabe's made such a scene about it, I've come to realize that I belong in this district with Ben and the aunts."

Everyone around him sucked air. Time stood still for a few tight moments.

"Are you *nuts*?" Luke finally rasped. "Gabe Glick's attitude and his refusal to change it are two of the best reasons to *not* become Amish."

"I figured you'd see it that way, and I understand," Ira replied. He took a deep breath, meeting the intense gazes around him. Nora, Wilma, and Millie looked at him with wide, identical eyes, but their faces expressed wonder rather than doubt. A big grin was stealing across his oldest brother's face.

"And what finally brought ya to this conviction?" Ben asked as he grasped Ira's shoulder. "I've been waitin' to hear ya take some sort of stand, little brother. *Gut* for you, goin' in this direction!"

"Oh my," Millie murmured. "This is a big switch from what you've been sayin'."

"And I hope you'll bear with me, Millie," Ira hastened to reply as he squeezed her hand. "It's the big picture I'm seein'. If we younger fellas don't join the Old Order, our faith has no chance to evolve away from attitudes like Gabe's. Bishop Tom — and Vernon and Ben — have newer ways of lookin' at our life, and I want to be a part of that vision. It's the right thing to do."

Nora gazed intently at him. "I'm proud of you, Ira," she said. "You've come a long way since we first met — when, frankly, I had serious doubts about a guy your age dating my sixteen-year-old daughter."

Laughter softened the tension of the group gathered around him, and Ira relaxed. If a strong woman like Nora believed in his motives — in *him* — he surely must be on the right track. "*Denki* for sayin' that. I want only the best for Millie," Ira insisted. "And if she's not ready to join the church yet, I'll be patient. It's a big decision, and we all need to make our choices for the right reasons."

"Which is another question that's slapping me in the face," Luke remarked. "I've not heard you say one thing about your belief in God, and you've never paid much attention in church or gotten into evening Bible readings and such. I'm hearing more about social issues than religion —"

"And that's a place for faith to start," Ben interrupted patiently. He winked at Ira. "After all, most fellas don't take their instruction until the right young lady puts them in the mood to get married. Had I not been engaged to Polly Peterscheim back in the day, I wouldn't have joined the Old Order when I did, for sure. But even though she threw me over for a wealthier beau, that little mustard seed of faith Jesus talks about had been planted."

Ben gazed toward his new house on the hill. "So after years of wanderin' the Midwest in my farrier wagon, my faith made me the right man for Miriam when I found her last fall. If such a new direction — a whole new life — was what God had in mind for me, I don't doubt that He's got wonderful-*gut* plans for you, as well, little brother."

"I think you're smart to hitch in with the likes of Bishop Tom — and Vernon," Nora joined in. "Vernon reminded me a while back that Jesus commanded us to *love* one another, above all the other man-made rules and regulations. Somehow Dat's lost sight of that," she went on with a sigh. "So it's in my best interest to shift his vision as much as I can with my love, instead of resenting his hard attitude."

"Ya said a mouthful there, Nora," Ben murmured.

"I'm so glad ya see it that way, Daughter," Wilma spoke up. "I'm movin' to your house while your *dat*'s under the ban, but that's not to say I don't love that pigheaded fella I married so many years ago. I'm just makin' a point, hopin' he'll feel it faster."

"Like a needle piercing fabric," Nora murmured with a chuckle. "Can't sew things together without poking a few holes."

As they all chuckled, Millie's grandmother smiled at Ira full on. "I like what I'm hearin' now, Ira," she murmured. "I've sometimes wondered about ya bein' so much older than Millie, yet who am I to judge? Gabe's fifteen years ahead of me, and it's worked out. Mostly."

Millie's nervous giggle made everyone smile. Ira felt so relieved now that the most important people in his life understood and supported his big decision. He glanced up toward Ben's yard, where the women were carrying out bowls of chilled salads, baskets of fresh bread, and platters of sliced ham and cold fried chicken. It pleased him to know that this Sunday ritual, eating a common meal with everyone in the church community, would remain a part of his life. These gatherings were where all the best talk and sharing of life events happened — not to mention being a place to latch onto good, solid food like he and Luke couldn't rustle up at their apartment.

"What say we eat? All this serious talk's made me plenty hungry," Ira teased.

Luke gave Ira's shoulder a playful punch. "I'm glad *some* of your priorities haven't changed."

As they all walked back up the hill, Ira smiled. Luke was making jokes and Millie was holding his hand. Ben and Nora had expressed their support, and Wilma appreciated his offer to help move her out of the old Glick farmhouse. All felt very right with his world now, even though he'd changed his path dramatically. *And I thank Ya for that, Lord, and for standin' by me while I stated my intentions.*

Later that afternoon, Millie entered her grandparents' dim kitchen and stopped. Dawdi stood at the kitchen sink, spooning up tomatoes from a quart glass canning jar. When he glared at her and Mammi, Millie wished she could disappear into thin air to avoid the confrontation she knew was coming.

"I see ya didn't bother to bring me anything from the meal, after ya filled your own bellies and stayed to gossip," he groused.

Mammi straightened her shoulders. "Gabe, I've told ya time and again that home-canned vegetables need to be boiled in a pan before ya eat them," she said in a voice that wavered a little. "But ya don't listen — to me or to Bishop Tom — which is why Millie and I are goin' to Nora's house while you're under the ban."

Dawdi's spoon clattered into the sink. "That's not part of the bargain!" he retorted. "It's wrong to leave me alone — and even more wrong to take up with an Englischer when ya know *gut* and well I can't get on by myself."

"I'm doin' this so's you'll know how it feels to be shut out," Mammi said in a stronger voice. "Just like you've shut Nora out — just like ya haven't considered the way Tobias Borntreger was the one who sinned all those years ago and brought us all to this sorry state of affairs. I'm callin' it tough love."

"And I'm callin' it flat-out *wrong*," Dawdi countered angrily. He started toward them, pointing his finger at them. "You're the wife, Wilma. It's your place to see to my needs, even if it means I'm to eat at a TV table and ya don't talk to me much."

Millie heard the door open behind her and was relieved to see Ira stepping inside.

"So have it your way. Fetch a TV table from the hall closet," Mammi replied as she eased farther away from him.

"Easy now, Gabe," Ira warned. "Let's you and I sit here at the table while Wilma and Millie pack."

"Help yourself to the brownies in that pan," Millie said, gesturing toward the other end of the counter. "We'll be back in a few, Ira. *Denki* for helpin' us."

Millie led her grandmother out of the kitchen as quickly as the older woman could walk. While in many ways Mammi was stronger than she had been, spending most of the last few years in bed had weakened her muscles. Millie was glad her clothes were downstairs in the small room Mammi had been using during her extended illness. After they folded her dresses and underthings into a suitcase, Millie urged her to rest while she packed her own belongings.

Mammi's lips twitched. "After I sit for a minute, I'll pick our dresses and what-not out of the clothes hamper. We can wash them tomorrow at Nora's."

Millie had been so wound up from dealing with Dawdi, she hadn't realized why Mammi had had so few dresses to pack. She pulled an old gray duffel from the closet. "Stuff the laundry in this. Dawdi'll rant about us takin' our dirty clothes but not his."

As she hurried upstairs to her room, Millie wondered if her mother had experienced this same sense of desperation when she'd been sent to live with Mammi's sister. This conflict and confrontation was tying her stomach in knots. Millie packed fast, praying her grandfather gave them no further trouble as they left — hoping Ira wasn't bearing the brunt of Dawdi's foul mood.

Denki, Lord, for providin' us a place to stay, and for Nora's determination to love Dawdi even when he's mean to her. Help me to be a gut *daughter. Strong like my mother.*

Millie carried her two suitcases to the waiting rig while Ira ushered Mammi outside, carrying her careworn suitcase and the duffel. It felt odd to ride away from the old farmhouse as though she intended to be gone for a long time. She worried that her grandfather would get sick or hurt himself — perhaps intentionally — to get back at her and Mammi for leaving him.

Millie hated thinking such thoughts about her grandfather. He wasn't the same steadfast man she'd known when she was younger. It seemed his hatred and bitterness had crippled his heart as surely as arthritis had bent his body.

When they got to the big house on Bishop's Ridge Road, Nora held the door so Millie and Ira could carry in the luggage. "Let's put you in this room off the kitchen, Mamma," she said, pointing them in the right direction. "And Millie, I've got a spare room upstairs between my bedroom and my studio. You'll have a view of the river, and you can make it your own space. I'm so glad you're both here!"

Nora's enthusiasm lifted Millie's spirits. It was fun to be staying in this large, airy home filled with her mother's bright colors. When she and Ira got to the upstairs room Nora had described, Millie went to the window. If she looked to the far right, she could see the mill wheel. The rest of her view was filled with wildflowers, trees, and the ripple of the flowing, sun-dappled river.

"I think I'll be just fine here," Millie murmured.

Ira came to stand beside her. "Your *mamm*'ll see to that," he replied. Then he gently turned her to face him. "About my joinin' the Old Order . . . I, um, *meant* it when I said I'd wait for ya, Millie. You're awfully young to commit to the church or to me. I don't want to deprive ya of your *rumspringa* — especially now that you're dealin' with your *dawdi.*"

Millie's heartbeat quickened. He was hinting about marriage someday, without expecting her to reply. "That's sweet of ya, Ira. I'll have time these next several weeks to think things through. But I'm glad ya decided about your faith," she added. "Glad ya went your own way instead of followin' Luke's example just because he's your brother and your business partner."

Ira lowered his mouth to hers for a tender kiss. "We'll be fine, Luke and I. Nothin'll change, far as how the mill's to be run — and if he goes the Mennonite route, it'll be easier to keep some of the power equipment we've set up."

Millie nodded. "It'll all work out," she mused aloud. "And I have a feelin' that *work* is what'll get Mammi and me through Dawdi's shunning. After that, we'll see what God's got waitin' for us. Thanks for helpin' me through today, Ira."

He kissed her again and then smiled. Even with the ridge around his head where his hat had flattened his hair on this warm day,

Ira looked very strong. Very masculine and attractive. "You're welcome, Millie. I'll see ya soon, all right?"

"I'm countin' on it."

CHAPTER TWENTY-ONE

In the wee hours of Wednesday morning, Miriam took a break from rolling out piecrust dough to amble around the Sweet Seasons dining room. The baby was very active — a blessing that made her smile as she wrapped her arms around her growing girth. Andy Leitner had told her it was better to move around every now and again rather than to stand in one spot for so long while she baked, so these little trips between the wooden tables in her café were just what the doctor ordered.

When she reached the front window, however, she frowned. Across the road at the Glick place, every room was lit up. *Again.*

Miriam hugged her little miracle as she considered what to do. She'd taken Gabe some food yesterday afternoon, and he'd seemed grouchy but grateful. Ben had tended the livestock chores and looked in on their aging neighbor at dusk. He'd said Gabe was restless but basically all right. So why had the lights remained on these past three nights since Wilma and Millie had moved to Nora's place?

Miriam had wondered if Gabe was afraid of the dark — yet she thought his penny-pinching ways would've kept him in one illuminated room to save on lamp oil. It was probably difficult for him, being by himself in that house, although he'd done all right when Wilma had been hospitalized in recent years.

"Have the lights been burnin' all day, too, ya think?" she murmured as she swayed with her baby. When nobody else was around, Miriam often conversed with her unborn child because it deepened her connection to the wee one she was so eager to see and to hold. "Let's make a phone call and then get back to work, shall we?"

Miriam strode through the kitchen and out the back door to the white phone shanty. She wouldn't be able to set aside her fears until she'd called in some knowledgeable help.

"*Jah,* Andy, it's Miriam," she said when the clinic's message machine prompted her. "Stop at the café first thing this morning so we can talk about Gabe, will ya? I'll have somethin' fresh for your breakfast whenever ya can get here."

When fifteen fruit pies filled her ovens, Miriam sat on a tall stool to form long logs of dough for cinnamon rolls as she considered the day's menu. Local gardens had overflowed with produce lately, and she'd been happy to pay her sister Leah, her daughter Rachel, and Nazareth Hostetler for the boxes of red and green sweet peppers, onions, and tomatoes that sat on her kitchen floor. She had also cleaned out her deep freeze at home — had brought over remnants of bread loaves, along with stale biscuits and muffins — that would make tasty bread pudding for the breakfast buffet.

"And what if I put crushed pineapple in it today, punkin?" she asked the baby as she arranged thick spirals of dough on baking pans. "Baked pineapple and bread pudding combined, sweet and creamy with milk and eggs —"

When the baby kicked, apparently excited about this suggestion, Miriam laughed. "*Jah,* you're right, honey-bug, the fellas will gobble that concoction right down. I'd better make a couple-three big pans of it."

Two hours later, when Andy knocked on the back screen door, Miriam was drizzling frosting over her pans of warm cinnamon rolls. "Come on in," she called out. "Your timing's perfect. I'm finishin' up these goodies for the bakery case."

As her future son-in-law stepped into the kitchen, he peered into a pot of simmering sausages, gazed at the lineup of pies cooling on her countertop, and shook his head in amazement. "You've made all this stuff *already?*" he asked as he removed his straw hat. "How do you *do* this day in and day out, Miriam?"

Shrugging, she reached for a small plate. "It's always been my purpose to feed people. Cookin' and bakin' is what I know. Here — enjoy your breakfast."

Andy gazed at the fresh confection as though it were a treasure before he began to unwind it. "There's nothing like the smell of cinnamon and the softness of a warm roll. *Wow,*" he murmured after he took his first bite. "So what's this about Gabe? From what I hear, Millie's been to visit him and —"

"*Jah,* Ben and I have been lookin' in on him, too," Miriam remarked as she continued working. "But every room in his house has been lit up since Wilma left. That doesn't set right with me. Gabe's so tight, he won't turn on his furnace in the winter until his windows frost over."

Stuffing another bite of roll into his mouth, Andy went into the dining room to peer across the county highway. "I see what you mean," he remarked as he returned to the kitchen. "So tell me this about Gabe. Has he always been such a surly man, or has this moodiness come over him just recently? I was shocked at the way he talked back to Bishop Tom on Sunday."

"*Jah,* retired preachers don't act that way, even when they've got a bone to pick," Miriam confirmed. "Gabe's always been hard-headed, but this business about refusin' to forgive Nora has me worried. Maybe it's guilt eatin' away at him, in spite of —"

"And maybe there's a physical imbalance at work, too," Andy mused. "I'll take my medical bag and check him over. While I understood Wilma's reason for getting out of the house, I figured something like this might arise once Gabe was left on his own."

"*Denki* for understandin'. We've seen enough drama of late, without havin' something happen to Gabe," Miriam replied. She reached for a white paper sack. "Take him a couple of these rolls — and let me know what's goin' on after you've looked him over, all right?"

"Will do. And by the way," he added with

a boyish grin. "Rhoda and I have set the wedding for Thursday, September twenty-fifth. You're the first to know."

"Congratulations! I'm so happy for the two of ya," Miriam said gleefully. "And by then Rachel should be recovered from birthin' her wee one, too."

"The baby and God already have their calendars marked, so we'll go along with whatever they've decided," Andy teased as he put his hat on again. "It'll all work out."

"*Jah,* it always does."

"And meanwhile, you should be putting your feet up every chance you get, Miriam." He gazed at her with the no-nonsense expression she'd seen a lot during her recent appointments with Andy. "We don't want the mother of the bride sidelined with complications on our wedding day. You should be hiring some extra help, so you'll be covered when your due date arrives in December. Right?"

"*Jah, jah,* I've been thinkin' on that," Miriam murmured as she frosted the last of her rolls. "You and Ben are fussin' over me like I'm some helpless girl who's got no clue about childbirth. I figure havin' triplets gives me more experience than either one of you fellas has had."

"Just advising my favorite patient," Andy

teased as he went to the door. "I wouldn't pester you if I didn't love you, Miriam."

As the screen door closed, Miriam's heart swelled. She was a blessed woman to be welcoming such a compassionate man into her family. Her Rhoda couldn't possibly have found a better match, even from among longtime members of the Amish faith.

She sent up a prayer on Gabe's behalf and then went on about her cooking. The bread pudding filled the kitchen with the heavenly sweet aroma of pineapple, and the Italian sausages scented the air with their spicy perfume, as well. Miriam sautéed fresh onions, bell peppers, and tomatoes for a rich red sauce to add to the meat.

She sang to the baby while she worked, as happy as a woman could possibly be. She was giving Naomi and her daughter Hannah a good start on the day's lunch offerings — and when they arrived in about half an hour, she'd think about getting off her feet for a while. Maybe.

As Nora gazed through her binoculars, her insides tightened. From her second-story bedroom window she was watching Andy Leitner's horse-drawn clinic wagon roll up the lane to Dat and Mamma's house. While she, Mamma, and Millie had noticed that every room in the place had been lit up for the past few nights, Mamma was adamant about not checking on Dat after Millie reported that he was getting by. Nora sensed she'd better waken the two of them anyway.

She slipped into the adjacent bedroom, savoring the sight of her sleeping daughter's face. "Millie," Nora whispered as she leaned close to the bed. "Millie, we should get up."

"Mmm?"

"*Jah,* come on, sweetie," Nora insisted. "Andy Leitner's over at Dawdi's. We need to be ready if he goes to the hospital."

Millie's eyes flew open then. "Dawdi's sick?"

"Maybe my hunch is a false alarm," Nora said as Millie swung her feet to the floor. "Maybe I'm a worrywart."

"Mammi thinks he's out of his head, burnin' all the lights," the girl countered as she took a fresh dress from the closet.

"I'll wake her and keep an eye out over there. Can you pack us something that'll be easy to eat?" Nora asked. "If Andy takes Dawdi in for medical care, we might not get home for a while."

Millie frowned as she twisted her long hair into a bun. "What about the gals who're comin' today to get your store ready for its grand opening?"

"We'll change the cleaning frolic to another time — if we need to," Nora added. "I could be jumping to all sorts of conclusions."

"Same ones I've jumped to," Millie remarked. "Dawdi's not been himself for a long while, and Mammi and I probably tipped him over the edge when we left. But I sure hope not."

On the way downstairs to rouse her mother, Nora stepped back into her room to peer out the front window again. Andy's wagon was still parked in front of Dat's house —

But Andy's coming down its ramp with a gurney. That can only mean one thing.

When Nora hurried down the stairs and into her mother's room, she was relieved to see that Mamma was out of bed and groping into her clothes. "You all right, Mamma? I was just ready to —"

"Heard ya walkin' around upstairs, talkin' to Millie," she said in a worried voice. "If something happens to your *dat* because I walked out on him, I'll —"

"Let's not go down that road," Nora interrupted emphatically. "Andy can handle whatever's going on, and he'll let us know about it."

Nora went back up to slip into her own cape dress and *kapp,* watching out her bedroom window as she dressed. By the time she'd scribbled a note to the ladies who were coming to help her clean, the lights at Dat's were blinking out room by room, as if each window was an eye closing in sleep. Andy would've called an ambulance if he'd found her father in serious condition, so Nora took comfort from the methodical way the local nurse was preparing to leave the house.

When Nora got downstairs, Mamma and Millie were in the kitchen tucking some snacks into a canvas tote bag. She was pleased that they had made themselves at home here so quickly, and grateful to be getting reacquainted with them at long last. It seemed they'd gone through one crisis after another since she'd come back to Willow Ridge, yet Nora believed they were stronger as a team than any one of them could be separately while this situation with Dat unfolded.

"I'm going to tape this note to the shop door," she said, waving her paper. "Be back in a few."

"We'll start walkin' that way, in case Andy needs anything done at the house," Mamma replied. "Awful nice of him to look in on

Gabe — it truly is."

The August morning already felt dense with humidity, promising a scorcher of a day by noon. Nora taped her note to the barn door with a sigh. She'd been looking forward to the cleaning frolic, gratified that so many ladies had volunteered to help her prepare for the opening of Simple Gifts — but Dat's health was a higher priority, even if her shop wouldn't be in perfect condition when her merchandise started arriving. As she joined her *mamm* and daughter at the end of the lane, Andy's horse-drawn wagon was rumbling toward them on Bishop's Ridge Road.

"Why am I not surprised to see you ladies here?" he asked as he stepped out of his unique vehicle.

Nora took heart from Andy's composure, his easygoing smile as he greeted them. "So — what can you tell us about our patient?" she asked. "I've been watching ever since your wagon pulled up at the house."

"No secrets in Willow Ridge," the nurse replied with a chuckle. "A visit to the emergency room is the best way to keep him under observation while we get him hydrated again and get some oxygen to his brain."

"Never did drink enough water," Mamm

muttered.

Andy nodded. "I also suspect he's suffering from sleep deprivation. He was, um, seeing mice scamper across the ceiling while I checked his vital signs."

Millie's eyes widened. "He's not been sleepin' through the night for a long while — at least since I've been helpin' with Mammi," she remarked. "He falls asleep in the middle of a sentence sometimes —"

"That's a common symptom," Andy remarked.

"— and jerks awake after wee little naps," the girl continued earnestly. "But he denies doin' that, of course. He didn't realize I could hear him rummagin' around in his room at night."

"Here's our chance to fix those things," Nora said. "Shall I follow you in my van, Andy?"

"Or can we ride with Dawdi — if it won't confuse him?" Millie added. Her expression suggested she was eager to see inside Andy's wagon yet apprehensive about her grandfather's condition.

"Might be a *gut* idea if he has some company," Andy replied with a nod. "I gave him a light sedative when I hooked up his IV, but if he decides to yank it out while

I'm driving, you'll be there to hold his hands."

"But if he's snoozin', we're gonna let sleepin' dogs lie," Mamma insisted. "If Gabe's seein' mice, there's no tellin' what he'll think if the three of us show up all at once, like we're gangin' up on him."

"Excellent point," Andy said as he opened the driver's door a little wider. "You can sit in the built-in seats where I usually draw blood or consult with patients. When we get to the hospital, I'll let you check him in at the admissions desk. I think he ought to stay at least overnight for observation."

After Andy helped her mother step up into the wagon, Nora preceded her daughter into the most interesting rig she'd ever seen. It looked like a very basic examination room, with cabinets and medical instruments along the walls above the cushioned seats Andy had mentioned. Colorful posters presented inside views of the body's major organs and a fetus growing inside its mother. Most of the space was filled with the gurney, where Dat lay with a little hose up his nose and a bag of clear fluid hanging on a pole beside him.

He looks so old and fragile beneath the sheet, Nora fretted as she gazed at him. He was dozing, so she lifted a finger to her lips to suggest silence.

Mamma and Millie nodded. They quickly took seats, as though they, too, were struck by how Gabriel Glick, the preacher who'd railed about their sinful disrespect on Sunday, seemed to have drifted beyond his earthly ability to communicate. Andy clucked to his Belgian and the wagon rolled into motion. It seemed almost like a wake, with nothing to look at except her frightfully quiet father, so Nora was relieved when they pulled into the entrance of the hospital in New Haven about twenty minutes later.

Nora couldn't miss the surprised expressions on the faces of the people who watched them emerge from Andy's unique horse-drawn wagon. Once they were inside the hospital, however, several of the personnel wearing scrubs greeted Andy as though they knew him well.

"You ladies finish checking him in," Andy advised, gesturing toward the admissions desk, "while I wheel him into an exam room. I phoned ahead so they'd know we were coming," he explained.

Once again Nora was grateful that a skilled medical professional had settled in Willow Ridge. The admissions clerk already had her father's file in the computer and only needed some information that Andy hadn't been sure about.

"Mr. Leitner requested one of the rooms in our unit for Plain patients," she said as her fingers danced on the computer keys. "He was pretty sure Mr. Glick has no insurance —"

"*Jah,* that's correct," Mamma spoke up.

"— so whose name shall I list as the contact person, where the bills will be mailed?" the clerk continued in a business-like voice.

"That'll be me, Nora Landwehr. His daughter." She had no idea how she would pay her Dat's medical expenses, but she doubted her parents had enough savings to cover this visit either. "Number one, Bishop's Ridge Road in Willow Ridge," she finished.

As she, Millie, and Mamma took chairs in the waiting area, Nora realized how she had taken insurance for granted while she'd been living English. She'd purchased the required homeowner's policy when she'd bought Hiram's house, just as she'd continued her auto policy when she'd gotten the van — but she hadn't been Plain when she'd acquired those items. She hadn't considered what she'd be risking when she opened her new business . . . a big barn filled with other people's original handmade items. What if the store caught fire? What if a storm took off the roof and rain ruined her merchandise? How would she possibly reimburse the clients who were consigning their items in all good faith that they'd be paid for?

In all good faith. As Nora tried not to nip her lip, these words echoed in her mind as though Vernon Gingerich had spoken them. Good faith was the core belief, the very essence of Plain living, in sunshine and in shadow. Families and neighbors looked after their own — but what about those who weren't members of the church district? How would she fare among the Old Order Amish of Willow Ridge if she joined the Mennonite fellowship near Morning Star and then lost her proverbial shirt?

Maybe Hiram made a good point, telling me I should have more backing from a bank.

Andy Leitner's smile lifted her clouds of doubt as he pulled a chair over to confer with them. "Gabe's resting in his room now that the doctor's checked him over," he reported. "You can peek in on him now, or you can come back with me when I do my rounds this evening. I strongly suggest you go home and let him rest —"

"So's we don't get him riled up and undo the *gut* you've done for him," Mamma

335

remarked. "I'm for that."

"He'll feel better after the IV and the oxygen have had a chance to work, too." Nora smiled gratefully at Andy. "So you come here to do rounds, just like a doctor? That's pretty special."

He shrugged, grinning. "My whole setup's special, thanks to Bishop Tom allowing me some extra telephone and electrical privileges," he replied. "You might not know this, but last winter when I was getting established in Willow Ridge, Miriam and Ben asked the folks at their wedding to donate to my new clinic in lieu of giving them gifts. They ran an ad in *The Budget* asking for donations, too, so nearly all of my building renovations and my wagon were paid off within a few weeks. It was the first time I'd witnessed Amish generosity in action, and it made a believer of me."

"Wow," Nora murmured. "Your story just sent goose bumps up my arms. That's incredible."

"Yes, to me as an outsider peering in, it seemed Miriam and Ben had put a miracle in motion. I was amazed that everyone in the community had placed their health and welfare in my hands with unshakable faith," he said. "So checking on your *dat* — or on whoever winds up in the hospital — is a very small way for me to pay back their enormous trust in me."

"We're glad God sent ya our way," Mamma said as she rose stiffly from her chair. "Shall we head home? You've got plenty to do besides hangin' around with us."

Once Andy had rolled his gurney into the wagon and collapsed it, they took off for Willow Ridge. The ride back was more relaxed, as they talked about Andy and Rhoda's upcoming wedding, as well as the possibility that Seth Brenneman and Mary Kauffman might soon tie the knot.

"That's the young widow who's livin' in the new house that Seth's built between the Lantz place and the Brennemans'," Mamma explained to Nora. "What with so many young folks gettin' hitched and new houses goin' up, our little town's changin' a lot."

"Mary's kids, Annie Mae Wagler's little brothers and sister, and my two were in the live Nativity we put on Christmas Eve," Andy remarked as he drove. "*That* was a first! We had one of Tom's cows, and the Kauffmans' miniature pony, a couple of Dan Kanagy's sheep —"

"And folks from miles around came to see it, too," Millie added. She passed around the oatmeal cookies and brownies she'd packed, which she'd originally made to serve during the cleaning frolic. Andy handed Nora a white bag from the bakery.

"No sense in letting these fabulous cinnamon rolls get stale," he said. "But I'll warn you — they're messy!"

Nora discovered the truth of that as she unwound the outer layer of a roll and had to quickly lick the melted frosting from her hand to keep it from dripping on her dress. Millie leaned close with a napkin, and then they all started giggling. It was good to relax now that they knew Dat was being cared for.

But Nora gaped at an even sweeter surprise than Miriam's roll as they pulled into her driveway. Several rigs were parked alongside the barn, where the door was propped open. A handful of women were stepping outside to drop wet, dirty rags in the grass. What a sight, when Mary and Eva Schrock waved at the wagon and then called into the building. By the time Andy halted the Belgian, more than a dozen women were hurrying toward them with anxious faces. Little kids darted outside, eager to run off some energy.

"Is Gabe gonna be okay?"

"When we saw ya takin' off in that wagon —"

"Oh, but it's *gut* to see the three of you gals with smiles on your faces!"

"— we figured to go on with the cleanin' frolic so's your store would be tidy for your big openin' day." Mary's voice carried above the rest of the excited chatter.

Nora could only stand there gazing at their relieved faces, which were flushed from scrubbing. She let Mamma announce the basic details of their trip as everyone listened earnestly. Along with the Schrocks, she saw Annie Mae, Rachel, Miriam's sister Leah Kanagy, and a young woman she'd seen in the yard after church Sunday but hadn't yet met. A few ladies from the Mennonite church in Morning Star had come, as well. Then Lizzie stepped outside to empty her buckets of scrub water before coming over to join them.

Gobsmacked didn't begin to describe the way Nora felt. Despite the midday heat and humidity, and despite her absence, these generous women had spent their morning scrubbing *her* store, out of the goodness of their hearts. Nora realized she'd unintentionally left the door unlocked, yet the compassion on these friends' faces told her they would've been disappointed had they not been able to help her while she was tending to her Dat. How amazing was that?

Nothing like this would've happened while you were living English.

It was a humbling thought, a reminder that humility was a hallmark of these gentle women — an attribute to which she should aspire as she became one of them. "Please! Come to the house and we'll take a lunch break," Nora insisted above the chatter. "Millie and I made fresh lemonade and sandwiches and cookies —"

"And we all brought food to share!"

"Oh, I've been waitin' to see your house, Nora!"

"We made a lot of progress this mornin', so it'll be *gut* to take a load off, *jah.*"

As their excited chatter swirled around her, Nora felt inexplicably happy. These women were her new friends, and they seemed eager to share their lives and get better acquainted. Maybe it was the worrisome morning she'd spent, but Nora felt a sudden surge of emotion rush through her.

The ladies fetched their pans and coolers from their rigs, and then Mary Schrock and Mamma led everyone toward the house. Millie was walking arm in arm with Annie Mae, while Lizzie was chatting with Leah Kanagy as little Ella rode her hip. The gathering felt like a picnic instead of a hot, sultry day during which her friends had worked until their dresses were sweaty. But then, that's why Plain women called such events *frolics*. Frolics were the time-honored way to turn hard work into a day of visiting and fun.

When Nora spotted Rachel Brenneman clutching her back and swaying with the weight of her unborn child, she hurried over. "Please tell me *you* haven't been scrubbing floors or climbing ladders or —"

Rachel laughed. "Not me, Nora! I've been keepin' the kids out of the way so their *mamms* could do all that heavy-duty stuff."

"Even so, you've had quite a job," Nora replied as they slowed their pace. "Who *are* all these kids?"

Rachel pointed to each cluster in turn. "Those two are Andy's — soon to be Rhoda's, ya know. Taylor and Brett, they are, and they'll be goin' to the schoolhouse with the Amish kids when classes start in a couple weeks," she replied. "And that pair, Lucy and Sol, belong to Mary Kauffman, the gal Seth Brenneman's gonna marry. And then there's Annie Mae's younger sibs — Josh and Joey are the twins, and Timmy and Sara are followin' along with Annie Mae."

Rachel's eyebrows rose expressively. "I shooed all of them inside earlier, when I caught sight of Hiram's big black car," she murmured. "He kept on drivin', though, so I think we'll be all right now."

Nora frowned. "What do you mean, *all right*?"

"Oh, ever since Annie Mae brought the little Knepp kids back from Higher Ground — after she'd seen Hiram's um, *girlfriend,* chasin' them with a paddle — we've been watchful," Rachel replied matter-of-factly. "There's just no tellin' what meanness Hiram might think of next, after the way he whacked off Annie Mae's hair a while back."

"*Jah,* Bishop Tom told me about that," she murmured. "Ira says Hiram's girlfriend has left him now —"

"She got smart, then," Rachel replied with a huff. "She wasn't much older than Annie Mae, ya know. What a *mess* that man's made, meddlin' in so many lives."

As they entered the house, Nora considered what Rachel had said about watching over the younger Knepp kids — about their father wreaking such emotional havoc. *Words to the wise,* she reminded herself. But with her houseful of guests, she had much more pleasant matters to oversee.

Her mother and the Schrocks were getting out paper plates and utensils while Lizzie and the other women set out the food. Millie filled pitchers with cold, fresh lemonade, and Annie Mae steered the kids toward the bathroom to wash their hands.

During her years away from Willow Ridge, Nora had forgotten how Plain women worked so effortlessly as a team, no matter whose home they were in. For the first time since she'd bought this house, she was glad the kitchen was so large and open, with so much counter space. Many of these women had much smaller areas for entertaining, yet she sensed any one of them would've held this lunch break at her own home, because hostessing came as second nature to them.

Note to self: invite these women over to have some fun! They're your neighbors and they want to be your friends.

Once the ladies began to fill their plates, Annie Mae brought over a pretty young brunette who was holding an alert baby on her shoulder. "I just realized ya don't yet know Mary Kauffman," she said to Nora. "And this is her little Emmanuel, who was the star of our live Nativity last Christmas Eve."

"I heard about that this morning," Nora replied, grinning as the baby gripped the finger she offered him. "It sounds like you've made yourself very much at home here in Willow Ridge, Mary."

"*Jah,* it was God's own hand that got me

to town in time for Seth — and nurse Andy — to deliver my son," she replied. "Had Aunt Miriam not kept the kids and me at her place over the winter, I don't know what we'd have done after my husband died."

Once again Nora was struck by the compassion that flourished here, grateful that she, too, was being enveloped in the love of the locals. "It was Miriam who alerted Andy to check on my *dat* this morning," she remarked. "We really need to throw that woman a party before her baby comes."

"*Jah,* for sure we do! What a fine idea." Mary's eyes sparkled as she gazed directly at Nora. "Would you have room in your new store for some Amish dolls? I've mostly been a quilter, but with moving into the new house — and getting married soon — I'm thinking to sew some projects that don't take so long. It'll be a way to bring in a little cash while I'm looking after my family."

"Amish dolls!" Nora exclaimed. "Those would be a perfect addition to my merchandise!"

Mary lit up like a girl who'd won a prize at a party. "I'll sew some as soon as I can, then! *Denki* so much!"

As Nora steered the two younger women toward the serving line, she marveled again at the industrious ways of Plain women.

They kept up with their housework, raised their kids, and were helpmates to their husbands, yet they looked for ways to make some money in their spare time — whenever *that* was. It made her feel like a slacker in comparison.

But now that you've found your way, look how far you can go! And you can take these friends along for the ride, selling their crafts in your store.

Nora sighed with a sense of great satisfaction as she picked up a paper plate. Everything seemed to be falling into place now, in ways she'd never imagined when she'd decided to move here. Was it her imagination, or had God been paying closer attention to her since she'd come back home?

Chapter Twenty-Two

As his Friday afternoon was winding down, Luke looked at his refrigerated display case and wished he knew of someone — probably female, with a good eye — who could arrange the mill's displays better than he and Ira did. With another weekend almost upon him, however, he didn't have the luxury of wishing for what he didn't have. He stacked the small containers of goat cheese and butter as tightly as he could. Then he replenished the cartons of cage-free chicken eggs and closed the glass door.

It would have to do. He had to restock the shelves with bags of coarse-ground corn grits, multi-grain baking mixes, and rolled oats before he could quit for the day.

"Quite the place you've got here, Hooley. How's business?"

Luke straightened slowly to his full height, quelling the urge to glare at Hiram Knepp. He had *not* heard the bell on the shop door, so he suspected Knepp had slithered in through the milling room — which probably meant he'd been snooping around before he'd entered the store. Ira was out fetching more eggs and taking checks to their suppliers, so there was no telling how long his uninvited guest had been here.

"Doing fine, thanks," Luke hedged as he moved toward the dry goods shelves. "What can I help you with?"

Hiram shrugged noncommittally. "Thought I'd drop by to see if your store measures up to the rave reviews from some of my Higher Ground flock. Your good-looking neighbor can't say enough about the traffic you've been getting since your grand opening."

"Nora?" Luke asked. Then he kicked himself for taking Hiram's bait. He sensed the banished bishop was fishing rather than shopping, because he doubted Nora would discuss his customers — or anything else — with Knepp, after her encounter with him in the diner.

"Nature girl Nora," Hiram mused aloud in a suggestive, faraway voice. "Nora *au naturel*. But then, you *know* she doesn't wear anything under those innocent-looking Plain-style dresses — which actually gives a man a lot more to think about than how she used to pour herself into her English clothes."

Luke pressed his lips into a tight line. If he responded, it would imply that he did indeed know what wasn't under Nora's dresses. And if he said nothing, Knepp would carry on about how he'd gotten way beyond first base with her while Luke had not. "You're out of line," Luke muttered. "And why are you telling *me* this stuff?"

"Because you need to know that the redhead next door now has a silent partner," Hiram replied without missing a beat. His dark eyes glimmered. "Nora realized her business was seriously underfunded, so rather than risk a shortfall before she even opened her doors, she . . . opened to me," he explained with a rakish shrug. "I've bought back the barn, which reduces her overhead to nothing and gives her a cash cushion —"

"This is nonsense," Luke countered with a glare. "Maybe you ought to move along so I can get some work done."

Hiram's knowing laughter echoed beneath the high, beamed ceiling. "Consider yourself warned, Hooley," he stated as he went to the door. "My partnership comes with certain perks — which means you're out of the picture now, as far as Nora's concerned.

She didn't want to tell you herself, knowing you'd be upset, so I've saved you a nasty confrontation and a whole lot of humiliation, right? You know how feisty she gets when she's . . . up against a wall."

The jangle of the bell intensified Luke's rising fury. Although he suspected Hiram was full of manure, spouting lies about Nora and her financial affairs, the foul odor of his story was more than Luke could stand. Just the hint about Nora not wearing under-things had sent his imagination into over-drive, his jealousy into high gear. All he'd seen of Nora this week was her black van coming and going as she prepared to open her shop — and because consigning dozens of different items from so many clients required a lot of time, he hadn't bothered her. Luke had hoped to catch her this evening, to offer her dinner out and some time off they both surely needed.

But his attitude was changing. There were things a man just had to know, questions he had to ask, to be sure a woman wasn't play-ing him false.

Luke looked out the back window of the milling room. Nora's van was parked behind her barn — or was it Hiram's barn again? He didn't want to believe Nora had given such a snake the time of day, much less her physical affection — but maybe she hadn't had any say about it. Maybe Hiram had sniffed out her money problems and used them as leverage to get whatever he wanted from her. The excommunicated bishop had a talent for basing his lies on just enough truth to trip up the most rational observer. Luke decided to straighten out this story once and for all. *Right now.*

As he strode across the lot between the mill and the big red barn behind Nora's house, Luke reminded himself not to jump to assumptions — not to force Nora's hand if she'd been caught between Hiram and a hard place. But he had to know. Even if she didn't utter a word, the truth would be written all over her fresh, freckled face at the mention of Knepp's name.

The door to her shop was propped open, so he walked in.

A lemony freshness lingered in the air and ceiling fans stirred the late afternoon stillness. A wide wooden stairway now led up to the loft, where a sturdy railing doubled as a rack for hangings. Nora had already hung several of her unique banners, and she was up there fastening the edge of a large quilt, which served as the central focus of the display.

"Luke!" she called out cheerfully. "I was

hoping to see you — to maybe do something tonight. And here you are!"

Without a word Luke bounded up the stairway, his boots making enough racket to fill the barn. It seemed like the perfect sound effect — like a hammer hitting a nail — considering what he had to say to this woman, who was acting as though nothing had happened between her and Hiram. Nora was wearing that bright red, pink, and orange checked dress he liked, but she'd removed the cape and had shoved the sleeves up her arms — probably because she was hot.

Hot *doesn't begin to cover it,* he thought as he imagined what she wasn't wearing beneath her calf-length dress. "Yeah, I had some ideas about dinner out tonight, but then I heard some interesting tidbits —" He grabbed Nora by the shoulders. "Hiram tells me you and —"

"Well, *that* should tip you off," she protested, wide-eyed.

"— he are partners now," Luke continued in a harsh voice. "I was going to ask about renting your pastureland for more of my grain crops — which would mean a very nice income for you. But maybe the land isn't yours to rent anymore, eh?"

Nora scowled, struggling to break free

from his grasp. "What on earth are you talking about?"

"And maybe the barn is Hiram's, too — not to mention certain *perks*," Luke blurted. His pulse was pounding so loudly he could hardly hear what he was saying. Nora smelled so fresh, looked so young and vulnerable, that if he found out she'd gotten intimate with Knepp, he didn't know how he would keep his hands off her.

"After the way he cornered me at the — do you *really* believe I'd —"

"He tells me you don't wear underwear, Nora. How would he know that?"

Somehow Nora wrenched herself away from him. Before Luke saw it coming, she slapped his face so hard he staggered backwards.

"Get out! I don't have to listen to this!" she cried. "I thought you were different from other guys, but *no* — you're a horse's rear end just like all the rest of them." She burst into tears. Then she started backing away from him as though he'd scared the daylights out of her. "Get moving — before I call the sheriff," she added in a quivering voice.

The throbbing in Luke's cheek brought him back into focus. He gingerly rubbed his face, amazed at the power Nora's slap had packed — and aware that she'd knocked some sense into him. But it was too little too late.

He'd been the world's biggest fool.

He'd accused her falsely. He'd made her cry. He'd insulted her. Worst of all, he'd probably lost her. After what he'd just insinuated about her and Hiram, why would Nora ever want anything more to do with him?

"I — I'm sorry," Luke rasped.

"Yes, you are — a sorry excuse for a friend," she hurled at him as she pointed at the door. "Out! *Now.*"

Luke knew better than to protest or plead his case. He went down the staircase a lot slower than he'd gone up it, and when he reached the door, he left without looking back at her. The sound of her sobbing followed him outside.

Stupid, stupid, stupid. Hiram set you up and you fell for it. Kiss her good-bye, idiot.

Nora wasted no time locking the shop door. Then she plunked down on the bottom step of the stairway and tried to figure out what had just happened. She'd been riding high as her displays fell into place, tagging a few last pieces before she'd figured on calling Luke to go someplace for supper. Mamma and Millie had moved back to the house when Dat came home from the hospital, so she was on her own again.

But *no.* Hiram had obviously spun a juicy tale or two, and Luke had gotten caught in his web.

She held her face in her hands. If she recalled those fast-flying moments of their argument correctly, Luke believed that Hiram had reclaimed the barn and maybe the pastureland. As part of the exchange, the ex-bishop had apparently received some sexual favors and a very intimate knowledge of her dressing habits. Had Nora not been so upset, she would've laughed out loud at such outrageous insinuations.

But Luke had believed them. Luke had lost all sense of perspective, and most likely he'd come here immediately following Hiram's tale-telling.

Nora could easily imagine the ex-bishop sitting in his classic Cadillac somewhere nearby, watching Luke storm over here and then watching him slink away. After Rachel had told her how everyone went on alert whenever they spotted Hiram's distinctive car, Nora sensed she needed to take the same precautions. If the ex-bishop's live-in lover had left him, he was on the prowl for another one.

Hiram probably figures that with Luke out of my life, I'd welcome him. He'll try to entice me with the financial assistance he's already told Luke about, because he knows I'm . . . vulnerable. Uninsured and underfunded.

There was a time when Nora would've kept this situation under her *kapp,* too embarrassed to admit the fix she was in — or foolish enough to believe she could outfox Hiram. But today's incident took her back to another barn that had belonged to another bishop who'd counted on her humiliation keeping her quiet.

Never again, Nora vowed as she rose from the wooden step. She went into the restroom and splashed cool water on her face, considering what she should do. Then she turned off the fans and the lights and locked the store before hopping into her van. With any luck, she wouldn't find too many folks in the clinic at this time on a Friday afternoon.

Nora was surprised to see Andy manning the front desk when she entered the empty waiting room. "Wrapping up another busy week?" she asked in the most chipper voice she could muster.

"And I get the evening off for *gut* behavior," he replied happily. "I'm really pleased with how well your *dat*'s doing with his new CPAP machine. We strapped the mask over his nose, turned on the air flow, and he fell asleep within minutes. Once he got some rest and oxygen and fluids in the hospital, he was a model patient."

"Happy to hear it," Nora replied. "Mamma and Millie felt a lot better about going home when they saw such an improvement in his mood. Who knows how many years he'd been suffering from sleep apnea, what with Mamma being the sick one for so long?"

"I'm glad it was such a simple fix. Atlee's already rigged up an adapter so Gabe can run his machine on a car battery." Andy smiled kindly at her. "We'll hope that this improvement in your father's health will result in improved relations with his family, as well."

"*Denki* for saying that," Nora whispered. "Our prayers will be answered, I believe." She took a deep breath, willing herself not to backslide into the emotional turmoil she'd driven away from a few moments ago. "Where might I catch Rebecca? Has she gone back to her apartment already?"

"Nope, she's upstairs in her office." Andy swiveled in his chair and tapped a button on the desk console. "Rebecca, can Nora come up for a visit?" he said into a speaker.

"Sure!" came her immediate answer. "I'm working on her website as we speak."

There was an elevator in the waiting room, but Nora chose the stairs. She composed her thoughts, prayed a little, and by the time she stepped into the upstairs hallway, she felt confident enough to discuss her situation without getting overly emotional. She saw no need to mention Luke's name or to take the chance that their spat would become the topic of conversation at the Sweet Seasons.

"Nora! What do you think?" Rebecca said as she gestured to the large screen of her computer monitor. "Look everything over to be sure I've got the details right. Your visit has saved me calling you about this."

Nora's mood improved immediately as she gazed at the home page header, where her quilted black cows welcomed visitors to the Simple Gifts website. She clicked on the various links, skimming the text on each page. "This looks so cool," she murmured gratefully. "The photos of the quilts and Matthias's horse collars really give a feel for the whole store."

"Anytime you want to update those with shots of new merchandise, it won't take me but a few snaps of a camera and a few clicks of the mouse," Rebecca said. "Is your grand opening information correct?"

Nora returned to the home page and then nodded. "I really like the way you used Ben's design from my outdoor sign to co-ordinate everything. I think he's going to mount it on the barn soon."

"This is so exciting," Rebecca said, glee-fully patting Nora's wrist. "If you'd like my help that Saturday, I can probably be there in the afternoon. I bet you'll have a lot of business that day."

Nora kept gazing at her lovely website, gathering strength for the favor she wanted to ask. "What I could really use is some advice," she murmured. "I just heard some startling insinuations that make me think Hiram wants to worm his way into my busi-ness. He, um, has guessed that I'm a little short on cash flow —"

"And he's a genius at manipulating such situations to his own advantage." Rebecca's tone suggested that the mention of Knepp's name had put a bad taste in her mouth. "You've probably heard how he tried to take over Mamma's café, and how my English dad prevented that from happening by becoming her landlord."

"It'll probably take something that radical to keep Hiram out of my hair, too," Nora said with a sigh. "But I hate to ask a total stranger to —"

"No, no, don't look at it that way," Rebecca insisted as she grabbed Nora's hand. "I've told Dad about the store you're opening. He's predicted you'll draw so much more tourist traffic to Willow Ridge that Miriam might need to consider enlarging the Sweet Seasons."

Nora's eyes widened. "Well, I like the sound of that, but I still hesitate to —"

"Dad *loves* this little town," Rebecca interrupted earnestly. "He partners with Derek Shotwell, the banker in New Haven. I think both of them would have an interest in keeping Simple Gifts financially secure. A lot of families here bank with Derek, so both men are dedicated to seeing that Willow Ridge doesn't go down the primrose path the way Higher Ground and Hiram's other undertakings have. Just a second."

Rebecca grabbed her phone and hit a speed dial button. "Dad, hi!" she said. "What's up for supper tonight? Nora Landwehr — the gal who's opening the consignment shop? — has an interesting business situation you might want to consider. Can you join us?"

When Rebecca raised her eyebrows, silently asking if Nora was *in,* Nora nodded quickly. Rebecca winked at her as she chatted with her dad for a few moments more.

Who knew? Nora mused. In the blink of an eye, she was making a connection she wouldn't have attempted alone. The New Haven banker's involvement eased her mind, too — although she doubted Rebecca's father would be difficult to deal with. Miriam seemed totally independent, as far as the way she handled her business. That's what Nora wanted, too.

"Awesome! We'll see you at the pizza place in New Haven in half an hour . . . love you, too, Dad." Rebecca clicked her phone off. "Let's see what he says, Nora. I hope I didn't just rearrange your Friday night."

Nora laughed, letting out the breath she'd been holding. "You're *amazing,* Rebecca. How can I ever repay the favor you've just done me?"

"Oh, I'm not promising that my dad will help you," she said as she cleared her desk. "But he'll listen to your concerns. He'll have ideas about how to keep Hiram's paws off you and your store."

Nora nodded, deeply relieved — even though her fight with Luke had merely *suggested* things Hiram might try. But forewarned was forearmed. She was still upset at Luke for jumping to conclusions about her relationship with the devious ex-bishop, but maybe he'd handed her the key to remaining her own woman. It was a gift she'd thank Luke for — one of these days when the red haze of misunderstanding between them had dissipated.

That evening as Nora prepared for bed, she felt a new sense of hope. Rebecca's dad, Bob Oliveri, was a middle-aged fellow with a business sense she truly admired. He was going to talk with Derek Shotwell about setting up business insurance for her store, with provisions for backup funding if ever she needed it. He'd seemed genuinely happy to help her thwart Hiram before the bishop could undermine her financial security.

"Hiram can spot a tiny hole beside your fence and burrow into your life before you realize it — and before you realize he has no real power to control you," Bob had said. "The bank's backing, and my involvement with your store, are as much about your peace of mind as your financial security, Nora."

As she slipped between the sheets, Nora gave thanks for the new friend she'd made over a pizza. Bob was right: Hiram had power only because vulnerable women

believed he did. Bob had no interest in owning her barn or getting involved in the day-
to-day operation of her store. He was simply
investing in her success and in the future of
Willow Ridge. Nora believed in him. His
smile and firm handshake had assured her
that he was as gratified by this transaction
as she was.

Here's another gift You've given me, Lord,
Nora prayed as she settled into the mattress. *Your hand has been leading me all
along, and it's time I said yes to Your call. I'll
speak to the preacher Sunday about being
baptized into Your fellowship of believers.
Denki for Your patience while I figured all this
out.*

CHAPTER TWENTY-THREE

When Nora pulled into her driveway Sunday after noon, her head buzzed with the discussion she'd had with Preacher Stephen Zimmerman while her heart still sang the hymns from the church service. She entered the kitchen and kicked off her shoes, delighting in the coolness of the linoleum floor as it seeped into her bare feet. She felt ravenous yet too excited to eat.

There was no backing out. She was to be baptized next Sunday!

Nora leaned into the open fridge, grasping a pitcher of lemonade as she searched for something quick to eat —

Was that a knock at the front door?

Nora went to answer it and nearly dropped her pitcher. On her front porch stood her father and mother, Millie, and Lizzie and Atlee. "Um — come on in!" she stammered as she unhooked the screen. "I just got home from church. Wasn't expecting company."

Millie stepped inside with a lidded rectangular pan. "This is a visiting Sunday for us —"

"And we've had quite a lot to visit about," Lizzie chimed in as she carried little Ella in her padded basket.

"*Jah*, can't recall the last time all of us sat around the dinner table together," Mamma remarked happily. She handed Nora a platter of brownies covered with waxed paper. "We're hopin' you'll join us for supper tonight, Nora, so it'll truly be *all* of us together."

Nora's heart stood still. Did she dare believe she'd be *welcome* at her parents' table? The brownies smelled *sooo* good. Her stomach rumbled loudly.

"We've got a big watermelon chillin' in a dishpan of ice, and Bishop Tom said he'd bring the ice cream." Millie sighed with pleasure as she gazed around the front room. "Your place is so pretty, Mamma. Your hangings must be in the shop now, *jah*?"

"They are," Nora replied. Then she held up the pitcher. "Lemonade, anyone?"

Millie and Lizzie joined Nora in the kitchen to fill the glasses, their faces alight with a surprise. Nora was dying to know what this visit was all about, yet she didn't want to ask too many questions too soon. Instinct told her to let the conversation play itself out in its own good time. When she caught a whiff of the frosted banana bars Millie was setting out on a serving plate, Nora snatched one and jammed it into her mouth.

"Sorry," she murmured as she chewed. "This is my dinner —"

"Then have one of Mammi's brownies, too," Millie insisted as she held one up. "Ya don't want to be fallin' over in a faint when ya hear what Dawdi's come to say."

Nora's eyebrows flew up as she polished off the banana bar. Then she savored the rich cocoa flavor of a brownie that tasted exactly as she remembered from her childhood. Rich and chewy, with walnut chunks. As they passed the glasses of lemonade to everyone and started the goodies around, she took a seat on the couch. Was she getting her hopes up too high? Or were her dearest prayers about to be answered?

As Nora told Ella how pretty her yellow dress was and chatted for a bit with Lizzie, she felt her father watching her. She didn't meet his gaze right off, but when a break came in the conversation, Nora looked at him. He sat in the chair nearest her end of the couch, calmly rocking forward and back. His eyes were clear behind his rimless glasses and his beard looked clean and fluffy. He was still awfully thin, but he seemed stronger — mentally alert, and taking his time about speaking to her.

Finally Nora could stand the suspense no longer. "It's *gut* to see you looking so healthy, Dat," she said. "Much better than when you were riding in Andy Leitner's wagon with hoses up your nose and hooked to your arm."

Her father smiled. "Amazing, what that little breathin' contraption on my bedside table has accomplished," he said in a clear voice. "When your mother and Millie and Bishop Tom told me what-all I'd been doin' and sayin' every time ya came around me, I was — well, I honestly can't recall a lot of it. That's no excuse. But it tells ya how far gone I was . . . in more ways than one, Nora."

Nora sucked in her breath. *Dat had spoken her name!* He was gazing at her, showing no signs of rancor or rebuke. "I'm glad Andy checked you out when he did —"

"I've come to ask your forgiveness. Daughter."

Nora blinked rapidly and swallowed hard. Everyone in the room was focused on her and Dat, gripping their glasses. Holding their treats instead of eating them.

"This doesn't come so easy for an old fella who's set in his ways," her father went on in a voice that sounded raspy with nerves. "I spent most of the morning apologizin' to these other folks in our family. I know Jesus has expected much better of me than I've been givin' to any of them."

Dat sighed, gripping the arms of the wooden rocking chair. "I stared death in the face a couple times while I was out of my head — knowin' I was by myself in that house because I'd gotten too cranky for your dear mother to tolerate me," he murmured. "That's when God reminded me how He struck Saul down in the road and blinded him for persecutin' Christians. Said He could just as well knock the stuffin' out of me for treatin' folks so mean and hateful."

Her mother leaned closer to squeeze Dat's arm. "But it's forgiven and forgotten now, Gabe. That's the grace of Jesus at work."

Dat patted Mamma's hand. "I'm lucky. I got another chance to make amends before I go." He focused on Nora again, his expression rueful. "I vaguely recall spewin' at ya in the café, Nora, callin' ya the Devil's own name. And I'm sorry I did that. Real sorry."

Nora swiped at the tears that were streaming down her face. "Well, I did show up from out of nowhere and sort of backed you into a corner," she murmured.

"And I spouted off again, that Sunday Bishop Tom told me I was to repent," he went on with a sigh. "Don't remember what-all I said, but it was surely as uncalled-for as the other vinegar I spat at ya."

"Apology accepted," Nora replied in a tiny voice.

"But I'm not done yet!" her *dat* insisted. He sucked in a deep breath, gazing around the circle of people who sat with them. "I realize now that I spent sixteen years of my life shuttin' ya out, believin' ya to be responsible for the baby ya carried," he admitted sadly. "When Lizzie and your *mamm* told me what Tobias Borntreger had done — how he swore ya to secrecy and said ya were goin' to hell if ya told anybody about him, well —"

Her father's head dropped so his chin nearly hit his chest. As he removed his glasses to wipe them with his handkerchief, Nora realized the lenses were wet.

"I had to chew on that for a while," Dat continued. "Part of me had never understood why ya refused to name the fella who got ya in trouble. Since everybody's been insistin' these past few days that it really was Tobias, I've had to adjust my thinkin'. A *lot.*"

"I'm sure you did," Nora murmured. The tightness was slowly leaving her body. Her heart was pounding but it no longer throbbed painfully. It was more like the gentle meter of the hymns she'd sung this morning, keeping a steady, reassuring beat as her father's words came through. "As I've thought more about it, I've realized you reacted like any Old Order *dat* would've —"

"*Jah,* but I felt like I'd been stabbed with a knife, straight through my heart, Nora, all those years I didn't know where ya were . . . how ya were doin'," Dat said, covering his nerves with a cough. "When I insisted that no one ever speak your name again, it was mostly because I was . . . afraid to hear it. Afraid I'd back down from a decision that went along with our ways, because what I'd done to ya caused me more pain than I could talk about."

Nora's eyes widened. In all the times she'd imagined her father offering his forgiveness, she hadn't expected him to reveal his emotions this way. Gabe Glick had never been known to go soft about *anything*.

"So I've come to say that I really can't forgive ya, Nora —"

Her heart clutched painfully. Had this

discussion been a cruel joke? An act, to suck her in?

"— because it wasn't you who committed the sin," Dat went on doggedly. "But ya asked, so I do forgive whatever ya feel needs forgivin'. And I — I hope you'll return the favor to an old man who stands corrected about a lot of mistaken assumptions, for a lot of wasted years."

"Oh, Dat." When Nora mopped her face with the back of her hand, she noticed that she wasn't the only one in the room who was crying. She set her glass on the coffee table and knelt on the floor, gazing up into her father's wrinkled face as she grasped his hands. "I forgive you, too, Dat. I want us to let go of the mistakes we made and start fresh."

He gripped her fingers, breathing in ragged bursts. Mamm and Millie and Lizzie were blowing their noses. Even Atlee sat wide-eyed and silent, too moved to watch her and Dat.

Time felt suspended. Nora knew she would recall this pivotal moment for the rest of her life. *Years* she had longed for her family's acceptance and her father's change of heart, and today — thanks to God's grace and Andy's medical attention — she had received so much more than she'd asked for.

Dat stroked her hands with his leathery thumbs. He seemed as overwhelmed by this momentous occasion as she was, even as the deep lines of his face relaxed into a smile. "We've invited Tom and Nazareth, and Ben and Miriam, to join us for supper tonight," he said. "I'm gonna ask them if I can do my kneelin' confession next Sunday, rather than lettin' another month of shunnin' separate me from my family."

"I think Bishop Tom'll go along with that," Nora whispered. "He's a very forgiving man."

"We're hopin' you'll come to church with us that mornin', Nora," her mother said. "The calendar says August, but to me it feels more like Easter — a resurrection of your *dat*'s true spirit."

Nora withered inside. After so much positive momentum had brought her family together again, she hated to hesitate with her answer. Should she postpone her baptism? Or should she disappoint her parents?

Lizzie leaned forward. "Has somethin' else come up, Nora?" she asked. "A cloud just shadowed the sunshine on your face."

Sighing, Nora decided to tell the truth — to reveal who she was and who she was

371

becoming. "Next Sunday I'm to be baptized into the Mennonite fellowship in Morning Star," she murmured. "Preacher Stephen and I believe I'm ready."

This time the silence wasn't as awe-inspiring as the earlier moments they'd shared, yet no one appeared upset, either. "*Jah,* you've said that branch of the faith fits ya better than our Amish beliefs do," her mother remarked.

Dat squeezed her hands a little harder. "It's not what I've been prayin' for," he murmured, "but after all your years of livin' amongst the English — and after the way Tobias played ya so false when ya were barely Millie's age — I'm just glad you're returnin' to Plain ways."

"I — I could ask Preacher Stephen to postpone my baptism to the next Sunday," Nora stammered. "I'm sure he wouldn't mind if —"

"Stick with your plan, Daughter," Dat said with a nod. "None of us knows when Jesus might call us home. If I've been reinstated into the church's *gut* graces and you've been saved, we're both better off. Readier for the Judgment Day."

Nora let out the breath she'd been holding. While thoughts of death and judgment were far from her mind, her father's sentiment made sense. And it made peace with the differences in the faiths they each embraced. "That's a *gut* way to look at it," Nora replied. "*Denki* for understanding why I want to follow a different path."

"Even if you stayed English, you'd still be our Nora," Mamma spoke up in a shaky voice. "After watchin' how Miriam's embraced her Rebecca, even though she'll never be Plain, I can do no less. God brought ya back to us, and I won't turn away His gift because of a few religious differences."

"That says it all, Mamma," Nora murmured. "I can't add a single thing."

As Luke gazed out the open window of the apartment above the mill, he braced himself for Ira's return. His younger brother was coming home from supper at the Glick place, walking alongside Nora as though it were the most natural thing in the world. As their laughter drifted up to him on the evening breeze, Luke kicked himself yet again.

That could be you beside her. Get a grip and get over yourself.

When Nora and his brother reached the intersection of the county blacktop and Bishop's Ridge Road, they slung their arms around each other in parting. Luke bristled. There was nothing romantic about their gesture, but the carefree nature of their loose embrace sent envy through him like a jagged lightning bolt.

Soon Ira opened and closed the mill door downstairs. As he took the steps two at a time, he called out, "Should've been there, Luke. Everybody asked where ya were."

Luke watched Ira enter their small front room, irritated at his buoyant mood. His brother had the nerve to wave a covered foil pie pan at him, his dark brows arched above teasing brown eyes. "Wilma felt sorry for ya and sent ya a go-box," he said as he set the package on the kitchen counter.

Luke inhaled the aroma of fried chicken, realizing how hungry he was. "What'd you tell them?"

Ira shrugged. "I said you were lickin' your wounds after —"

"You did *not*!"

"— a lover's quarrel," his brother continued cheerfully. "What else could I say? It's the truth."

Luke stood up to look out the other window, where he watched Nora's kitchen light come on. "And what'd Nora say to that? If that's what you really told everyone —"

"Guess you'll have to ask *her,* ain't so? What's your problem with that, anyway?" Ira demanded in an edgier tone. "What with Gabe takin' her back into the family, and Nora gettin' baptized into the Mennonite church next Sunday, you'll never find her in a more forgivin' mood. Go talk to her!"

Nora was getting baptized next Sunday? Although this information came as no surprise to Luke, he hadn't realized the fetching redhead was so close to becoming a church member. And with Ira taking his instruction, probably to join the Old Order in another month or so, Luke felt a gnawing emptiness in the pit of his stomach.

Merely a month ago Nora had turned Willow Ridge on its ear by buzzing into town in her shiny red convertible and short-shorts — and his brother had been a free-wheeling bachelor enjoying an extended state of *rumspringa.* Two people Luke admired for their rebellious sense of fun-loving freedom were settling down, signing on to accept responsibilities he'd *so* enjoyed avoiding.

Where did that leave him? It was probably only a matter of time before Ira married Millie, too. And if Nora met up with some fellow in the Morning Star congregation . . . Mennonite couples had to be baptized into the church before they could marry, the same as Amish couples . . .

Do you have to be as stubborn as you are stupid? Is Hiram going to win this one?

"I really don't get you anymore, Luke," Ira remarked with a disgusted sigh. "You used to go after every little thing you wanted from your women, and you got it! Now you're mopin' around — *poutin'*! What are ya, thirty or thirteen?"

"Lay off."

"Fine. Have it your way," Ira retorted. "After all the roads you and I've run together, I never figured ya for a quitter, Luke. Or a coward."

Luke let that last remark pass. It came too close to the truth.

"And ya know *gut* and well that if ya keep this up, Bennie and the aunts'll be quizzin' ya, and buttin' into your private life," Ira went on. "Whatever ya did to Nora — or whatever she did to you — it's gonna keep chewin' on ya until ya kiss and make up. *She* seems just fine. Which tells me you're stewin' in your own juice."

"Okay, so you're right," Luke snapped. "And it's none of your beeswax, so lay off, got it? I'll handle it."

Totally irritated, Luke tromped downstairs and strode across the back lot toward the riverbank. His mind buzzed with opening lines, apologies, and other clever yet heartfelt words that might regain Nora's affection, but he paused to sit on the big boulder to get his script just right.

From this vantage point Luke could see Nora moving in her kitchen, and shortly after the light went out in that room another one flickered on upstairs. Thoughts of her undressing, getting ready for bed, tormented him — but he'd waited too long. No decent man would knock on her door now, even though it was only nine o'clock and not quite dark.

So Luke sat there for a long while, watching the fireflies drift up from the grass. The lights in the houses around Willow Ridge blinked out as the darkness deepened. It was a peaceful scene, with the river murmuring its lullaby and a few bullfrogs singing along with the cicadas as they'd done for countless years.

But change was in the air.

CHAPTER TWENTY-FOUR

"Matthias, this saddle looks fabulous!" Nora said as he positioned it over a sawhorse she'd draped with a striped blanket. "I'm so glad to have some masculine things in my store instead of just girlie stuff."

His smile brought back memories from when they'd been much younger, going to singings on Sunday evenings. "With so many hobby farms around here, maybe some of those English folks'll realize they could be buying their tack locally," he remarked. "Rebecca gave me the idea for these tote bags with the fold-over flaps. What do you think?"

As her neighbor lifted two tooled leather bags from his box, Nora let out an appreciative *oooh*. "These could be computer bags, or purses, or carryons, or — well, whatever anybody wanted them to be," she replied. "I didn't know you made pieces like these, Matthias. I might have to buy one of them myself."

He shrugged almost shyly. "Doesn't hurt to branch out from the usual harnesses and horse collars," he remarked. "Now that you're opening a place to display stuff like this, a lot of the locals might think of things they could be making in their spare time. I — I'm glad you're back, Nora."

Her heart fluttered at the hopeful expression on Matthias Wagler's chiseled face. He'd lost his pregnant wife, Sadie, to an asthma attack a while back, and now he was sharing his home with Adam and Annie Mae — not to mention teenage Nellie and the four younger Knepp kids. No doubt he was feeling a bit displaced these days.

"It's *gut* to be here with my family again," she replied. "And such a relief to have all the secrets out in the open and the mysteries about Millie revealed."

"*Jah,* I wondered where you'd gone all of a sudden, back then," he replied. "When rumors about you having a baby started around, I didn't want to believe them. You weren't that kind of girl, Nora — and when folks quizzed me about it, as though the baby might be mine, I set them straight, too."

"*Denki* for that," Nora murmured. She suspected Matthias was working up his courage to suggest a date, but he was a member of the Amish church, so there was no point in encouraging a romantic relationship. "Things fell into place pretty fast once I bought this property," she said. "It's wonderful that Millie has accepted me as her mother — and come Sunday, I'm getting baptized into the Mennonite church, and the next weekend the store opens. That's a lot of progress in a short time!"

Regret flickered in Matthias's eyes, but then he smiled. "You've not allowed any grass to grow under your feet," he agreed. "Guess I, um, should've figured from your pretty print dress that joining the Willow Ridge church wasn't part of your plan. But I wish you all the best, Nora."

"*Denki,* Matthias. It's nice to be welcomed back."

After they hung three horse collars on the wall to complete the display of Matthias's work, he got into his open wagon to return to his harness shop down the road. When he was nearly there, he waved and Nora waved back. If their lives had gone differently, maybe the romance that had been budding between them would've bloomed into something rich and rewarding.

No sense in regretting what might have been — with Matthias or with Luke, Nora reminded herself. She'd been disappointed when her neighbor on the other side hadn't come to supper Sunday night and hadn't made any effort to talk with her this week. It hadn't been polite of her to slap him so hard, but Luke's remarks about Hiram had been way out of line. If he approached her, she would accept his apology before it was all the way out of his mouth — but Luke would have to make the first move.

The crunch of gravel made her turn to watch a horse-drawn wagon loaded with furniture come up her driveway. Aaron Brenneman, the youngest of the brothers who ran the local cabinet shop, grinned at her as he halted the massive Belgian. Seth hopped down from the other side of the seat.

"How's it goin', Nora?" Aaron called out. "If you'll open the door, Seth and I'll put this stuff wherever ya want it."

As Nora hurried ahead of them, she was glad she had a big barn door that slid sideways on a track. She'd arranged her store to make it easier for clients with larger pieces to move them in — and for buyers to haul them out. "I've saved you a spot on the main level, front and center," she called over to them.

"*Denki* for not makin' us haul these pieces

up to your loft!" Seth replied with a chuckle. He and his brother were carrying a dining room table between them as though it required no effort whatsoever, but she could tell it was solid and heavy.

When they'd angled the table on the floor the way she wanted it, Nora buffed away their fingerprints with a rag while they went after the chairs. The finish was a beautiful shade of walnut in the center and it darkened as it reached the edges — an effect she'd never seen anywhere else. The backs and the seats of the six sturdy chairs were finished in the same way, and when all seven pieces were in place, the set was a sight to behold.

"Wow," Nora murmured. "When I imagined opening a store that featured Plain pieces, I never dreamed I'd be carrying furniture like *this*, guys."

Aaron shrugged modestly. "No point in makin' stuff nobody would want," he remarked. "We'll get that sleigh bed in here now. Ya want it right there?"

Nora nodded when he gestured toward a nearby nook. She was already imagining how the bed would look draped in one of the Schrocks' quilts, with a crocheted rag rug from her Cedar Creek supplier on the floor beside it. A few minutes later, after

Aaron and Seth had carefully set the bed down, she ran her rag over its beautifully carved, curved headboard.

"Did I hear that you and Mary have set your wedding date?" she asked the older Brenneman. "Congratulations!"

"*Jah,* we're tyin' the knot in a couple of months," he replied. "Mary's been so busy of late, movin' into the house, I didn't realize she was sewin' up a few things for your store. Be back in a few!"

Nora blinked. Seth returned to hand her a big plastic sack, and when she peeked inside, she saw not just one or two Amish dolls, but a whole family of them!

"Oh my word!" She grinned at the two men. "If you'll bring me that empty mattress box beside the door, I can make up this bed with embroidered sheets and a quilt. These dolls will be sitting pretty on top of it! Tell Mary I'm really tickled that she's already made so many of them."

The Brennemans hadn't even pulled their wagon out of the driveway before Nora was fitting a set of pale yellow sheets over the mattress box. Embroidered butterflies of pink, fuchsia, and blue embellished the pillowcases, which were edged in a variegated crocheted border of the same colors — the sort of handiwork that looked so romantic in a bedroom, but which few women had the time or inclination to craft these days. After she'd tucked Eva Schrock's flower garden quilt into the sleigh bed's frame, she folded the crocheted edge of the sheet over it.

Arranging Mary Kauffman's family of faceless Amish dolls on this quaint, feminine bed made Nora smile. With their solid-colored Plain clothing, *kapps,* and a broad-brimmed hat on the bearded father, the dolls made the perfect addition to the display.

"Looks like your store's really taking shape, Nora."

Nora turned to grin at Vernon Gingerich. "I was so engrossed in arranging these new pieces, I didn't hear you come in," she admitted. "It's like playing house, but on a bigger scale. It's a huge dream coming true."

"I can see that. It's written all over your face, dear Nora," the kindly bishop replied. "I've brought you the pottery and rugs from Cedar Creek, along with a little gift."

"You've saved me a trip. *Denki* so much." Nora followed him out into the bright sunshine, to the enclosed surrey that held boxes of ceramic pieces and a stack of colorful crocheted rugs. But before he removed these items from his double rig, Vernon lifted a table through the back door and placed it on the ground.

Nora sucked in her breath. The table was about three feet wide and five feet long, made of cherrywood and polished to a lovely gloss. Its rounded corners were set off with identical carved roses in full bloom, so perfectly crafted that they might have been real flowers.

"I thought you weren't going to consign anything to my store," she said. "This is such a fabulous piece, Vernon. It would surely bring hundreds of dollars at your auction."

"It's not for sale. I made it for you, Nora."

Her mouth fell open. "I — I don't know what to — thank you so very much," she stammered. "What a treasure."

Vernon's blue-eyed gaze embraced her. "I thought a new storekeeper could surely use a place to do her bookwork, or merely to sit for a minute when her customers don't require her attention. Work and rest," he went on in a more eloquent tone. "They both belong in our schedule as we go about the business God has called us to."

"I know where I want to put it, too," Nora said. "We've got a space right outside the office, where we can tend to the record keeping while we watch the store. My daughter, Millie, will be helping me, you know. And — and Dat and I have made our peace," she added in a rush. "We Glicks are all together as a family again."

"The *gut* news traveled fast, from Bishop Tom's barn phone to mine," Vernon replied with a chuckle. "We're both glad that God's wisdom has settled over this situation, and that your *dat*'s health has been restored, as well. I see those two things working together, as two parts of the whole blessing."

After they placed the table and its matching chair on the dais outside the office, Nora and Vernon unloaded the crates of pottery and the rugs. The bishop said his good-byes and headed down the road, leaving Nora to contemplate the selection of beautiful pottery as she unpacked it. The bowls, pitchers, vases — and dinner place settings for four — glowed on the new shelving. Nora arranged one place setting of the dishes on the dining room table, loving the simplicity of their warm ivory color, which was accented with rings of rust and cobalt around the edges.

She positioned the largest of the rag rugs, crocheted with fabric strips in deep rose, cream, and yellow, beneath the Brenneman table. She hung the other rugs from hanger bars that extended out from the wall so customers could get a good look at them. After she put a folded paper placard on the table, telling about the Brenneman brothers of Willow Ridge, she made similar signs about Zanna Ropp in Cedar Creek, who had crocheted the five colorful rugs, and Amanda Brubaker, who'd created the pottery.

Nora's rumbling stomach told her it was time for a break, but she wandered back to admire the cherry table Vernon had made for her. It seemed the perfect place to put a monitor for the security camera system, so she quickly set it up. With the push of a button, she began watching the various nooks and display areas of the store rotating on the screen. Plenty of space remained for her or Millie to do bookwork on the table —

Nora gripped the top of the chair. On the screen, she saw Hiram Knepp entering the shop. When he noticed the swivel of the camera that was mounted above him, he flashed a cocky smile at it — at her — and then wound his way between the displays to where she was standing.

"You've had quite a stream of gentlemen callers, Nora," he said in a silken voice. "I was wondering if I'd get my turn."

Goose flesh raced up Nora's spine — the *willies* that hit her when something creeped her out. Had Hiram really been watching the comings and goings at her store all morning? Or was he just saying that to frighten her?

"You are the queen of *heat* in that pink print dress." Hiram stopped mere inches away from her, well aware that he'd invaded her space and trapped her against the table. "It calls to mind the color of a woman's skin between her —"

"What do you need?" Nora interrupted brusquely. "I'm ready to go —"

"You lead and I'll follow. You know what I need," he whispered suggestively. He raised a finger to her face but Nora smacked it away.

"Leave! *Now,*" she snapped. She inhaled, trying to control the sick, woozy feeling in her head. Her first impulse was to call the sheriff, but her phone was in the office. If Hiram cornered her in there, she'd be very, very sorry.

"What kind of talk is that for a lamb who's to be baptized in a few days?" Hiram asked in a voice edged with sarcasm. "If you were a seeker in *my* district, I'd have you on your knees begging for my —"

"But Nora's *not* in your district," came a loud male voice from the doorway. "I've got the sheriff on speed dial, Hiram. Wherever you take off to, he'll know it's *you* in that vintage black Caddie, won't he?"

Oh, thank you, Lord! Nora prayed when she spotted Luke and heard the solid tattoo of his boots crossing the floor.

Hiram eased away from her, but he didn't appear ready to leave. "There'll come a day when Hooley won't arrive in the nick of time," he remarked caustically. "Then you and I can become partners on more than just a business level. You know you need me, Nora. I *know* too much."

"You don't know *beans,*" Nora blurted. It was exactly the wrong tone, the wrong attitude for dealing with Hiram — or was it? Maybe she could end this farce once and for all — if Luke would play along. Would he do that for her? Or had he come to pay her back for the way she'd slapped him and told him off? His face looked ruddy and set, his eyes as hard and green as marbles.

Slipping her arm around Luke's waist, Nora gazed up at him with an expression of utter, head-over-heels love. "What you *don't* know, Hiram, is that you were exactly right at the diner," she said boldly. "When you told me I was a thoroughbred yoked to an ox? Well, Luke and I *are* a team now — engaged, matter of fact. We're both the best of our breeds, so I *don't* need you. And I have never *wanted* you. Got it?"

Luke pulled her closer, kissing her temple as a chuckle rumbled in his chest. "We've been comparing notes, Nora and I," he went on. "And all that stuff you told me about being her silent partner and buying her barn is a pack of lies, Hiram. She's got bank backing, like any smart businesswoman."

Hiram opened his mouth to refute Luke's statement, but Nora was ready for him.

"Same thing goes for that story you told me about Ben financing Luke and Ira's mill," she asserted. "And you did *not* lower the price of this property for me. You made a killing on this place — raised the price so your crooked Realtor would get a bigger commission. The loan officer in New Haven confirmed my suspicions."

Hiram smirked. "Who's been filling your pretty head with such —"

"Lay off!" Nora blurted. "I find it *disgusting* that you're putting the moves on me — and that you insinuated Luke left a woman in the lurch, back in Lancaster. Matter of fact, every woman I know thinks you're disgusting — including Miriam and Jerusalem," she continued in a voice that rang around the rafters. "So why do you keep making a fool of yourself? Why don't you get a clue and go after *stupid* women, Hiram?"

The slightest flicker in Hiram's eyes told Nora her arrows had found a soft spot.

"That's why Delilah left you, too," Luke continued without missing a beat. "That black dye's a poor cover for the old goat you really are, butting into everybody's business with your lies. Delilah and Nora have got your number — and I've got a number ready, too."

He pulled a cell phone from his pocket and positioned his thumb over a button. "So what'll it be? Will you get out of Nora's face — out of our lives for good?" Luke demanded. "Or do I let Officer McClatchey know you're driving with expired license plates?"

Hiram's eyes widened before he could cover his reaction. "Fine," he muttered as he turned to leave. "But don't believe for a minute that you can tell me where to go or with whom to spend my time."

As her uninvited guest made his way between the displays, Nora kept her arm around Luke, maintaining their appearance as a team. Her heart was pounding too fast and her legs felt wobbly, but she dared to believe she'd gotten rid of Hiram Knepp — at least for a while.

"Hey, Knepp?" Luke called out.

Hiram turned, scowling.

"That underwear you said was missing?" Luke went on in a knowing tone. "You got it all wrong. It's pink and frilly and made of silk."

Hiram pivoted. After a few moments a car engine roared, and then gravel pinged against the outside of the barn as he raced away.

Nora let out the breath she'd been holding. "Are his plates really expired? How'd you notice *that* little detail?"

Luke reached into his shirt pocket and pulled out two small, curled-up slips of plastic film that were tattered around the edges. "I'd have been here sooner, but I had trouble lifting the edges of these renewal stickers off his plates with my pocketknife."

Nora laughed out loud. "So are you going to call the sheriff?"

Luke shrugged, easing away from her. "I'll let Hiram wonder about that for now. He can get new stickers at the license bureau. But like he said, we can't tell him where to go or who to see."

"Yeah, but he knows we're wise to the lies he's been telling us." Nora sat down in her desk chair to keep her knees from buckling. "I'm not sure why you showed up when you did, but *thanks,* Luke. Hiram's full of hot air but he still gives me the creeps."

CHAPTER TWENTY-FIVE

Luke realized he was breathing in and out in time with Nora. He wanted to grab her and kiss away her fear — her huge hazel eyes took up half her face as she gazed up at him. She was so grateful for the way he'd rescued her, he could probably ask for anything he wanted.

But he held his breath for a few heartbeats so his fantasies wouldn't run away with him. He knew some of the stuff she'd said had been designed to get Hiram out of her store, but when Nora had put her arm around him — when she'd said they were engaged . . .

Was that part of her ruse, too? Was Nora pulling one over on Hiram, the same way *he* had peeled off the Cadillac's license plate stickers? Hiram could replace those, but Luke wasn't so sure he could handle it if Nora had only been toying with his emotions.

Should he reveal why he'd come over?

How he'd been a fool for believing Knepp's lies? Luke decided to start slowly, to clarify a few major points first. He hoped he wouldn't regret delving into the issues their confrontation had raised.

"When I looked out my upstairs window and saw Hiram's car parked behind the windbreak of evergreens across the road," he began, "I realized he's probably been hiding there periodically, ever since you moved here. Spying on you."

Nora's mouth formed an O but no sound came out. She looked ready to crawl underneath the desk. "Stalking me," she whimpered. "That's horrible — but what can I do? The windbreak's not my property, so —"

"We can tell Dan Kanagy what's going on," Luke suggested. "Wouldn't hurt to trim those evergreens and the vines that've grown between them. Ira and I could make pretty short work of that."

Luke stopped before he volunteered any more of his time or emotional involvement. As pieces of their conversation with Hiram came back to him, he figured he had to be careful about how he used that information.

"So Knepp said you were a thoroughbred yoked to an *ox*?" he murmured. "I've been compared to a lot of animals over the years, but most of them were more, well — graceful. Certainly sexier."

Nora bit back a laugh. "But an ox is strong and dependable, and he *gets the job done,*" she remarked. "And only a fool would get crossways with an ox."

Luke smiled. Was that the tiniest hint at innuendo in her teasing tone, her arched eyebrows?

"Think of it this way," Nora went on. "Would you rather be considered an ox or a snake? I know which one I'd prefer to be hitched up with."

Hitched up with. Nora was referring to Hiram's yoke imagery rather than marriage, of course — yet her words made his heart wander down a more hopeful trail. *Too early to jump to such conclusions. Focus on the answers you need to hear.*

"So Hiram told you I left a trail of trouble back in Lancaster?" Luke ventured, watching Nora's expression. "What did he mean, saying I left a woman in the lurch?"

"That phrase could cover a lot of sins," Nora replied. "I see it as another of Hiram's attempts to manipulate me. Another lie to make you look bad."

"Glad to hear that," Luke murmured. "While I'm by no means as pure as the driven snow, I was *careful* about sowing my wild oats. If you know what I mean."

"I believe that," Nora whispered. "You've always told me what you wanted to do with me, but when I asked you to slow down, you showed me total respect. I really appreciate that, Luke."

Appreciation was fine, as far as it went, but Luke had wanted more from Nora from the moment he'd first laid eyes on her — not to mention after he'd kissed her. The open expression on Nora's sweet face made him want to kiss her *now,* but he had another point or two to clarify first. "Why'd you tell Knepp we're engaged?"

Nora clasped her hands in front of her white apron, her gaze never wavering from his. "Why'd you give him so many details about my underwear?" she countered. "That bit about the pink silk was an interesting touch."

Nora had him there, and they both knew it.

"Can't a man have his fantasies?" Luke blurted. "I was just fighting fire with —"

"You could probably have more than fantasies if I sensed a bit of . . . repentance."

Luke's throat went tight. His previous encounter with Nora came back in all its inglorious detail as he glanced at the wooden staircase and up to the loft level, where a magnificent quilt was hanging. "I owe you that," he agreed with a sigh. He paused to pray — asking God for the right words, because he doubted they would flow out without divine intervention.

"Nora, I was way out of line when I stormed over here and accused you of being Hiram's — *partner,*" he said, quickly replacing a harsher word. "I'm sorry I let his insinuations get me all riled up —"

"You were green with envy," Nora recalled in a breathy voice. "This might sound strange to you, but after the way my ex lost interest and left, it was kind of gratifying to see a man get so worked up over me — so angry about who might be getting what he wanted for himself."

Luke sucked in his breath when Nora came over to grasp his hands. Her face had regained its usual glow as she gazed up at him with eyes that shone like wild honey.

"I accept your apology, Luke. And I'm sorry I slapped you so hard," she said. "The way both of us sometimes fly off without thinking, I suspect this won't be the last time we apologize to each other."

That implied a future, didn't it? Luke wrapped his arms around Nora, resting his head on hers. While he'd come here to rescue her today, *he* was the one who'd been sprung from a trap of his own making. It felt so good to hold Nora this way, to feel her forgiveness and erase the doubts Hiram had fabricated.

"Is this where we kiss and make up?" he murmured.

When Nora tilted her head, Luke settled his lips over hers. She reached up to twine her hands behind his neck, driving him crazy when her fingers toyed with his hair. He pulled her closer, daring to kiss her more fervently . . . awash in the waves of her acceptance and affection —

"Well, *this* looks hopeful," a familiar voice said behind them.

Luke didn't break the kiss immediately, and it pleased him that Nora didn't jump away like a scared schoolgirl. "Mmm," he murmured against her *kapp.* "Later."

"Jah. Please," she whispered back.

Luke flashed his older brother a smile. "Preacher Bennie," he teased. "Too bad you didn't get here earlier for the *real* action."

"Jah, I'm glad Hiram didn't run you down, considering the way he took off," Nora remarked as she loosened her hold on Luke.

Ben's arching eyebrows expressed the exasperation they all felt whenever Hiram showed up, but then he smiled at Nora. "I brought the sign for your store," he said. "If my brother's agreeable, I think the two of us can get it mounted above your entry."

Nora's smile brightened the entire shop. As she hurried outside to see the sign, Luke told himself he'd do well to put that sort of happiness on her face every chance he got.

"Penny for your thoughts," Ben murmured as they followed her.

"I'll keep them to myself, thanks," Luke teased. "But let's say that Nora's given me a *lot* to think about in this past half an hour."

Ben clapped him on the back. "Imagine that — *you,* thinkin' about what a *gut* woman's told ya instead of runnin' around like a wild, aimless rooster. And our youngest brother soon to join the Amish church," he added. "I hadn't figured on seein' either of those events anytime soon, yet here they are!"

Ben stopped in the door way, smiling pensively. "It's gonna be quite a harvest season for the Hooley family, what with Miriam carryin' our firstborn and your new mill doin' so well — a harvest of blessings!" he added happily. "I'm a thankful man, Luke."

As they stepped outside, Luke was glad his brother hadn't launched into a full-blown sermon, yet Ben's words had summed up their family's situation perfectly. Luke usually balked at talk of blessings and settling down, yet he felt curiously contented — relieved after this morning's encounter with Knepp, and hopeful about what he'd shared with Nora.

As Luke watched Nora running her hands over the wrought-iron lettering of the sign, admiring its curving vines with roses on each end, he knew what joy looked like. He was witnessing the fulfillment of Nora's biggest dream, and he felt honored to be a part of it.

SIMPLE GIFTS, her sign proclaimed in white ironwork. As he went to fetch a ladder, Luke whistled the tune to that beloved song. And when was the last time he'd whistled when he worked?

It really was a gift to be simple. Luke was finally figuring that out.

CHAPTER TWENTY-SIX

Nora bustled about the kitchen early Sunday morning, groaning as she burned her toast. Then she spilled her coffee and nearly slipped in the wet spot before she could wipe the floor. She did *not* want to be late for church, yet it seemed everything she did took twice as long or turned out wrong.

Be still and know that I am God.

Nora bowed her head, breathing deeply. *And I am Your Nora, and I'm making a bigger mess of things than I need to, right?* she replied silently.

Peace . . . My peace I give to you.

"I'd appreciate it if You'd keep me from running off the road between here and Morning Star, too," Nora murmured as she grabbed her purse. "The way things are going —"

When she went to lock the front door, Nora saw Millie hurrying up the driveway, waving. How could she remain out of sorts at the sight of her dear daughter, who'd come to join her on this very special morning?

"Hope it's all right that I come to church with ya," Millie panted as she reached the door.

"What a fine surprise!" Nora replied. "I'm glad for your company, sweetie. Let's get going or we'll be late — and that wouldn't look good!"

Millie laughed as they hurried to the van. "Are ya scared?" she asked as they took off. "I would be."

Nora inhaled deeply, reminding herself to concentrate on the curves in the road while she chatted with her daughter. This felt like an important topic of conversation. "*Jah,* my nerves feel like hungry hens are pecking at me, but it's only stage fright," she mused aloud. "Nothing I can't handle."

Millie nodded, looking her up and down. "Your dress is a real pretty shade of red — like dark cherries. Or wine."

"When Preacher Stephen said he'd be talking about the first Pentecost as part of my baptism, I thought this color would be appropriate without looking too flashy."

Her daughter's laughter helped Nora relax and put her minor troubles into perspective again. "And it's a solid-color fabric instead of a print. You'd pass for Amish — not that I want ya to change your mind," Millie added quickly.

It was a sentiment Nora appreciated as they whizzed past the Schrock place. "What'd Mammi and Dawdi say when you wanted to come with me instead of being in church with them today?" she asked. "It'll be a big deal when your *dawdi* makes his confession. He's hoping to get out of four more weeks of his ban — which is an unheard-of favor to ask of Bishop Tom and the others."

Millie shrugged. "I don't get to go to the Members' Meeting," she pointed out, "so I'd rather be with you, Mamma. It's really special that you're gettin' baptized at your age. A lot of folks would let it slide by, thinkin' it didn't matter anymore."

Nora's eyes widened. She let the part about her *age* pass, because the rest of Millie's response touched her. "That's a really important observation — and *jah,* if I were still living English, I doubt I'd be going to church at all," she replied. "But if I declare that I'm following Jesus from here on out, I believe it'll change the whole world for me."

Millie nodded, listening carefully.

A few minutes later Nora parked in the

lot alongside the plain white Mennonite church building with its two single doors on the front, one for women and one for men. Other families were arriving, calling out greetings to each other and to her. It felt good to introduce Millie to these people who were quickly becoming her friends. She and her daughter filed inside with the other women and took their place on one of the pews in the simple sanctuary.

Preacher Stephen began the service with a prayer. The first hymn enveloped Nora in the richness of the four-part harmony this congregation embraced, and not long after their song, the minister began his sermon.

"As we celebrate the baptism of Nora Landwehr, I've chosen to talk about the first Pentecost, as told in the book of Acts," Stephen said. He smiled at Nora and began to read from the Bible.

" 'And suddenly there came a sound from heaven as of a rushing mighty wind,' " he recounted with enthusiasm. " 'It filled all the house where they were sitting, and there appeared unto them cloven tongues like as of fire, and it sat upon each of them. And they were all filled with the Holy Ghost and began to speak with other tongues, as the Spirit gave them utterance.' "

As Preacher Stephen continued his sermon, Nora felt as though he was talking directly to her. What a wonderful sensation it was, to compare the experience of Jesus's apostles to her present-day situation.

"The first Pentecost is considered the birth of the church," he went on. "It was the day Peter preached his first sermon, and later in the passage we learn that nearly three thousand believers repented and were baptized. I can't say that my first sermon initiated any such response."

All around Nora, men and women in the congregation laughed along with the minister. Nora relaxed, smiling at Millie. She felt more comfortable in this place every time she came here to worship among these friendly people.

"And as the Holy Spirit came upon those followers of Jesus, so shall Nora be blessed with His presence today," he went on. "We should note that although the apostles began speaking in different tongues, they weren't babbling. These Galileans spoke in dialects that were understood by the many visiting Jews and foreigners who were in Jerusalem that day for a sacred celebration at the Temple.

"Even so for us today," Preacher Stephen said as he leaned forward, "the Spirit speaks to us in a language each of our hearts understands, if we'll listen for His call."

The minister invited Nora to the baptismal font, and from that point she entered a state of her own private awareness. She answered the questions she and Stephen had discussed previously . . . a pitcher of water was poured over her head . . . someone handed her a towel as the final words of the baptismal ceremony were spoken. When she'd blotted her face and hair and put on her *kapp,* Nora felt sanctified — and relieved. Millie was beaming at her. The others in the congregation were smiling, too. Then she got a jolt that had nothing to do with the coming of the Holy Spirit.

At the end of a pew near the back of the church, Luke sat gazing steadily at her.

Luke enjoyed the surprise in Nora's eyes, even if he'd have to explain his presence at church —

Who are you kidding? She already knows why you're here.

As Nora resumed her seat beside Millie, Luke realized that he was the surprised one. Why did Nora look more appealing to him now than when he'd first gone over to meet the hot redhead who'd moved next door? Watching her baptism had made him feel twitchy, as though one of those tongues of flame mentioned in the sermon had settled on his head. Yet Luke felt ready to consider what that sensation might mean.

He'd come to show his support for Nora, mostly. He would've understood if she'd skipped religion altogether, after what that long-ago bishop and her father had done to her. Yet she'd found a faith that fit her better than the Old Order Amish ways, and she'd made her stand. She'd committed her life to Christ despite all the excuses she might have made.

Luke admired a woman who could do that at this stage of her life. He admired a lot of things about Nora, and that was a first for him. Other women had turned his head with their good looks and flirtatious ways — and Nora had done that, too. But she was rock solid. She was a survivor, and she was nobody's doormat. Nora believed in a cause bigger than herself, and she'd forgiven him for being such an idiot —

What other reasons do you need? State your case before somebody else does.

After the benediction Luke headed outside to wait in the shade, knowing folks would congratulate Nora. He was pleased that Zeb Schrock and some of the other men came up to chat with him. He liked the way nobody was pressing him to join the church, and that these Mennonites didn't require an instruction period. These folks believed that if you were ready to follow God, He was waiting to embrace you. They weren't focused on sin and suffering for it. They believed in moving past mistakes and making improvements, a doctrine he found very refreshing.

At last Nora stepped out into the bright sunshine, along with several of the women. Mary and Priscilla Schrock were talking about Nora's grand opening. Their happy chatter rang around the parking lot, and Luke was glad Nora had found a new group of friends who welcomed her and Millie. If they knew she was divorced and that Millie had been born out of wedlock, they showed no sign of hesitation — no inclination to stand apart from her, thinking Nora's former English life might contaminate her relationship with them.

Her past has been washed away by her baptism. She's writing on a clean slate and everyone wants to know where her story will go now.

As though she felt him watching her, Nora turned to look at Luke. She smiled and then turned back to her conversation, silently stating that it was his move. While others he'd dated had come running when he'd beckoned them, Nora was too self-assured for that. She intrigued him. She didn't *need* him, which gave him even more incentive to pursue her.

When he saw Preacher Stephen step outside, something prodded Luke to go shake his hand. He'd been impressed by this man's down-to-earth faith, and before they'd chatted for very long, Luke surprised himself. "I'd like to talk to you sometime soon about being baptized. Joining your church."

Stephen's smile made his eyes sparkle. "I'm always happy to hear that," he replied. "We'll set up a time whenever you're ready."

No getting out of it now, his thoughts challenged. After years of avoiding such a commitment, Luke was surprised at how easily the words had come — and at how comfortable he felt, now that he'd stated his intentions to the Mennonite minister. He'd never been one to think much about the role God played in his life, but he was pretty sure the Lord had brought him to this church service today — and that divine intervention had guided Nora into his life when he'd needed her.

Luke didn't intend to tell Nora or his family about his decision just yet. He wanted the most important people in his life to believe that hooking up with a woman wasn't the only reason he'd decided to follow Christ. That kind of church membership was for younger guys.

As Luke crossed the parking lot, he savored the flutter of Nora's deep red dress in the breeze, and the way she held her head high. The red hair beneath her *kapp* was still wet and mussed from the water Preacher Stephen had poured over it, yet she didn't seem anxious about her appearance. He stopped a few feet behind her, letting her finish her conversation.

When Nora turned, her smile dazzled him. "Luke, it's so *gut* to see you," she said. "Millie and I are going to the common meal in Willow Ridge now. Care to join us? It's at the Wagler place."

His heart began to hammer. He would already be perfectly welcome there, where his brothers and aunts would be eating, but Luke felt as if he'd just been invited on a special date. "I suppose I could —"

"Mammi and I roasted a big batch of chicken yesterday," Millie chimed in. "And we made a bowl of fresh kale salad, too."

Nora chuckled. "I'm taking a tray of pickles, olives, and raw veggies. Nothing to *cook* that way, you know."

Luke laughed. "Sounds better than

scrounging around in my fridge," he re-marked. "Go ahead and eat, if you want to, since I won't get home as fast in my rig —"

"We'll be waiting for you," Nora replied firmly.

Luke liked the sound of that. A *lot*. And when he arrived home in his rig, it was gratifying to find Nora watching for him from her porch swing. She started across the yard and met him as he unhitched his horse.

"Millie went on over to eat?"

Nora smiled. "Ira's there, you know."

"But you and I are *here*." Luke steered her into the shade of the stable and stole a kiss. When he released her, Nora took a kiss of her own, slower and deeper.

"Why not stay here awhile?" he hinted. "Just the two of us."

"It would take Millie two seconds to figure out what we were doing," Nora replied without missing a beat. "And Mamma's waiting to hear about my baptism, and I need to find out how Dat's confession went. But I *want* to stay here with you."

Luke's pulse sped up. After Nora got her relish tray from her fridge, they strolled over to the Wagler place, where almost everyone in town was loading a plate at the long serv-ing tables. When Nora looked up at him, holding his hand, it felt so natural. So easy. Even when he saw Annie Mae Wagler grinning at them like a sly cat, Luke felt good about being seen by the much younger woman he'd once run the roads with.

Annie Mae's found her happiness and you've found yours, he realized. *It's all good.*

And it wasn't just Annie Mae watching him with Nora. His aunts, Jerusalem and Nazareth, came to chat with them, as did Ben and Miriam and many of the others. While he'd hidden himself away with the other women he'd dated, Luke felt comfortable attaching himself to Nora . . . making a statement about their relationship among these people who wanted him to commit to something. To *someone.*

Wilma's roasted chicken tasted fabulous. Millie's kale salad — ordinarily a dish he would've avoided — surprised him with its apple chunks and tangy dressing. Even the bologna and cheese sandwich he'd taken seemed special, maybe because Nora was eating the other half of it.

As Nora's father approached their lawn chairs, Luke smiled at him. Was it his imagination, or did Gabe Glick look twenty years younger? The bitterness that had once etched Gabe's face had disappeared.

"So you're a Mennonite now?" Gabe

asked Nora in a light voice.

"*Jah,* they took me — and God didn't send any lightning bolts through the roof to stop the baptism, either," she teased. "How'd *your* morning go?"

Gabe laughed out loud at her joke. "Mission accomplished. Confession accepted," he replied. "Thanks to you, mostly, because you'd already forgiven me."

"Just as you forgave me, Dat," Nora replied as she took his hand between hers. "I'm glad your confession went the way we'd hoped. I feel so much better now, being your Nora again."

It was a touching conversation, a reunion made possible by great faith. Rather than feeling embarrassed by such talk, Luke felt the healing of the Holy Spirit at work right before his eyes. Another phrase stuck with him for the rest of the afternoon, as well, while he visited with folks beneath the Waglers' trees.

Being your Nora.

Luke nipped his lip. Even though he'd only met Nora a month ago, he felt compelled to speak up. For days now his inner voice — the Spirit, perhaps — had been nudging him to declare himself. The idea of committing to a woman for a lifetime scared him, yet Luke believed it was finally time to state who he wanted to be when he grew up.

It was a major step. But as he gazed at Nora, Luke realized that all the days of his life had been leading him to this time, this place, this woman.

He was ready. At long last, he was ready.

CHAPTER TWENTY-SEVEN

When Nora went to unlock the store on Saturday, dawn was a pink glow on the horizon, yet nearly a dozen colorful balloons were tied to the door handle, flapping gently in the morning breeze.

Who got here so early? she wondered as she rushed toward the barn. *Happy Birthday!* the tag on the balloons said. But no one had signed it.

Nora looked around, thinking Millie might pop out from behind the building — but a tingling sensation made her turn to face Luke's upstairs apartment at the mill. She waved and blew him a kiss. Maybe he wasn't up yet — and maybe someone else had given her these balloons — but instinct told her that Luke might've surprised her this way. He'd been attentive all week, even as he'd kept enough distance to intrigue her.

When she unlocked the door, Nora stood in the entryway to breathe in the essence of

Simple Gifts. Matthias's leather goods and some scented sachets and candles made her shop smell as inviting as it looked. *And if I say so myself, Lord, the store is a feast for my eyes. Yet another gift You've made possible.*

Nora admired the quilts hanging from the loft railing and the Amish dolls on the sleigh bed. She smiled at the displays of pottery, handcrafted toys and rocking horses, beautifully embellished linens, one of Bishop Tom's Nativity sets, Preacher Ben's wrought iron trellises, and so many other wonderful items. For years she'd dreamed of owning a store, but this reality surpassed her wildest fantasies.

"Mamma! It's your big day!" Millie called from the buggy coming up the driveway. "And happy birthday to ya, too!"

Nora ran alongside the rig to where Lizzie parked it behind the barn. She was immediately wrapped in an excited hug from a daughter who was nearly as tall as she was. What a blessing, to hold this fine young woman after so many years of wondering about her. "*Denki,* Millie," she murmured. "*You* are my best present ever. It'll be a *gut* day even if I don't sell a thing."

"Puh! You'll be callin' your suppliers to restock their displays before ya close up today," Lizzie predicted as she helped Mamma down from the buggy. "Everywhere I go, folks're talkin' about coming to Simple Gifts."

Nora grinned, hugging her mother and her sister-in-law. "All of us Glick women together for my birthday breakfast — now *that's* a treat!" she said. "I've got a card table set up on the porch for us."

From their baskets, Lizzie and Nora's *mamm* took a pan of divine-smelling breakfast casserole, pastries from Miriam's café, and a fresh fruit salad. As they ate and chatted, Nora couldn't recall a birthday so happy. When they finished, she gave her mother and Lizzie a tour of the store and its merchandise so they'd be familiar with everything when customers started coming.

"How about if you remain in the loft, Lizzie, while Mamma and I circulate on the main level?" she suggested. "Millie's a whiz at running the cash register, so if she can stay there — at least when we've got customers — that'll keep the traffic flowing. Rebecca's working this afternoon, and I suspect Mary and Eva Schrock will take a turn then, too."

"They might have to stay in their own shop," Mamma said with a wide smile. "Once folks see your place and the mill, they'll eat at Miriam's and take in the Schrocks' quilts and fabrics while they're there. You just wait and see!"

Nora felt as giddy as a girl as she waited for nine thirty. She arranged a self-serve cooler of lemonade and a coffeemaker on a small table, with a big tray of cookies Miriam and Millie had baked for her grand opening. She was checking the restroom when a familiar voice came from the doorway.

"Can I be your first customer, pretty please? Before I start work at the clinic?"

Nora laughed. "Rebecca! It's so nice of you to stop by —"

"When I brought your labels yesterday I spotted some stuff I just *have* to have. I don't want it to be gone when I come to help," Rebecca said gleefully.

Nora watched Rebecca move from one display to the next with a shopping basket on her arm, choosing embroidered hankies, scented soaps, three Amish dolls, and one of the tooled leather bags Matthias had made. "I don't want to take your display," she remarked as she went to the cash register, "but I also want a place setting for four of that fabulous pottery."

"I'll write that in my notebook," Nora said as Millie began to ring up the order. Then she hugged Rebecca. "You've already made my day!"

Rebecca laughed and hugged her back. "Just you wait, Nora," she said. "The photos on your website — and the beautiful way you've set up your store — make you a shoo-in for Willow Ridge's Business of the Year award."

Nora's eyebrows rose. "There's an award for that?"

"There should be!" Rebecca said as she took her bagged purchases. "I can't wait to see what's sold by the time I come back later."

In a few minutes cars and buggies began pulling in, and the women driving them looked as eager as Nora felt. "Come on in!" she called out to them. "What's a grand opening if I can't open early?"

Happy chatter filled the store as English and Plain women exclaimed over the items on display. A few men moseyed in with their wives, impressed that Nora was carrying wrought iron and saddles. Nora welcomed everyone, directing them to sign her mailing list at the refreshment table. She was refilling the lemonade cooler when a man called out, "Nora Landwehr? Got a present for you!"

Nora's jaw dropped. The flower arrangement coming toward her was so large, she couldn't see the deliveryman's face until he set it on the checkout counter. "Thank you so much," she murmured.

Millie's eyebrows rose. "And I wonder who *that* might be from?" she teased.

Nora plucked the gift card and stuck it in her apron pocket. "I don't know, but it's going on the Brennemans' table, because it's too huge to sit anywhere else."

Nora arranged the bouquet on a placemat at the opposite end of the table from the place setting of pottery. A riot of tiger lilies, gladiolas, hydrangeas, snapdragons, and other colorful flowers encouraged her to inhale their fresh fragrance. When she could stand the suspense no longer, Nora stepped into the office to read the card.

Luke's familiar printing made her heart pound. *Happy Birthday, Nora. I'm Proud of You. I Love You. Luke.*

Nora sucked in her breath. She glanced out the window, noting that her parking lot was full — as was the mill's — but she grabbed her phone anyway.

"The Mill at Willow Ridge," Luke answered in a businesslike tone. "How can I help you?"

"You can pick me up off the floor," Nora murmured. "Luke, your flowers just came and I — I don't know what to say!"

His laugh was low and maybe a little nervous. "You'll think of something."

For a moment, Nora drew a blank. She *did* love Luke, but this wasn't the time to have that conversation. "Come to the house after our stores have closed, okay?"

"Exactly what I wanted to hear," he replied with a chuckle. "I'll be there around six. Right now we're swamped, and I see you are, too. You *go,* girl."

As she hung up, Nora wanted to dance and sing and throw her arms around Luke, but she did have a store full of customers. And that was almost as fabulous as seeing Luke's declaration that he loved her. *Almost.*

As the day passed, Nora encouraged Mamma to sit at the Brennemans' table and be the greeter. When she relieved Millie at the cash register, Nora punched a button that tallied the day's sales and nearly fell over. More than a thousand dollars had flowed in! As she stuffed a bunch of the cash into a bank bag to keep in her office safe, Nora felt almost light-headed. Giddy, yet seriously amazed.

Bless her, Millie was restocking and straightening the displays — and directing customers to the photo albums Rebecca had made for her, so folks could see some of the items that had already sold out. When Rebecca arrived at one thirty, Nora let her run the cash register.

"Didn't I tell you this place would be a huge success?" Rebecca whispered as she came behind the checkout counter.

"I sure hope my crafters can replenish my stock early this week," Nora remarked. "I never dreamed we'd sell so much in one day."

"Think of all the women who'll be happy to hear that," Rebecca replied. "You're going to boost a lot of area families' incomes, Nora. It's a ripple effect — you're touching more lives than you ever thought possible."

Around three o'clock, Nora encouraged Lizzie to take Mamma home. Her mother looked exhausted but happy as she rose from her chair at the walnut table. "What a glorious day," she said as she wrapped her arms around Nora's waist. "I'm so glad I got to share it, too."

"It wouldn't have been the same without you, Mamma," Nora replied quietly. She couldn't help recalling her first day back in Willow Ridge, when she'd feared her mother had died in bed. How far they both had come, and Millie and Lizzie with them.

It was five o'clock before the last customers left the store. "What a find!" one of the

English ladies said as she and her friends went to the door with their sacks. "We'll come earlier in the day next time —"

"And thanks for taking my order for a rocking horse and a set of those pretty sheets," her friend chimed in. "Your shop has so many wonderful things in it!"

When the door closed behind them, Nora turned the sign in the door to Closed and sank into one of the Brennemans' chairs. She grinned at Rebecca and Millie and they all started laughing.

"Can you *believe* what people bought today?" Nora crowed. "Bedroom sets and quilts and pottery — and a ton of little stuff!"

"I don't think anybody left without buying or ordering something!" Millie said as she perched on the edge of a chair beside Nora.

"You'll need to be ready for crowds like this all during autumn, when folks like to be out driving," Rebecca said. "And then it'll be the Christmas season! I'm so glad I got to help today, to see all your hard work pay off, Nora."

"Ah, but it was your website design and Internet savvy that got shoppers to come," Nora pointed out gratefully. "Otherwise, we'd be just another store in the Missouri countryside waiting for folks to find us. I couldn't have done this without you, Rebecca."

Rebecca shrugged modestly as she grabbed her purse from under the counter. "I'll see you girls next Saturday. I'm meeting Dad for dinner."

"And I'm helping Ira deliver checks and pick up eggs for the mill store." Millie stood and opened her arms wide. "This was such a great day, Mamma. I'm so glad ya wanted me to help."

As Nora embraced her daughter, she blinked back grateful tears. "You gave me a chance to be a part of your life again, Millie," she replied in a breathy voice. "For me, that's been the best blessing of all."

When her two helpers had gone, Nora let out a long, tired sigh. Her legs ached. Her head swam with details she had to see to — following up on orders for her crafters, and tallying their sales to figure their checks, and —

Luke's bouquet reminded her that there was more to life than doing business. Perhaps the element of Plain living she most admired was the insistence on keeping the Sabbath as a day of rest rather than as another day for retailing. And her rest started right this minute.

Nora took the gift card from her pocket. *Happy Birthday, Nora. I'm Proud of You. I Love You. Luke.* She shut off the security monitor, the fans, and the lights and wrapped her arm firmly around the vase holding the flower arrangement.

As she crossed the yard, she saw Luke waiting on her porch. Her heart thrummed. Though she'd been burned by the man who'd provided her ticket out of dead-end poverty, Nora knew Luke was different — a down-to-earth fellow that Tanner Landwehr would dismiss with a lift of his salon-tanned nose as he sped off in his high-dollar car with his new trophy wife.

Nora now felt at peace with that. Tanner's leaving her was the best thing that could have happened, because then she'd allowed God to step in and lead her back to Willow Ridge and her family. A whole new life. A whole new faith.

"Congratulations, Nora-girl," Luke murmured as he patted the seat of the porch swing. "Your store's a hit — and then your customers came to visit mine. Good thing I saved back a few things for our supper."

Supper. The last thing Nora wanted to do was feed this man, but that would only be fair if he'd brought the food.

"I'm cooking your birthday dinner, okay?"

Nora nearly dropped the flower arrangement before she set it on the porch floor. "That's the best offer I've had all day."

"More offers where that one came from," Luke hinted as she sat down beside him. "But I'm reminding myself to woo you. To let you make the next moves."

Nora rested her head on his shoulder and slung her arm around him as he pulled her close. "You're smarter than you look, Hooley," she teased as he bussed her temple. "Your flowers and note still have my head spinning."

"As well they should. I was trying to get your attention."

"One request," she murmured.

"Only one?" Luke's chuckle rumbled in his chest. "It's your birthday. Milk it for all it's worth."

"I do want to spend my time with you, Luke," she whispered, "but it's only been a month —"

"I'm every bit as scared of a forever relationship as you are, Nora," he admitted. "But with you, I see the potential for a day-to-day adventure instead of a life sentence. That's a major change of perception for me."

Nora lifted her head to gaze into Luke's deep green eyes. He didn't waver. Didn't wiggle his eyebrows or try to hide behind humor or innuendo. "You've never sent anyone flowers before, have you? Never told another woman you loved her."

You've put your foot in your mouth now! What if he says —

"Nope."

Nora let out the breath she didn't realize she'd been holding. Luke was thirty, with a string of sweethearts in his past, yet he'd saved those three words — along with an important part of himself — for this day. For *her.* "Wow. Thanks," was all she could manage to say.

"You're welcome," he replied softly. "I'm glad you understand that confession. And value it."

Luke kissed her then. Nora fell into the luxury of his lips and the slow, easy way he engaged her. When her stomach rumbled loudly, he chuckled. "Shall we hit the kitchen? I only know how to cook one thing —"

"And it'll taste fabulous, no matter what it is," she assured him. "I'm so starved, I could eat the wrapper instead of the bread and not know the difference."

Luke held the screen open while she unlocked the door. He went back for her flowers and a grocery sack he'd brought along. When he'd set everything in the kitchen, he turned one of the chairs so it faced away from the table. "Have a seat," he insisted. "You're going to sit on your throne while I take care of you. No arguments."

Nora's eyes widened. Luke ran warm water into her dishpan and then reached into his sack for a greenish bottle. As he drizzled some foaming gel into the water, aromas of eucalyptus and chamomile filled the kitchen.

"Time for a soak," he said as he knelt before her with the frothy water. He gently removed her shoes and socks. "You should invest in shoes with more cushion and support, Nora. We can't have these fabulous legs wearing out before their time from the hours you'll spend on the hard floors in your store."

Nora let out a long sigh when Luke placed her feet in the warm water. He took one foot between his hands and began to knead the tired muscles, lavishing extra attention on her calves, the ball of her foot, and her arch.

Her head fell back and her eyes closed. When Luke Hooley had first swaggered over to introduce himself, Nora could *not* have imagined him on his knees, paying such loving attention to her aches and pains —

much less offering to cook. "Ohhh," she moaned as he continued his massage. Then she chuckled. "You were born to serve, Luke."

His laughter teased at her ears. At her heart. "It'll only get better," he murmured as he picked up her other foot. "It's the *do unto others* thing, and I'm going first. Looking forward to the payback."

"Ah, the Golden Rule as it was originally intended." Nora opened her eyes to find Luke gazing up at her. "Where I've come from, it was usually restated as *he who has the gold, rules.*"

"But you're Plain now. The giver — and receiver — of simple gifts." Luke finished her other foot and placed it back in the warm, fragrant water. "If I'm to keep to my honorable intentions, I'd better get myself to the stove. You're a beautiful woman, Nora, and I'm a needy man."

Once again his words surprised her. She'd never figured Luke for a guy who would admit his deeper feelings. It was so gratifying that he insisted she was beautiful, and that he wasn't hustling her with his heady words.

"Skillet?"

"Bottom drawer of the stove," Nora replied.

"Toaster?"

"In the pantry, where the solar panel plug-ins are."

Luke smiled at her as he spooned butter from one of Bishop Tom's little tubs into her skillet. "You're not going to get wired for electricity, are you."

Nora liked it that he'd made that a statement rather than a question. "I've adjusted to using lamps and gas appliances, so I can't see tearing into the walls to install wiring."

"Good girl."

Nora liked the way Luke said those words as an endearment rather than a term that diminished her. "I feel helpless sitting here while you —"

"Is helpless a bad thing?" he countered with a laugh. "I enjoy doing this for you, Nora . . . thinking about how I'll render you helpless in a different way one of these days."

As images of intimacy filled her head, Nora's breath escaped her. How was it that the man at the stove could make her crave lovemaking with the merest suggestion of it, while Tanner's affections had often left her —

That's behind you. Go with the flow . . . with Luke.

He cracked six brown-shelled eggs into

the skillet, unwrapped a packet of sliced bread that looked like Miriam's, and stepped into the pantry to use the toaster. "Plates?" he asked.

"Above the sink, to the left."

Luke smiled. "That's where Ira and I keep ours, too." He sprinkled the crackling eggs with salt and pepper and gently broke the yolks with a spatula. Then he reached into the grocery sack again. "A few chunks of leftover ham, a little of the aunts' goat cheese, and we'll be all set."

Nora heard the toaster pop. She sat in awe of the way he'd organized his cooking so everything was ready at the same time. When he set two plates of scrambled eggs and toast on the table, Nora grabbed a dish towel to dry her feet.

Luke took the towel from her and deftly massaged from her toes to her calves. Then he turned her chair around to seat her, and leaned over her shoulder for a kiss.

"This looks so awesome," Nora whispered. "Thank you, Luke."

"Happy birthday, sweetheart."

When he grabbed her hand and bowed his head, Nora couldn't resist peeking at him between her half-closed eyelids. Luke's handsome face looked serenely at ease as he prayed silently, and his hand cradled hers as though it were a treasure. *Guide me, Lord. If this is too good to be true, too soon —*

"Dig in," he murmured a few moments later.

Nora didn't have to be told twice. The eggs were a calico of yellow and white with pink chunks of ham and little globs of melted goat cheese. The first mouthful nearly made her faint. "I'm in love," she gushed.

Luke's laughter filled the kitchen. "You mean I could've just scrambled you some eggs that first day you came, and you'd have fallen for me?"

"Ah, come on. Where's the adventure you were wanting in *that*?" she teased as she loaded her fork again. "From here on out, *you* will be cooking the eggs, because mine never turn out this way."

Luke bit into his toast, holding her gaze. "From here on out, eh? I like the sound of that."

Nora's heart fluttered. "Do you think we could make it work, Luke?" she dared to whisper.

"You're the one with marriage experience. I'll trust your judgment."

Nora waved off his remark. "My time with Tanner was nothing like I'd dreamed it would —"

Luke gently laid a finger across her lips. "But it led you back to Willow Ridge. To me," he pointed out in a low voice. "We probably won't be *perfect* together, but I'll give it my best shot if you will."

Nora laid down her fork to really look at Luke. His wavy brown hair had a ridge in it where his hat had been, his sea-green shirt was rumpled, and his gray suspenders had seen a lot of wear, yet the sincerity on his handsome face was drawing her in . . . making her believe in fresh starts and blessings she hadn't counted on when she'd come back home.

"You're on," she murmured as she squeezed his hand. "Let the adventure begin."

WHAT'S COOKIN' AT THE SWEET SEASONS BAKERY CAFÉ?

Because I love to cook as much as Miriam and Naomi do, here are recipes for some of the dishes they've served up in HARVEST OF BLESSINGS. With summer in full swing and autumn just around the corner, the women in Willow Ridge are cooking with fresh vegetables from their gardens, and they're also trying recipes that use the grains available at the Hooley brothers' new mill. You'll find these flours and grains at most larger grocery stores — my favorite brand is Bob's Red Mill.

I constantly read Amish cookbooks, *The Budget,* and Lovina Eicher's weekly newspaper column, The Amish Cook, so I can say yes, any convenience foods you see as ingredients are authentic!

I'll also post these on my website, www .CharlotteHubbard.com. If you don't see the recipe you want, please e-mail me via my website to request it, plus bookmarks — and let me know how you like them! I hope you enjoy making these dishes as much as I do!

~Charlotte

COLD WATER WHITE CAKE

Here's the recipe Miriam baked for Annie Mae and Adam's wedding cake. As with most Amish recipes, it's made with simple everyday ingredients, and the beaten egg whites produce a cake that's lighter than a cake from a box mix. Using two 9-inch pans will make a standard two-layer cake, but this amount of batter also fills a 9 × 13-inch pan or a 2-inch deep 10-inch round pan. Don't wait until someone gets married to try it!

4 egg whites
2 T. baking powder
2 cups sugar
1/2 cup shortening (Crisco, for instance)
1 cup cold water
1 tsp. vanilla extract
2 1/2 cups flour

Preheat oven to 350°F. Cut wax paper to fit the bottoms of two 9-inch round cake pans.

With the paper circles in place, spray the insides of the pans with nonstick coating.

Beat the egg whites with the baking powder until stiff peaks form. In a separate bowl, cream the sugar with the shortening, then mix in the cold water, vanilla, flour, and a pinch of salt. Fold in the egg whites.

Pour the batter into the prepared pans. Bake for 35–40 minutes, until the cake springs back when touched in the center. Cool the cake layers for 15 minutes in the pans before turning them out onto wire racks. Carefully remove the paper and cool completely before frosting with your favorite frosting (or see the recipe for Buttercream Frosting at www.CharlotteHubbard.com).

Kitchen Hint: *Cupcakes are so popular right now, and this recipe works well for those! Spray a muffin pan, or use cupcake papers. Check for doneness after about 10–12 minutes. This recipe makes a sweet, moist cake that freezes well, whatever form you bake it in.*

PEPPERMINT STICK ICE CREAM

This refreshing ice cream has to be one of my favorites! For a more colorful dessert, use both red and green starlight mints.

3 cups cold heavy/whipping cream
1 cup cold whole milk
1 cup sugar
3/4 cup crushed peppermint candy
1 1/2 tsp. peppermint extract

In a large bowl, whisk the cream, milk, and sugar until sugar is completely dissolved. Stir in the candy and the extract. Pour into the frozen bowl of an ice cream maker and freeze according to manufacturer instructions until mixture is soft-set, about 20 minutes. Pour mixture into a container (a glass bread pan works well), cover, and freeze 2–3 hours until nearly solid.

Kitchen Hint: *You can also add a few drops of pink or green food coloring for extra color.*

FIVE-GRAIN QUICK BREAD

This has become my favorite go-to recipe for bread that requires no rising. The mix of grains produces a dense, satisfying loaf with a touch of sweetness that complements soups or tastes great toasted for breakfast. Try it with peanut butter and jelly, or spread on some goat cheese or cream cheese!

1 cup 5-grain rolled whole grain cereal (or old-fashioned oats)

2 cups whole wheat flour

1 cup all-purpose flour

1/3 cup packed brown sugar

1 tsp. baking soda

1 tsp. cream of tartar

1 tsp. salt

1/4 cup cold butter or margarine, chopped

3/4 cup golden raisins and/or dried cranberries

1 egg

1 1/2 cups buttermilk

Preheat the oven to 375°F. Line a cookie sheet with parchment paper. Reserve 1 T. of the cereal. In a large bowl, mix the remaining cereal, the flours, brown sugar, baking soda, cream of tartar, and salt. Cut in the butter using a pastry blender (or rub in with the tines of a fork) until the mixture resembles coarse crumbs. Stir in the dried fruit.

In a small bowl, beat the egg and buttermilk with a whisk or fork until blended — reserve 1 T. of this mixture. Stir the remaining liquids into the dry ingredients until just moistened. On a floured surface, knead the dough 5 or 6 times until it holds together. Shape the dough into a 7-inch disk, place on the cookie sheet, and cut a large X across the top, 1/4-inch deep. Brush the top with the reserved buttermilk mixture, and then sprinkle the loaf with the reserved cereal. Bake for 30 to 35 minutes, or until the top is golden brown and the loaf sounds hollow when tapped. Cool before serving.

Kitchen Hint: I use Bob's Red Mill 5 Grain Rolled Hot Cereal, but using old-fashioned oats won't change the flavor/texture of the bread a lot. To save some time, I also use my food processor to cut the butter into the dry ingredients.

Another Hint: If you don't have buttermilk, you can put 3 T. of lemon juice or vinegar into the measuring cup and then add regular milk to the 1 1/2 cup mark. Let this thicken while you're mixing the dough.

WHOLE GRAIN PANCAKE MIX

Finally, my quest for a really good whole grain pancake mix has ended! The secret to this mix is putting the oats through the food processor so they become like flour, which produces a smooth, silky pancake that's a lot fresher and tastier than you get from a box mix. Warning: the bulk recipe below makes a LOT of pancake mix. I made half this recipe and got enough mix to fill a gallon zipper bag and make about six of the recipes below. Once you try this, you'll understand why Miriam was so tickled to get Nora's food processor!

Bulk Mix
6 cups old-fashioned rolled oats
3/4 cup wheat germ
3/4 cup brown sugar
9 cups whole wheat flour
3 cups instant skim milk powder
1/2 cup baking powder
3 tsp. baking soda
4 tsp. salt

With the food processor running, pour in the oats, wheat germ, and brown sugar. Turn off the processor and add the flour, skim milk powder, baking powder, baking soda, and salt. Pulse just until blended. Place mixture in a sealed container or zipper-style plastic bag and store in the fridge or freezer.

Whole Grain Pancakes
2 eggs
2 T. vegetable oil
1 cup milk
1 tsp. vanilla
1 1/2 cups whole grain pancake mix

Beat the eggs in a medium bowl with the oil, milk, and vanilla. Stir in 3/4 cup of pancake mix. Let stand 5 minutes. Heat the skillet or griddle on a medium setting, wipe with oil, and use about 1/4 cup of the batter for each pancake. Cook until bubbles form on the top, then flip to cook the other side. Adjust burner heat to keep cakes from scorching. Cover the cakes with foil and keep them warm in a 200°F oven until all the batter is used up. Makes 9 or 10 five-inch pancakes.

CARROT GINGER SOUP

This is truly a soup for all seasons, as you can either serve it hot as a side dish or first course, or chilled as a refreshing light meal on a summer day. Even kids like carrots, so this is a great way to get more servings of healthy veggies into your family's meals.

2 T. butter
1 small onion, diced
12 medium carrots, peeled and sliced
4 cups vegetable or chicken broth
1 T. or more grated fresh ginger or powdered ginger
1 cup orange juice
Salt, pepper and/or lemon pepper, and dill to taste

In a large pan or Dutch oven, melt the butter over medium heat and sauté the onion and ginger for about 5 minutes. Add the carrots, and sauté for a few minutes. Add the broth and bring to a boil. Turn heat to low, and simmer carrots until tender, about 30 minutes. Transfer soup to a blender or food processor in batches, and puree until smooth. Add orange juice and seasonings. Reheat and serve.

Kitchen Hint: *This soup keeps well in the fridge for several days, or you can freeze it.*

MAKE-AHEAD MASHED POTATOES

Here's the perfect dish for entertaining, when you want real mashed potatoes without the last-minute hassle. I love to make these on Saturday so we can enjoy mashed potatoes after we get home from church, usually to go with a roast I've put into the Crock-Pot.

2 1/2 pounds red or Yukon Gold potatoes
2 T. butter
1/4 cup milk
3 oz. cream cheese
3/4 cup sour cream
Salt, pepper, garlic powder, and other
   seasonings, to taste

Peel the potatoes and cut into chunks. Boil

them in salted water until tender, and drain. Beat in the remaining ingredients until the potatoes are well mashed and the cream cheese is blended in, and place this mixture into a sprayed microwavable dish or a 2-quart casserole. Cool, cover, and refrigerate.

To reheat, cover with a microwave-safe cover and microwave on a medium setting for about 8 minutes, until steaming hot. Stir and heat a bit longer, if needed; OR, cover the casserole with an ovenproof lid or foil and reheat in the oven at 350°F for about 45 minutes. Serves 6–8.

Kitchen Hint: _You can use margarine instead of butter, and you can also replace the sour cream with plain Greek yogurt._

CHEESY BAKED ONIONS

This was a recipe I found stuck in Mom's cookbook. Part of the enjoyment in making this dish comes from recalling how she _loved_ onions, and part of it is following the recipe written in her distinctive, back-slanted handwriting. Sweet, creamy, and decadently rich, this makes a wonderful side dish for any sort of meat. You can make it the day before and reheat it.

6 medium or 4 large yellow onions
1/4 cup butter or margarine
1/2 cup beef or chicken broth
1/2 cup whipping cream
2 T. flour
1/2 cup grated Parmesan cheese
Salt and pepper to taste
1 cup shredded Swiss cheese

Peel the onions and slice them thick. Sauté them in the butter or margarine until tender, adding water if necessary. Place in a 2-quart baking dish sprayed with nonstick coating. In a separate bowl, stir together the broth, cream, flour, Parmesan cheese, and seasonings until blended. Pour this mixture over the onions and top with the Swiss cheese. Bake uncovered at 350°F for about 45 minutes, until the mixture is bubbly. Serves 6–8.

CORNBREAD CASSEROLE

Here's the ultimate comfort food, made from ingredients you can keep on your shelf to whip together at a moment's notice. When I serve this or take it to a potluck, I rarely get any because the bowl's empty by the time I get to it!

1 15-oz. can whole kernel corn, drained

1 15-oz. can creamed corn
1 box (8 oz.) Jiffy corn muffin mix
1 cup sour cream or plain Greek yogurt
1/2 cup butter, melted
1 egg
Salt, pepper, dill weed to taste
1 1/2 cups shredded cheese of your choice,
   divided

Preheat oven to 350°F and spray a 9 × 9-inch baking pan or a quart-size baking dish. Mix all ingredients, saving back 1/2 cup of the cheese. Pour the batter into the prepared baking dish and bake for 45 minutes or until the center is set. Sprinkle on the rest of the cheese and return to the oven for another 5 minutes.

Kitchen Hint: Feeling decadent? Stir crumbled bacon or ham chunks — up to a cup — into the batter.

PINEAPPLE BREAD PUDDING
We love bread pudding and we love baked pineapple, so when I decided to try blending the two, it was *outrageously* good, moist and creamy and sweet without a lot of added sugar. It's great for breakfast, and it's also a yummy dessert.

5 cups cubed stale bread
2 cups milk, scalded
1/4 cup butter or margarine
1 20-oz. can crushed, juice-packed pineapple, undrained
3 T. cornstarch
3 eggs
1/2 cup sugar
1 tsp. vanilla
Cinnamon

Preheat the oven to 350°F and spray/grease a 2-quart casserole dish. Place the bread cubes in a large bowl. To scald the milk, heat it until it's steamy, melt the butter in it, and then pour this mixture over the bread cubes. Stir. Pour in the pineapple, cornstarch, eggs, sugar, and vanilla and stir everything together until the eggs and sugar are well-blended with the bread mixture. Pour the mixture into the prepared dish and sprinkle with cinnamon. Bake for about 45 minutes, or until the center is loosely set. Serves 6.

Kitchen Hint: *You can scald the milk in the microwave — takes about a minute, depending upon the wattage of your microwave. You can also reheat leftovers in the microwave by covering them loosely with a wet paper towel to preserve the creaminess.*

SAUSAGE, SWEET PEPPERS, AND ONIONS

Zesty and chock-full of vegetables, this makes a hearty sauce to serve over your favorite pasta, spaghetti squash, or rice. If you use fresh tomatoes, as Miriam does, first dip them in boiling water and peel them, then core, cut them into chunks, and smash them in the pan. Add canned tomato juice if needed, so the other vegetables will have enough liquid as they cook.

1 lb. Italian sausage, links or bulk
2 28-oz. cans of diced tomatoes with juice OR 6–8 large, very ripe fresh tomatoes
1 or 2 large onions, cut into chunks
2 green bell peppers, cut into chunks
Several fresh mushrooms, cleaned and halved
1 24-oz. can or jar of spaghetti sauce
Liberal amounts of basil, garlic powder, lemon pepper, dill
2–3 bay leaves
Salt and pepper to taste
1 6-oz. can of tomato paste

If you use bulk sausage, brown it in a Dutch oven and drain the excess grease. If you

448

prefer Italian links, boil them in a Dutch oven until nearly done, cool slightly, and then cut them into bite-size chunks. Set meat aside.

Pour the tomatoes, with juice, into this same Dutch oven and add the onion and green peppers. Cover and cook over medium heat until vegetables soften, stirring so the tomatoes don't scorch. Add the mushrooms and the meat, stirring well. Pour in the spaghetti sauce, then add the bay leaves and the other seasonings — be generous! Lower the heat and simmer, covered, at least a half hour, stirring occasionally. Remove the bay leaves and stir in the tomato paste to thicken the sauce. Serve bubbly hot.

Kitchen Hint: _Add any other veggies (chunked zucchini, summer squash, cooked Italian/ Roma beans, cooked carrots) and increase the tomatoes and sauce to accommodate them. This recipe also works well in a crockery cooker if you sauté the vegetables before you add them. Like any good sauce, this one tastes best if it's allowed to sit for several hours (or overnight in the fridge) to allow flavors to blend. Freezes well._

EASY ROASTED CHICKEN

Here's a recipe that expands easily to feed a crowd. While this version calls for baking in the oven, you could cook larger amounts — four or five chickens, say — in an electric roaster by increasing the other ingredients according to how many birds you cook.

1 chicken, cut into desired serving pieces
1 stick butter or margarine, melted
1/2 cup white vinegar
Lawry's seasoning salt

Preheat oven to 350°F. Spray a 9 × 13-inch pan and arrange chicken pieces in a single layer. Mix the butter/margarine and the vinegar and drizzle over the chicken. Sprinkle with the Lawry's seasoning. Bake uncovered without turning the chicken pieces. Check for doneness after an hour and bake longer if necessary (meat should be starting to separate from the bones).

Kitchen Hint: *Avoiding salt? Season the chicken with garlic powder, salt substitute, some lemon pepper — whatever flavors you prefer. It'll still taste great!*

OVERNIGHT KALE SALAD
WITH APPLES

I really wanted to embrace kale, but until I found this recipe I tossed more of it out than I ate. The difference? This salad marinates for several hours, so it soaks up the sweet-sour dressing. The apples and dried cranberries make it even tastier!

3 T. apple cider vinegar
3 T. olive oil
Salt, pepper, and sugar/sweetener
1 apple, any variety
5–6 cups fresh kale
1/2 cup dried cranberries

Pour the vinegar and the oil into a large lidded container (a one-gallon ice cream tub works well). Add sugar or sweetener to taste, along with some salt and pepper, then rotate the container to blend these ingredients. Wash, core, and cube the apple into the container. Wash the kale, cut out the tough stalks, and slice the leaves into ribbons. Add the kale and cranberries to the salad, put on the lid, and shake well to coat the kale and apples. Chill for several hours, preferably overnight, shaking occasionally. Serves 4–6. Keeps well in the fridge for 2 or 3 days.

LUKE'S SCRAMBLED EGGS

This is more of a technique than a recipe, and ever since I read about this method I've not scrambled my eggs any other way! Simple, quick, and delicious for breakfast or after a busy day when you don't feel like fussing over food.

1 T. butter per person
2–3 eggs per person
Salt and pepper
Shredded cheese, cubed ham, bacon bits as
  desired

Spray a small skillet and melt butter in it over medium-low heat. Break the eggs directly into the butter, and season with salt and pepper to taste. When the whites start to become white, gently break the yolks with a spatula but don't stir and don't flip anything over — allow some yellow and some white to remain distinct as you gently move the mixture around in the skillet. While the eggs still look wet, add any additional toppings (cheese last). Remove from the heat before the eggs look dry. Enjoy!

The employees of Thorndike Press hope you have enjoyed this Large Print book. All our Thorndike, Wheeler, and Kennebec Large Print titles are designed for easy reading, and all our books are made to last. Other Thorndike Press Large Print books are available at your library, through selected bookstores, or directly from us.

For information about titles, please call:
  (800) 223-1244

or visit our Web site at:
  http://gale.cengage.com/thorndike

To share your comments, please write:
  Publisher
  Thorndike Press
  10 Water St., Suite 310
  Waterville, ME 04901